MW01504671

UNEXPECTED RUFF AIR

UNEXPECTED RUFF AIR

A Novel

Russell Goutierez

ISBN 9798319202482

Front Cover Photo © 2000 Erik Frikke

Back Cover Photo © 1982 Captain Mike Martin

See the Acknowledgements section for details on each photo.

Cover and interior designs by the author.

DEDICATION

In memory of Mom and Dad, with love and gratitude; and to the people of Muse Air/TranStar, who did their very best to make flying beautiful.

"You can't deregulate this industry. You're going to wreck it!"

* * *

President Signs Airline Deregulation Bill
By Constance Clifton, *Washington Globe* Staff Writer
Wednesday, October 25, 1978

WASHINGTON, D.C. – President Carter on Tuesday signed controversial legislation ending government regulation of the nation's airlines. The President hailed the law as a victory for consumers, promising lower fares and better service…

PROLOGUE

AUGUST 9, 1987
TAMPA INTERNATIONAL AIRPORT

In hindsight, the warning signs hadn't just been there, they had flashed and twinkled like Vegas marquees. Failing to grasp what they foretold had already cost Drew dearly. Reality had shattered his rose-colored glasses, yet the inevitable result still seemed impossible even as it unfolded before his eyes.

The concrete beneath his feet, smudged and stained by countless arrivals and departures, still radiated heat absorbed hours before. The cicadas were in full voice and the usually pervasive odors of kerosene and jet exhaust had faded in favor of a surprisingly pleasant bouquet: freshly mown grass, briny bay water, and even a trace of tropical blooms.

When flights operated, passengers scurried past the concourse windows above and workers crisscrossed the apron like industrious ants. At half past ten on a Sunday evening, the stark gold light from the vapor lamps revealed nothing but a few parked airliners and the ground equipment that would attend them come morning.

He loved this spot. There was something magical in watching the airport come alive in the predawn silence or sticking around after a shift as the operation slowed. Soaking up the unique ambience of aviation—the thunder of takeoffs, the orderly pinpoints of light defining the airport, even the jets slumbering at their gates—had never failed to recharge his spirit.

Until now.

Arms crossed tightly, he stared at the familiar T-tailed silhouette awaiting takeoff. Rhythmic flashes from its strobes and beacons framed a row of softly glowing windows and the whine of idling turbines drifted on the wind.

In the darkness beyond, an approaching blaze of lights gradually assumed the stubby form of a 737, Piedmont's last daily inbound from Charlotte. The arriving jet touched down, tires yelping on contact, and slowed with a roar of reverse thrust.

A few seconds later, the waiting MD-80 trundled onto the runway and lined up for takeoff. In the timetable, this was AirStar 888 to Miami, just another of 17,000 daily US commercial flights. But as its engines spooled up, a tidal wave of pride, heartbreak, and bittersweet memories crashed over the quiet observer.

Yes, much more than a flight was about to depart.

ONE

JANUARY 1984
NEW ORLEANS, LOUISIANA

Maybe the worst thing about the sales job fiasco was that Drew had asked for it, literally and figuratively. He had jumped at the opportunity, and why not? Slogging away on Streak Air Cargo's second shift had provided a solid footing in Operations; commissions could ratchet his pay up by at least a third; and there would be no nights, weekends, or suck-ass on-call duty. The promotion would look great on his resume, and it came with the keys to a year-old Ford sedan. Gravy train!

Like any good house of cards, the new gig was impressive early on but tottered alarmingly at the first hint of a breeze.

The Ops crew was a team, one that got the job done but had fun along the way and helped each other when things went wonky. Streak's sales types worked alone, coming together only for occasional meetings or to throw back a few at happy hour.

Most of the reps acted more like bitter rivals than colleagues. Nobody exchanged ideas or feedback until someone blew a presentation or lost an account. Then nearly everybody became big-mouthed, chest-beating "experts" who told the offender and anyone else who would listen how things should have been handled to begin with. A female presence would have tempered the pack mentality, but the same pig-headed professional misogyny found throughout much of the business world still prevailed at Streak as well.

Constructive direction was fine, but the open criticism and second-guessing was frustrating. The new rep also dealt poorly with rejection, a serious impediment for salespeople in any economic climate and a fatal one given the cutthroat competition the oil bust had spawned in the New Orleans air cargo market.

On the money front, a sales rep's base salary was actually a cut compared to Ops even without factoring in the loss of overtime and increased hours. Worse, counting on commissions turned out to be financial quicksand. Accounting calculated them based on the previous month's billing, so if clients' traffic took a nosedive for whatever reason, their rep's pay did the same. Living check to check was tough enough without the amounts bobbing like yo-yos.

Then there was Marty. When Drew walked into a so-called training session with some company-issued sales training pamphlets, his new manager yanked the packet away and Frisbee-tossed it across the room. It sailed wide but suddenly curved sharply up and left, stalled, and dropped right into the trash can.

Ignoring the pupil's perplexed look, Marty celebrated the improbable bullseye by throwing his arms up and shouting, *"Pistol Pete wins it at the buzzer!"*

More calmly, he added, "You don't need that."

What followed was informal to say the least. Nothing on sales, but Marty enthusiastically described methods for acquiring hard-to-find event tickets, where best to wine and dine customers, and, curiously, which "gentleman's clubs" had the curviest dancers. When the trainee steered the conversation to sales techniques and strategies, Marty waved dismissively.

"Don't worry about that crap, Junior," he said, straightening his tie and flicking away a speck of lint ballsy enough to have landed on one worsted wool shoulder. "Sales isn't about 'techniques.' It's about relationships."

My ass! Like this takes a degree in sociology or personal after-dark tours of Bourbon Street? Christ, it's not brain surgery. All I need to do is get in front of the customer and show them we can move their freight faster and cheaper.

Drew didn't push it, not wanting to appear uncoachable right out of the gate. He failed—or perhaps refused—to even consider the possibility that Marty was right.

By half past six, everyone else but the boss was gone from the sales side of the office. Drew looked up from a stack of client files, expecting Marty to simply say goodnight. Instead, he assigned a make-work chore that wouldn't challenge an intern, then said, "That'll be good experience for you, Junior."

Working late was part of the job, but what was this? The task took until almost eight and he was two hours more on the files. Worse, the petty stay-late projects and inexplicable insistence that they were "good experience" became a frequent ritual, each instance more irksome than the last.

Next came two weeks spent tagging along on sales rounds. Any hope that first-hand observation would provide the needed insight faded fast. Instead, his enthusiasm faded in direct proportion to the time spent with Marty.

"This is Junior," the boss would say. "I'm *trying* to show him the ropes," his inflection implying the task was akin to hiking Antarctica. Everyone would then ignore the trainee as the conversation meandered about and on rare occasions found its way to business, or what passed for it with Marty. Some of his manager's offers to potential clients made it tough to keep his face disconnected from the drop-jaw shock bolting through his brain. But questionable tactics aside, Marty brought in the numbers and regularly scored major victories over the competition.

Secretly longing for his old job back in Operations didn't help. In retrospect, life in Ops had been a walk in the park. Monday through Friday, four to midnight, with the first couple of hours spent on paperwork, any special shipments, dispatching pickups, and routine tasks like posting updates to the various references they used. The drivers were generally back to the airport with the freight and overnight packages about the time Drew, his colleague Brock, and Stan, the warehouseman, finished up dinner. By then everyone else had gone home, so they could crank up the radio and talk as candidly as they pleased about whatever came to mind.

Sure, the job had its moments. The occasional avalanche of sheer volume that buried them till the wee hours; so much data entry that glowing green characters lingered in his vision even as he fell asleep at home; working two Saturday mornings a month; and carrying the on-call pager until Monday morning. With luck, it remained so quiet as to warrant a battery check. Occasionally, it buzzed like an angry hornet day and night. And sometimes, the little gray box seemed to possess a malevolent omniscience, demanding attention only a few times but choosing exactly the worst moments with unsettling precision.

Best of all, the Ops crew got on well and had fun, with plenty of jokes and pranks. Stan did dead-on impressions of everyone from President Reagan to Michael Jackson—the one of Marty was particularly funny—and Brock cracked everyone up by ad-libbing hilarious faux lyrics to whatever song came on the radio. There was even quiet time when Brock and Stan went out back for a smoke. Drew would walk out front, prop the door open in case the phone rang, and watch the planes. He enjoyed those moments the most, even if each reminded him that air freight had never become the stepping stone to an airline job as he had hoped.

Someday, he would tell himself as the colorful jets came and went.

Yes, Ops was pretty peachy. Sales, not so much. Even after poring over the customer files and going on orientation calls, how his predecessor had secured the accounts to begin with remained a mystery, much less how to go about keeping them. Shippers sometimes chose the competition even when Streak had the clear advantage and, just as often, the reverse. Many decision makers grimaced as if passing a broken sewer pipe when handed a proposal. Some didn't even bother with a courteous once-over before tossing it aside, the painstakingly researched price comparisons and transit-time analyses never to be read.

Drew finally had to admit, much to his chagrin, that sales apparently *was* more about relationships, though his definition of the word had never included the shameless glad-handing, schmoozing, boozing, ass kissing, occasional strip club "business dinners," and plain old bullshitting that Marty's did. Marty enjoyed the game, reveled in it, even rightfully considered himself some kind of sales artiste extraordinaire.

Drew's tolerance for the obligatory shtick had started low and continued to plummet, but he saw no choice but to make the best of it.

* * *

Two weeks later, on an exceptionally cold morning, Marty waved him over as the Sales meeting broke up. Mondays were admin days, spent planning the week's calls, but fifteen minutes later Marty's Crown Vic was screaming down I-10 into the city. Drew fastened his seatbelt while Marty, coffee and cigarette in hand, drove, sipped, puffed, and preached.

"You gotta listen to these guys, buddy, you gotta play the game! Those assholes from Emery, are you kidding me? You think they have anything we don't have? Shit no! But they did their homework"—Marty pointed accusingly, cigarette clutched between manicured fingers— "and you didn't."

Right. Nothing we don't have. Nothing but a whole goddam fleet of planes!

Emery flew its own cargo-configured 727s and DC-8s, a huge advantage over forwarders like Streak who were stuck with using scheduled airline service. Knowing this to be the sorest of subjects, always summarily rejected as an excuse, he chose to amp it up instead. When Marty got unreasonable, you had to boomerang it right back.

"Marty, that's horseshit! The shipping manager is from Palm Harbor, Florida and went to the University of Miami. He's married and has twin ten-year-old sons. He couldn't care less about sports but likes to sail. What was I supposed to do, buy him a boat?"

Marty looked sideways in exasperation.

"Son, you think *that* pussy wears the pants? C'mon, man, he's been there what, six months? The warehouse supe, Boudreaux, routes the freight. He's been there since Billy Cannon's run"—1959, as any local sports fan knew—"and bleeds purple and gold. And who's looking good for the SEC title next year?"

Next year? The football season just ended!

Marty went on, slowly, as if addressing a restless kindergartener.

"LSU and A-la-*bam*-a, that's who!"

After letting that critical point marinate, he continued, now talking around his cigarette.

"We're losing out on ten K a month in freight over an autographed football and a couple of fifty-yard-line seats? Uh uh, podna."

"What's that got to do with anything anyway? We can actually beat Emery by half a day to six of their top ten destinations and our rates average five cents less a pound."

Marty removed the cigarette and sighed, expelling a cloud of smoke so big it wreathed his head.

"Where's the warehouse supervisor?"

"What?" replied Drew, baffled. "You mean Boudreaux?"

"Yes. Where is Mr. Boudreaux?"

"I don't know, in the warehouse?"

"Exactly. In the warehouse on Tchoupitoulas Street in New Orleans, Louisiana. Where he's not is in Receiving at any of your 'top ten destinations.' And if he's not there, what's he not doing?"

Bewildered silence.

The boss went on, "He's not waiting on those parts, so he doesn't give a shit if we beat Emery by a few hours! The pallet probably sits on the customer's dock that long anyway before anybody touches it. We're five cents less, so what? He's usually billing it back to his customers. If we were a day faster or fifteen cents a pound less, maybe you'd have something there we could use."

Marty paused for effect, pointing again as he continued.

"This is important, Junior, so listen up: it doesn't have to be fastest, just fast enough. Not cheapest, just cheap enough. That means every rep's nuts are in the same vise and every goddam shipper has a free pass to squeeze away for whatever they can get." A note of resignation crept in at the end, which Marty punctuated by powering down his window, crushing his empty coffee cup, and pitching it out in disgust.

Another long drag followed. Drew glanced over and did a double-take, shocked at how old the other man suddenly looked, how much wear and tear lay hidden beneath the swagger and constant preening. The difference was startling, like viewing a seated corpse made up for an open casket. The effect was such that he almost jumped when Marty turned and asked, "So, Junior, where do you think Boudreaux's gonna be, courtesy of us and not those pricks from Emery, on Saturday, November fifth?"

That one was easy, and he hammered it up for full effect, pumping his fist and raising the volume with each word.

"Tiger *fuckin' STADIUM!"*

Marty returned his eyes to the road, accepting the unsubtle parody with a droll grin and blowing out another billow of smoke.

"Very good, Junior," he said. "Sometimes you belong on the short bus but you're learning." The vulnerable moment was gone, the return to normality complete.

Wait, did I imagine that?

Marty went on, eyes taking on a faraway look and jaw tightening with determination as if his will alone could shape the outcome.

"That's right, chief," he said quietly, almost talking to himself. "Tiger Stadium. When the Crimson Tide comes rollin' in to Baton Rouge, old Boudreaux's gonna be on the LSU bench with a cheerleader on his lap if that's what we have to do."

The customer's facility shared the street with a line of drab, nearly identical warehouses tagged here and there with graffiti. Trucks rumbled by, fouling the chilly air with diesel fumes. As they started for the door, Marty said, "You're lucky these guys didn't sign a contract. Watch and learn, Junior, 'cause I'm gonna save your ass while I jam a telephone pole right up Emery's."

Sure you are.

After a considerable wait, the receptionist ushered them in. She didn't offer to take their coats or even try very hard to camouflage her distaste. Mr. Boudreaux looked confused by the introductions.

"I thought his name was Junior," he said to Marty.

Boudreaux's office had three gray partitions. The fourth side was a three-story exterior wall topped by a ten-foot band of windows. No doubt some enterprising architect had envisioned an interior flooded with natural light, a fine goal now defeated by decades of yellowish grime that clouded every pane's center and blocked most of their corners completely.

With no ceiling, there was little to keep out the oily odor, high-pitched *thum-thum-thum*, and occasional metallic shrieks from the shop floor. The only personal touch aside from a few family photos was a faded purple and gold pennant from LSU's '59 Sugar Bowl appearance.

After the obligatory small talk, Marty described their proposal. Mr. Boudreaux's response was predictable. He had taken the meeting out of respect for Marty, but his word was his bond and he had given it to Emery. He dug his heels in even further at the mere mention of putting anything in writing.

Then Marty stood, picked up his coat and his unopened briefcase, and said, "Well then, sir, sounds like you're all set. We thank you for your time."

Drew followed hesitantly, confused at the apparent capitulation. Even Boudreaux seemed to be caught off guard.

Turning to go, Marty paused and casually asked, "So Mr. Boudreaux, what'cha think about 'dem Tigers next year?"

The supervisor relaxed and his eyes brightened. He smiled and said it looked pretty good if they could get past 'Bama. "At least we get 'em in Death Valley," he added.

Marty, the picture of innocence, tossed his line into the water.

"Ya'll going to that game?"

Boudreaux's smile widened. "Oh yeah, man. Great seats, too, right on the fifty!"

"Well, good. I heard you're a big Tiger fan, so I phoned a friend who works at LSU and talked him into a couple of sideline passes for the 'Bama game. You know, a little customer appreciation gift, hoping we could do some business. So it's too bad about Emery and all that but I'm sure they'll do a good job for you."

Boudreaux snapped up in his chair.

"Sideline passes?!"

Marty had carefully selected the fattest, juiciest bait he could find, set the hook, and now he yanked hard on the pole. Yes, he had sideline passes and more. Much more. Should Boudreaux see fit to make a written deal, Marty could toss in a posh tailgate party hosted by Tiger boosters. A two-year pact would warrant two seats in a plush Superdome suite for the Bayou Bengals' season-ending rivalry game against Tulane. And, Marty said, including overnight letters and packages would garner two choice tickets to the Super Bowl.

Drew, standing with coat in hand and already trying to hide his astonishment over the uncommonly rich offer, shot Marty a surprised look.

The Super Bowl?

Besides, forget the overnight stuff. It was worth a good twenty-five thousand a year but even Emery knew that was a dead end. The maddeningly untouchable Federal Express had carried the next-day traffic for years. Still, you couldn't blame a guy for swinging for the fence and the boss had obviously called in some major markers to do it.

Marty looked over with a confident wink as they accepted Boudreaux's invitation to sit down again. Cups of coffee appeared courtesy of the receptionist, who was suddenly as warm as the java. She took their coats, then set a little tray of hard candies on the table between their chairs. Meanwhile, Boudreaux was stepping lively toward the shipping manager's office, Streak's previously ignored proposal in hand. He knocked and disappeared through the door.

I'll bet he's just figuring out how many crumbs to toss us to grab some of the goodies.

Forty-five minutes later, after ironing out a few details and a brief, deferential audience with the sailing aficionado, they left with a signed two-year all-traffic agreement worth well over a quarter-million dollars in revenue.

Drew could hardly contain his amazement at how Marty had coaxed their wary, uncooperative prey to emerge from his comfortable hiding place, swim eagerly to the surface, and basically leap into the boat.

Yet another cigarette in hand, Marty said, "The yacht club's holding a regatta in May." He blew out a perfect smoke ring. "I reserved four of their best seats. Send sailor boy the tickets with our thank-you note."

"A regatta? On Lake Pontchartrain?"

Marty turned with a raised eyebrow and deadpanned, "No, on the Industrial Canal."

Drew laughed, then said soberly, "That was primo work back there. I didn't even bid for the overnight stuff. The file said Fed Ex has…or had…it locked up." As painful as it was to say, Marty had earned the compliment.

"Go big or go home, Junior. My father taught me most any job is doable if you use the right tools. That's your job…find the right tools. Find the right button and push it, as long and as hard and as often as you have to."

The thought of having snagged that monstrous commission with a little determination and creativity of his own went down like a swig of sour milk. The monthly check would probably pay Marty's mortgage for the next two years.

At the office, Marty pointed at the coffeemaker and motioned toward his office. A moment later he rose, took the steaming cup and waved Drew to a chair. Settling into a half-roost on the edge of his desk, he put aside his cockiness and affected the role of earnest mentor.

"All I've been trying to tell you, Junior, is that these people aren't getting paid any more money or taking home any trophies because the freight gets there a little earlier or they save a few cents a pound."

Setting his cup down, he touched the side of his head and said, "You're very good at using this, and sometimes that works. But you better learn and learn quick what every good salesman knows." Dropping his hand to his chest, he tapped above the heart and went on, "Most people are making decisions from here."

This was the guidance he had needed. Maybe he should have been more open-minded despite Marty's eccentricities.

This guy's a pompous ass, but he knows how this works, that's for damn sure. Maybe—

Marty's hand dropped again, this time to his crotch, where he grabbed a handful and went on with a lecherous smirk.

"Not to mention here!"

Seeing Drew's eyes widen in surprise, he let go and said, "Hey, just 'cause you don't like it doesn't mean it's not true. Some of these guys, they get laid, we get paid! What's our motto, Junior? 'Whatever it takes.'"

"But—"

"No buts!" Marty shrieked, face contorting as he jumped to his feet and jabbed a finger in Drew's face. *"I said whatever the fuck it takes!"* Several flecks of spittle sailed out as unwelcome emphasis.

He snatched up his cup, splashing coffee onto his desk, and stomped out.

Drew, incredulous, stared at the empty doorway.

A few seconds later, Marty stuck his head back in, smiling.

"What'cha waitin' for, Bubba?" he asked cheerily. "Come on, I'm buying lunch!"

TWO

The first Saturday in March dawned gray and raw. An umbrella-mangling wind howled through the leafless trees, lopping a good ten degrees off the forty announced on the radio.

Drew, up early, made fast work of breakfast and headed out on wet streets smeared with the reflections of traffic signals and streetlights. Leaden clouds hid half the GNO Bridge's superstructure and shortened several downtown skyscrapers too. Ragged, misty streamers hung below the overcast and the rain only occasionally lightened to drizzle, all poor omens for the parades scheduled later.

Light traffic put him on the bridge ten minutes later. Gusts buffeted the car and streaked the broad Mississippi with whitecaps. A ship maneuvered cautiously around Algiers Point, riding low in the brown water under a colorful mosaic of stacked containers. Only a few vehicles, and even fewer hardy pedestrians, waited at the ferry landings. The tourists would have a rough time if the sternwheelers went out today, rough enough that a few queasy unfortunates would no doubt jackknife over the railing and toss their coffee and beignets into the swirling current.

He reached mid-span lost in thought, the river far below. That cadaver-like glimpse of Marty on the drive downtown had foreshadowed his own potential destiny with bone-chilling clarity. Weeks of restless indecision had crystallized into resolve, and one thing was certain after what followed: there was no going back.

After the knock, Marty had waved him in with a smile and said, "What'cha got, Bubba?" The smile faded fast as he read the resignation letter. There was an eerie calm, but his surprise soon morphed into something from a horror flick, as if he was transfused with the raw, unimaginable forces that enable volcanoes to instantaneously obliterate a hundred square miles. His face reddened, his eyes bulged and stared unblinkingly at the page, and his hands began to shake.

Drew started to rise, concerned that maybe a blood vessel had burst and started hosing the gray matter. He settled back when Marty didn't keel over but erupted into a vitriolic rant so shrill neither the closed door nor the flimsy veneer walls prevented the entire staff from getting it practically verbatim. Even Stan the warehouseman later quoted several explicit phrases.

Drew's reaction ran the gamut in about forty-five seconds: shock and dismay to deep embarrassment to anger to indifference and eventually, he had to admit, some secret enjoyment. Marty, who usually wouldn't tolerate a stray wrinkle in his shirt, became sweaty and disheveled, his tie off-center and freshly barbered hair mussed. He was pacing around and hadn't even begun to wind down.

Should I just walk out?

He waited, holding on to the irrational hope that they could eventually discuss loose ends like how the accounts would be transitioned to a colleague.

Fat chance. Marty was still breathing fire and despite Drew's best efforts, his mind wandered. He already knew what he would do next and thus considered himself ahead of the game. Back in high school, his boss at a part-time job had chimed in during a conversation about future plans.

"You guys think getting what you want is the hard part in life?" Mr. Lynn had asked. "No. It's *deciding* what you want, 'cause once you do, you go balls to the wall until you get there."

Well, given the present situation, the balls must go immediately and fully to the wall.

As dreams go, one could argue that an entry-level airline job hardly qualified, even if its genesis was one of his earliest memories: mashing his three-year-old face against the window of a World Airways charter carrying military dependents to

Okinawa. As the 707 cruised westward, he had spent hours mesmerized by the magnificent blue Pacific and a sky filled with cloudscapes that looked fresh from the brush of God. All these years later, he could still close his eyes and see that sunset, countless shades of pink, gold, purple, and orange in a tableau so grand it wrapped around the curvature of the earth. Later, the night shimmered with what seemed like a billion stars. Once the flight arrived, being somewhere so vastly different from where they had boarded seemed impossible and wondrous.

That flight planted a seed, a passion nurtured by contented hours wandering the world with the likes of Gann and de Saint-Exupéry and constructing a fleet of model planes. Most of the collection was long gone; fragile and tough to pack, one move or another had crushed nearly all beyond repair. The *Spirit of St. Louis*, a Black Sheep Corsair, Robin Olds' Phantom, an American 707 Astrojet…all shared the same inglorious fate. Only one of his creations remained intact: a '60s era jet, the tiny replica hardly longer than a playing card and bearing the markings of the U.S. Navy's Blue Angels. The sole survivor of a four-plane set, its flawed paint and misaligned decals were obviously the imperfect but devoted work of a child and the little artifact meant all the more to him because of it.

Serling's airline histories, Captain Len Morgan's *Vectors* columns, and Arthur Hailey's novel *Airport* and its movie adaptation only sharpened his focus on the industry and made him wonder whether he could be part of it someday. The summer job at Streak felt like a first step, so he decided to postpone college, promising himself it was only for a year. Yet here he was while his high school classmates had already flipped their tassels. Worse, freight forwarding, especially at a company without its own planes, bore far more resemblance to trucking. Time had drifted away like the tide, carrying his hopes further and further into improbability. Now he would have his chance!

Marty did not appreciate the resulting faint smile. The manager stopped mid-sentence, capping his outburst with a notably creative insult that used the f-word as a verb, adjective, and noun. Seizing Drew's keys and company ID, he stood sanctimoniously as the now-former sales rep grabbed his belongings.

In essence, enduring the tirade earned his final paycheck. Well, that and walking a freezing mile on the road by the railroad tracks to call a ride because he was too embarrassed to ask to use a competitor's phone. But if listening to Marty throw a tantrum snagged him two weeks' pay and a head start on his job search, so be it, hike and all.

Some unpleasant truths lurked in the shadows, obscured by the relief of escaping Marty and the excitement of a fresh start. He had failed to think through the position's nature or responsibilities before plunging in. Upon finding them disagreeable, he had let dissatisfaction steer him along the path of least resistance instead of confronting his own issues. In his anger at Marty's condescending treatment, it never occurred to him that perhaps his manager was simply measuring his mettle—mixing in a little hazing for tradition's sake—and that things might have improved over time.

Nor had he considered the full chain of consequences. It could alienate customers, many of whom disliked change; the burdensome hiring process would have to be repeated; accounts would be vulnerable while other reps were spread thin; Marty's superiors would question his judgement in promoting Drew to begin with; and the mess left behind would bog down anyone else seeking to make the leap from Operations into Sales.

Perhaps worst of all, the new beginning was starting off the same way: charging off into unknown territory with insufficient recon. Years would pass before experience and responsibility forged his character to where he could objectively examine the entirety of it and confront some uncomfortable facts: his own demons and shortcomings were equally if not more to blame, and there was a much wider gap than he thought between the person he was and the one he aspired to be.

Off the bridge and onto I-10, the Superdome squatted off to the right like some enormous stalkless mushroom. Inside it, crews had removed the "Mardi Grass" artificial turf to reveal a concrete floor that would soon host a lavish Mardi Gras party. He had been inside many times but was still amazed that an entire parade could end its route inside, floats, marching bands, flambeaus and all.

Drew's take on Mardi Gras had changed with age. Fun was a given but realistically, if you had seen one Carnival, you had pretty much seen them all. The day itself was essentially a citywide social experiment wrapped in what would one day be called a rave, and had few rivals as an interesting forum for observing human behavior.

The faces changed but the roles seldom did, and yin always tagged along with yang. There were Bible-belt tourists in tucked-in button-down shirts; inebriated women who coaxed extra parade throws by nonchalantly flashing their breasts; international visitors mingling with mellow locals; overworked police, some blasé while others cracked skulls with little provocation; and wandering among them all, that semi-permanent cadre of lost souls always drawn to places like the Quarter and Key West and the Haight.

Mardi Gras threw them all together, dressed many in outlandish costumes, mixed in enough alcohol to float a supertanker, then turned it all loose downtown and called it Fat Tuesday. Neophytes no doubt expect some level of restraint given that the setting is, after all, the streets of an American city. But some of the sights and sounds—and smells for that matter—of Fat Tuesday in downtown New Orleans could turn a flamethrower on such charming naiveté, not to mention propriety itself.

Would this be his sixteenth or seventeenth Carnival?

Damn, this year makes seventeen.

Though not a native, he called New Orleans home, having lived in the Crescent City nearly twice as long as all the other places combined. The continuous shuffle between various army posts in Texas, Okinawa, and California had left many of his childhood memories a blur. Each time they moved into new quarters, it seemed he barely knew his playmates' names before Dad's new orders arrived. It was frightening to clutch his mother's hand as the movers drove away with the family's belongings reduced again to a flatbed load of shed-sized crates stenciled with yet another new destination. As with most military brats, the turmoil was old hat by the time he was five or so, but undercurrents beyond his understanding were also at work. Only many decades later would the emotional repercussions of this nomadic life unveil their role in shaping his psyche, for better and worse.

Dad finally retired at Fort Ord near the California coast. Only one more move would be in the offing once he and Mom agreed on where to settle, or that had been the plan. Dad wanted to go home to New Orleans; Mom preferred Dallas, where she had family. Neither would budge, so they agreed to compromise and make a home in San Antonio, relatively near to both and convenient to Fort Sam Houston's facilities, an important consideration for military retirees.

But the transition from combat-decorated Master Sergeant to civilian life wasn't easy. Rank, hash marks, and ribbons are in effect a resume worn on service members' uniforms, and Dad's was respected and admired. But this meant little on the outside. In fact, his Army service was often detrimental in the tumultuous late 1960s, as was his age, though he was only forty-five. Prospective employers were brutally candid: some called him too old for a new career while others worried about military retirement pay diluting his commitment. He tried working at a bank and then the county hospital, but San Antonio never felt like home, rekindling the relocation debate.

Mom gave in and they headed for New Orleans, where another army, this one of uncles, aunts, and cousins, welcomed Drew and his siblings and quickly initiated them into local customs. His favorites were snowballs on a hot afternoon and Monday evening's traditional dinner of red beans, rice, and warm butter-soaked French bread. The talk was usually about the local economy, the oil business, Louisiana politicians' latest bizarre antics, and the hapless but entertaining Saints.

Many of his aunts and uncles had since passed and most of his cousins had families of their own. How fast the time had gone!

Near the airport, a cream-colored airliner suddenly emerged from the low murky overcast, roaring directly over the car, condensation trails streaming behind like white ribbons tied to each wingtip. The name "Ruff Air," rendered in huge cursive letters, ran from the wings nearly to the cockpit windows.

Traffic had stopped so he watched the landing. Two gray puffs of spray announced touchdown. The wing spoilers rose and the huge metal petals of the "bucket" thrust reversers deployed, creating a curtain of mist behind which the plane disappeared.

He couldn't help but smile at the sight. Perhaps it boded well for the errand he was there to run.

* * *

The rain continued on and off through Monday night but all the krewes managed to roll. Then, as if directed by Zeus himself, the front blew through with impeccable timing. Fat Tuesday dawned freezing cold but perfectly clear. Millions of celebrants, many costumed and as many already tipsy at an early hour, swarmed Downtown, the suburbs, and especially the Quarter.

All three TV channels had coverage. The helicopter shots were like watching bees on a hive, the people gravitating toward floats like metal shavings to a magnet. Zulu, Elks, Crescent City, Grela...all threw their favors under a sky as purely blue as a gas flame. His Majesty Rex, King of Carnival since 1872, reigned in grand style, an improbably pleasant end to an otherwise bleak Carnival season.

Well, pleasant for most. For others, all that would remain tomorrow were epic hangovers and dicey attempts to stitch together cryptic shreds of memory. The city would haul away tons of garbage, pay city staff thousands of overtime hours, and discharge most of the Orleans Parish Prison's overnight guests.

Whatever the best or worst of the day, Drew's activities were pedestrian in comparison. His airport expedition had yielded a stack of employment applications and he spent the extra annual holiday filling them out. He honored one Carnival tradition, periodically scarfing down another piece of king cake and watching a few minutes of the parade coverage.

Each break restarted the introspection that had spurred him to action.

Why did I wait so long?

Good intentions had died by the wayside, starved by his poor choices. He had gradually realized how those decisions had methodically washed away paths once rife with possibilities. Time and circumstance culled one promising course after another until nothing remained but a dark trap called the here and now. Marty and the sales job disaster were the catalysts that brought it all into sharp relief: if his life was to be what he wanted it to be, it might be now or never.

Still, even Drew had to admit that resigning might have been a brashly proactive move considering he did not have a job of any sort, an interview scheduled, or so much as a lead.

I have some money saved, he reassured himself. *Sure, I may have to start low and pay my dues, but how hard can it be to get an entry-level position?*

A glance at the pile of applications broke his reverie. Four hours and a spare typewriter ribbon later, he stood in the Gretna post office reflecting on the hope the envelopes in his hand represented. The addressees included majors like Delta, Eastern, Trans Global and Pan Am along with Piedmont, Southwest, Ozark, Royale, and Ruff Air. He dropped them into the mail slot, casting his fate in a new and compelling direction, confident he would get a call within a few weeks.

* * *

St. Patrick's Day came and went, but no one called. Surprised, Drew phoned each carrier to get the manager's name for a follow-up letter but failed because the local phone listings weren't local, they went to reservations centers. Annoyed at not having asked the names while picking up the applications, he sent the letters with a generic greeting.

Spring blossomed, children hunted Easter eggs, and flags went up for Memorial Day, all without even a nibble. Flickers of doubt danced around the rapidly receding edges of hope. He kept busy, having lunch with Brock a couple of times a month, joining some friends to visit the World's Fair, reading stacks of library books, and riding his bike. He had cut expenses to the bone and had plenty of savings left. He shoved the doubts aside.

I'll be fine.

By June, he rarely left home. He told himself he had to be available for calls but in reality, just getting up, showering, and dressing had become an effort. He shaved twice a week if that and badly needed a haircut. The answering machine received intense scrutiny whenever he ventured out and returned to find no messages. He even rode up to Time Saver and made a test call from the pay phone to verify the thing was working. Occasionally he simply stared at the glowing red zero as if sheer desire could somehow cause the phone to ring and place an airline representative eager to hire him at the other end.

His outlook darkened with each passing day. He was unnerved by his dwindling bank account, depressed that not a single airline seemed remotely interested in him, and concerned that some disqualifying defect on the applications had slipped his notice. Had he thought to keep copies, he would have combed through them again and again.

Mom, whose concern for his well-being had steadily escalated as time passed, suggested a fill-in job to get some money coming in. He thought it over.

No. I need to be available for an interview when someone calls.

But no one called.

THREE

Late on a broiling Tuesday afternoon, his reserves of money and hope both at new and drastic lows, Drew's spirit neared surrender. He was half-heartedly reading the want ads when the phone rang. He ran for it, paused to collect his thoughts, and answered. A young woman asked for him and identified herself as Kelly, an administrative supervisor with Ruff Air. They were hiring part-time; was he still interested in interviewing?

Drew had waited so long for such a call and was so surprised it had finally come that he stood tongue-tied. Fortunately, he recovered quickly.

"Yes, absolutely."

"Are you available tomorrow? It's really short notice and we can—"

"Yes!" Later he wondered whether the emphatic interruption had come across as interest or flat-out desperation.

"Great! Ask for me at the ticket counter at eight."

Once he stopped whooping in celebration, his excitement evolved into stony determination not to blow this precious opportunity. He checked the time, scrambled out to the car, and got through the barber shop door right before they flipped the sign to "Closed."

He grabbed a burger on the way home and spent the evening preparing for every question he could imagine being asked. Explaining the departure from Streak and being unemployed for so long would be the thorniest assignment. He mulled the best approach while dusting off his dress shoes and touching up the shine.

He woke early, ate a quick breakfast, hacked off four days of stubble, showered, and dressed. At the airport, he chewed up a breath mint, popped into a men's room for a final mirror check, and approached the Ruff Air ticket counter at exactly the specified time.

A petite woman with mocha skin, beautiful eyes almost amber in color, and a name tag identifying her as Regina took his name. She asked him to wait to the side, then made a brief call. She and the other agents cast several furtive glances his way, perhaps sizing him up. After a minute or two, a trim brunette appeared through a door leading through the wall behind the ticket counter. Her attire was the same as the agents wore: dark blue skirt and vest with a white blouse and patterned scarf tie.

"Drew, I'm Kelly. Thanks for coming in. This way."

She guided him through the door and down a hall into a back office which featured a glass wall looking out on the apron. Flights of several airlines were in various stages of arrival and departure, instantly capturing his attention and triggering an involuntary grin.

Kelly grinned too. "Pretty cool, yeah?"

He nodded. "Yes, very."

"Please," she said, indicating her visitor chair, a battered gray metal fold-up with PROPERTY OF C & S AIR LINES stenciled on the back. Looking over his application, she asked about a few things, noting his responses, then said, "The pay is $6.25 an hour, plus 20 cents an hour extra for afternoon shifts. There are ways to pick up hours and there's overtime, too. I'll tell you more about that if Barb decides to bring you on."

She asked him to wait and disappeared into the adjoining office. The shock of hearing the pay rate took a second to wear off. He started calculating. At 25 hours a week, the annual total was about a third of his former earnings. He hadn't known the pay was so low, but at this point, he was all in one way or the other.

Large destination posters in metal frames adorned the walls. Each featured a clever three-dimensional paper sculpture photographed against a deep blue background with the corresponding city's name spelled out beneath. An old-fashioned movie camera represented Los Angeles, the actors on the "film" cut out like paper dolls; an art deco hotel and palm trees touted Miami; and the famous "Welcome to fabulous Las Vegas" sign invited visitors to Sin City. His favorite was the one for New Orleans—an elegantly intricate depiction of a sidewheeler complete with lacy railings, curling bow waves, fluttering pennants, and "smoke" pouring from its split-top stacks.

Kelly reappeared and ushered him into the station manager's office. It also had the ramp view but just two items on the wall. One was a takeoff shot of a Ruff Air DC-9 noticeably smaller than the one he had watched land a few months before. This was especially obvious because the long, distinctive ending stroke on the word "Air" was almost comically lopped off. Exhaust had blackened the rear end and the plane had almost a disheveled look, to the extent a commercial airliner could. More puzzling was a black and white photo of a tumbleweed. Against the wall, under the framed photos, was a credenza with chrome legs and scuffed woodgrain veneer which held a model of a Ruff Air jet, some books, neat piles of paperwork, and a scanner which emitted a murmur of radio traffic.

A tall woman came around from behind the desk, which was clean and orderly but had seen better days. She had black hair, green eyes, a warm smile, and a firm grip to match her direct manner. She introduced herself as Barb, motioned for him to sit, turned off the scanner, and got right down to business. Pen poised for notetaking, she said, "So tell me about yourself."

He did, then answered other questions until she eventually tossed him the hot potato.

"Help me understand why you left your last position."

He explained as well as he could, which really wasn't very well.

"So," she said, "it sounds like it really wasn't a good fit for you."

Sounds so much better when you put it that way.

"Why do you think this will be better?"

He laid it out, highlighting his operational background, fitting his skills with the job description as he understood it, and handing over copies of commendations earned through the years.

Her pen was busy. Without looking up, she said, "You left your other job months ago. Why haven't you gotten another one in the meantime?"

He thought a moment and answered from the heart.

"I probably should have, but getting into the airline industry means an awful lot to me."

"Why?"

Though careful not to overdo it, he shared his intangible motivations, touching on his passion for aviation and airlines, and finished by saying, "It's always felt like what I'm supposed to be doing."

She scribbled another note and continued, "The money isn't much to start. Can you make it on what we pay?"

Drew said "Absolutely!" while thinking, *I hope so!*

"Good. It doesn't sound like a lot but there are ways to pick up plenty of hours, both straight and overtime."

Kelly called Barb away for a few minutes, which he spent watching the activity outside and pondering the tumbleweed. When she returned, he waited quietly as she finished up her notes, paper-clipped them to the copies he had provided and slipped it all into a manila folder labeled with his name. A glimpse of its contents revealed the follow-up letter he had sent, in which she had highlighted several lines.

Barb rose and offered her hand.

"I discuss hiring decisions with the supervisors. We'll let you know."

Drew thanked her for her time and the chance to earn a place on her team. She was tough to read, but he left feeling cautiously optimistic. Was it reality or wishful thinking?

Curiosity about his potential employer prompted a stop at the main library on Loyola, where he asked a research librarian what information might be available. He expected little and was pleasantly surprised when she compiled an impressive collection of material.

A 1980 *Time* issue featured a brief piece on the plain-spoken W.W. Ruff and his new venture. After decades of success as an airline executive, Ruff finally had the means to run his own show. He laughed out loud at Ruff's blunt take on finally being top dog: "This time I won't be taking orders from a bunch of horse's asses!"

Looking around self-consciously, he thought, *How refreshingly direct!*

On microfilm were various local and wire service features describing off-beat promotions Ruff Air had cooked up, like the one tying in their unique non-smoking policy with Great American Smokeout Day. Smokers could sign an affidavit pledging to kick the habit and trade four unopened cartons of cigarettes for a free return ticket. To keep costs reasonable, the sale lasted just two weeks and only a few seats were set aside on each flight. The media ate it up and plenty of people, including some non-smokers savvy enough to act the part, took advantage.

Each Ruff Air location then shipped its considerable haul of ciggies to headquarters, where the airline's founder presided over a parking lot bonfire that attracted the attention of a wire service stringer, a couple of TV stations, the *Chronicle* and *Post*, and two watchful engine companies from the Houston Fire Department.

A deeper treatment by *Air Transport World* provided additional insight. Mr. Ruff had done an excellent job of raising capital. His reputation and business sense inspired investors' confidence and soon the startup's war chest ranked among the biggest ever. Conservative by nature, Ruff initially leased two McDonnell Douglas MD-80 series jets configured with 155 leather seats, all Coach class. The maiden trip in July 1981 flew with high hopes, optimism, and the pride that came with seeing shiny new planes in the air.

The excitement lasted two weeks, until the air traffic controllers' union went on strike after a long and contentious standoff with the Federal Aviation Administration.

Ruff had almost thirty years in aviation, and though others would unfairly be credited for much of his best work, his management prowess was legendary. But launching Ruff Air on the assumption the controllers wouldn't strike nearly sank his new airline right out of the blocks. Reduced airway capacity forced Ruff Air to cancel sixty percent of its schedule in the first week. With no interline agreements—arrangements under which carriers honored each other's tickets—there were few rebooking options and the airline had to refund most of the fares. Still, Ruff remained confident because the strike would eventually be resolved as they all are.

Then President Reagan fired every controller who ignored his ultimatum to end the strike and barred them from ever returning to federal employment. The time required to rebuild the ATC system dimmed Ruff Air's chances considerably. Saved by resisting the urge to make a splashy and expensive debut, the airline gamely struggled through those early troubles but burned most of its cash in the process. The balance sheet had been seesawing between red and black ever since.

Drew winced, hoping the outlook had improved.

There had been expansion and changes, like the addition of a First Class cabin, but W.W.'s straight-shooting style hadn't filtered down to marketing. The airline chose to call First Class "Preferred" and Coach "Competitive."

He shook his head. *Wouldn't that confuse people?*

There was more, plenty more, in extensive and disheartening detail, about the wrecking ball Congress had crashed through the industry's status quo with deregulation.

From the dawn of American commercial aviation, the federal government had held all the cards in an iron fist. Any carrier flying between states had no choice but to play those dealt to them. The Civil Aeronautics Board controlled every fare and while flying wasn't especially affordable, the system motivated outstanding service since it was the only basis on which airlines could compete.

Uncle Sam also drew the route map. Profitable or not, airlines could not add or drop a destination without plodding through a route case before the CAB, a process that too often felt about as rapid as continental drift. This made meaningful planning essentially impossible. Carriers had to maintain service indefinitely in money-losing markets and couldn't expand in promising new cities when opportunities arose. If carmakers played under similar rules, the government would have prohibited the Ford Motor Company from building Mustangs no matter how many unsold Edsels crowded its empty showrooms.

After laboring under such autocracy, one might think airlines would welcome deregulation, and some did. In fact, one avid proponent was W.W. Ruff, then an executive at an ambitious intrastate carrier. But among the majors, only United was in favor. A partial or more gradual loosening of federal control might have received a warmer response but as it was, many shared the reservations held by the future leader of American Airlines, Robert L. Crandall.

Never one to mince words, Crandall had torched a deregulation advocate with a notably candid aside in 1977.

"You fucking academic eggheads! You don't know shit!" he railed. "You can't deregulate this industry. You're going to wreck it! You don't know a goddam thing!"

Few would ever label Crandall a diplomat, but many would call him a prophet.

Objections notwithstanding, deregulation became the law, freeing airlines to charge any fare and fly wherever they wanted. Only a few constraints remained, such as limited landing slots at congested airports like LaGuardia and Washington National. The swift transition and resulting Wild West environment left airline leaders and executives blinking and squinting in the harsh light of sudden choice. As one carrier's president told a reporter off the record, "For fifty years we couldn't scratch our asses without government approval. Now they say we can do anything we damn well please. That takes some getting used to."

For most, perhaps, but not for Harding Lawrence, who made his name with a 1960s makeover of stodgy Braniff that turned heads all over the country. The cabin crews got wild and stylish Pucci uniforms and the airline backed up its "End of the Plain Plane" advertisements by painting its aircraft from a palette so vibrant that people called it the Easter Egg Fleet. The airline embraced the notoriety, eventually dubbing the Crayon box of paint schemes "Flying Colors."

When the constraints of regulation ended, Lawrence believed the government would soon reconsider and slam shut the window of opportunity. Braniff rushed to expand, adding new routes all over the country, at one point opening more cities in one day—sixteen—than they might have in twenty years under the old system. In that heady rush of optimism, no one at Braniff dreamed their airline would soon become a cautionary tale, the first of many to have their corporate necks wrestled into the guillotine of a merciless new reality. Braniff had become the lead lemming in an industry rushing headlong into financial disaster, and in May 1982, it reached the cliff.

Staggering under its financial obligations, out of cash, and rebuffed by potential merger partners and new investors, Braniff declared bankruptcy. The airline matter-of-factly informed its workers via Mailgram of a "temporary cessation of work because of circumstances beyond the company's control" and stranded thousands of passengers by immediately grounding its planes.

Employees, bewildered and under siege, had nothing left but shattered pride, memories, and a final paycheck many banks declined to honor. Many wept openly at the sight of their kaleidoscopic fleet clustered forlornly on the DFW ramp, knowing in their hearts the Flying Colors would never fly again.

The abrupt downfall, the first major airline failure in five decades, shocked the country. Forget profits; most carriers' very survival was in question. When one went under, what followed had more in common with a Serengeti kill than traditional corporate America. The survivors tore at the carcass for anything worth salvaging but instead of meat and bone, the scavengers sought landing slots, aircraft, equipment, and facilities.

Some familiar names disappeared from the skies and more eventually would. Their fleets went to competitors at fire sale prices or were parked in colorful herringbone rows in the preservative low humidity of various desert storage points. The end came so suddenly on several sorry occasions that airport staff reported for work to find the locks changed, guards around the aircraft, and schedule boards stripped. Even the names of the airlines themselves were gone from behind the ticket counters and gates, leaving ghostly outlines that mocked the anxious employees as they and their customers milled about trying to make sense of it all.

The carriers still afloat were slowly bleeding out, marginally solvent and bobbing in oceans of red ink, desperately hammering and sawing at the chains and anchors that would ultimately drag many under. High costs, volatile fuel prices, inflexible management, obsolete equipment, labor troubles, unprofitable routes, an evolving clientele…all came together to create an extraordinary whirlwind that ripped away generations of conventional wisdom. In all the thrashing about, dozens of smaller communities either lost air service or had it reduced to a few daily frequencies to hub cities—funnels through which nearly all air travelers had to pass.

Passengers loathed connections to the point of making them a punchline. One joke about Delta's monster hub declared that when people died, those meriting Heaven went nonstop while the devil's conscripts were forced to suffer through one last connection in Atlanta.

But deregulation also brought opportunity. Entrepreneurs near and far jumped into the aerial fray and airlines sprang up seemingly overnight. The most well-known was People Express, whose astounding growth almost defied belief. Only two years after launching service between Newark and Buffalo with second-hand 737s, a People Express 747 touched down at London Gatwick. Along with this ambitious poster child came aspirants like Air Atlanta, America West, Jet America, Pride Air, Air South, Midway, Air Hawaii, New York Air, Air Chaparral, and Ruff Air itself. Just about anybody who could scrape together some capital and a few airplanes decided to try their luck. They seemed unaware that the objective—consistently making money flying people from one place to another—had confounded the best business minds ever since the St. Petersburg-Tampa Airboat Line boarded inaugural airline passenger A.C. Pheil in 1914.

Most newcomers flamed out as quickly as they formed, the ink hardly dry on new stationery, their existence barely a hyphen on history's timeline. Even People Express would be gone within a few years, swallowed up by Texas Air Corporation.

The rest, big and small, old and new, were roiling with change and uncertainty, fighting for their lives, no holds barred. Ruff Air was—so far—a rare survivor among deregulation's stepchildren, trying to find its place in a shrinking flock aptly described by a *Time* headline as "Small Birds in a Big Sky."

Drew sat back and looked at the ceiling.

Holy crap!

Suddenly a memory popped into his head, a crisp October morning in 1978. Dad, sipping coffee and working his way through the *Times-Picayune* as he did each morning, had laid two sections of the paper aside for his son. A couple of months into 11th grade, he had always been a bookworm and having the sports helped pass the long ride to West Jeff down in Harvey. Today there was some lagniappe on the Business page too, something about airlines and the government.

Drew had dashed in, sitting down long enough to devour some toast and gulp down a glass of orange juice.

"Thanks, Dad," he said on his way out the door.

He loved aviation even more than the Saints, so today Manning and company would have to wait. President Carter had signed the Airline Deregulation Act, and below that article was a piece speculating on potential ramifications locally. According to both, big changes were on the horizon, but nobody really knew what.

He had looked out the window, thinking. The law was supposed to increase competition by abolishing a bunch of rules, but so what if airlines didn't have to wait on some bureaucrat's approval to change a price or open a new city?

Seriously, is this really such a big deal?

Well, now he had his answer.

After returning the materials and thanking the librarian, he headed home, grimly hoping he hadn't made a terrible mistake. It didn't really matter; when Ruff Air made an offer—he couldn't bear to contemplate that they might not—there was no choice but to swallow any misgivings and follow it through.

* * *

Kelly phoned again early the next day. She offered a cheerful good morning followed by a single question: "Can you start tomorrow?"

They agreed to meet at the ticket counter at seven sharp.

He stood quietly after hanging up, staring down at the phone, unable to muster even a smile. There was no elation, no relief. If anything, he felt tired and old. He sat down on the edge of his bed, shifting his gaze to the floor and then to his reflection in the dresser mirror. Instead of the expected joy, it took everything he had not to break down and weep.

He laid back and watched the ceiling fan's slow revolutions. It was mid-afternoon when he woke up. Groggy and no happier than before, he dug around and scrounged up a pathetic meal of Pop-Tarts and Dr. Pepper that took maybe a minute to wolf down and that long only because he nuked the pastries to warm them. There was nothing on TV and he didn't feel like reading. He took out his bike, couldn't think of anywhere he wanted to ride, put it back.

What's the problem here, bro? Isn't this what you've been waiting for?

Maybe a shower would help. He stripped and stepped in.

Under the hot, relaxing spray, the clutter in his mind gradually cleared. He hadn't realized how far he had sunk into despair, how much the financial strain and long months of watching his hopes fade had chipped away at his spirit. The unexpected offer from Ruff Air was still unreal, slowly working its way into his consciousness. The more he thought about finally achieving his goal, the faster the doubt and stress and weariness followed the soap lather down the drain.

The money part would be iffy for a while and his sojourn at the library had definitely fostered a twinge of apprehension. Should he have been more careful of what he'd wished for? Time would tell, but the wish had come true, and by the time he had toweled off and dressed, he was fired up and determined to make the most of it.

F O U R

Friday morning, refreshed and renewed, Drew grabbed an apple and left before dawn. He refused to bet a punctual arrival against the perpetually tangled rush-hour traffic on the GNO Bridge.

There was thus enough time to read the paper over a more substantial breakfast, watch a couple of departures from the arched main terminal's observation deck, and play two games of Asteroids. It was still ten to seven when Kelly, coffee in hand, found him standing nervously near the ticket counter.

"Oh," she said, "you're here already?"

You have no idea.

"Sorry," she went on, "I would have bought you a cup."

"Thanks, but that's okay. I don't drink coffee."

With a little laugh she said, "Don't worry, you will. Come on, let's start on your paperwork."

Two hours later, the newbie again sat in the back office, but this time the view didn't capture his attention. Instead, he inspected two laminated ID cards, the first bearing his name, photograph, employee number, date of hire, and his new employer's logo. The other was similar but issued by the airport. Most intriguing was the small green plastic fish dangling from the clip, its meaning a mystery. Issued with his IDs by Kelly, who only smiled enigmatically at his quizzical glance, it was perhaps a trout, though not well crafted and thus hard to identify with certainty.

She again shepherded her charge into Barb's office, where the manager spoke about the operation, the chain of command, and her expectations. She was polite and businesslike, yet a flinty strength simmered beneath the surface. She didn't smile often but when she did, it lit up her face and lent balance to a somewhat stern demeanor. Though not explicitly stated, it was clear that woe awaited those who disappointed her.

Drew still wondered about the tumbleweed but held back, worried the question would sound stupid, and then it was too late. Barb rose, wished him luck over a handshake, and directed him back to Kelly.

The admin supervisor was on the phone, so he waited by the window, stomach tumbling with the anxiety of starting a new job. He would gladly take the butterflies over the dark months of worry. Watching the activities on the ramp, he couldn't believe he would be out there with them soon.

Some of his zeal obviously showed. Kelly smiled as she hung up, beckoned him over, and said, "You're an airline guy, I can see it already."

"I hope so. I've wanted this for a long time."

"You'll do fine. Okay, off we go."

She explained the various airport roles, the training regimen, and how the staffing worked. Teamwork was essential for any airline to succeed, especially at smaller carriers where economic realities forced them to operate with fewer staff and less equipment. She emphasized that carrying one's own weight, and more when necessary, also directly influenced one's prospects for advancement.

Ruff Air's new hires started as part-time Customer Service Representatives. Referred to as CSRs, they initially worked only on the ramp, known in airline parlance as "below the wing": handling baggage, servicing lavatories, directing aircraft at the gate, and performing all the other tasks involved in "turning" a flight.

Upon becoming proficient, which meant both procedural competency and appropriate esprit de corps, newcomers earned the privilege of training "above the wing" in customer contact activities such as ticketing, check-in, and baggage service. The instruction eventually progressed to Operations, where agents computed aircraft weight and balance, assigned gates, and communicated with flights via radio. The idea was to qualify every CSR to perform any role.

"Working all the jobs makes it fun," Kelly said, "'cause once you're trained, you'll do something different almost every day. It never gets boring."

Some CSRs even doubled as reserve flight attendants, which Ruff Air called Inflight Service Representatives or ISRs. Regulations mandated the minimum number of cabin crew based on an aircraft's capacity. Economically, keeping reserves was impractical anywhere but their base at Houston's Hobby Airport. Elsewhere, if an ISR could not fly for whatever reason, an FAA-qualified local employee filled out the crew. Avoiding cancellations more than justified training and overtime costs.

Supervisors managed customer service and ramp operations, with lead agents beneath them—one assigned to the ticket counter, the other to the gates. Leads served as floaters, stepping in wherever needed and empowered to make decisions that didn't require supervisory approval.

"Why isn't there a lead agent on the ramp or in baggage service?"

"Good question. There's no need. Both are pretty cut and dried, but ticketing gets complicated at times and when you get into working oversold flights and such, there's always something for the gate leads to do."

"How do they pick leads and supervisors?"

"It's the same basic merit and seniority process."

"So," he asked, "you have to earn your way up? Makes sense, does every airline do it that way?"

"No, there's one other I know of but a lot go on straight seniority. Mr. Ruff doesn't think that should be the only basis for putting people with customers or giving them authority. Don't get me wrong though, seniority is still up there with the Holy Grail around here."

"What about going from part-time to full-time?"

"When full-time shifts open up, they're offered to part-timers in order of seniority."

"What about days off?"

"That's part of the bid. The schedules are awarded by seniority."

"Vacation?"

She smiled. "Guess."

"I'll go with seniority."

"Yep. We even assign lockers that way. Yours is on the bottom back in the corner by the way. I'll show you in a minute."

He looked at the employee number on his ID, which was also his own seniority number: 1974.

Kelly continued, "Memorize that now; you'll be asked for it a lot. And don't worry, it's slowed down a lot but with transfers and people leaving for whatever reason it still goes pretty quick. Rondell's the number three part-timer and he's only been here two years."

"So there aren't two thousand people ahead of me?"

"Nope. They don't reissue employee numbers if someone leaves so it's only about twelve hundred and that's in the whole company. You only have to worry about the CSRs and really only the part-timers here if you get down to it."

"The pilots have their own list then?"

"Yep, and so do the ISRs, TSRs, the mechanics...let's see…oh yeah, Dispatch too."

"TSR, is that for Telephone Service Representative maybe, like the people who take reservations?"

"You're close. It's actually Telephone Sales Representative, but very good! You catch on quick! Now for shift trades and LWOP."

The last thing sounded like "ell-wop."

"And what?"

"Leave Without Pay, LWOP. There's a sign-up sheet and if we have more people than we need based on the load forecast, some can go home. That's also awarded by seniority. As far as shift trades, it's pretty simple. If you want to work and someone else wants off, you fill out a trade request. If it's approved, you come to work for the other person. If you want off, it's the other way around."

A quick facilities tour followed, then there were several personnel forms to fill out, including one authorizing payroll deductions to cover the $200 cost of his uniforms. When he finished and handed them back, he asked, "Hey, by the way, what's with the picture of the Ruff Air plane on Barb's wall, the smaller one?"

She beamed. "Oh, that's 'Spike'!"

Years before, Ruff Air had urgently needed a plane pending new deliveries. Briefly leasing a small DC-9-30 that had rolled off the Douglas line in 1968 provided the cheapest, quickest option. The jet was powered by tired old engines and packed with well-worn coach seats, having been flown for 15 years by a European carrier before being traded back to Douglas.

The problem wasn't age; DC-3s built in the 1930s were still flying passengers in some places. This airplane just had a litany of minor but vexing issues, some disquieting but none unsafe, and addressing them made little sense on a short lease. It lacked the noise-suppression technology becoming common, drawing complaints from both passengers and people on the ground; whistling cabin doors invited uneasy glances, especially from ISRs, who were strapped into their jumpseats next to the leaky seals; pilots grumbled that it flew like a lead sled; and rampers quickly learned that kneeling on someone's checked garment bag while stacking luggage was the only way to avoid picking up itchy little fiberglass strands from the bin walls and floor. This happened in most aircraft but Spike was the worst, often leaving CSRs scratching like flea-ridden monkeys.

But employees' affection for the little jet had somehow grown in inverse proportion to the bedeviling idiosyncrasies. Eventually purchased by an Alaskan cargo company, Spike's old Ruff Air colleagues obviously remembered him with fondness, however misplaced.

"Who named it 'Spike'?"

"Our maintenance director—after his dog. That's not a coincidence. You'll see pictures of Spike all over the place. And watch for ship six seventy-three, we named it after him."

She was getting a little misty. "Boy, those were crazy times. Hectic as heck, but a lot of fun. I miss that little guy."

Her eyes refocused and she went on, "Well, we better get back to your paperwork." She left him with a binder of employment policies to review. He replaced it on the shelf an hour later and initialed a document called the Read Log to affirm his understanding.

Kelly then pointed him down the hall to the "training room," which wasn't a classroom, rather a storage area heavy with the smell of old cardboard. Some school-style desks with chipped wooden chairs were wedged into one corner amid racks of boxed baggage tags and blank ticket stock. In another corner stood three life-size color cutouts of W.W. Ruff, his hands posed as if holding an advertising sign someone could position in a slot.

The trainee closed his eyes, rubbed his temples for a moment, then opened the first manual and began memorizing airport codes. There were hundreds, many of which he knew from his days at Streak. Some destinations were logical enough, like MIA for Miami and AUS for Austin; others were obvious but easy to confuse, like SJC for San Jose, California, SJO for San Jose, Costa Rica, and SJU for San Juan; and to make things especially interesting, some that were both easily confused *and* less than obvious, like MCO for Orlando and Kansas City's MCI.

As for New Orleans' MSY, the city built the airport over the Moisant Stock Yards, named for aviation pioneer John Bevins Moisant. The intrepid airman's accomplishments were nearly inconceivable given his short time as a pilot. On only his third time aloft, he was the first aviator to carry a passenger over a city, Paris. His sixth flight achieved another milestone, flying the first known passengers to cross the English Channel by air—his mechanic, Albert Fileux, and Moisant's cat, Mademoiselle Fifi.

The feline eventually logged some 14 flights at his side, surely a record for nonpilots in aviation's early years. As a kitten, she slept in the pilot's coat pocket, but as she grew, he had to wrap his aircraft's leather seats with a special durable type of rope to accommodate her scratching—a lesson learned at the cost of five shredded seats. He even secured her litter box to the floor, making it very likely the first airborne lavatory ever.

Moisant transferred his French pilot's license, becoming just the thirteenth registered pilot in America. And, perhaps apropos in a city noted for its historic cemeteries and voodoo, he tragically perished in a 1910 crash near the future site of the cattle pens and the airport that would bear his name. Incredibly, Moisant died less than nine months after learning to fly. Whether Fifi was absent or survived the crash is unknown, but she spent her remaining days cared for by Moisant's sister.

Another page listed airline codes. Like those for airports, many were self-evident, like AA for American and EA for Eastern. Ruff Air's was RX since the authorities had long ago assigned the more obvious choice, RA, to Royal Nepal Airlines. Each carrier also had a three-digit numeric identifier and a three-letter international code as well.

Next came the fleet. Having kept up with airliner evolution, he was familiar with the types Ruff Air flew: ten McDonnell Douglas MD-82s on lease along with six smaller DC-9-50s, bought surplus from a European carrier.

The Douglas Aircraft Company had made a lot of hay with the DC-9 type since its 1965 introduction. The original DC-9-10 series tipped the scales at around 90,000 pounds fully loaded and its Pratt & Whitney turbojets produced nearly 30,000 pounds of thrust. This made the jet so nimble and responsive that Mexicana pilots nicknamed it *el raton super loco*—"the super crazy mouse."

Douglas expanded and refined the design into –20, -30, -40, and –50 variants, enabling customers to choose whichever performance and seating capacity options fit their operation. To pilots' collective disappointment, however, engine power hovered around its original rating while the airplane's maximum weight grew with each iteration.

The 1970s brought demand for an even larger version, resulting in the DC-9-80. By then, the manufacturer had stretched the original design's length by some 44 feet and modernized its engines and systems so thoroughly that the DC-9 designation was sometimes a sales-hindering anachronism. A 1967 merger had created McDonnell Douglas, so the type was renamed the MD-80 series. Its initials had inspired the affectionate nickname "Mad Dogs."

Marketed as the Super 80, these rugged, reliable jets quickly became an industry favorite. For consistency, Ruff Air called their smaller version the Super 50. Both had twelve First

Class seats—he noted the airline no longer called it Preferred—but the Super 80 could accommodate eighteen additional passengers in Coach.

Flying only two variants made a lot of economic sense. The pair shared many of the same parts; in addition, training was easier and far less costly, especially for pilots, who could fly either one.

He shook his head.

Sixteen planes.

Majors like American, Trans Global, and United had hundreds of jets with many different seating configurations.

A surprising footnote informed him that Ruff Air coded its flight numbers. Those flown by a Super 50 started with a 5 and the ones operated by Super 80s began with an 8. Employees and perceptive travelers could thus determine which aircraft type would operate a particular flight.

The long morning of reading and memorization had spawned a pulsing rock right at the base of his skull. He downed a couple of aspirin while hurrying to his thirty-minute lunch in the cafeteria out on Concourse C. The people shuffling forward to fill their trays reflected the industry's vocations and the colors of a half-dozen airlines. He joined the line, self-conscious at having no uniform to wear, not to mention the fish, which had already elicited several knowing chuckles. He assumed it to be a badge indicating his new-hire status.

Reading more training material as he ate, he was glad the airline split trainees' first few days between course work and on-the-job training. This was designed to improve understanding by placing the book knowledge in the context of actual operations.

His train of thought derailed when some new arrivals joined the lunch line—svelte Southwest flight attendants in their trademark orange hot pants and white knee-high sidelaced boots.

Hoping no one had noticed his wide-eyed distraction, he hurriedly closed the binder and inspected Ruff Air's signature-style logo while finishing off his sandwich. An advertising trade magazine at the library had described the creative process, quoting a handwriting expert who claimed the logo conveyed "confidence, attention to detail, loyalty" and other qualities potential customers presumably valued. The mark was distinctive and eye-catching, but confidence and loyalty?

I must be missing something.

Soon he was outside scouting the best route to the Ruff Air Operations office, where he would train with a supervisor. He had overstayed lunch and now faced the prospect of walking across the hot concrete. Retracing his steps through the terminal would be much more comfortable but take twice as long.

Can't be late so I better get going.

A Ruff Air tug rounded the corner at high speed. The driver noticed Drew and startled him by swerving over and skidding to a halt.

A thin man with flowing brown hair and a Fu Manchu mustache sat at the wheel. Several boxes of printer paper or forms were stacked beside him. Drew could see himself in the man's mirrored aviators, distorted as if in an amusement park funhouse.

The driver nodded once and looked at him in silent expectation. Finally, he asked, "Aren't you going to Ops?"

Drew nodded, glancing at the boxes blocking the passenger seat, which obviously would not stay put if placed on the tug's narrow rear deck. He said, "Yeah, but…."

Another silent moment, then the driver raised his face to the sky as if savoring a cool rain.

"Jesus Christ," he said with a deep sigh and a shake of his head. "Newbies."

He waved at the back of the tug.

"I don't have time to draw you a picture, Einstein. Get on and hang on."

Drew climbed up and saw no choice but to sit facing backwards. As he looked for a way to hold on, the tug demonstrated one of its less obvious attributes. Sturdily constructed and clad in thick steel plating, their purpose was to pull baggage and lav carts. They were also powerful enough to occasionally pinch hit for the heavy pushback tractors. And despite their homely appearance, they took off like a bat out of hell when a leadfoot punched the pedal.

The tug leapt forward without warning, nearly dumping him and his binder full of papers onto the pavement. Only a flailing foot's chance landing on the towing gear kept him from tumbling off. After a moment, he finally managed a tenuous grasp on the seat back.

They zipped across the airport, dodging a Trans Global 757 pushing off its gate, lumbering fuel tankers and catering trucks, a remarkably loud Florida Express jet, and an American tug towing a long train of metal containers. The speed, serpentine path, and pungent mix of exhaust and fuel vapors made the passenger a little dizzy, especially when he tried to look around, so most of these were seen only as they receded into the distance.

After passing a solitary suitcase laying far from any gate, Drew leaned forward and shouted over the noise.

"Shouldn't we pick that up?"

The driver shook his head and shouted back. "Not our bag, not our problem!"

Nearing the concourse, the man hit the brakes so hard that the tires left black streaks on the concrete. By the time Drew clambered down, the driver had already taken the boxes from the passenger seat and was about to disappear through a black door stenciled with OPERATIONS under the omnipresent cursive logo.

Inside was a space featuring a cracked floor and more destination posters, though unframed and attached with thumbtacks. Someone had used more tacks and black thread to show Ruff Air's routes on a faded Gulf Oil highway map of the fifty states. A few empty holes marked destinations that must not have panned out. The lights emitted a low buzz and one tube flickered unpredictably as if it had a tic. To the left were a couple of doors and in front of them, the top half of a woman's head behind a chest-high counter.

The rampers, seated on ancient plastic chairs and a threadbare sofa, had been chatting and sipping soft drinks or coffee. Everyone paused and looked expectantly at the newcomer, but the tug driver called out before he could speak.

"So what's your name, man?"

He laughed at the response. A woman with curly red hair said, "What's so funny about that?"

"Drewbie the newbie," the man cackled. "It's perfect. Oh, and nice fish."

The redhead said, "Hey, you carried the fish once upon a time too, Mister Rob, and I happen to know a few stories. In fact, tell me again how long it took you to move up to agent training?"

The woman behind the long counter stood, smiled, and extended her hand.

"Hi, I'm Peggy. Please, just ignore the peanut gallery." Nodding toward the office door, she said, "Grayson's expecting you but he had to go upstairs. Have a seat and he should be back in a sec."

An unseen radio came to life. "New Orleans Ops, Tumbleweed Eight Sixty-seven in range with eight point one."

The rampers rose and filed out the door, donning leather work gloves and hearing protectors that looked like stereo headphones.

Peggy responded, "Tumbleweed Eight Sixty-seven, New Orleans copies you in range with eight point one, take gate Seven Bravo on arrival."

"Roger, Seven Bravo for Tumbleweed Eight Six Seven."

Drew asked, "Tumbleweed?"

"Our air traffic control call sign. Lots of airlines have them. Like Pan Am, their flights are 'Clipper such-and-such' on the radio. British Airways is 'Speedbird' and America West is based in Arizona, so they're 'Cactus.' Air Florida is gone now, but they were 'Palm.' My favorite, besides ours of course, is China Airlines. They use 'Dynasty.' How cool is that?" She chuckled. "With five thousand years of heritage, I suppose they've earned it."

"What does 'in range' mean?"

"Well," Peggy said, "it meant just that way back in the early days of radio, that the plane was close enough to hear them calling, usually about ten minutes before landing. The radios are way better now but the purpose is the same, so we'll be ready when they get here."

He was also curious about what "eight point one" referred to but decided to ask another time. There was obviously a lot to learn but now the framed photo in Barb's office made sense. And this was nothing like school or his previous jobs–this was fun!

"Can I go out and watch until Grayson comes back?"

"Absolutely! Leave your stuff on the table there."

He set his binder down and started for the door.

"Drew!"

He turned and caught the battered hearing protector Peggy tossed to him.

"You'll need those," she said. "Welcome to the asylum, and good luck!"

FIVE

Drew thanked Peggy and rushed out the door as Grayson, his trainer, was coming in.

"Whoa!" Grayson said. "Easy there." He stuck out his hand and said, "You Drew? Good! Follow me!" His Texas accent was as thick as his mane of salt-and-pepper hair.

As they walked, the rookie watched the crew stage assorted ground equipment around yellow caution lines that followed the shape of a parked airplane. There were baggage carts; a large, boxy apparatus with "GPU" stenciled on it; the lavatory service cart, streaked with blue stains; a tow bar; and a squat, brawny pushback tractor. All were painted the same cream as the aircraft, with nicks and scrapes that either revealed the dark metal beneath or were touched up with paint that was the same color but didn't quite match. A catering truck and fuel tanker rounded out the waiting entourage.

One man positioned the tow bar so a ramper could quickly attach it to an arriving aircraft's nose gear. The red-headed woman trotted over to the GPU and soon it barked, hesitated, and finally clamored to loud, smoky life. Piled next to it was a black bundle of cables as big around as a fire hose. The woman grabbed the brick-sized plug on the end and lugged it over next to the tow bar. After looking around to ensure everything was in place, she clambered atop the pushback tractor.

Grayson stopped and said, "Stay here and get a sense of what's goin' on. I'll be back in a few minutes."

Drew nodded, looking toward the runway. Within seconds, the first of several imminent arrivals rolled by, thrust reversers open and engines roaring. The plane vanished behind the end of Concourse B then reappeared, taxiing to the gate near which he stood.

As it approached, the woman atop the pushback tractor raised her arms like a football referee signaling a touchdown. The training manual identified this as the stance of the marshaler, who guided the captain in parking.

The concrete had soaked up heat all morning and the apron temperature was nearly 110°, but he was too excited to notice any discomfort. Sweat blasting from every pore, he stared, captivated, as the flight turned up the line. With it came a unique aroma, a mishmash of oiled machinery, scorched rubber, hot metal, jet fuel, and exhaust. The noise was like a blowtorch fed through concert amps. He pressed his hearing protector cups tighter against his ears, but that was no better.

A ramper waiting to place the wheel chocks nodded and grinned sympathetically behind his sunglasses.

Arriving with the flight was amazement.

I can't believe they're going to pay me to be out here!

The redheaded woman atop the tow tractor used hand signals as the jet rolled up the yellow line. Sweat already darkened much of her blue uniform, the back of which had "Ruff Air" in the ubiquitous cursive lettering. Her hips wiggled as she moved, kind of wagging out in the opposite direction of her signals. When the plane closed in, she lowered her arms to her sides, then raised both in an arc, slowly bringing her hands together over her head. This indicated the decreasing distance between the Super 80's nose wheel and the hash mark labeled "S80" that bisected the yellow line. Accordingly, the captain slowed the plane to a crawl.

As the tire rolled onto the mark, she brought her hands together and the aircraft stopped. She cued the man with the chocks, who placed one ahead of a main gear tire and one behind. Another worked the huge GPU umbilical plug into a socket near the nose. The redhead held up her fists with her thumbs pointed toward one another, brought the thumbs in together, then opened her left hand and struck her palm from below with the still clenched right fist. This meant "chocks in" and "ground power connected." One of the pilots flipped some switches and the engine noise ebbed.

Nearly simultaneously, the jetbridge accordioned out; the redhead hopped down and helped pull empty carts up next to the fuselage; a tan-shirted woman exited a truck marked "Dobbs" and began guiding the driver to the galley door; a fueler opened a panel under the right wing, hoisted up a massive nozzle, and locked it onto a fitting; a tug brought the lav cart up under the left engine; and a ramper opened the forward cargo bin, hopped up, and climbed inside. Soon bags were being rapidly unloaded.

The gate CSR had promptly opened the cabin door and made a welcoming announcement. Deplaning passengers could be seen passing by a little gap between the jetbridge canopy and the fuselage. The gap closed as the CSR worked some controls to extend the canopy, snugging its edges up to the plane.

So far, less than a minute had passed. He had watched ground crews work before but had never considered how many tasks were involved in "turning" an airliner. Doing it quickly would obviously take an impressive combination of teamwork, hustle, and communication.

The last bag appeared at the bin door within ninety seconds. The man standing there placed it on the cart as the chauffeur for his trip across the ramp arrived. The planeside worker unhooked two carts of outgoing luggage and quickly attached the load of new arrivals. The tug darted off toward the terminal, tow bars clanking and bags teetering precariously as Rob maneuvered in the tight quarters.

Now the rampers reversed the process. A moment after the last bag was in, a pair of legs appeared in the open bin door. Their owner dropped to the tarmac, closed and locked the bin door, and helped move the cart away.

All this occurred twice more as the number of cream-colored jets occupying gates on Concourse B grew to three. The training material had detailed all of this. Seeing it happen concurrently at three gates underscored why everyone had to chip in. By comparison, the figures working around the 727s over at Concourse C seemed to be moving in slow motion.

There was no gender differential, either. The women did everything the men did, something Kelly had mentioned. "Why not? Sure, we might need a hand with the heaviest stuff. Other than that, what's so special? But watch the looks from those old-school OAL guys—oh, that stands for Other Airlines—they're a riot. Most of them, nobody but a mechanic or a senior ramper can push a plane. Then we're pushing and it's a five-foot, hundred-pound cutie with a ponytail doing it as well as they can. Drives 'em batty."

Processing everything took a back seat to just staying out of the way. The adrenaline was flowing and Drew was ready to help, but there wasn't much he could do. The only time available for training was between flights.

Then Grayson returned and motioned him over. Feeling like a scrub suddenly called into the big game, he listened with rapt attention as the supervisor gripped his arm. Hearing was difficult over the racket from the ground power unit and a passing 737, but pulling up one hearing protector earcup actually made it worse. Grayson leaned closer, close enough to provide a whiff of sweat and aftershave. The supervisor was yelling, the intelligible words sounding like "Aft…trash…ISR…hurry!" This and some demonstrative gestures sent Drew jogging back to stand beneath the cabin door situated forward of the left engine.

The door swung open and he looked up, arms outstretched to catch the garbage sack he presumed someone would drop. He was ready for the trash but not at all prepared for the someone.

Suddenly the ramp was as silent as a mountain dawn. The massive jet vanished, leaving only the doorway overhead. Because framed in it was a stunning five-foot-ten raven-haired beauty with electric blue eyes. She wore the ISR uniform of a navy skirt, white blouse with scarf tie, and camel-colored peplum vest. The knee-length skirt was quite plain except for the generous slit up one side. The edges had worked apart—almost certainly by design—to reveal about a mile, he guessed, of toned calf and thigh sheathed in sheer nylon.

He was still standing with arms out, eyes wide, and mouth hanging stupidly open when the thud of the bag hitting the concrete jarred him back into the world. The ISR never missed a beat. She grinned, winked, waved, and closed the door.

Sensing something in his peripheral vision, he looked over to see the pushback driver looking impatient behind his shades. Grayson's hearing protector was around his neck, replaced with a headset featuring a hanging mouthpiece and a cord plugged into a jack below the cockpit. The tow bar bracketed the nose gear and the gate CSR, who had retracted the jetbridge, now peered around the edge of it, probably wondering why nothing was happening.

Grayson was sweeping one hand out and yelling. He couldn't be heard but his lips could be read and his body language was unmistakable anyway: *"Move! Move!"*

The supervisor turned to the tractor driver, held up a fist, opened it quickly, then motioned toward the tail, signaling "brakes released, clear to push." The tractor's engine growled and the airplane rolled backwards, gathering speed. The newb grabbed the surprisingly heavy sack, which thankfully hadn't split open. It reeked and had a hole somewhere that left a glistening trail.

A low-hanging wing fairing would have knocked him upside the head had he not ducked. Bending down while struggling backwards with the trash bag, his right foot caught on his left and he fell down. Scrambling to his knees, he grabbed the bag and crawled clear. Grayson was watching for traffic but the tractor driver glanced over in surprise as he went by.

Drew felt foolish, a feeling that deepened as the story made the rounds. Some of his new colleagues snickered when they saw him, and the evening shift was somehow aware too. He mentioned this to Peggy, the Ops agent, who said, "Listen, child, those scientists who say nothing can travel faster than light? Well, they've never seen something go through an airline. But don't worry about it. Newbies have done a lot worse."

The rest of the week entailed learning and practicing procedures. Grayson had simple expectations: understand how to do something and why you were doing it, then do it safe and do it right. For each task, he quizzed trainees on the rationale behind it, then corrected or elaborated on the response to ensure solid comprehension. They started one afternoon with simple, common-sense items like lifting properly, always using hearing protection, and scanning for "foreign object debris," or FOD.

Jet engines could vacuum items off the ground, potentially causing considerable damage. Airlines lost millions annually to FOD so rampers kept a sharp lookout for obvious things like rocks, ID tags, and suitcase handles or latches, but also pens, coins, paper clips, keys, nuts, bolts, tools, nails, screws, bits of wire and other miscellany.

"When I was with Braniff in Minneapolis," said his colleague Henry when the subject came up, "I stepped on a hockey puck that must have fallen out of somebody's bag. Twisted my ankle pretty bad."

The next morning's lessons started beneath a Super 80 that had spent the night. Pointing to a metal pin inserted in the nose gear mechanism, Grayson asked, "See that?" It would be hard to miss since the pin had a long red streamer saying REMOVE BEFORE FLIGHT in faded white letters.

"That's the steerin' pin," Grayson said, going on to explain that on arrival, a ramper moved a small lever and inserted the pin to keep it in place. This disabled the captain's ground steering apparatus and allowed the nose gear to freely rotate through a given range during pushback. After disconnecting the towbar, the telephone talker pulled the pin and held it aloft for the captain to verify its removal. Cross-checking was important; few things were more potentially embarrassing than having a pilot try to turn a taxiing jetliner only to find the controls locked out. The plane would have to stop and sit there until someone could drive out and remove the pin.

"Okay," Grayson said once they were back inside, "what do you think are the two main reasons for preventing aircraft damage?"

"Well, it must cost a lot to fix them."

"Correct. And?"

Drew thought it over. "We might have to cancel some flights until they can get an extra plane here to take over for the broken one?"

Grayson snorted.

"Extra plane?" His hand swept in an arc. "Son, does this look like American Airlines? Does this patch here say Eastern? We got no spares. Only the big boys got spares, and only at their biggest airports. You're right, it's the revenue we lose, but when one of these birds is belly up, we're a three-legged dog until Maintenance gets it back in service."

While everyone understood the whys and wherefores, warding off complacency could be difficult. One policy required verifying vehicle brakes with a "safety stop" when approaching an aircraft. This could feel redundant after hours of uneventful trips planeside, especially in a rush. But as a few people learned to their dismay, sometimes brakes seemed to choose to fail the one time they went unchecked. And as Grayson reminded everyone, "Just remember, if you bend an airplane 'cause you didn't do a safety stop, clear out your locker and head on down the line."

He coached people gently the first time and emphatically enough the second that a third error was clearly best avoided. What pushed the supervisor's hot buttons most were people failing to learn from mistakes or making ill-considered, boneheaded moves, either of which revved him directly to redline.

Drew would discover this for himself soon enough.

* * *

Monday afternoon, Grayson provided training on the ground equipment, going over their operation and having the pupil demonstrate his proficiency. Making turns while towing carts was the trickiest, especially when Grayson hooked up a train of four.

"Don't cut it too sharp," the supervisor advised. "You'll run the corners together." In too tight a turn, one cart's corner would collide with the one ahead. Judging the turning circle took several tries.

After Grayson declared his satisfaction, they toured relevant destinations in the battered company pickup. First up was the bag room, called "T-Point."

"Stands for 'transfer point,'" Grayson explained. Next, they visited the remote dump tank where rampers emptied the lav cart—carefully staying upwind—then Trans Global's maintenance office.

"Too expensive to base mechanics at every station," said Grayson. "So we farm it out everywhere but Houston."

The circuit concluded at Delta's cargo facility since they accepted Ruff Air's infrequent high-priority "next flight out" shipments under a similar agreement. Drew smiled at the friendly razzing from those who knew him from Streak.

On the way back, he asked, "I saw an article once that said Ruff Air called First Class 'Preferred.' Why did they change it to First Class?"

Grayson chuckled, then looked over and asked, "What would you say if you come up to the counter and I offered you an upgrade to Preferred Class?"

"I'd say, 'What's Preferred Class?'"

"Bingo. Every last customer. And we said, 'Well, it's like First Class.' And everybody said, 'Then why don't you just call it First Class?' Couldn't answer that, not the way I'da liked to." The last line came with a smirk.

"What did you want to say?"

"That these marketing consultants that think up all that fancy-ass crap never took a Res call or worked behind a counter or gate podium in their life. If they had, they'd have figured that out to begin with."

"Why is the call sign 'Tumbleweed'?"

"Well, they used 'Ruff Air' when we first started up, but then some hotshot who writes about airlines said we was nothin' but another dusty little tumbleweed blowin' around Texas. Captain Michaels told Mr. Ruff we should stick it to that clown by takin' 'Tumbleweed' for our call sign. Whiskey Whiskey loved it. Yes sir, 'bout the last thing you ever want to do is tell that old bastard he can't do something."

Whiskey Whiskey? Oh, right. It was the phonetic pronunciation for Mr. Ruff's initials.

"What about the weird marketing stuff, like the smokeout thing?"

"There was some guy come from Allegheny or somewhere behind all that. Some of it worked, some didn't, and finally he got too big for his britches, so the old man showed him the door. They don't do much of that anymore."

They rode in silence for a minute, then Grayson asked, "Where'd you say you read about all that?"

"The main library on Loyola."

Grayson seemed to be musing on something. Finally, he said, "You're going to hear a lot of stuff going around, rumors and so on, most of it bad. Don't believe anything until you see it from the company. We ain't in the best shape but we ain't circling the drain, either. Continental and us might end up beating each other's brains out at Hobby but old man Ruff knows what he's doing."

"Why does Continental care about Hobby?"

"Same reason Braniff cared about Dallas Love," the supervisor replied. He described how both had invested heavily in hubs they had to defend—Braniff at DFW and Continental at Houston Intercontinental. Determined to crush Southwest at Love Field, Braniff had cut its fare to half of its pesky opponent's, knowing the smaller airline couldn't match without going bankrupt. But Southwest had eventually won the critical Dallas-Houston market, their strategy so brilliant it would one day become a business school case study.

Southwest realized most Dallas-Houston customers were business travelers expensing their trips. Wagering that a tempting incentive might persuade them to pay a higher fare, they began offering adult passengers on the route a free fifth of whiskey, bought in bulk far cheaper than the fare difference. The liquor—delivered by lovely flight attendants in their eye-catching uniforms—proved immensely popular. The gamble paid off, temporarily landing the airline among the Lone Star State's largest whiskey distributors—while destroying Braniff in the Dallas-Houston market.

Continental, being similarly entrenched at Houston Intercontinental, hadn't taken kindly to Ruff Air's incursion at Hobby. Continental had to add flights there to avoid losing lucrative business travelers, but this left them competing against themselves. Each Hobby passenger, even on Continental flights, represented another empty seat to fill at Intercontinental.

"And Whiskey Whiskey," Grayson went on, "Well, for whatever reason he seems to enjoy being a burr under their saddle." He sounded half amused and half apprehensive.

A less enraptured newcomer, especially one with so much riding on a job, might have found some of Grayson's remarks disconcerting.

Back at Ops, the supervisor observed operation of the ground equipment again, this time with no coaching. The newb started up, operated, and shut down the ground power unit and demonstrated the maneuvers appropriate to each vehicle. When he finished and parked the pushback tractor, Grayson walked over and checked that it was out of gear and the brake was properly set.

"Any questions? Okay, you got the form?" He laid the paper on the tractor, scribbled his signature, and handed it back.

"Good job," he said, "but remember, you got to do it right each and every time. My ass is on the line right next to yours."

* * *

Two days later, the gang indulged in a time-honored tradition. A maintenance issue delayed an inbound flight, creating an unusual hiatus between arrivals. Taking Drew aside, Grayson convincingly lamented the delay and gravely declared that more were possible if they couldn't borrow a critical piece of equipment.

"It's called a 'bin stretcher,'" the supervisor explained. "See, bag bins ain't fully pressurized, and when they're empty, you got to set one of these up in there to keep the walls from sagging in up at cruise altitude." He held his hands out wide like a fisherman talking up a fine catch. "It's about this long, looks kinda like one of them pogo sticks kids bounce on, or maybe a shower curtain rod, but thicker and with a flat plate at each end."

Eyeing Drew solemnly and clapping him on the arm, he continued, "I need somebody I can depend on to find us one. Try Continental first, they prob'ly got a spare."

"But you told me the other day that Continental hates us. Why would they loan us one?"

"We're all in the same boat when it comes to this stuff, just tryin' to get by," Grayson said. "Nobody cares about them front-office peckerwoods and their pissin' matches."

So off he went to find a bin stretcher. Continental didn't have one, but helpfully suggested he try Eastern next. They didn't have one and neither did Piedmont, but their Ops guy recommended he try Royale. This seemed odd; Royale flew fifteen-seat turboprops to smaller markets like Lake Charles and Lafayette. As he suspected, the young lady said, "Ours won't fit a Super Eighty or DC-9. Try Delta."

There, the agents looked at each other earnestly, reaching an unspoken consensus. "Trans Global," said one, emerging from behind the counter to guide him out with a smile that was almost suspiciously polite. "They're *definitely* your best bet."

In TGA ops sat a gruff, bulldog-faced giant, a man so large he almost looked like an adult seated at a preschooler's desk. His thinning gray hair was slicked back and his sleeves barely restrained massive biceps above forearms that bulged under tattoos of anchors and eagles. A patch on his shirt bore the name Frank and six embroidered bars, symbols Drew would learn each represented five years' service.

Frank laid a pencil down on a partially completed report and looked up with bushy brows raised, anticipating a legitimate business-related request. As he listened, his expression gradually soured into a scowl.

Frank stood up, glanced down at the fish, pointed with a meaty finger, and spoke with a voice that boomed like the report of an artillery piece.

"Listen, kid, and listen good, 'cause I don't have time for this horseshit. They're screwin' with ya. There ain't no such thing. Go tell 'em all to stick that goddam 'bin stretcher' up their asses. That goes for every last one of them idiot jerkoffs that passed you around before they sent you over here to bother me. Now get your sorry ass outta here!"

After a brisk exit, Drew jumped aboard the tug and glanced back at the door.

Holy shit!

Donna jumped up as he came back into Ops. Emoting theatrically exaggerated concern, she said, "They didn't send you to Global, did they?"

"Oooooh, yeah," he said, then shook his head at having fallen for the gag and joined in the laughter. Having taken just 17 minutes to return, albeit with Frank's "assistance," he had earned the unofficial Fish Flash award as the fastest newb to catch on.

Peggy told him later how one unsuspecting mark had toured the airport for almost ninety minutes diligently searching for her imaginary prize, a fifty-foot spool of "flight line." That newbie got revenge, if inadvertently, when her radio battery coincidentally died. Now short their colleague and the tug, the pranksters had to push the lav cart—torturously heavy when empty and nearly immovable when even partially full—to and from the next two arriving aircraft.

Both nearly took delays, significantly diminishing the hilarity. Grayson only tracked the victim down after a lengthy quest of his own. Having exhausted the options on each concourse, the eager, conscientious young lady had driven across the airport to a remote maintenance hangar. Grayson found her there, gamely trying to explain exactly what she was seeking to a group struggling to look interested and concerned even while stifling their laughter.

Out at the next arrival, Grayson instructed Drew to climb into the baggage bin and slide the bags to the door. After a minute, the supervisor stuck his head in the door. "I have to go to Five Bravo for a minute. Keep 'em coming!"

The bags piled up but soon started disappearing again. He pushed the last bag to the door, scrambling after it in a duckwalk but still too tall to keep his upper back from bumping along against the low overhead.

To his surprise, the person offloading the luggage wasn't Grayson, but Barb. Her hearing protector looked decidedly out of place with a pantsuit and she had broken a nice sweat. Drew hopped to the ground and helped her push the cart to where they could connect it to a tug. After hooking it up, she turned and asked, "Everything going okay?"

He nodded. She smiled, patted him on the arm, and strode off toward the Ops office.

Grayson returned a few minutes later.

"Hey, why was Barb down here?"

As if it should be obvious, the supervisor said simply, "She saw we needed the help."

Next was another trash detail, but not time-critical since departure was minutes away. As Drew waited at the aft door, he noticed a first officer doing the pre-departure walkaround inspection. The pilot wore a necktie printed with the body and head of a large fish. The tail was right below the knot and the fish's head filled the tie's bottom.

This was too great a coincidence. Drew walked over and asked, "Do you have time for a quick question?"

"Sure," the pilot responded.

"What's with the fish?" He held up his own to explain his curiosity.

"Tradition," the pilot said. "Newbs have to wear it. I'm the 'lowest form of life in a cockpit' and you must be the 'FNG' around here."

Drew nodded. He was indeed the effin' new guy in New Orleans. A taxiing DC-10's warm jet blast made them both turn away and hunch down, the pilot holding his hat on. When it lessened, the pilot smiled, flashing perfect white teeth. He stuck out his hand and said, "I'm Alberto. Call me Bert."

"I'm Drew. Let me know if you see a bin stretcher." The pilot laughed, obviously already familiar with that particular trick.

"Don't feel bad," he said, "the senior ISR swiped my coat on the way to LAX one day and sewed the end of one of the sleeves shut. We were halfway to the hotel shuttle by the time I figured out why I couldn't get the damn thing on." They both laughed this time.

"Hey, one last thing…when you guys call in range, you give a number, 'with eight point five' or whatever. What's that mean?"

"It's our fuel onboard in thousands of pounds."

"Pounds? Not gallons?"

"Has to do with density and having a consistent way to measure. It's probably a hundred degrees down here but in a half hour we'll be up where it's about fifty below zero." He held his hands up, moving them closer together then farther apart as he spoke. "A gallon's volume shrinks or expands depending on temperature, but no matter how much space it takes up, a pound's always a pound."

"Thanks, I really appreciate it."

"Any time." Gesturing up at the plane, the pilot continued with a grin, "I could talk flying all day but they say I have to take these people to Houston." Bert shook hands again and said, "Good to meet you. Take care and good luck to you," then returned to the pre-flight.

Drew clocked out when his shift ended, but didn't leave. He spent an hour studying procedures, then another watching the evening shift work arrivals, watching for more nuances. He drove home late that evening, drained and smelling of jet exhaust but feeling deeply content and almost proud of his fish. Along with this quiet satisfaction was something else he had never felt for a job or place of work. It took him a while to hunt it down and tag it.

Ruff Air felt like home.

SIX

Upon completing ramp training, new CSRs were eligible to have a regular shift, or "hold a line," on the bid. Kelly took him aside to explain the process.

"There are separate bids for full-time and part-time. Both work the same way. On the full-time bid, Henry is most senior, so he always gets his first choice. Connie is second, so she has to choose two lines. If her first choice isn't the same line Henry took, she gets that line. If it is, she gets her second choice and so on down the list. You're last on part-time, so for now, you get what nobody else wants. But remember," she said, looking up into his eyes for emphasis, "always bid what you *want*, not what you think you'll get. Someday you won't be at the bottom."

Ranking his choices was fun at first, but with no hope for a desirable schedule, the novelty faded quickly. When the results went up, the bottom line was just that—the misfit toy of schedules, 3:00 p.m. to 8:30 p.m. with Tuesday/Wednesday off.

Still, having a routine felt good, repetition left him more comfortable in his role, and the ability to trade away or pick up hours was pretty sweet. People used the privilege in different ways. Most part-timers seldom traded time away and hunted hours like hyenas chasing dinner. Their opposites were a couple of full-timers with breadwinning spouses who freely admitted to only having an airline job for the travel. They gave away every possible minute, swapped ramp shifts for the counter because they hated being sweaty, and always signed up first for LWOP. Everyone else was fairly balanced, taking off when needed and occasionally working extra hours to pay off a bill or save for something special.

Drew needed the money and loved being at the airport, so he took every opportunity to pick up extra hours. If a morning ramper wanted off early, he could punch in and work in their place until 2:30, then start his regular shift 30 minutes later. With luck, he might have the chance to cover for an evening ramper until 11:30. He could also trade for full shifts on his days off or even work doubles, picking up both morning and evening shifts or a full morning before his regular start time.

Trades were straight time and working doubles made for very long days, but he didn't care. Being a ramp rat was a blast. Getting paid to do it was almost a bonus! In one notable two-week pay period, he averaged almost twelve hours a day for thirteen days, collecting a check covering 134 straight time hours, five hours holiday pay, and thirteen hours overtime. It added up nicely, even at six bucks and change an hour.

Other benefits included shedding the ten or so extra pounds picked up during his Sales stint plus eleven more. When his 3:00 PM shift started, the air felt like wearing a wool poncho steeped in hot water. That and the constant exertion had the last of his fat reserves cowering in a corner.

Drew enjoyed most of the newbie chores, even unofficial ones like the "gumbo run." The crew of Tumbleweed 557 had no time to eat during stops and crew meals weren't catered. The pilots, arriving from Tampa one day, half-jokingly asked whether someone might grab them some gumbo from the cafeteria. Thus began a tradition. A ramper brought takeout containers to the gate; the CSR delivered them and collected payment. It was tough during OSO—off-schedule operations like weather delays—but the rampers always managed to make time and the crews appreciated it. Everyone took pride in timing it right, starting back as the flight landed so the gumbo was good and hot.

This was also a two-way street, which Donna explained one day.

"My girlfriend Sandy works in Midland," she said. "Used to be they couldn't get Blue Bell ice cream out there, so Captain Michaels brought them some in a cooler! On the radio, he says,

'Tumbleweed Five Seventeen in range with seven point four—and a half-gallon!'"

Dumping the lav cart was no fun, but he didn't mind the long trip to the tank. Getting out to the airport's farthest reaches, where he could see the comings and goings and just enjoy being outdoors, was refreshing. Arthur Hailey's fictional Mel Bakersfeld was right about the numbing effects of spending too much time in terminals and offices; it was cathartic to "stand at the distant end of a runway once in a while and feel the wind in our faces." Well, at least in decent weather. It sucked when storms rolled through, driving through downpours in the open seat wearing raingear that was hardly worth the trouble. It had to be *really* great fun in mid-winter.

Drew befriended his crewmates and was especially fond of Peggy and Donna, the feisty redhead. Peggy was older than most and had lived in the south all her life. He couldn't imagine what she must have endured and witnessed as a Black woman during the Jim Crow years and he respected and admired her grace, dignity, and kindness all the more for it. As for Donna, he liked her bold spirit, unfailingly upbeat nature, and generosity. Both always greeted him with a smile and something nice to say.

When he inquired about the photos of youngsters taped inside Donna's locker door, she replied, "I heard about how airline employees were volunteering their time and passes to escort children who need medical treatment. The hospital care is free, but their families hardly have enough money to keep a roof over their heads so there's no way they have enough to travel."

She pointed to one of the pictures. "See this little girl? She had four brothers and sisters and her whole family lived in one of those twenty-foot containers you see on ships. All these kids, unless an adult can accompany the child, they don't get treatment and for a lot of them, that means they'll die or have to live with awful handicaps or diseases. I've done it three times now and I truly believe those trips might be the most important thing I'll ever do in my life."

There were tears in her eyes and something else, a sadness perhaps alluding to her own backstory and its role in her determination to help others.

Donna also shared his love of everything that flew, an affliction she called "aviation fascination." She pointed when a new Southwest 737-300 taxied by and said, "Look at the intake on that thing! They had to flatten the bottom of the nacelle so it doesn't scrape the ramp!" Later, in Ops, she mentioned the same pilot Grayson had, Captain Mark Michaels, and his museum-worthy collection.

"Grayson told me he's the one who suggested 'Tumbleweed'."

"Yep, that's him. Watch for his layovers, or even long turns, and ask. He's always got something interesting to share. Pictures, timetables, schedules, logbooks, all kinds of historical stuff. One day he had a Douglas diagram marked with four of our planes on the assembly line! It was so cool! Hang on, did I ask him to Xerox it for me? I think I did!"

She retrieved the page. Titled "DC-9 ASSEMBLY AND RAMP STATUS" and dated July 26, 1982, the sheet featured a blueprint-style depiction of the Douglas Aircraft Company's Long Beach plant. Tiny silhouettes represented aircraft in various stages of construction, testing, and delivery. Notations, some typed, others handwritten, showed line numbers—a manufacturer's permanent designator based on production sequence—and customer's two-letter codes. These included Air California, Aeromexico, Venezuela's VIASA, Republic, ALM of the Netherlands Antilles, and Frontier along with Ruff Air. Three little outlines were outside awaiting pickup and had 1071-RX, 1072-RX, and 1073-RX written next to them, while 1074-RX sat across the way being prepped for its first flight. Captain Michaels had added Ruff Air's eventual registrations next to each.

"Can I copy this?"

"Of course!" His interest brought a smile to her face.

Donna often made or brought treats like popsicles or brownies and a particular shift favorite was sun tea. She would fill a huge jar with water and Luzianne tea bags when they came on shift, leaving it to steep while they worked five or six turns. Sitting in the shade sipping fresh tea poured over cups of crushed ice made for a nice break after hours on the blistering tarmac.

To his surprise, he found a complimentary letter in his mail folder after clocking in one day. He had noticed a baggage ID tag on the apron weeks ago and picked it up as trained. That wasn't unusual, but mailing it to its owner was. Tags were usually tossed since they were inexpensive and easily replaced. This one was different, a nice leather holder sheathed in a custom-made needlepoint cover resplendent with colorful flowers arranged around an elaborately monogrammed "S." Someone had devoted considerable effort to creating it, so he brushed off the loose dirt, copied the address onto an envelope, and mailed it to a Mr. and Mrs. Shanklin in Marble Falls, Texas.

Mr. Ruff's executive assistant opened Mrs. Shanklin's letter two weeks later. She told how her great-grandmother had made the cover special for the newlyweds' honeymoon trip to New Orleans. Mrs. Shanklin was heartbroken to find it missing upon their return and elated at receiving it. She was now a Ruff Air customer for life and would tell everyone she knew to fly the airline every chance they got.

Drew was glad that his feeling had proven correct and proud to receive the commendation from Mr. Ruff's office despite the admittedly modest effort involved in returning the tag.

The recognition was soon common knowledge.

"Wow," commented Donna, "you already got an 'atta boy' from Whiskey Whiskey? Great job!"

Things were going well, enough that his rapidly expanding job knowledge and sheer enjoyment of the work unconsciously escalated his comfort level right past confident to borderline cocky. It wasn't intentional, simply human nature at work, but Fate dutifully took notice and must have worn an expectant smirk as it perched patiently, intent on humbling him.

The wait wasn't long.

At mid-afternoon on a Thursday, the sun baked the still, humid air but the thunderstorms had taken a day off. Drew had drawn the mundane chore of chocking, a duty so simple as to always be the first entrusted to newbs. The triangular rubber chocks, about eighteen inches long, effectively immobilized vehicles or aircraft.

He had worked a double the day before and was midway through another. He was beyond exhausted, but all he had to do was stand safely clear until the marshaler gave him a hand signal, then place one chock ahead of the tire nearest him and one behind. An elementary task, yet it became his undoing, and spectacularly so.

Parking an airliner involves more than meets the eye. The simplest mechanical method uses a rubber cylinder suspended horizontally. The pilots stop when the cylinder touches the cockpit windows. Effective, but limited by the difficulty of adjusting the tube's height for different aircraft types. The other end of the spectrum was cutting-edge automated systems using lights and arrows to guide pilots with no need for a marshaler. But few airports had such devices and those that did often found them problematic. So more often than not, the task still fell to a ramper standing atop a pushback tractor.

The marshaler had to ensure the wings had sufficient clearance, keep the pilot centered on the lead-in line, and help the captain slow gently to a stop right on the painted mark. Each aircraft type using the gate had a corresponding mark and hitting it aligned the plane's door with the jetbridge. This was especially critical for Ruff Air. While newer jetbridges could maneuver to and fro on huge tires that acted like casters, those on Concourse B were an older, fixed design, far less agile and useless if not quite lined up.

These overlapping duties lasted at least a stressful half-minute. Marshalers had to safely accomplish them over and over, in blinding sunlight and inky darkness, in all kinds of weather, always appreciating the fact that they were guiding a large, costly machine laden with fragile human occupants and enough fuel to fill a swimming pool. Having an aircraft strike carelessly parked ground equipment, incorrectly positioned jetbridges, or inattentive personnel was embarrassing, expensive, occasionally tragic, and more common than one would think.

But the corporate emphasis on safety felt a little like lip service at times, coming out of one side of an airline's mouth while spiels about keeping schedule came out the other. Ruff Air's standard ground times seemed ridiculously short. Jets belonging to major carriers spent forty-five to sixty minutes at the gate for domestic flights and far longer when going overseas. Deplaning, unloading, cleaning, reloading, fueling, catering, and boarding a Super 50 in fifteen minutes, or the larger Super 80 in twenty, even with a full ground crew working, was very tough. Also, since departure and arrival times influenced the desirability of airlines' flight listings in computer reservations systems, taxi and flight times lacked any meaningful buffer, even for common occurrences like weather deviations or air traffic congestion. These realities played out almost every day all over the system and left everyone feeling they were always behind the eight ball.

"Why can't they see we need more than fifteen minutes?" Drew asked after a particularly frustrating shift.

"'Cause Southwest does it in ten," Grayson replied.

"What?"

It was incredible, but true, if not quite apples to apples. Southwest kept things remarkably simple. There were no meals to cater and no assigned seats. Customers used plastic boarding passes that the gate agents collected and reused. Their employees also exemplified hustle and teamwork. Flight attendants were already tidying the aft lavs even as people stood to collect their carry-ons. The cabin crew stayed right behind them as they deplaned, collecting trash and straightening up as they went. It wasn't easy; planes often looked like windblown landfills even after short flights. The last passenger stepped off a clean airplane that was ready for immediate boarding. Their rampers took the same fast-paced approach, aided by the fact that fewer customers checked luggage on Southwest's relatively short segments.

Since airliners only make money at cruise altitude, such efficiency went right to the bottom line while providing another incalculable competitive advantage: surveys showed again and again that customers most valued schedule frequency and reliability. Some delays were unavoidable and uncontrollable but regardless of cause, one thing was certain: they inexorably snowballed and wrought havoc on a carrier's schedule for the rest of the day.

Considerable effort went into making schedule. Pilots increased speed, trading fuel for time, requested more direct routings, and shortened taxi time by choosing the closest suitable runway.

Ground crews turned late-arriving flights as quickly as possible. An 11:45 a.m. arrival due out at noon might arrive at 11:48 but leave on time if rampers could "pick up" three minutes with a twelve-minute turn. If they took the whole fifteen minutes, the 12:03 departure was late by a customer's watch but the local station would avoid a "chargeable" delay by not exceeding the allotted time.

There were, however, a few aces up employees' sleeves. Major airlines employed an automated system that registered the combination of closing the main cabin door and releasing the brakes to transmit the official "out" time (leaving the gate). Landing gear retraction triggered the "off" time (takeoff). A ground-based receiver then updated the computer system. Such precision allowed no fudge factor whatsoever. But to save money, Ruff Air and many other low-cost carriers opted to stick with the old-school method of having the pilots report the official times via radio after takeoff. Sometimes an understanding captain would magically erase a brief delay by providing a favorable, if false, out time. Such adjustments, strictly forbidden, occurred fairly frequently because the honchos had no way to determine how long a particular flight actually took to taxi out.

The ongoing emphasis on punctuality produced a subtle but palpable fixation on saving time. This might seem praiseworthy but could also result in ill-considered shortcuts or honest mistakes, some with disastrous potential. One disturbing episode had occurred the spring before.

An advancing front drove heavy, violent squall lines into most of the southern U.S. and the Gulf of Mexico. Six Ruff Air jets were converging on Moisant: the regular afternoon rush of three, two trips affected by air traffic delays to Florida, and one needing fuel due to extended hold times in Houston.

Donna, working Ops, had gates 5B, 7B, and 9B but was scrambling to find three more amidst a crush of delays and cancellations. American granted use of 11B after canceling their inbound DC-10; Piedmont agreed to let Donna squeeze in a turn at 15B, which would be 13B but for the superstitious airport authority having skipped that number.

Recipients of such courtesies returned the favor when the tables turned because the cooperating airline took an enormous risk. If the timing was tight and the intruding flight developed a problem, the accommodating manager could end up answering embarrassing questions from headquarters about incurring a delay waiting for a competitor to vacate his or her own gate.

Donna still had an orphan despite her efforts. Tumbleweed 820, inbound from Houston and continuing to Miami, had been in range a couple of minutes and would be the flight left standing when the music stopped. Donna had banked on the trip at 9B getting out in time but the crew had reported a mechanical issue, just what she needed on top of everything else. More flights would arrive soon for the other gates so they were out of the equation. Already far behind schedule, 820 would have to idle in a remote area nicknamed the "penalty box" until a gate became available.

Oh well, they can't go anywhere anyway until ATC lifts the ground stop.

The phone rang ten seconds later.

"Ops, Donna."

"Hey Donna, it's Randy in Dispatch. ATC canceled the ground stop so get your Florida trips out ASAP."

She groaned as she hung up. It sucked, but 820 would just have to wait.

Unless…

She called Randy back and described her idea. He was agreeable so she consulted the counter lead and finally the FAA ground controller in the tower. When 820 called on the ground, Donna grinned with satisfaction and directed the crew to park on the opposite side of Concourse B in a large open area of the apron.

There was no jetbridge but Super 80s had built-in rear airstairs. Only thirty or so passengers were deplaning and about the same number headed out, one of whom happened to be a helpful CSR on personal travel. No seat assignments were needed since the flight wasn't full, so she "worked" the flight by collecting tickets and directing the outbound customers to wait by the correct door.

The Houston ground crew had dumped 820's lavs and catered for both legs. Randy the dispatcher had explained to Donna that the crew could leave the number two engine running as long as the chocks were in and the cockpit manned. This eliminated the need for ground power and saved the time required for an engine restart. Finally, the plane could taxi away from the open space without a push.

Two CSRs, hastily drafted from the ticket counter, handled the ramp duties. The pair rushed around as best they could in blue pumps, ignoring the heat and the wind whipping their navy skirts as they worked. Meanwhile, an ISR escorted the arriving passengers, several of whom covered their ears against the noise, across the hot concrete and upstairs to the concourse. The CSR who was collecting tickets left the stack on the 9B podium and guided the customers down to the airplane.

Staffing was thin; the only gate with two CSRs was the busiest one. But with help from Barb, the supervisors, and a couple of other employee travelers who pitched in, the flights were starting to leave. A mechanic had even resolved the maintenance issue, a burned-out bulb.

Downstairs, Rob returned from the inbound baggage area, where he had simply unhooked the cart to save time. He would toss the bags on the carousel after dropping off the ten or so outbounds. The CSRs detached the bag cart and loaded the luggage while Rob drove around to the nose. He carried what some jester had dubbed the "Elevated Flight Document Transferal System"—a capped foot-long piece of PVC pipe duct-taped to a broomstick—and held it up so the captain could take the rolled-up dispatch papers through an open cockpit window. Rob raised the stick again to collect the signed copy, then circled back to pick up the now-empty baggage cart as an ISR raised the airstairs.

One CSR pulled the chocks, the other directed the Super 80 away, and the two exchanged a high-five as Tumbleweed 820 taxied out after an extraordinary nine-minute turnaround.

All the flights were leaving and 820 joined up as tail end Charlie as they moved out to the active runway like a line of circus elephants. Such a procession of company jets, over a third of the entire fleet, was a rare and exhilarating sight that motivated a couple of employees to grab cameras from their lockers.

The ground crew's swell of pride and accomplishment lasted until the fuelers walked into Ops fifteen minutes later and one asked, "Hey, what happened to Eight-twenty? Wasn't it in range about forty-five minutes ago?"

Donna smiled and said, "You're funny, Jeff. Eight-twenty's long gone." She playfully drew out the word "long" and consulted the stat log before continuing, "They left with everybody else. Let's see their off time…yep, almost twenty-five minutes ago."

Jeff stared at her as if she had spoken a foreign language. He queried his partner with a glance and got a shake of the head in response.

"Gone? How can it be gone? It never even came to the gate."

Donna responded with a statement that sounded like a question, as if to remind him of something that should have been painfully obvious.

"Because we used apron parking on the other side of the concourse?"

But as she finished speaking, a shadow of doubt appeared on her face, placed there by the recollection of something she should have done and her uncertainty as to whether she had done it. Handling the accustomed three simultaneous turns was challenging, let alone double that number. She had called for an extra tanker, but had she later informed the fuel contractor that Tumbleweed 820 would be using nonstandard parking?

Jeff laid that issue to rest in dramatic fashion.

"Apron parking? Well, we never saw 'em so they didn't get any fuel."

Donna rocketed out of her chair, eyes wide.

"What? Oh my God!"

Anxiety surged through the room, manifesting itself most in Donna, who was the only one who could do anything about it. She fumbled for the desk mic, knocked it over, righted and keyed it, and tried to steady her trembling voice.

"Tumbleweed Eight-twenty, New Orleans Ops."

She hoped the crew still had one radio on Ruff Air's Moisant frequency; otherwise, she would have no choice but to phone Air Traffic Control and ask them to contact the flight on her behalf, taking precious time and undoubtedly bringing some inquisitive ears over along with the flight crew.

Her mind was racing. Fuel was heavy and carrying extra, called "tankering," cost money. Each flight usually got only the amount needed for a single leg plus the appropriate reserve. With the delays, maybe the crew fueled for both segments at Hobby and simply forgot to notify her.

That has to be what happened. Because if not…

Her face had drained of color. Though only a few seconds had passed, she whispered, "Come on, come on, come *on!*"

"Go for Tumbleweed Eight-twenty," said a voice from the radio, an undertone of curiosity apparent. Something was off if a station recently departed was calling.

Donna suddenly realized she was about to do something that made her profoundly uncomfortable: question a professional flight crew about one of their most fundamental responsibilities.

The radio spoke again.

"New Orleans, do you have traffic for Tumbleweed Eight-twenty?"

Finally, meekly, she managed, "Sir, will you please verify your fuel status?"

Silence, during which the pilots no doubt glanced at each other in surprise.

"Roger, stand by."

There followed an uncomfortably long pause, during which Donna turned even paler, then a terse response.

"New Orleans, Tumbleweed Eight-twenty. We're coming back."

Donna said later she would never forget the edge in the captain's voice, not fear but an instant and uneasy comprehension of what had happened and what the consequences might have been.

As crash investigators know, most accidents don't result from one monumental error or malfunction. Small but crucial human decisions combine with innocuous and often unlikely events to form an insidious chain leading to disaster. Removing any one link dissolves the sequence and the trip becomes another safely operated flight, one of many thousands each day worldwide.

In New Orleans that day, the three extra arrivals coincidentally piled up with the afternoon rush; the sudden end to the Florida ground stop erased any flexibility Donna had; and she couldn't stand the idea of leaving passengers waiting for an open gate. Under pressure, she forgot to inform the fuel company dispatcher about the nonstandard parking, then, with no suspicion of anything amiss, had inadvertently prepared an incorrect weight and balance form based on the fuel she expected to be taken on.

Changes of plan were so common that neither fueler felt any undue urgency when only five of the expected six inbounds appeared. One of the CSRs sent to work 820 wondered why there was no fuel truck but figured Ops would have ordered one if needed. The flight crew, the last line of defense, had somehow left the quantity unchecked because of the rushed ground time, an ill-timed interruption of preflight checks, or perhaps both. Finally, this particular Super 80 was one of only four overwater-equipped Ruff Air jets, meaning it carried the gear necessary to fly direct routings to Florida. The other three-quarters of the fleet had to stay closer to shore.

Had the error remained undiscovered, the chain completed, the last of Flight 820's fuel would have run through the turbines about halfway across the water. The engines would have flamed out high over the Gulf at a point where land was so distant and the sky so crowded with dangerous storms that even the most skillfully flown glide toward the coast would have ended in a desperate water landing. After the ditching, unquestionably a violent one considering the conditions, those still able would have scrambled to evacuate, fighting off panic as heavy seas tossed the aircraft and slide rafts like bathtub toys and salt water cascaded in through the emergency exits.

Instead, the crew informed the passengers of a "minor mechanical issue" that would require a "precautionary" return to New Orleans. Jeff the fueler quickly finished his work and Tumbleweed 820 departed again, more delayed than ever. The passengers never knew the real reason, though some likely noted that no fueling occurred during the first stop and was the only obvious activity during the second. In any case, the incident never became public. The company quietly suspended the flight crew for two weeks without pay and Donna received a written reprimand, the only tarnish on an otherwise exemplary record.

The elephant in the room—a surly gray beast named Constant Push to Meet Marginally Realistic Schedules—grazed on, ignored.

With everything going so well, a week or so of chocking flights under his belt, thought patterns left in disarray by working so many hours, a sincere desire to contribute, and the continuous drive to make schedule, complacency's trap was set.

From his view, the puzzle looked complete. But one crucial piece was missing, a fairly common occurrence that by chance hadn't happened during his time handling the chocks. The possibility would have been instantly apparent with more experience or anything close to his usual wits. As it was, the wild card torpedoed and sank his growing confidence when Tumbleweed 534 pulled into the gate.

SEVEN

The Super 50 operating Flight 534 landed nineteen minutes past its scheduled arrival time. Following an early morning departure from Dallas Love Field, the plane had flown to Houston, Orlando, Miami, and Tampa before heading west again.

The ramp crew was ready—almost. The newest one was juggling several upcoming trades, debating whether he could take them all. That would mean postponing several pending errands and some overdue car maintenance—again.

Drew tugged his gloves tighter, wriggled his hearing protector into the best fit, and picked up the chocks when the jet taxied into view.

I should really get the car stuff done.

The captain slowed and turned up the line.

But give up eight hours just in case it's not finished in time? If I have it there at seven, they should be done by noon…

The main gear tires stopped rolling. Distracted, Drew placed the chocks—without waiting for the signal to do so. As he jogged toward an empty bag cart, the engine noise, normally ebbing at this point, instead began rising in pitch and volume.

Wait, what's with that?

He found the answer atop the pushback tractor, where Chuck, the marshaler, stood with his hands a foot apart above his head.

Drew's eyes went wide and his heart leapt into his throat with the realization of what he had missed: just because an aircraft stopped didn't mean it had reached the proper position! The Super 50 hadn't rolled quite far enough up the line, so the captain was adding power to nudge it to the mark—unaware that some inattentive knucklehead had prematurely chocked the main landing gear.

The horrifying possibilities of the next few seconds flashed through his mind. Pulse pounding, he realized there would be no stopping the jet's momentum if it jumped the chock under power. It would bolt forward even as the captain instinctively yanked back the thrust levers and both pilots jammed hard on the brakes. With luck, the marshaler might leap clear, but after the tow tractor sheared off the nose gear with a metallic screech, the jet would plow into Ozark's ground-floor Ops office. Immediately above it was a concourse window where several smiling, waving people—unaware of their sudden peril—watched friends and loved ones arrive.

The ISRs, up disarming the slides, would be thrown to the floor, into bulkheads, or onto seats and passengers. Likewise for the inevitable eager beavers already in the aisles and the carry-ons they were even now schlepping from the overheads.

He had to signal Chuck, but his body refused to cooperate, as if he were in a nightmare trying to outrun a monster through wet cement.

Move, shout, wave, do something for Christ's sake before it's too late!

He darted sideways to where Chuck could see him, yelled *"Stop! Stop! Stop!"* and crossed his wrists over his head to signal the same. But the marshaler was watching for the nose wheel's expected advance, not for frantic gesticulations from a flustered ramp rat newbie.

Jumping up and down and waving his arms, he kept shouting in the forlorn hope of being heard over the spooling engines. Running toward the nose, forearms again crossed over his head, he noticed Rob approaching. The bag runner had obviously perceived something was amiss because he skidded to a stop, yanked the parking brake, and vaulted onto the tarmac, waving too.

Chuck finally saw Drew and instantly signaled the pilots to cut power and apply the brakes.

Relieved as the engine noise waned, Drew signaled that the chocks were in and pointed to the tires. This prompted

Chuck to kneel and lean sideways so he could see, then to pivot, look at the CSR on the jetbridge, and point at her and then the airplane. She understood the unspoken question, squinted one eye as she gauged the cabin door's alignment, then looked back and shook her head. The aircraft would have to move forward before the passengers could deplane.

Chuck directed his attention back to the cockpit with palms out, a gesture the pilots correctly interpreted as meaning "wait," followed by the "chocks in" signal. Face red and jaw set tightly, he then turned and signaled for the chocks to be removed.

As luck would have it, powering up had inched the aircraft forward far enough to wedge the chock tightly underneath the massive tire. Cursing his stupidity, Drew kicked at it from several angles, first stubbing his toe then bruising his heel. He dropped to his knees, desperate, pawing fruitlessly at the heavy rubber. Rob sprinted over, knelt, and pushed as he pulled, all to no avail.

Grayson rolled up in the pickup and jumped out nearly before it stopped moving.

He didn't do a safety stop! Drew's training forced the ridiculously ill-timed observation into his head.

The supervisor took in the scene—plane stationary short of the mark, equipment still staged, rampers standing expectantly, the jetbridge retracted—and fixed an incredulous glare on Drew.

"What in Satan's flamin' hell is going on here?" he roared.

Fate's smirk was now a satisfied cackle.

Grayson quickly saw the only solution: attach the tow bar, push the plane back slightly, remove the chock, then tow it to the mark. Nearly five precious minutes ticked away until the gate CSR could finally open the door. Passengers could be seen through the cabin windows, waiting impatiently, most standing with their carry-ons and some undoubtedly making snide remarks about airline service these days.

Once the dust settled, the captain descended the jetbridge stairs to conduct the walk-around. He stopped to speak with Chuck, who turned and pointed at Drew.

Uh-oh.

Rob arrived with a cart of bags just in time to witness this.

"My friend," he said, "you are royally and completely screwed."

The captain clapped Chuck's arm and started checking items as he made his way around the plane, beckoning to Drew when his path reached the rear bin area.

The embarrassed newb limped over, toe and heel both throbbing.

"I hear you're the one who chocked us."

"Yes sir, I'm sorry about that. I really screwed up."

The pilot eyed the fish hanging from Drew's ID then looked up, examining the tail.

"Why'd you drop 'em early?"

He stammered out his explanation. As dimwitted as he sounded to himself, he could only imagine what the other man was thinking.

But the captain surprised him. Removing his hat, he rubbed his forehead while looking off at nothing and said matter-of-factly, "Well, Drew, fatigue does that. We always have to be mindful, and that goes double when you're tired. We all make mistakes…" His voice trailed off as he turned toward the concourse, the upper-level window now empty, as if imagining for himself what might have happened. He continued, "…but we could have ended up with some bent metal here, or worse. A lot worse."

Drew nodded and stared at the concrete, uncomfortable with the captain's eyes on him. He was unsure whether to feel encouraged or unnerved that the captain had taken the trouble to learn his name.

"And I have to tell you, buddy, I sure was starting to wonder how we had that much power on and still weren't going anywhere." The captain replaced his hat, shook his head, made a little sound like "Huh!" and walked away.

The audience with Grayson later that afternoon was markedly less cordial. Drew sat uncomfortably for long minutes, given no chance to speak, eyes on the floor, face crimson with embarrassment. Nothing could make him feel any worse than he already did. Again and again, he relived his desperation before Chuck noticed his frantic signals and the horror when his mind's eye conjured the Super 50 jumping the chock and crashing through the concourse wall in such authentic detail that he felt he had actually witnessed it. Those terrible seconds had seared everything there was to learn into his conscience. He would never forget that electric jolt of adrenaline and alarm, and he would never let his mind wander again.

Grayson's anger ran its course. He said, "Drew, you're too smart to make that kind of jackass move." He waved at a shelf of manuals. "Always remember, every last thing you read in them procedure books has a reason behind it. Like my Daddy used to say, 'work your mind and mind your work and you'll be fine'."

The supervisor paused and his face grew pensive.

"No way this is staying under the rug. We'll both be going upstairs, probably tomorrow, so be ready. In the meantime, pray the captain don't feel the need to bend old Demerest's ear about this." Drew had already heard enough about the salty, imposing chief pilot to hope Grayson was right. Profiled in a recent newsletter, Captain Demerest was a retired base chief pilot from Trans Global, notable for his gruff, direct demeanor and a striking resemblance to the Rat Pack entertainer Dean Martin.

The rampers made up two wasted minutes and the captain wiped out the remainder with a generous out time. Grayson's inevitable visit with Barb would be anything but pleasant, and having others take risks to cover for him made everything worse. The miscalculation occupied his thoughts during every idle moment until quitting time, the drive home, and several fitful hours spent trying to fall asleep.

* * *

The next afternoon, the ticket counter banter dissolved into an uneasy silence as Drew approached. The last thing he heard before the hush was, "No way, he's gone."

That can't be good. The sick feeling that had been lounging around in his gut all day suddenly jumped up and ran around screaming.

Grayson was in the back hall and motioned him into the training room.

"Barb wants you in her office right now and copy this, amigo, she is fit to chew roofin' nails. She met me at the door this mornin' and kicked my ass halfway to Baton Rouge. You deserve to hear it straight. This here's prob'ly adios."

His heart sank. While dire consequences were a given, he hadn't allowed himself to consider that unemployment might be among them.

When Kelly saw him, she stood and meekly pointed at Barb's door, her expression suggesting she might be about to watch a shelter worker put down an injured puppy.

All this paled in comparison to the chill in the manager's office. Grayson hadn't exaggerated; Barb's cold stare was worthy of a fish market tuna. A slight tilt of her head indicated he should close the door, never a good sign.

"My current plan," she said, "is to fire your ass."

Drew looked at the floor. For an instant he was a child again and heard his father's voice.

A man doesn't make excuses. He accepts responsibility, learns from his mistakes, and moves on.

Resigning himself to his fate made candor surprisingly easy. He looked her in the eye and said, "I deserve it."

But Barb didn't drop the ax.

"Out of sheer morbid curiosity, please explain, or at least try, one thing. What the *hell* were you thinking?" She added a dusting of sarcasm before he could answer. "Maybe you can serve as a cautionary tale in training."

He never quite figured out the source of the ensuing flash of insight. He had believed that exhaustion was why he had screwed up, but now a deeper, more distasteful truth revealed itself. Vanity and cockiness, not in his nature, had gained a foothold through his excitement over the job and his success—to this point—at learning it.

He hadn't understood before, so he was surprised to hear himself admit, "I thought I had the job down pat and that kind of put me on autopilot."

Frostier than ever, she said, "I sure hope there's more to it than that."

He gazed out the window, then at the ceiling, reluctant to say it. How could he not have seen the possibility?

"I guess I really didn't think about the plane stopping before it was in the right place. I'd been chocking for a week and that never happened."

Sarcasm stepped aside for outright mockery. "Wow, that *never* happened in a *whole week?*"

She sat back in her chair, letting him sweat. Finally, she said, "Grayson's more forgiving than I am. He actually seems to think you've learned your lesson. But do you really understand what could have happened?"

He looked at the floor again.

"Yes, ma'am, I do. I saw in my mind what might come next if the plane jumped the chock. I saw it crash through the building. I heard people screaming. And I knew I could never live with myself if someone was hurt or killed because I screwed up." Returning his gaze to Barb, he went on, "I knew all of it in this one intense moment and I've thought about it ever since. Grayson let me have it, and I deserved it, but believe me, he's right. I had learned my lesson before we even got the plane towed to the right spot."

The meeting had already gone longer than expected. He wouldn't grovel but figured he might as well show interest in staying employed.

"This was as stupid as stupid gets but please let me earn back your trust. As short-handed as we are and as long as it takes to hire and train people, it makes sense to keep me around, at least for now."

The green eyes didn't even flicker. After a long moment, Barb swiveled her chair around and took her own turn staring out the window. One minute turned into three. He waited, trying not to squirm, wondering if he had failed and she meant for him to leave.

She turned back and said, "I appreciate honesty and I respect people who can admit mistakes and learn from them. Grayson went to bat for you and so did the captain by the way. He called me this morning and said before I dealt with you, I should think back to some of the things I did when I was 'new and starry-eyed' as he put it. Nothing this dumb, but he has a point. He and everyone else covered your ass so I don't have to try to explain this...*idiocy* up the food chain. And yes, we'll be short-handed if I fire you. If *any* of those things was different, you would have been gone before we even had this little conversation. Is that clear?"

He nodded.

"No trades for a month, and your margin for error is now zero. If you think I'm overstating that, just try me. Is that also clear?"

"Yes ma'am, very. You won't regret this."

Another long, icy glare.

"I'd better not." She picked up some papers, began to read, and growled, "Get out of here."

Kelly had her hand out to take his keys and ID when he emerged, and everyone in Ops gaped in open surprise when he walked in. Even the unflappable Grayson stared goggle-eyed from his office door.

Donna flew off the sofa, hugged his neck, and said, "Wow! You survived *that* dumbass move? Will wonders ever cease?" She meant no offense and he took none.

Chuck the marshaler was less excited.

"Look, man," he said, "we're not playing with goddam Tonka toys here. Pull your head fully and forever out of your ass or go find another job. That scared the living shit out of me."

Regina chimed in, perhaps trying to help by lightening the mood.

"Speaking of," she said, "we haven't had that much 'fun' since Rob dumped the lavs on the apron."

The ripple of laughter left Rob, on a trade and thus not in his hidey-hole at T-Point, looking sullen and embarrassed.

"Okay, what's *that* about?"

Donna told the story, which mirrored his own error in that haste had made waste, though much more literally.

"Lisa and Demarcus both called out sick. They had, well, it's pretty gross but I guess it was food poisoning or something. You know that little place down Airline, the one down past the turnoff to cargo?"

"Sure, we ate from there all the time at Streak."

"Well, they split a shrimp po-boy the night before so I don't know if it was the shrimp or what but whatever it was, they were both living in their bathrooms for a couple days. Ha! Pretty ironic considering what happened because of it. Anyway, morning shift was way short and boy, they were scrambling! They barely got the bags off and on, much less getting over to dump the honey wagon. So right when we came on, Grayson told Rob to go dump it and get back here 'cause we had three about to call in range. So Rob *flies* over there and back—big surprise—and gets back just in time for the first arrival."

She went on with difficulty, stray giggles interrupting the narrative as she tried not to laugh.

"He gets up there, hooks up the drain hose, pulls the handle, and out comes the donut"—the drain plug, so named for its shape—"but Speed Racer was in such a hurry that he forgot to close the bottom valve, the one the stuff runs out of into the dump tank. This disgusting, reeking lav gunk comes flowing out of the plane down into the cart and keeps right on going, *pouring* out onto the ramp! That hose is about four inches wide you know, so who knows how much he spilled, and of course the concrete was hot enough to scramble eggs. It was so…repulsive! Just disgusting, blue and brown and clumpy with God knows what. And the smell! Ugh!"

Donna's face contorted, the sight and stench clearly still locked in her memory. Several in her audience made faces too.

She continued, "So this United tug driver sees it and he stops and is pointing and yelling and waving so hard he looks like one of those navy guys with the signal flags. Rob thinks the guy's screwing with him somehow, so he waves back. We all start yelling but the GPU was down again so Rob can't hear us 'cause he's right up there by the APU. Finally, Grayson gets his attention and does the 'cut' sign"—she mimicked the motion, moving her hand across her throat—"but Rob's still not getting it, so Grayson keeps doing it faster and faster and faster."

With this, Donna's hand flew comically back and forth and Grayson interjected, "Damn near pulled my arm out of the joint."

Rob, sulking in a corner, said, "You guys suck."

Donna went on as the others laughed. "Rob lets go the handle, but of course it always takes about three tries to get the stupid donut seated. We had a huge mess by then."

Drew shook his head, his face involuntarily puckering at the thought of the vile spill.

"Who cleaned it up?" he asked. "And how?"

"Well, we called the fire department and one of those trucks with the water gun on top came over and hosed it out of the way so we could push, then they washed it down the storm drain. Can you believe it, we didn't even take a delay!"

"New Orleans Ops, Tumbleweed Five Forty-one in range with six point six," said the radio, cueing everyone to start gearing up. Grayson caught Drew's eye, waved him over, and said quietly, "The ice don't get no thinner but at least you're still skatin'. Don't waste it."

On the drive home, the episode at 7B and the tense discussion with Barb played over and over in his mind. He was almost afraid to think of either for fear that one or both might somehow turn out differently. He couldn't be mad at Barb, Chuck, or anybody else but himself.

Crossing the bridge, the shimmering skyline to the left and the dark Mississippi below, he forced himself to let it go. Still, it was long after midnight by the time he drifted off into a restless sleep.

EIGHT

Others having lobbied on his behalf was humbling. Grayson in particular was gambling his own reputation by refusing to write the newbie off. The supervisor said nothing about the whispers questioning his judgement, and anyone who broached the subject received a stare that led the inquisitor to look away and change the subject. When Drew tried to thank him, Grayson stopped him with an upraised hand and said, "Just don't make me sorry."

Those words became a mission. He kept a low profile, always hustled, and happily claimed any available overtime. Since Barb's punishment only applied to trades, the OT helped soften the financial penalty until the embargo expired.

He also looked for other ways to be useful, volunteering for extra duties like washing the equipment or repainting the caution lines, and sent more baggage tags back to their owners. Several people wrote complimentary letters, copies of which went to Barb, who sent him brief, cool notes acknowledging his thoughtfulness.

As the summer heat began to fade, so did the chocks mess. Drew, under close supervision as trainees obviously were, earned the endorsement necessary to push aircraft off the gates. He found the steering similar to backing up a trailer, the differences being the advantage of facing the direction of travel and that the "trailer" could be 150 feet long and weigh 75 tons. Like everyone, he had some cringeworthy moments but proved a quick learner. Pushing became his second-favorite ramp duty behind manning the headset that connected the ground crew with the pilots.

Everything seemed to have finally come together, though Barb had never retracted her warning, which remained fresh in his mind. The fast-paced environment worked to his advantage, bringing new challenges every day that helped keep memories short. There were some cutting remarks now and again but that came with the territory. The comments became less caustic over time, more like friendly jabs. As Donna said, the time to worry was when people *stopped* ribbing you. Besides, he wasn't above roasting a wayward colleague if the situation warranted.

His stock rose again when Sylvia, a gate lead, wrote a commendation. He came upon a chaotic scene at 7B while headed up to clock out one evening. RAATS was down so the CSRs were assigning seats with numbered stickers from a chart. A long line occupied both and an irate woman had Sylvia cornered. On top of everything else, the flight was overbooked and there were three pre-boards, two in wheelchairs and one family with small children. The crew couldn't help because one flight attendant was waiting to take tickets and by regulation, the other two were aboard.

He tapped a CSR on the shoulder and she turned, trying to rein in her exasperation at the interruption until she saw who he was.

"Anything I can do?"

She nodded with relief. "If you can help those two and that family over there so we can board, that would be great."

By the time he returned, things had calmed down, so he asked whether the CSRs needed anything else. They didn't, so he went home, thinking nothing of it until Grayson summoned him a few days later. Sliding Sylvia's letter across the desk, the supervisor gave what for him amounted to a speech.

"Nice job," he said. "Keep it up."

By and by the chocks mess was all but forgotten and an exciting milestone pushed it even further into the rearview mirror.

Airline employment's ultimate privilege is "nonrevving," or as formally titled, Nonrevenue Space Available (NRSA) travel. Simply stated, it's the ability to fly anywhere at little cost, albeit on standby. If flying Ruff Air, staff and their immediate families traveled free in Coach and paid only ten dollars if First Class was open. Employees traveling on other airlines used standby Industry Discount passes. A number denoted the discount offered against the full coach fare: ID50, ID75, and sometimes even ID90, where the traveler paid just ten percent of the other carrier's fare. Hotels and car rental companies, cognizant of airline employees' influence in steering passengers their way, also offered significant discounts.

With a pass or ID ticket in hand, and a cheap room and car waiting, even shiny new ramp rats could take excursions otherwise far beyond their means.

Nonrev travel presented unique opportunities. For instance, short getaways and even day trips worked nicely. The previous week, several colleagues had hopped the morning nonstop to Tampa. They rented a car, slipped into swimsuits in a convenience store restroom, and filled a foam cooler with ice, drinks, and snacks. After dashing across the causeway spanning Tampa Bay, they were soaking up the sun on Clearwater's gorgeous white sand beach an hour before lunch.

That evening, as the sun touched the horizon under a majestic mural of purple and orange, the group brushed off the sand and salt, posed for a photo with the Technicolor sunset, and piled into the car. Hurrying back to the airport, they took turns testing modesty and flexibility while changing into acceptable travel attire in the back seat.

Day trips were hectic, a total blast, and cheap to boot. The Clearwater foursome paid less than twenty dollars apiece, riding free in Coach and splitting the cost of lunch, the cut rate rental car, gas, and refreshments. The bargains didn't stop at the border either. Donna's passport had stamps from almost every continent, and the previous year she had flown to Los Angeles on Ruff Air then to Auckland using an ID90 on Air New Zealand. The total airfare amounted to only a few hundred dollars.

Nonrev travel was also the second most popular topic when people learned he was an airline employee. "Are you a pilot?"—as if no other possibility existed—was always the first question. With many women, he wryly noted the spark of interest in their eyes as they inquired and how quickly it died when he answered no. People also assumed every woman to be a "stewardess." Either way, what came next was always, "So do you get to fly for free?"

Few industries boasted such a desirable privilege. Different from a benefit in that it could be revoked, nonrevving really was fantastic—most of the time. After minimal arrangements, a traveler simply filled out a pass, boarded his or her flight of choice, and flew off to whatever fun or adventure awaited. Spontaneity was part of the allure; Peggy described how some nonrevs took what became known as "Weather Channel vacations," in which the nicest forecast from that network determined their destination.

There was, however, one gigantic caveat. Traveling on standby could occasionally be grueling, as evidenced by a joke making the rounds: "Have you heard about the new Holiday Nonrev Doll? Wind it up and it sits at a gate for three days."

Full flights stranding nonrevs for days wasn't the least bit implausible, especially at times like Thanksgiving or Christmas. They sometimes ended up taking bizarrely circuitous routings cobbled together from whatever connecting flights might be open. The last resort was renting a car and driving to an airport with better flight availability or all the way home. Relatives eligible for NRSA travel often fared even worse due to their limited knowledge of travel alternatives and their inability to research them on the fly in airline computers.

NRSA privileges started ninety days after the hire date, and Drew began seeking advice a few weeks before the big day. Awaiting an arrival one evening, he asked, "So Rob, you ever been stranded somewhere trying to get home from a nonrev trip?"

"Shit yeah, Drewbie," Rob replied from behind the ever-present mirrored aviators. "Everybody has. Let's see, drove Vegas to L.A., that actually happened to me twice. Once from Key West to, get this, *Orlando*, man. Got to Miami, no seats. Lauderdale, West Palm…nothin'! Goddam cruise traffic. Another time from San Antonio all the way back here in this crappy rental LeBaron that looked like the Dukes of Hazzard had driven it about ninety thousand miles."

Drew laughed out loud.

"I'm serious, man, I thought that piece of shit was gonna disintegrate right there on I-10."

"Was that the worst time?"

"No way. The worst was Hawaii. Continental canceled two straight widebodies. They had about forty nonrevs already and I'm standing there with my ID75 watching seven hundred tourists cry into their leis. I was in deep shit, man. Took 'em *three days* to move that sunburned herd—three days! Ended up getting the last seat on a United redeye to Chicago, then American to Denver, TWA to St. Louis, and Ozark back here. Talk about a long freakin' trip? I needed another vacation to recover from getting home."

Rob shook his head in disgust. "Ended up giving away three shifts so I didn't get my ass fired plus it cost me a crapload to call long distance and beg people to come in for me. And *then* that asshole Brent says he won't take the last shift I need unless I give him twenty bucks *and* swap with him on Thanksgiving so he can be home for dinner. What was I gonna say? That prick."

He spat on the concrete. "Sometimes it really, really blows. Always have a plan B."

Everybody repeated the same mantra. Peggy's take was practical as always.

"Flights look great, then suddenly fill up. Planes break down, weather socks you in, anything can happen. And you'll be at the bottom of the list every time," she warned. "Trade off an extra day or have an ID ticket in your back pocket just in case. Better yet, both. And buy it before you leave. If you don't need it, get a refund."

"What happens if you don't get back?"

She looked up from her weight and balance sheet. "Suspended without pay the first time. Second offense, or if you're on probation? Bye bye."

"Really?"

"Yes, really. It's happened twice since I've been here."

Still curious, he flipped through the policy binder to the NRSA section. There it was, couched in corporate formality: *Employees on standby personal travel should always have alternative travel plans. The company considers failure to report for a scheduled shift, or reporting late, due to employee's inability to board a flight while traveling on stand-by status to be an unexcused absence punishable by disciplinary action up to and including dismissal.*

No matter how well things had been going, Barb's hatchet would surely be sharp and swift if he was late.

Everyone added something to watch out for: booking levels, travel patterns, day of the week, special events, no show factors…the problem for new nonrevs was trying to see everything in context. Novices lacked the perspective to fit all the pieces together.

Constant daydreaming about potential destinations didn't help. Several people suggested a day trip but by then his sights were set on San Francisco. He had last been there as a child during the family's residence at Fort Ord. It was a long trip to shoehorn into a few days, but he managed to swap his evening shift on Monday for one ending at eleven that morning. He would catch a one-stop that landed before dinnertime, allowing him Monday evening, all of Tuesday, and most of Wednesday. The flights out and back were wide open.

As the trip grew closer, he focused more on the city's many attractions and that he was about to jet out to California because that's where he felt like going. This was it, the culmination of the dream kindled long ago as an entranced little boy stared out the window of a 707.

But if Joyce was right about mistakes being the portals of discovery, there were clearly a few more he needed to explore. Even the cloudiest crystal ball would have shown what might lay ahead for an excited first-time nonrev who neglected to properly complete his trip preparations.

First Class was available—and his choice of window or aisle to boot. He had just settled into the wide blue leather seat when an ISR approached, offered a newspaper, and asked his preference of champagne, orange juice, tea, coffee, or soda. He marveled at his good fortune as Tumbleweed 841 climbed out over the marshes lining Lake Pontchartrain's southern shore, the mottled colors sort of resembling camouflage.

The short hop to Houston was smooth and they arrived a few minutes early. Hobby was busy; four Ruff Air jets were at gates, a couple more taxiing, and one sat on a maintenance pad with mechanics on mobile scaffolds tending to each engine.

As the jetbridge extended, a lav service truck—*Damn, must be nice!*—came alongside, joined by a fuel tanker and catering truck. Noises from below; the bin doors opening. Thumps and metallic clicks and clanks from the galley, where empty carts were being replaced with full ones. People milled about looking for bin space and rechecking seat numbers.

Everyone put their things away, took their seats, and buckled up. Thuds as rampers closed the bins. A CSR did a P.A. then stepped onto the jetbridge.

"Ready, guys? Okay, have a good trip and we'll see ya next time."

"Thanks, Lyle. Bye!"

One last thump as the CSR closed and secured the cabin door.

Another voice announced, "Prepare for departure."

The ISRs fitted the slide activation bars into floor brackets, arming the escape chutes. If an evacuation became necessary, someone—ideally an ISR, or at worst a passenger who had actually read the safety card—would peek through the door's tiny window and either open the exit or direct people elsewhere depending on the conditions outside.

The plane began rolling smoothly backward. A glance at his watch showed it was exactly departure time, and he felt a rush of pride by association.

The ISRs served lunch once the jet reached cruise altitude. Nonrevs only received whatever meals remained once revenue passengers were served. The crew had a list, but Peggy said they appreciated subtle confirmation since keeping track could be troublesome, especially on full flights. She suggested something like, "Thank you, I'll wait to be sure everyone has a choice."

The line elicited a smile and nod from the ISR, whose wings said Melissa.

He eventually got what he hoped for, grilled chicken strips with honey-mustard dipping sauce. Each tray featured polished silverware wrapped in a cloth napkin; small glass salt and pepper shakers; a coffee mug; a short beverage glass; a saucer-sized plate with a wedge of cheese, some grapes, and a croissant; a bowl of chilled fruit slices; and even a miniature box of chocolates. Beverages included a variety of libations and while most others took full advantage, he chose ginger ale.

Once the trays were picked up, he headed for the lav but found it occupied. Melissa was straightening up the galley, sliding the carts back into their matching openings and locking them down. She looked up, smiled, and said, "Hi. Thanks for the heads up before. I'm Melissa."

"Drew," he said, shaking her hand.

"Glad you got a meal. Sometimes they don't cater us full up front."

"It was great. I was surprised though that they were all chilled plates."

"They have to be," she said, gesturing toward the galley bulkhead. "Our planes have no ovens."

"No ovens?"

"Not a one. They're heavy—more weight, more fuel you know—and they break about every five minutes, or it seems that way. I thought it would be a disaster when I came here, but it's not like ovens do much more than warm up the stuff they try to pass off for hot food anyway, right?"

Realizing she was speaking louder than intended, she peeked up and down the aisle, then continued, "The caterers have come up with lots of great stuff and the passengers love it. The chocolates don't hurt either."

"So you flew for somebody before?"

Her eyes grew wistful. "Continental, for fourteen wonderful years. Yep, the 'Proud Bird with the Golden Tail.'" She frowned and said, "And two more after the merger. Then they laid me off and I landed here. It's a fun place to work but starting all over at the bottom just about killed me. And actually,

I'm lucky. I know people on their fourth, fifth, even sixth airlines, and a lot of times they had to move for every new job. There have been divorces, drinking problems, bankruptcies, even suicides. It's too much, having to start over again and again. A lot of people don't understand yet, but this industry will never be the same again."

"Divorces? Suicides? Seriously? I didn't know that. Damn."

"It's really sad and it's not over yet."

As for the merger, Texas Air Corporation had taken over Continental in 1981, keeping the more widely recognized brand. The company filed bankruptcy two years later amid accusations that the true purpose was to dismantle nettlesome labor agreements. The contracts were voided and about half the workforce jettisoned. Those who stayed accepted drastic pay cuts. The resulting upheaval left thousands like Melissa looking for work. As with tens of thousands of others, she knew nothing else, loved the business too much to leave it, or both. And here was the seniority system's large and ugly albatross: you can't take it with you.

When airlines failed, top executives often walked away with financial security and a high-paying new title elsewhere. Everyone else started over as newbies again, which was humbling for all, financially strenuous for most, and absolutely devastating for rank-and-filers with even a few years invested. Senior captains who had commanded 747s to London, Rio, and Hong Kong ended up short-hopping the country as first officers on 737s. Flight attendants accustomed to Paris layovers found themselves flying six trips a day on short-haul turboprop turnarounds. Agents, rampers, and mechanics who'd waited fifteen years for day slots with one weekend day off could only hold graveyard shifts with midweek days off.

Management employees didn't live or die with seniority but still had to start all over, often in a new city after a self-paid move.

Though people tried to make the best of it and move on, the turmoil had taken a terrible human toll.

She tried to smile and said, "Don't get me wrong. I love it here and I'm glad to have a job." Her smile waned and her eyes welled. "I'm sorry, it's just tough sometimes."

He didn't know what to say. Seeing this, she touched his arm and said, "It's okay. There's nothing to say."

The lav door opened and a passenger emerged. Melissa nodded toward the open door with a sad, wry little grin, as if reluctantly bundling up her heartbreak and locking it away again.

The ride west was smooth, only a few bumps ("light chop" in pilot P.A.-speak) crossing the Rockies. There was plenty to see in the terrain: forests, deserts, mesas, canyons, and the Continental Divide's awesome, angular peaks, most wearing a five o'clock shadow of pine forest. Farm fields were colorful quilts made of squares, rectangles, and even dots where the center-pivot method delivered irrigation. Towns laid out in grids often reminded him of computer circuit boards cut to shape and laid on the land. Some of the remote areas had unusual patterns, circular spots joined in a huge chain-link pattern by what must be unpaved roads. Maybe oil wells or military sites of some kind?

He drifted off while pondering it, waking to Tony Bennett's voice a half-hour later, destination-themed music being part of Ruff Air's in-flight flair. After Tony went on about cable cars and the blue and windy sea, Otis Redding took over from his perch on the dock of the bay as the fledgling nonrev returned to his aerial sightseeing.

Here were wide freeways swarmed by colored dots; downtown San Jose, smaller than its bay-straddling cousins to the north; and residences on narrow lots that made subdivision streets look like zippers splayed across the landscape. Further on was an airport, notable because three buildings there looked like huge gray Twinkies. They could only be Moffett Field's airship hangars, built decades before to house Navy dirigibles and among the world's largest free-standing structures.

On final approach, another song suggested everyone wear flowers in their hair. Of more concern was how the plane descended until the bay rushed by so close it seemed the pilots had decided to ditch. At what seemed the last possible moment, the runway threshold flashed by followed by a firm thump. The main gear touched down, rose slightly, and settled as the wing spoilers deployed. They were twenty-one minutes early ("favorable winds," the captain explained) and with the time change, he would be downtown by late afternoon.

The Bay Area was as beautiful as ever, the weather perfect except for a slight blue haze masking the distant hillsides. He grabbed a newspaper for the shuttle ride, finding in it a bicycle rental ad. This was a touring method he hadn't considered but made perfect sense. He enjoyed riding at home and could cover a lot more territory too. He walked the area around the hotel that evening then mapped out a cycling plan.

Early the next morning, he got a bike at a rental place near Pier 39. Sea lions barked in the background and a unique blend of waterfront aromas wafted on the damp air—the salty bay breeze, seaweed, fish, food cooking, a street vendor's popcorn. Then he was wheeling down past Fisherman's Wharf, the Coast Guard station, through Fort Mason, and into the Presidio. He had to dismount on the steepest inclines, catching his breath while walking the bike and self-consciously watching locals pedal by.

Back in the saddle, he rode on to a place with a view of the magnificent Golden Gate, amazed to see cyclists and pedestrians flanking the traffic streaming back and forth. Should he ride over to Sausalito? His acrophobia politely tapped him on the shoulder and asked whether he had lost his mind.

Well, I'm here…might as well make it memorable.

He soldiered up a few more climbs and gingerly made his way out onto the bridge.

Memorable turned out to be an understatement. The GNO Bridge crossed the Mississippi about 170 feet above the water; the Golden Gate was a third again as high. Being in the open at that height left him feeling weirdly vulnerable. The crosswind, gusty, damp, and chilly, only made it worse. His discomfort spiked up to terrified a time or two but soon enough the sights overpowered his fear and left him almost euphoric. The rocky vistas of the Marin Headlands, the city, the bridge itself, the water traffic…there was so much to see! On the far side, he coasted at speeds ranging from sedate to breakneck depending on the decline and ultimately found a promontory east of Horseshoe Bay.

Few vantage points had ever impressed him more. The panorama included Tiburon, Angel Island, Alcatraz, the San Francisco skyline, the Golden Gate, and of course the bay itself. He spent nearly an hour watching the ships and boats come and go. Sailboats seemed to be everywhere, tacking this way and that, knifing through the water at the head of a whipped cream arrow, some so fast they raised rooster tails of spray in their wakes.

He rode on to Sausalito and ate lunch in a waterfront café. On the ferry back, he read brochures picked up here and there, pausing only to examine Alcatraz as they passed. Apparently tours of the island prison were available. There was so much he wanted to do!

He stopped by the Alcatraz tour office but the kindly woman there shook her head.

"I'm sorry, sweetie," she said. "These things are usually sold out within an hour or two. There's none left by this time of day."

Oh well. Next time.

Climbing through the World War II submarine USS *Pampanito* at Pier 45 brought real perspective to a favorite book, *Run Silent, Run Deep*. He had toured the equally tiny confines of USS *Drum* in Mobile, so he knew what to expect. Still, it was astonishing that 80 officers and crewmen could occupy such a space for months on end.

A framed photo featured one of *Pampanito's* sister subs bravely standing out to sea, dwarfed by the massive Golden Gate. How must sub crews have felt, fighting thousands of miles across the vast, angry Pacific with no one to count on but their shipmates and their complex, cantankerous vessel? Each port call brought news of more subs that were, in official Navy language, "overdue from patrol station." By war's end, 52 U.S. subs and over 3,500 of their buddies—nearly 20% of the entire submarine force—would remain on "eternal patrol," never to return.

Only the unforgiving sea knew most of their resting places. In some cases, even diligent post-war investigation failed to reveal their fates. With those stakes, what must it have been like to leave the Golden Gate behind or to see it appear through the fog on a homeward journey?

These somber thoughts lingered on the walk to a nearby deli. Finishing up his ham and Swiss on sourdough, he wondered whether he should have taken more time off. Peggy, among others, had urged him to do so. But lose money to be cautious? The Wednesday 4:00 p.m. departure through Houston was wide open and some half-hearted trade feelers found no takers anyway. He could have left at noon, with the later flight as backup, but the Muir Woods were already a time casualty. He didn't want to write off Lombard Street and the Coit Tower too.

Unwillingness to cut his trip short or trade away good money led to a classic rookie mistake: fixating on the number of open seats as if it was the only venomous snake in the nonrev grass.

Any experienced pass traveler knew relying on one flight was beyond foolhardy. Drew thought he was being conscientious, waking early on day two to call Res and check the bookings. Assured everything still looked great out of both San Francisco and Houston, he dressed, checked out, and dropped his bag with the concierge. Outside, there was bright sunshine under clear skies like the day before. He hit everything left on his abbreviated list and even squeezed in an hour at Fisherman's Wharf and a ninety-minute boat tour, shooting pictures until he ran out of film. All too quickly, it was time to go.

The queue waiting at Hyde and Beach was long enough to be a worry. A cable car arrived, and after passengers hopped off, workers rotated it on a huge turntable for the return trip— an interesting process to watch. Drew, fidgeting near the end of the line, barely made it aboard. He grabbed a brass handle and swung himself up onto a small side platform. The operator worked the long lever controlling the grip, rang the bell, and soon the car clacked, jerked, and clanged its way uphill. Traffic weaved around it and the street's incline occasionally steepened such that a death plunge back down the hill seemed inevitable. Visitors revealed themselves by clinging nervously to the handholds and casting uneasy glances at the slope. Everyone else read and chatted.

Twenty minutes later, he retrieved his carry-on from the hotel and caught an airport shuttle. While grateful that this would now be part of his life, there was something missing—someone special to share it with. Work had been too hectic to even think about dating but now seemed like a good time to start. Squeezed into the van with other budget-conscious travelers, he gazed out the window and contemplated some possibilities.

On the SFO ramp, an American Airlines flight engineer on her walk-around noticed what appeared to be hydraulic fluid under a DC-10 scheduled to take a full load to Dallas-Fort Worth.

As he arrived at curbside and headed for the Ruff Air counter, a blue-clad mechanic wrapped up a quick inspection of the leaky system. Looking down from atop a ladder, he shook his head and gave a thumbs down to the flight engineer, the trip's captain, and a few colleagues curious to see what was up.

While Drew waited to check in, a dispatcher in American's System Operations Control in Fort Worth marked the disabled DC-10 as OTS—out of service. No spare aircraft were available, so the dispatcher reviewed passenger counts and maintenance routings to see whether it made sense to "steal" another flight's aircraft to operate this trip instead. It didn't.

A Ruff Air agent placed his name on the standby list. On the walk to security, he noticed the lines at American's counter were very long. Some of the customers looked angry, their gestures and body language expressive even from afar.

The likely source of their angst became evident out on the concourse. Another agitated line waited at an AA gate, outside which a massive blue tractor was crawling away with a polished American widebody in tow. Drew had witnessed some cancellations in New Orleans. Though he hadn't yet had to face such unhappy customers, it had to be tough sledding. The DC-10 had about twice the capacity of Ruff Air's largest plane, so American could have over 270 angry people to rebook.

He shook his head, empathizing with both the stranded passengers and the American agents.

Man, that really sucks!
He had no idea.

NINE

American's ticket counter lead at SFO had a problem. Her people were already moving passengers booked on the canceled DC-10 to the next DFW nonstop and a Delta flight. She had also found alternatives for most of the connecting passengers. But what to do with the nineteen going to Houston and thirty-eight more headed for conventions in New Orleans? She frowned, typing furiously, scrolling through availability displays. Continental could accommodate a few Houston passengers but the other majors had…nada.

Come on, there has to be something…yes!

Soon American was rebooking fifteen Houston travelers and all the New Orleans people on Ruff Air 812—the flight Drew was counting on. Airlines welcomed such revenue and usually even took a few overbookings under the "bird in the hand" theory. Ruff Air's flight had been about 70% full and the American reroutes overbooked it by about ten. Still, there were usually enough no-shows to accommodate standbys.

But this flight's no-show factor was nowhere near average. Two large groups also headed to the New Orleans conventions were booked on RX812. Seasoned nonrevs were wary of group bookings because cancellations and no-shows were rare. Like two chemicals, inert when separated but explosive when mixed, the rebooked customers and the unusually low no-shows bulldozed his plans.

That something was up became obvious when people began arriving at the gate grumbling about a canceled flight, asking each other if anyone had heard of this Ruff Air, pestering the CSRs about whether they would get their AAdvantage miles, or all three. Cause for real, gut-tightening concern arose forty minutes before departure when a CSR keyed her mic and said, "For those passengers traveling on Ruff Air Flight Eight-twelve, Super Eighty jet service to Houston Hobby, some unexpected passengers from a canceled flight have unfortunately left us overbooked. If you are willing to take a later flight…"

The wait was downhill from there. The standbys worried themselves sick for the next half hour, all for nothing because they never stood a chance. The CSR crushed any remaining hope ten minutes before departure.

"For those passengers traveling standby on Ruff Air Flight Eight-twelve, we are completely full and will not be able to accommodate any standbys. Our next flight to Houston…"

Drew heard nothing more. Anxiety melted into despair as he sat with his head in his hands, berating himself for being so short-sighted. The very thing everyone had warned about again and again had blown up in his face. Even if another airline miraculously had seats to New Orleans, he didn't have enough cash for an ID ticket, hadn't brought his checkbook, and nonrevs couldn't pay with credit cards thanks to transaction fees. He hadn't even copied the station phone list, erasing the possibility of begging long-distance for someone to cover him.

He crossed his arms tightly and shook his head as he watched the Super 80 taxi away.

Well, that's that. God, how incredibly, ridiculously, unforgivably stupid!

His reflection caught his eye. Inexplicably, seeing how forlorn he looked almost made him laugh. Reality quickly dropped a wet blanket over any stray mirth. He waited, miserable, until the CSRs finished with the two volunteer oversales and the other disappointed standbys, then glumly requested a "meal listing." Unlike a reservation, listings didn't reduce available inventory but simply indicated a nonrev's intentions. Along with reservations, meal listings helped the caterers formulate a more accurate plan.

Noticing his expression, the young lady smiled sympathetically.

"What a bummer AA canceled. I guess lots of them are going to conventions in New Orleans. So which trip would you like to list on?"

He asked for the 8:15 a.m. departure the following day.

The agent replied, "The redeye's too much of an ordeal, huh? It's wide open out of here but I can't say I blame you."

His ears perked up.

"What redeye?"

Through sheer dumb luck, the airline's last daily flight—or, more accurately, the first the following day—had escaped his notice. Ruff Air 576 departed at 2:02 a.m. local and flew direct to Hobby for an 11:22 a.m. arrival. He could connect to New Orleans on Ruff Air's noon trip and with more good fortune, lots of it, might still get home in time.

But wait a minute...seven hours plus to Houston?

He had once been among those who confuse the term "direct" with "nonstop." Direct flights, like the SFO-HOU-MSY example he had missed, made one or more stops but without a change of aircraft or flight number. Still, even with a stop, this flight shouldn't take anywhere near that long.

"Is there more than one stop?" he asked.

Indeed, there was. Tumbleweed 576 epitomized the airline's whimsical call sign, meandering from San Francisco "direct" to Houston by way of Las Vegas, Midland-Odessa, Dallas Love, and Austin. This news tempered his excitement, eliciting a whispered *"Holy crap!"* as the CSR recited the routing. Regardless, he was ready to take on all comers for the title of most relieved nonrev in the history of San Francisco International Airport.

The trip wouldn't be pleasant or restful, but if all the "ifs" turned out to his advantage—both flights stayed reasonably close to their schedules, there weren't any traffic snarls on the GNO Bridge, he drove like a NASCAR hopeful at Daytona—he might be able to get home, shower, change into his uniform, and make it back before his 3:00 p.m. start. Failing to pack his ramp suit or stash it in his locker was another error of inexperience, one he found particularly irritating when it occurred to him somewhere over New Mexico.

Of course, first he had to get aboard and stay there. Standby status applied at every stop so he could get yanked anywhere along the way. There was no problem out of SFO and Las Vegas should be likewise since the flight was lightly booked. But the CSR frowned as she checked the loads further on.

"It'll be really close in Midland and Dallas," she said. "*Real* close." She smiled encouragingly. "But Houston-New Orleans looks good if you make it to Hobby!"

After nine-and-a-half interminable hours spent exploring the far corners of the airport, eating dinner, observing people and airplanes, reading every unattended newspaper or magazine and a couple he bought, and dozing fitfully in chairs seemingly the product of some sadistic design competition, Drew finally trudged down the jetbridge.

He stowed his carry-on, settled next to a window in Coach, and savored the thought of sleep at last. It was approaching 4:00 a.m. in New Orleans, but as luck would have it, he was wide awake. Every fall-asleep trick failed miserably. He gave up and stared out the window, taking stock as the jet rumbled out to the runway.

Let's see...I've been up for 20 hours, the time clock is 1900 miles away, my shift starts in 11 hours, and I have four stops, a connection, and a 90-minute trip home and back to look forward to. I am so...very...screwed.

And if he somehow made it, how would he be feeling when the end of his workday rolled around?

First things first.

The view after takeoff pushed his dilemma aside. The sparkling panorama ringing the blackness of San Francisco Bay stretched nearly to the horizon. A dark splotch in the sea of light caught his eye, its shape, orientation to the nearby water, and even the aerial vantage point all somehow familiar.

It's almost like a blimp shot...that's it, that's Candlestick!

The Saints had spent many a long Sunday afternoon in the blustery stadium when they came west to play the hated 49ers.

The plane continued climbing and turned east, revealing the cityscape with its iconic pyramidal skyscraper, the Bay Bridge, Treasure Island, and the floodlit Golden Gate beyond. The Super

50 steadied on course and leveled off at altitude a few minutes later. The gleam around San Francisco dwindled to a few pinpoints and clusters here and there and even these vanished in the utter blackness of Death Valley.

Sooner than expected, a distant glow appeared, quickly growing into a glittering, twinkling splash of colors embedded in an oasis of golden light that eventually filled the entire window. The final approach offered a look right down the famous Strip. Three-something in the morning on Las Vegas Boulevard looked like seven in the evening in some towns. What must it look like at its busiest?

Drew deplaned to stretch his legs since they were a few minutes early. Surprised to find slot machines near the gate, he got some change and tried his luck, achieving nothing but bolstering the local economy by a dollar or so a minute.

A couple of the boarding passengers looked decidedly the worse for wear, bleary-eyed, reeking of booze and cigarette smoke, their clothes and hair in disarray.

Soon the jet barreled down the runway for takeoff and the irony couldn't be ignored. Given the stakes and long odds, the odyssey's first stop being the world's gambling capital was only fitting.

I hope my luck runs better the rest of the flight than it did at the slots!

He mulled his chances as Tumbleweed 576 again climbed into the night. Overbooked trips early in the morning had to mean business travelers headed to meetings and appointments.

I really might be hosed.

The word overbooked, or its synonym, oversold, sent an icy stab of fear into any standby. Only the brave, naïve, or desperate tried to nonrev on overbooked flights.

The practice was widespread, effective, and almost universally despised outside executive suites. Proponents argued that retailers didn't have to sell a television or washing machine the day it arrived; the item could remain in stock until a buyer took it home. Unlike such durable goods, available seats on a given flight became worthless when the cabin door closed—

"spoilage" in airline lexicon. Given the money at stake, carriers became adept at deducing how many people would no-show and thus how many reservations should be accepted to ensure a full flight.

But the ideal outcome wasn't simply a sold-out aircraft. That was easy if fares were low enough. Airlines wanted each passenger to pay the highest fare they were willing to pay. This led to maddening price fluctuations, where two callers making reservations around the same time might pay vastly different prices. The steep fares last-minute travelers paid must have left some wondering whether they were buying an airliner instead of a ride on one.

Peggy had done her best to explain.

"Imagine a row of buckets, each marked with a ticket price and how many seats are at that price," she said one afternoon while they sipped sun tea under the concourse. "And say it's a really popular flight. They might only sell ten seats at the lowest fare and once those are gone, that bucket is full so they close it off. The next person wanting that flight gets the price in the next higher bucket, and so on."

"So it's kind of like the reservations are being poured into an ice cube tray? Once the first little chamber is full it spills over to the next?"

"Just like that. And the other way too, the cheaper seats may open up again if there are cancellations. I think that's what drives people nuts, the way the prices can bounce all over the place no matter when you book."

"But why not figure out the cost per seat and set a reasonable profit over that?"

"Well, as it was told to me, if they set a price, it might be more than one person will pay and less than another. Some people don't care which flight they're on as long as they get there on a certain day or even within a day or two, but others might be on a tight schedule of meetings and such. They have to be there by a certain time."

She pointed to the cup in his hand.

"It's like that tea. You might give a quarter for it right now, but how much would you pay if you had just walked out of the desert after a couple days? 'Variable demand' is what they called it. It really doesn't come into play here because we only offer a few fares. Now Delta and Eastern and American? That's a way different story."

Huge mainframe computers crunched historical and contemporary data, delivering amazingly accurate estimates based on a laundry list of criteria: city pair; month, day, and time of departure; and special events that brought more travelers at a given time.

The overbooking process, reliable but far from perfect, occasionally resulted in a few volunteers staying behind. This wasn't a concern since their compensation was far less than the revenue from filling otherwise empty seats. But sometimes no one volunteered, leaving gate agents no alternative than stranding paying passengers. Known as "involuntaries," they understandably vented their wrath with infamous ferocity.

Leaving involuntaries was bad enough, but sometimes the system misfired completely. Grayson had seen an extreme example first-hand. It involved a so-called circular routing, where a single aircraft flew from his old employer's hub in Kansas City to Los Angeles, on to Las Vegas, and from there back to Kansas City. Because reservation systems couldn't handle a flight number with the same origin and destination, the only way to sell tickets for all five city pairs was to assign two flight numbers. One covered Kansas City to L.A. or Las Vegas; the other was for customers flying from L.A. to Las Vegas or on to Kansas City, or from Las Vegas to Kansas City.

Because both flight numbers were "live" out of Los Angeles and Las Vegas, proper booking limits were imperative.

It was a holiday week and Grayson described LAX as "bustin' at the seams" that night. A gate agent, Rod, became increasingly apprehensive as an extraordinarily long line grew. He typed a few entries, studied the results, and wondered what was going on. The trip was overbooked by twenty, but who were all these other people?

Then his colleague Lydia turned to him. In in a small voice, she said, "Rod?"

Obviously distraught, she held out a ticket. "Look at the flight number."

It was the number originating in Kansas City. The only people traveling on that flight number should be claiming luggage or on the plane, not standing in line for a seat assignment.

They exchanged a look, both considering the same unthinkable possibility.

Rod checked the second flight number in the computer and there it was: a nightmare spelled out in green pixelated characters. One 737 was overbooked under both flight numbers, leaving nearly 300 people with reservations for 136 seats.

Rod had decades of experience but had never seen anything like this. He called the supervisor, who said she would be up ASAP. But she had failed to understand exactly what Rod was telling her and was tied up with something else. For forty chaotic minutes, Rod and Lydia, both too busy trying to sort it out to call again, worked to find some kind of solution. The only possibility was an extra section—an unscheduled additional flight—but while the Dispatch manager was sympathetic, he was also firm: there were no spare aircraft at LAX so that plan would entail canceling another full flight.

In hindsight, that would have been a brilliant move.

The customers' mood escalated from curiosity to restless concern. A passenger overheard something and word shot through the crowd that half of them would be left behind. A mob mentality began to fester and with it, the slide toward a potential riot.

As Lydia frantically dialed the airport police, Rod picked up the mic, quieted the rowdy passengers with a call for their attention, and briefly explained the situation. Grayson, nonrevving from a nearby gate, arrived within earshot as Rod wrapped things up with a proclamation that soon became airline legend.

"So that's what happened," he calmly declared in his soothing baritone voice, "but I have no idea how. In fact, ladies and gentlemen, there's only one thing I *do* know right now: these cheap bastards don't pay me nearly enough to deal with crap like this. Good night and good luck."

With that, he removed his ID, laid it and his keys on the podium, and strode off down the concourse under incredulous stares, no one more surprised than Lydia.

Loosening his tie, Rod didn't look back even when several police officers jogged by in the opposite direction.

With no way to determine who should stay or go, Dispatch ultimately canceled the trip. Lydia, the tardy supervisor, Grayson, and two cross-trained rampers spent over two hours taking abuse as they rebooked people under the watchful eyes of half the LAPD's airport detail. Grayson always ended the story in typically laconic fashion: "Now that there was a goat rope."

Drew pushed everything from his mind and tried again to sleep. No luck. He twisted this way and that, rested his head on the tiny pillow, then the seatback, then the window. Maybe it was the chill. A blanket warmed him up a bit but that was it. He turned sideways, gave up on that again, straightened out, and stretched his legs out as far as possible. This succeeded only in jolting awake the woman seated ahead when he accidentally kicked her foot. After apologizing quietly and profusely, he sat up, stretched to the extent possible and started his third perusal of the in-flight magazine.

An hour later, he forgot exhaustion and anxiety for a few minutes as the subtle blush of dawn caught his eye. A broad rust-colored band brightened to rose and then into a salmon pink blaze. After this vivid splendor, the color slowly faded to a cobalt blue that gradually grew upward as night dwindled away. Below, still steeping in the darkness, were farms, rural houses, and towns, some of the latter large enough to be surrounded by clusters of subdivisions that looked like tangled strings of white Christmas lights. Here and there, tiny pinpoints, two each of white or red, pushed pools of light along roads likewise invisible except where dotted lines of streetlights shone along their edges. The land eventually lightened, the rising sun turning a river below into a serpentine ribbon of molten gold.

As the descent began, the cabin pressure changed and the engines quieted. The spoilers popped up, acting as speed brakes, and the wings quivered under the disrupted airflow until the panels slowly settled as if lazily falling back asleep. Below, the tiny buildings, trees, and vehicles gradually grew until the world resumed the proper scale.

Fellow travelers could have mistaken the rookie nonrev for a terrified flier if not for the obvious reversal. In the air, he was fine; he only became distressed when the aircraft taxied in. Then he sat sweating despite the air conditioning, face creased with anxiety, the magazine he had been reading forgotten and crushed in his jittery hands. People came aboard, stowed their belongings, and took seats. He couldn't see any more empty ones, yet more passengers appeared, rooting around for space in the overhead bins.

He remained clenched up, certain his name would be called at any moment followed by instructions to gather his belongings and deplane.

The aisle finally cleared and a CSR's voice came through the overhead speakers.

"Good morning, ladies and gentlemen. Welcome to Ruff Air Flight Five Seventy-six, nonstop Super Fifty jet service to Dallas Love Field with continuing service to Austin and Houston Hobby. On behalf of our Midland-Odessa ground staff, thank you for choosing to fly with us today. We hope that when your plans again call for air travel, you'll once again think of us here at Ruff Air."

Minutes later, he slumped against the window with relief as the tow tractor headed toward the concourse, spewing black exhaust, with rampers trotting along behind. The suspense left him drained and dreading a repeat at Love Field.

The climb was a bumpy ride through sickly walls of gray broken by darker patches seemingly airbrushed in for effect. The cabin bucked and lurched, bouncing passengers' heads about in comic unison.

Grayson had provided a helpful tip.

"Watch the ISRs," he had advised. "If they don't look scared, ain't nothin' to worry about."

Soon the Super 50 broke out on top of the cloud deck. An announcement warned that while the air was smooth for now, turbulence could be expected during approaches and departures all the way to Houston. Still, the reward proved well worth the bronco ride. A cotton candy panorama stretched as far as the eye could see, complete with a touch of pink courtesy of the morning sun. The color was gradually replaced by a blinding white glare that made the sky above look even bluer.

The stop at Love Field brought fifteen more minutes of sick apprehension. Finally, the jetbridge moved jerkily away followed by the little jolt indicating the pushback tractor had begun its work. The ISRs hurriedly served beverages, and one paused long enough to say, "Wow, you've got some amazing luck going. We're really full today. Some big conventions in New Orleans is what I heard."

Austin wasn't supposed to be in doubt yet the bustle began anew. Few debarked and it was disconcerting—again—to see so many people in the aisle looking for bin space and vacant seats. There had obviously been a late wave of bookings.

Drew felt as if he'd been born and raised right there in 22A by the time they began the descent into Houston. He squeezed past his seatmates to go use the lav, a necessity he should have addressed earlier. The seatbelt sign illuminated as he slid the knob to lock the door.

The bouncing started again, amplified by proximity to the tail. Sideways, up, up, down, twice to the other side, up, down, up. He tried to brace himself, clunking his head and elbows several times while trying to keep his balance.

Jesus! And women envy us for being able to do this standing up?

He hurriedly washed up, splashed his face, and brushed his teeth, but still felt like a mere shower might fall short of a good steam cleaning.

The flight arrived four minutes early, leaving him grateful and guardedly optimistic.

Yes! I might make it!

This warm rush lasted the six glorious minutes needed to hurry to the connecting gate and learn Continental had canceled their noon flight to New Orleans. He needed every bit of self-control to rein in the resulting surge of frustration. Upon reaching the podium, the CSR shook his head and said, "Yeah, Continental wasn't that full but it doesn't look good. I guess there's some big conventions starting in New Orleans."

You don't say!

He took a seat in the gate area, dog tired and convinced he was doomed. The only thing to do was remain calm, wait patiently, and hope for the best.

The last confirmed passengers filed down the jetbridge as departure time neared, leaving fifteen or so standbys clustering around the CSR like rapt believers facing a tent revival preacher. Some carefully kept poker faces, worried but determined not to reveal it; others genuinely seemed past or above caring, resigned to whatever outcome awaited; and a distressed few stood as stiffly as stick figures, faces contorted, agonizing over the CSR's every word and move as if the boarding passes he wrote were death row reprieves. Emulating the blasé proved tough with so much riding on making the flight.

The CSR called names until everyone else boarded, then checked his computer one last time. With a sympathetic look, he said, "Sorry, buddy, that's it. Hang tight and I'll roll you over to the next trip when I get back." He leaned around, kicked loose the hook holding the door, and headed down the jetbridge. The door banged shut behind him.

Drew looked at the ceiling for a long moment, dejection and anger boiling inside.

I got so damn close!

He slammed his carryon to the floor, then stomped back and forth a few times. He picked up his bag, resisted the urge to throw it as far as he could, and strode off, no conscious destination in mind.

Twenty feet on, a nugget of wisdom buried in memory's nether depths chose this opportune moment to fight clear of the frustration and dart into his consciousness. The source was Rob of all people. He had sauntered over the day after their conversation about being stranded and said, "Hey Drewbie, remember I told you about being stuck up the creek in Honolulu? I forgot the best part. There were five people ahead of me for that last seat on United's redeye."

"Seriously? How'd you get on?

"No shit, man. When the agent shut the door, the next guy was a revenue passenger who missed his flight. He jumps up and takes off after a redcoat like a cheetah running down a gazelle. Right, man, it's United's fault you were too busy catching rays and checking out the ass on Waikiki to make your flight. Anyway, the agent comes back and says the computer is off and there's one seat. Beach boy was three gates down reaming the redcoat and then it was two honeymoon couples and me. No way either of *them* were splittin' up, so off I went. Ain't love grand? For once *I* was the leprechaun at the end of the rainbow."

"Nice."

Rob continued, "The counts are screwed up half the time anyway. I ain't the fastest learner but after that I never leave the gate 'til I'm looking at a tailcone heading for the runway." He had popped in a fresh stick of gum, grinned, and said, "I almost wish one of the lovebirds had gone so I could have seen the look on that asshole's face when he got back and found out he would've gotten on after all."

Well, I've got exactly nothing to lose.

He hurried back only to find he needn't have bothered. The flashing amber light below the jetbridge cab and the retracted canopy both indicated the CSR was about to pull away. But he didn't, and then came the thumpety-thump of running footsteps. As if recalling Rob's anecdote had somehow altered reality, the door burst open and the agent yelled, "Come on! There's a seat, mid-cabin, on the left. Hurry!"

Drew dashed aboard. An ISR grabbed his carryon and said, "It'll be in the coat closet. Go!" He heard the cabin door close and felt the aircraft begin rolling even as he rushed down the aisle, found the open middle seat, and squeezed into it, muttering "sorry" and "excuse me."

Fittingly, now that little rest time remained, even his relief wasn't enough to keep him awake. His head lolled and he was deep asleep before takeoff.

The landing rudely jarred him awake well under an hour later. He looked around groggily, needing a moment to remember where he was.

Damn, is this one of those ex-Navy types Bert talks about?

His friend had said former naval aviators sometimes needed practice making soft landings, accustomed as they were to firmly planting their Intruders, Tomcats, and Hawkeyes on pitching carrier decks.

Or maybe they're having the same kind of day I am.

Sleeping in the seat left his neck stiff. He tried to work it out as the Super 50 turned off the runway, promptly dozing off again during the taxi.

Roused by the arrival announcement, he checked his watch and found Chance had left a small parting gift: his marathon with wings was seven precious minutes early.

Peggy's variable demand explanation now made perfect sense. He would give almost anything to magically erase his obligations and slide back into deep, delicious sleep. Who cared where this airplane was going? But remembering what was on the line provided enough impetus for him to wearily deplane and race to the shuttle stop.

The wait for the employee bus seemed endless. Watching anxiously for it to round the corner, Drew realized he had forgotten to thank the Houston CSR, who could have—and arguably should have—closed the door. Maybe somebody knew a way to figure out who it was.

By the time the bus arrived, he was pacing like a hyperactive cockroach. He hopped off at the first stop, dashed across to the car, hurried home, and left a trail of clothes into the bathroom. After shaving, brushing his teeth, showering, and dressing in ten minutes flat, he rushed back to Moisant, parked in the ludicrously expensive hourly garage, and bolted for the time clock in an open sprint.

A moment of panic as he scanned the rack.

Where's my card?!

He spotted it behind someone else's. He fumbled, got it free, jammed it into the machine, withdrew it, and inspected the result—2:58 p.m.—with a heady rush of relief and elation. He might have bounded down the hall with a rebel yell had he still possessed the energy to do so, but was happy just to lean on the wall, panting, head spinning, with a goofy grin of satisfaction.

There was a technicality, however, and the grin faded fast as he remembered it: clocking in was only step one. You also had to be in your area ready to work at starting time.

Grayson punctuated this detail, leaning in the door and bellowing, "I don't know what you're so goddam giddy about, but we ain't got time for lollipops and lemonade! Get your ass downstairs!" But it was mostly for effect; he was chuckling as Drew hightailed it out.

There was no reason to share his story but who was he kidding? Before his gloves, ball cap, and hearing protector were out of his locker, a curious colleague remembered his desperate run for curbside a couple of hours ago. Idle during a lull and feeling a little nosy, she deduced what had likely happened and started perusing standby lists. Finding his name, she backtracked to his planned return the day before, saw the final passenger count versus the original bookings—obviously somebody had canceled a flight—and from there the rest was easy.

As he walked out ten minutes later to meet the first arrival, the circle already briefed on his near miss stood at four and was growing fast. He was genuinely confused when Rob pulled up planeside 25 minutes later and yelled, "Hey Drewbie, how was Frisco?"

"Great."

"Good, how 'bout Vegas? Midland? Love? Austin? Houston? I hope you're not tired. We've got a busy night ahead!"

You've got to be kidding me.

He shrugged in response. Rob chortled behind his mirrored sunglasses and drove away.

Back in Ops later, Peggy looked up with an expression that needed no interpretation.

Drew held up his hands, palms out.

"I know, I know, you told me."

"Do you have *any* idea how lucky you were? Any idea at all? Come around here, child."

She said it in a way that reminded him of Mom's tone when he was in enough trouble for her to use his first and middle names.

Sheepishly, he made his way through the little swinging door and sat beside her. She had pulled up the final load displays from Midland-Odessa, Dallas Love, and Austin.

Super 50s held 126 passengers. Peggy said, "Look at this, and this, and this." Each line of green characters to which she pointed was identical:

```
TOTAL PAX F 12 / Y 114
```

The nonrev gods had been beyond merciful. He would have been stranded, all hope gone, had just one more person shown up anywhere along the way.

"One more," Peggy went on. "One more and your butt would have been grass and Barb the mower. *Four times over!*"

This addendum naturally circulated in nothing flat. Most colleagues were empathetic; they had been newbs once too. But apparently, a few believed a flameout was inevitable before his probation ended. There were even whispers of a pool, with an over/under option available for those willing to risk an extra buck on exactly how long he would last.

TEN

Personally and professionally, the next few months passed uneventfully, with the dating scene a particular disappointment. Working so many hours barely left enough free time for laundry, let alone love. Asking a colleague out felt like asking for trouble, but there weren't many alternatives, so romance stayed on the back burner. On the bright side, each day brought his goal of passing probation that much closer.

Soon only two weeks remained until the hangman's noose would be removed from his professional neck, assuming of course Barb signed him off. Despite the smooth sailing of late, he still felt like a tightrope artist learning his craft with an unforgiving floor beckoning from far below. The knowledge that others were watching—some like circling vultures—only intensified his determination.

He had arrived early on a Friday afternoon and was watching the ramp action from the breakroom. A morning shift agent named Gail flopped down beside him, rested her elbows on the chipped, scuffed old table, cupped her face in both hands, and said, "Hey."

"Hey," he replied. She was in her ramp suit but had her purse and was wearing sneakers, so she was obviously headed home. Drew didn't know her well but had heard she was pleasant if direct.

"I need a big, big favor."

Like maybe a day off that no one else will cover?

"It's my son," she said, widening her brown eyes beseechingly. "He's going to be in the first grade play a week from Monday but I'm stuck on the counter. It's called 'Mr.

Hoppy's Carrot Farm Christmas.' He's Mr. Hoppy"—her hands simulated rabbit ears—"and I have to be there, Drew, I *have* to, but with Christmas coming up nobody else can cover me."

She went into overdrive for the final push.

"I can't really afford to take the whole day but I know you'd be working like three straight doubles so I wouldn't ask you to come in for half a shift and there's a special lunch too after the play so please? Please? *Please?*" She dragged out the last "please" for about three seconds while leaning over and hugging his arm, her lovely eyes and pleasant scent not hurting her cause one bit.

How does she smell so good after eight hours slinging bags?

Olfactory distractions aside, he was torn. With a crushing load of hours lined up, he planned to sleep in that Monday. That sounded especially sweet since his regular shift had been extended three hours due to the Christmas rush. Helping Gail would mean another eight hours of pay in the bank, but at a cost. He wouldn't be home until after midnight Saturday or Sunday. A third double with a 6:00 a.m. start would be brutal.

Gail had to be desperate to be asking this far down the pecking order. As Rob had mentioned, some took advantage of such predicaments by demanding money or other perks, but that didn't seem right. Someday the roles would surely be reversed and he would need a favor. Still, he should say no. But some odd psychological quirk made "no" a word he often had trouble saying when it would disappoint a woman. A couple of former girlfriends had uncovered this lever and used it to great advantage.

Then it clicked: Gail was stuck on the counter so the trade wouldn't be approved anyway. The company had issued him a customer service uniform—showcasing Payroll Department efficiency by immediately starting deductions for its cost—but he hadn't yet earned any training above the wing. Double trades, where he would work the ramp for someone who could cover Gail's counter shift, were frowned upon. Gail must have forgotten he wasn't signed off on the counter. Secretly, he was relieved. Sleeping in that Monday was well worth forgoing the extra money, and now he could do it with no guilt.

"I would, Gail, no problem, but I haven't been trained on the counter."

This defense proved as effective as Wile E. Coyote's umbrella against falling boulders. With two thumbs up for emphasis, Gail exclaimed, "No, it's okay! I already talked to Grayson and Mary. They both said since I'm working Express Check-in, they'll approve it. It's easy!"

The hands were flying. "All you have to do is remember a few entries"—she pantomimed typing—"and send the bags to the right place!" She fastened an imaginary destination tag onto an imaginary luggage handle, finishing with a cute little flourish. "See? Piece of cake!"

So he agreed, and if Gail noticed his reluctance, she ignored it. She delivered another enthusiastic hug followed by a brief tutorial covering the seat-assignment entries in Ruff Air's computer system.

Well, it wasn't *exactly* Ruff Air's. Trans America Airlines had developed and refined it through decades of effort and enormous monetary investments. While TAA had since rebranded as TGA—Trans Global Airlines—their electronic brainchild still carried its original name, a clunky Cold War-era moniker only a software engineer could love: Automated Universal Reservations Architecture, understandably shortened by users to AURA.

Launched around 1960, within a few years AURA was among the country's largest private real-time networks. TGA had approached several competitors early on, suggesting joint development of a system serving each carrier. When the others balked, TGA went solo. In time, most of the uncooperative would-be partners came to deeply regret their shortsightedness.

AURA's capabilities soon expanded far beyond reservations and fare pricing, encompassing ticketing, boarding passes, booking levels, and even cargo rates and tracking. The system handled operational tasks like planning flight routes and the optimal fuel load to fly them along with hunting lost luggage. It automatically adjusted passenger weight distribution through seat assignments and, once the load planner and gate agents entered final counts, calculated the aircraft's weight and balance.

TGA's flight crews then received the data instantly via a miniature cockpit printer as the plane taxied to the runway.

Just as impressive was AURA's ability to generate monumental piles of cash as computerized reservations systems quickly became a necessity. Deregulation had provided TGA with an eager flock of new customers, some of whom later accused Trans Global and other similar networks of gouging them with fees, poaching booking data, padding competitors' flights with ghost bookings, and various other forms of electronic voodoo. He had read of this and wondered if companies would really go to such extremes.

In any case, airlines near and far paid Trans Global to use AURA, choosing functionalities à la carte or buying the entire repertoire. Ruff Air opted for the most basic package—reservations, flight tracking, boarding passes, and some reporting features—but still forked over monthly licensing and transaction fees so hefty that the airline disclosed the amounts only when required by law.

As time went on, TGA's aviation brethren proved to be the tip of the revenue iceberg. The same way speedy jets revolutionized air travel, rendering propeller planes obsolete almost overnight, systems like AURA began replacing paper schedules and tariffs. Computers provided travel agencies instant access to worldwide flight schedules and millions of fare and route combinations covering almost every airline. Hordes of customers jumped aboard and soon little colored pins marking their locations swarmed the map mural at AURA's headquarters.

Over time, programmers further broadened their prodigy's talents, adding the ability to book hotels, rental cars, cruises, rail, tours and, eventually, complete vacation packages. Like airlines, TGA billed other travel merchants for licenses and transactions. The nonstop activity rang TGA's register around the clock, repaying the airline's original investment many times over.

The mainframe's location underscored its operational and fiscal importance. It resided beneath twenty feet of Midwestern prairie in a reinforced concrete bunker supposedly stout enough to withstand anything other than a direct hit by an

ICBM. So, as the joke went, even if the world nuked itself into smoking rubble, AURA would be up and running.

Such precautions were understandable; downtime, mercifully rare, brought the cash cow to its knees and every user's enterprise to a screeching halt. The dreaded SYSTEM UNAVAILABLE message caused "Noooo!" to be simultaneously uttered in an impressive assortment of places and languages, soon followed by prayers to a variety of deities that the interruption would be brief. Most were, as multiple redundant systems minimized major snafus. But when a big one came along, Murphy often seemed to personally author the scenario, then grab some popcorn and a front row seat to enjoy the chaos.

Early one Friday, shortly after dozens of carriers chummed the booking waters by matching a United sale, a hardware failure took down the main data line. Technicians estimated five hours to replace the failed component: four to fly it in on a chartered Lear and another to install it.

The backup line picked up the load and performed flawlessly for forty-six minutes, until a thrifty homeowner on a rented backhoe severed it while digging his own swimming pool.

TGA's operations and those of hundreds of AURA subscribers slowed to a crawl. Workers struggled to implement manual procedures, the situation ironically worsened by their unfamiliarity with the seldom-needed contingency plans. Technicians restored the system several hours later, but untangling such a massive ball of yarn took well into the wee hours of Saturday. Employees throughout the industry still used "Backhoe Friday" to describe those especially rotten days when everything that could go sideways, did.

A marketing clause permitted lessees to choose a name, no doubt so the leasing airline could advertise "its" computer system. Some HQ big cheese had grandiosely christened it the Ruff Air Accounting and Ticketing System, apparently without considering the resulting acronym: RAATS. Everyone pronounced it like the rodent, which was amusingly apropos. CSRs often exclaimed that very word when confounded by long, complicated formats. The inputs probably made perfect sense to some code writer who would never have to execute the commands with a tense, impatient passenger staring into their face and thirty more fretting and fidgeting in line.

Gail demonstrated the few simple entries he would need to know, pointing to each one on a small cheat sheet she had been kind enough (or, perhaps, presumptuous enough) to photocopy.

"What we'll do is put these in your PNR so you have them handy. You have a PNR, right?"

"A what?"

"How has nobody showed you that?"

She explained that "Passenger Name Record" or PNR was the official term for a reservation. Employees could book one under their own name and since everyone used the same fake flight number, anyone could pull up a colleague's PNR and leave them a message in the remarks section. PNRs were also useful for keeping notes handy, as Gail was suggesting now, and for staying in touch with friends in other stations.

"I'll show you that and how to get to the customer service ALM lessons too," she promised. "That's 'AURA Learning Modules' if you care what things stand for."

ALMs were computerized courses, including a set covering safety and ramp procedures he had completed.

"Doing the customer service series gets you *big-time* brownie points toward training above the wing," she explained. "And of course, that'll go a lot faster too if you know a little something about the formats."

Displaying a thick, spiral-bound tome divided by small colored tabs and filled with neat feminine handwriting, she recommended he also start his own notebook and practice whenever he found an open terminal.

There was no need to ask whether there were RAATS classes. As with everything else, Ruff Air agents learned on the job. He would later find that TGA flew its own greenhorns to a state-of-the-art multifunctional training center, housed them in dorms, paid them their salary plus a small per diem, and provided three meals a day during a formal six-week AURA course. Word had it the facility even sported faux ticket and gate counters for class practice along with after-hours amenities like a swimming pool, club room with TV, and even an arcade.

A separate building, still saddled with the obsolescent name Stewardess Academy, was affectionately nicknamed "Stew U." The classrooms and cabin mockups there stayed busy seven days a week providing initial and refresher training on a multitude of emergency procedures—the cabin crew's primary function—and the niceties of in-flight service. There was even an in-ground tank surrounded by replicas of fuselages and wings from which trainees could rehearse launching life rafts.

Gail was thorough and the role sounded simple enough. Drew felt reasonably confident as she hugged his neck tightly again—not an unpleasant experience, he had to admit—surprisingly kissed him on the cheek, and said, "Thanks! I owe you one!"

Nine days later, he stumbled into his apartment ninety minutes past midnight. Instead of scrubbing away the dirt, sweat, and charming scent of eau de kerosene as he usually did, he emptied his pockets onto the dresser, shed his uniform in a rank pile, double-checked both alarm clocks, and fell instantly asleep splayed across the bedspread.

Gail's heartfelt words of gratitude were little comfort when the jangling clock roused him at 4:00 A.M. Rubbing sleep from his eyes, he stumbled into the bathroom. The haggard reflection there looked more like someone headed for rehab intake than an airline ticket counter.

He had been eager to show his stuff above the wing. Now he just hoped to make it through the day.

ELEVEN

A shave and hot shower helped, then out came the new Class A uniform. Tying the necktie proved a challenge. He was out of practice and having difficulty keeping his eyes open also slowed the process. After he got it right, he carefully splashed his face with cold water in a largely futile effort to clear his head.

This is going to be a long, long day.

He inspected the unfamiliar attire in the mirror: pressed, white long-sleeved dress shirt, navy vest and trousers, patterned blue tie, and polished black dress shoes.

There is nothing, he thought with tongue firmly in cheek, *that makes a man look sharper than blue polyester!*

A stray flash of white caught his eye as he turned away: the manufacturer's tag, still stitched on the vest. Off came the vest and then the tag.

Yeah, that would have been smooth.

Fatigue circled like a starving shark on the long drive, slashing in every few minutes even with the stereo cranked and the sunroof cracked to suck in some freezing air. More than once, he caught himself nodding off and far more than once, a single question buzzed around his brain.

What in God's name was I thinking to take this trade?

The Plexiglas box at the shuttle stop offered little protection from the bitter wind. Nobody spoke; the only signs of life were little clouds of silver mist with each exhalation. They could hear the shuttle coming and people fifteen miles up U.S. 61 in LaPlace could probably hear it too. Its brakes emitted a tortured shriek whenever it came grinding to a halt, each instance so long and piercingly loud that it felt like it might actually cleave open his skull. He hopped aboard, fortunate to find a seat near the back. The passengers at the next few stops had to stand.

Years of hard use had left the interior worn and reeking of dried sweat and diesel exhaust. He wanted to offer his seat to one of the women, but it was impossible. At least 25 employees, all swathed against the chill, were stuffed inside. At first it felt good to be out of the cold, but within minutes the warmth inside grew oppressive, almost sickeningly so. Too bad, though; everyone was crushed together with hardly room to move, much less shrug off a coat. The brakes continued their protest each time they were called upon and the steamed windows blurred the lights and scenery outside into a scrolling impressionist mural.

He dozed off. An agitated gate agent was calling his name from an open jetbridge door. He was standing right there saying, "I'm here, I'm right here!" But he must have been mute and invisible because she ignored him, repeating his name over and over. As the bus approached the terminal, the person beside him interrupted with a gentle elbow to the ribs.

"What? I said I'm here," he mumbled before remembering where he actually was.

The American agent who had nudged him had kind brown eyes that were bright despite the hour. Her name tag said Angie, and as they waited for the aisle riders to shuffle past, she turned to him.

"Okay, you're here. Let me guess: evening guy on a trade?" Her accent was from the upper Midwest.

Embarrassed, he started to answer but a huge yawn took hold. There was no stifling it, so he covered his mouth till it subsided, then said, "Sorry. Third double in a row. Guess it shows, huh?"

She looked surprised. "Good grief. What, you're Superman?"

"No, he quit. Couldn't take the hours." She was even sweet enough to laugh at the corny joke.

The gaggle of employees walked into the dark, quiet terminal, their footsteps echoing, whiffs of the floor polish applied overnight hanging in the air. Drew enjoyed the surprisingly different look of the terminal when he worked such early starts. Empty of bustling crowds, it looked cavernous, the building's signature arched ceiling lost in shadows high above.

Ruff Air's ticket counter had three sets of adjoining work positions, divided by wells where passengers placed baggage for checking. A Skycap had already stacked the plastic bins used to protect soft luggage from the pulleys and sharp-edged snags waiting in ambush along the conveyor. The cursive logo's huge cream-colored letters spanned the entire dark blue backdrop except for the arrival/departure board listing twenty or so flights. The flanking counters belonged to Piedmont and American and they too were dimly lit and still.

The other CSRs and Mary, the lead, were in the office. Each had already retrieved their "bank," a zippered vinyl pouch containing exactly $75 cash for making change, a few forms, a small authentication ink stamp, and a die. The latter was a metal plate about an inch square with raised characters like a military dog tag. The identifying codes on stamps and dies traced a document's origin to a specific airline, location, and individual.

Seasoned agents always put newbies on notice with a warning that had probably been circulating since the DC-3 days: "It's called a 'die' because that's what will happen to you if you lose it!" Not literally of course, but the consequences would apparently be dire, though no one had yet explained why.

Along with his login, Kelly had assigned him the designator RX MSY 42Q. He was accountable for documents bearing that mark. She hadn't issued a bank, die, or stamp, but he wouldn't need them today. He would simply write his code on bag tags and boarding passes he issued.

The change in the lobby was astonishing when they went out 20 minutes later. Now brightly lit, the terminal bustled with passengers. Lines of ten or more waited at each counter position and more streamed back and forth beyond. The scene was similar at the competitors' adjoining counters. It was as if an unseen director had called "Lights!" and waved in a brigade of extras after the employees had disappeared into their offices.

Drew had never seen this seemingly instant transformation occur; he always went straight downstairs after punching in. For rampers, only the number of bags brought planeside indicated how busy the counter might be. This was different, far more personal. He tensed as he felt the customers' eyes on him and sensed their impatience.

Powering up the computer, logging on, and unlocking the drawer and cabinet took much longer than it should have.

Why didn't I think to come up here and practice?

From the drawer came a stapler, the credit card/ticket imprinter, and several pens. The cabinet had small compartments filled with destination tags in many colors along with bright red "Heavy" tags, blue ones indicating a connection in Houston, and large chartreuse "Voluntary Separation" tags. A passenger's signature on a VS absolved the airline for late-checked bags or any that already had damage.

The first departure was over an hour away, yet many passengers already appeared antsy. Suddenly, his responsibilities felt overwhelming. The cabinet held a thousand different tags, half of New Orleans waited restlessly in line, and the RAATS entries Gail had explained now seemed complex enough to launch a NASA rocket. An irrational anxiety grew, as if each customer's timely arrival to the gate was his personal obligation.

Finally, everything was ready. He motioned his first customers forward and said, "Good morning, may I help you?"

They were an elderly couple headed to Las Vegas. The man peered uncertainly at Drew, looked up and then back at him again, his eyes magnified by thick corrective lenses.

"Are you open then?"

Drew nodded and said, "Yes, sir" while mentally rolling his eyes. Another one of those people his colleagues laughed about, who magically lost their ability to read signs simply by passing through an airport door. The couple struggled forward, herding three matching bags.

Express Check-in was a picnic for even modestly experienced CSRs, but angst and a generous helping of sleep deprivation made it far more challenging than expected. The destination tags were different colors, but manufacturing inconsistencies and similarities in hues and airport codes could easily lead a CSR astray. For example, one might attach a peach-colored LAX tag in lieu of a tan LAS. Drew, bone-tired, rushing because of the long line, and flustered by the unfamiliar tasks, did exactly that to the luggage belonging to his very first customers.

Three things saved the day: he didn't put the bags onto the belt until he had finished with everything else, his was the end position farthest from the chute, and he remembered to use the confirming conversation Gail had taught him. As the misrouted trio began its long, winding trip to T-Point, Drew handed the man a folder containing their boarding passes, return tickets, and baggage claim checks.

"Okay, your boarding gate is Seven B like baker and"—he showed the claim checks stapled inside and read the destination as Gail had emphasized—"we have three bags checked to Los Angeles. Concourse B is down that way, then left. Have a great trip."

The old gentleman, confused, turned to his wife. "Do we stop in Los Angeles? I thought it was Houston." He asked Drew, "When we stop in Los Angeles we have to claim our luggage? What about Houston?"

The newb, mixed up as well, re-examined the claim checks and saw his mistake. The first bag was rapidly approaching the sharp turn leading through an opening in the wall. The other two followed like floats in a parade.

"Wait here!" He dashed off toward the far end of the counter.

The pace was busy enough for Mary to work a position instead of floating and he collided with her as she turned to place a bag on the belt. Instinctively wrapping her in a bear hug, he set her down on her behind, the bag in her lap.

"Sorry…sorry," he managed as he stumbled over her and kept going.

Lunging for the first and largest suitcase, he caught the handle as it rounded the turn. The other two piled up behind and the combined weight dragged him halfway through the curtain of heavy rubber strips across the chute's entrance. Fortunately, the task at hand prevented his imagination from serving up an image of his predicament. Had he envisioned the scene from everyone else's perspective, he might have simply given up once and for all, ridden with the luggage to T-Point, handed his keys and ID to the startled ramper there, and hitched out to the employee lot.

As it was, he muttered under his breath, scrapping with the luggage trio and the unyielding conveyor. He could keep the bags from going any further, but couldn't wrangle them back through the opening with the belt running.

It was a standoff, man versus Samsonite.

If only the damn belt would stop!

And as if his thoughts were wired into the controls, it did. Later, he would have sworn the battle lasted a good long minute, not the half dozen seconds Mary took to regain her feet, take three steps, and press the emergency stop. Bright red and the size of an English muffin, it was on the wall a few feet from the Express Check-in position. Pushing it would have instantly halted the belt and allowed him to retag the bags at his leisure.

Relief coursed through him until he backed out and looked into a sea of staring faces, their expressions saying everything. A few looked sympathetic, many more tried unsuccessfully to suppress smiles and guffaws, and some were laughing out loud.

Red with embarrassment, Drew started to haul the bags toward his position. Henry, the station's most senior CSR, touched his arm. Not unkindly, and with a wry grin, he said "Hey, maybe taking the new tags to the bags would be easier than the other way around. Where're they going?" On his response, Henry scribbled the flight number on three LAS tags. Drew tore off the claim checks, swapped them for the LAX tags, and replaced the bags on the belt.

Sweating and struggling to recapture his composure, he returned to his position and changed out the customer's claim checks. He took a deep breath, apologized for the confusion, and reassured the couple that their only stop was in Houston and they would only have to claim their luggage in Las Vegas.

The husband turned to leave but paused when his wife didn't. The elderly woman reached out with a wrinkled hand speckled with brownish spots. Drew hesitated, then extended his own.

She squeezed his hand and said, "You're having a tough morning, young man, but always remember this. No matter how bad things seem to be, it can change."

She smiled, squeezed his hand again, then released it and took her husband's arm. Drew was touched but had no time to get misty. The next customer, eyeing him with disdain and irked at the delay, was already stepping forward.

Mary climbed into the bag well, reached up, and flipped the sign above his head from "Position Closed" to "Express Check-in – Ticketed Passengers Only." No wonder the passenger had been confused!

Great. Just…freakin'…great.

He already felt moronic for mischecking the luggage; if getting stuck in the chute had been the whipped cream on that cold dish of stupid, here was the cherry on top. Yet the elderly couple had been patient, understanding, and kind despite his mistakes.

As Mary stepped down, she touched his arm and said softly, "Let's talk when things quiet down. For now, calm down and take your time, okay?"

Easier said than done. Some customers were still staring and more than a few remained openly amused. Still, the elderly woman's words rang in his head. He decided she was right.

The rest of the day will not *be like this.*

He took another deep breath, forced a smile, and took the next passenger's ticket envelope.

"That went well, didn't it? Where are you headed today?"

The lame attempt at humor actually broke the ice, causing the man to chuckle despite his impatience.

When the people were gone and the ticketing lobby relatively quiet again, Drew glanced at the terminal clock. It must have stopped; there was no way that only forty-five minutes had passed! But his watch and the tiny luminescent numbers on his monitor both confirmed it.

Mary walked up, smiling.

"Time flies when you're having fun, yeah? Don't worry, the next wave is already on the way." As she predicted, the lines built again within fifteen minutes.

They got a chance to meet briefly two hours later. The newbie, steeling himself for a reaming, feared it would get back to Barb. She no longer treated him like radioactive waste but hadn't rescinded her zero-tolerance policy either.

Instead, Mary's eyes met his and she said, "I owe you an apology."

"*You* owe *me* an apology?"

"Yep. When Gail asked about the trade, I said yes, but I meant to talk with you beforehand, to let you know what to expect and stuff, you know, like how seeing big lines of people can make you feel rushed."

"Don't we have to hurry when it's busy?"

"We have to hustle, yes, but you'll learn that hustling and hurrying are two different things, whether it's on the counter, the ramp, wherever."

His mind deposited him near gate 7B amid the sound of jet engines spinning up to power and the sight of Tumbleweed 534's main gear tire beginning to climb the chock.

"Yeah, I learned that the hard way."

"Right, the chocks. Sorry, I didn't mean that in particular. Anyway, when you're new, you have to concentrate on what you're doing and get things right. The speed comes with practice. You had a rough start, but you got it together and now you seem fine. Hang in there, and if you have any questions, just ask."

The atmosphere at Ruff Air was refreshingly different from any of his previous jobs. Supervisors (and peers for that matter) could deliver a forceful foot in the ass when necessary. There were one or two pissy little cliques, plenty of gossip, and a couple of jerks, but at crunch time, everyone got along and tried to do things right.

Drew got his share and more of ribbing but had earned most of it. Tormenting newbies was a sacred tradition anyway. But everybody did their best to help each other when push came to shove in the operation. A few weeks after the chocks deal, he had seen the captain who had advocated for him and started over to say thanks. The pilot waved him off with a little nod and a thumbs up. No words were necessary.

The camaraderie came up in Ops one day and Peggy said, "It's great, isn't it? The thing is, nobody with an airline job takes it because they can't find anything else. Everybody wants to be here. Not to say everybody is nice or well-suited for the work but most are good folks. You'll see when you travel more, the same kind of people are drawn to the industry all over the world. No matter where you are or whose logo is on the tail, a new friend or a helping hand is as close as the nearest airport."

The passengers kept arriving but serving them was actually fun once he got into a rhythm. He got the entries down and found he could chat with customers while (correctly) filling out their boarding passes and bag tags. Donna had mentioned that many people liked telling where they were going, who they were visiting and so on. He liked the personal aspect and was genuinely interested in all the different reasons people shared for their travels. Disengaging proved to be a challenge from time to time, sometimes because the back-and-forth was such a nice change from the dispassionate ramp, others because the passenger wouldn't stop talking.

The counter crew had a late morning breather and Henry walked down and shared a story. Like Melissa the flight attendant, he had given his heart and soul to an airline only to have the rug pulled out from under him. His first day with Braniff was the same week a Pan Am 707 brought the Beatles to America. Nearly 20 years later, the airline's failure had cast him adrift, another of deregulation's human flotsam. Such refugees accounted for many of Ruff Air's Moisant staff.

Henry said, "It was my third day on the counter and three or four of us were standing around chatting between rushes, like we are now. This man came up and asked, 'Excuse me, where's the nearest restroom?' Everyone heard him clearly…everyone but me. *I* thought he said 'restaurant.' And I was so new and eager to please I just about hurdled the other agents to get over there and impress this guy with my knowledge of the airport.

"I said, 'Well, there's a stand-up place right down here to your left if you're in a hurry or a nicer one a little further on if you want to sit down, relax, and enjoy yourself.'"

When the laughter subsided, Henry went on, "There was this weird quiet and you can imagine the look on the guy's face, and then he walked away. Somehow everybody kept from cracking up until the guy was gone."

He frowned and said, "You think you've got it bad with that chocks business? Let me tell you, honey, I heard about my little faux pas *forever*. Everywhere I went, it was 'Hey Henry, where's the restroom?' A couple years ago I was waiting to board in Miami and suddenly this voice yells down the concourse, 'Wherrrrre's the restrooooom?' It was a guy from MSP I hadn't seen in twenty-five years. I mean, call me queer all you want, I couldn't care less, but they'll probably carve 'Where's the restroom?' on my headstone. We all do stupid things when we're new. There's no magic bullet, you just have to stick with it. Trust me, you'll catch on."

He cocked his head and arched an eyebrow.

"Sooner or later."

Curious about the constant cautions to safeguard their dies, Drew asked, "What's the deal with the die and the change bank? I mean, I get the money part but what would anybody want with a die plate?"

The answer spotlighted one of the industry's little-known underbellies. As Henry explained, even with constant warnings to never leave die plates in the validator, it happened from time to time. Busy CSRs got tired of retrieving their die only to replace it in the validator a few moments later. Inevitably, someone would leave it there for convenience then forget about it when going on break or at shift's end.

Some airline aficionados were hardcore collectors who watched for untended items. Anything with an airline flavor—staplers, pens, counter cards, slide-in city name signage strips, and yes, even dies—regularly vanished.

Of much greater concern were those with more sinister purposes: scouts for counterfeiting rings.

Using stolen ticket stock and die plates, such profiteers produced fake wares possessing a disarming air of authenticity. Airlines and travel agencies constantly circulated stolen ticket numbers but checking them manually was time-consuming and simply impractical. Many holding fake tickets went on their merry way, the fraud undetected until the remittance coupons reached revenue accounting or were sent to the issuing carrier for payment. By then the bearer had long since traveled and the fare would never be collected.

When agents spotted bogus documents, the tell was usually something like a mismatch between the die plate airline code and that of the issuing carrier, a nuance no mark would ever notice but instantly apparent to anyone behind a ticket counter. Next came the unpleasant task of informing the passengers. They were seldom aware they had purchased worthless forgeries and shocked when told they must purchase new tickets.

Henry told of an occasion at Braniff where a church member's acquaintance claimed he could arrange cheap fares—if everyone paid cash. A group of 20 purchased tickets for a mission trip to Latin America. When the check-in agent saw something suspicious and inspected the tickets, all were found to be fakes and confiscated. The "good Samaritan" who had stolen their money was conspicuously absent, busy as he was slurping margaritas and appraising the tanned coeds frolicking in a Cancun resort's pool.

Technically, the full walk-up fare applied in such cases. Most supervisors tried to ease the blow by charging only the fare paid for the bogus ticket. Some went farther, knocking the cost down to the lowest fare sold for that flight. The betrayal was still a bitter pill, especially for those whose trips had to be canceled, such as the church group. They couldn't afford substitute tickets at any price.

Some, especially those who had misplaced or forgotten tickets, demanded free replacements, becoming irate when refused. Airlines' stance—that tickets were essentially like cash—only infuriated them more. The logic was sound, if unappreciated: passengers were not asked for identification, so anyone possessing a ticket could travel on it.

Though larger carriers were far more vulnerable to fraud, the potential for lost revenue made securing die plates serious business. With luck, a colleague would spot it in the validator and return it. Supervisors couldn't let it slide. Some were known to quietly hold the die to let the agent's deepening apprehension rub the lesson in a little. Discipline included dismissal if the die was never found.

Each CSR also had responsibility for their bank. These were stored within post office box-sized vaults accessible only to the CSR and station manager. Agents going off-duty double-checked their banks with verification by the counter lead. As such, the presumption was that banks contained exactly $75. Employees had been known to take ill-advised loans, intending to replace the money before their next shift. They were dancing in a minefield because the bank policy made the one on die plates look compassionate. Should an audit find other than exactly $75, immediate termination followed regardless of the explanation, some of which were heartrending.

Drew mulled this as he washed up for lunch, which took longer than expected. Each ticket page had a red coating that made carbon copies. The residue proved surprisingly tough to scrub off after a morning of pulling flight coupons. He had seen counter agents with red fingertips and wondered about that and the red smudges on their uniforms. Now it made sense. The smears resulted from people unconsciously adjusting their clothing. He checked his flanks and discovered red where he had retucked his shirt a couple of times.

Crap!

Fortunately, his vest covered them.

A near-stupor descended as he walked back from the cafeteria thirty minutes later. It was probably good that counter CSRs couldn't sit down and that humans lacked the equine ability to sleep standing up. He was about ready to give it a try.

About ten past two, a few people waited for express check-in. Mary, covering for a CSR on break, was at the next position. She had no one in line, so when they simultaneously finished their transactions, Mary beckoned the next customer in his line. Drew told her thanks, then froze for a second when he looked up into Marty's sneering face.

His former manager said nothing, just stood there with a scowl. After listening impatiently to the spiel about baggage checks and the gate number, he snatched the ticket folder away.

Shaking his head, he said, "You gave up a plush job with a company car for *this?* Boy, you pathetic." Besides the poor grammar, the insult missed its mark; Drew had never been more certain he was on the right path.

So he just smiled and said, "Have a nice trip, sir," in a tone that translated to *up yours.*

Mary leaned over and whispered, "What was *that* about?"

"Long, long story."

Finally, the clock hands snailed their way to half past two. He again splashed his face with cold water after wearily changing clothes, hoping things had gone better for Mr. Hoppy at Carrot Farm then they had for Mr. Drew at the Ruff Air ticket counter.

TWELVE

Drew sat silently during the shift change hubbub, sipping a cup of vending machine hot chocolate and staring at nothing. He answered robotically as people said hi and bye. With every flight full, his shift's end felt as distant as if seen through the wrong end of binoculars. Despite his best efforts and a frigid blast whenever someone opened the door, he felt himself winding down like a tired old grandfather clock.

Donna, chipper as always, made a show of checking his pulse and said, "Hey there buddy, you haven't flat-lined on us, have you?"

The "patient" shook his head and managed a muted chuckle.

He would have tried to rest before the first arrival but feared falling asleep. He would spend the time with Peggy instead. Grayson tore a page off the printer and handed it to him, indicating it was for the Ops agent, who was on the phone. The message, a load plan and weather update, made no sense to him but the teletype address caught his eye.

Peggy hung up and said, "Drew! How are you? I'm about to work up the load sheet for the next trip. Want to see how it's done?" He loved her warmth and willingness to share her knowledge and experience.

"I would, but first…" He pointed to the Dispatch message. "What's MSYOO? I mean, MSY is New Orleans, does OO mean 'Operations Office' or some such?"

"Yes, that's for Ops. There's a standard list. There's LL for baggage service—that one's easy to remember, think 'lost luggage'—RR for Res, MX for maintenance…let's see…KK for the station manager—don't ask me why on that one—and so on. Say I need to send something to Austin baggage service, I address it to AUSLL. It works for everybody, too. You just add their two-letter code. Go ahead, try me."

"Alaska's ticket counter in Seattle."

"Easy," she said, "S-E-A-T-R-A-S." She took on a mischievous look. "Come on, you can do better than that."

"Okay…hmmm…Lufthansa cargo in Frankfurt."

Her face went blank, then puckered in concentration. Finally, she said, "I was right, you *could* do better. Wait a minute…fudge, what's cargo? Okay, you got me, but hang on…" She ran her finger down a reference flattened under the crazed plastic covering the desk.

"Okay, wise guy, cargo is FF, so F-R-A-F-F-L-H. But see, seven letters let you send a message to any airline department anywhere! Now getting them to actually do anything with it? That's another story. Come on, let's do the load plan for Eight Fifty-five."

She gave a quick weight and balance intro. Tearing two legal-sized worksheets from a pad, she said, "We have to account for everything that'll be on the plane." To his unpracticed eye, the form was hopelessly intricate. There were columns of squares for writing in figures, then subtotaling and eventually totaling them.

He pointed to a rectangle with numerous converging lines over a grid labeled "CG Envelope."

"What's that?"

"That's where you 'plot the dot'," Peggy said, slipping carbon paper between the worksheets. "That shows whether the plane is properly balanced. The best way to understand CG—that's for 'center of gravity'—is to imagine the plane hanging from a string—"

"That'd be some string."

She grinned.

"It sure would, come to think of it. Anyway, if you *could* hang it, the CG is where the string would need to be attached for the plane to hang level both front to back and side to side. It's never going to be exact, and neither are the weights, but as long as they end up within the limits, it's good to go."

She went on to explain that AURA even allocated seat assignments based on optimal weight distribution.

"Some time, when you're on a half-full flight, watch how the people aren't all packed together, they're kind of spread all over," she said. "That's AURA's programming. Some people move but it's not enough to matter."

She swiftly wrote in the date, flight number, city pair, aircraft registration number, and captain's name. She showed him the weight calculations, filling in numbers as she went. Consulting tables of standard figures and averages, her fingers flew over the calculator keys.

Drew smiled, remembering something he had read long ago.

"What?" Peggy asked.

"Just remembering something funny from a book."

She stopped and looked at him. "Don't tell me you mean Fred Phirmphoot from *Airport?*"

"Yes! You read *Airport?*"

"I sure did, back in high school. It's one reason I'm sitting here now. Fred was something, wasn't he? 'Illinois to Rome, man. That's long spaghetti.'"

He finished the line. "'It don't pay off in marmalade.'"

They shared a laugh.

Returning to her task, she added preliminary estimates for the plane and crew; baggage, cargo, fuel, catering equipment and supplies; and passengers and carry-ons. Once finalized, Peggy would use these weights and the estimated ground and enroute fuel burns to get taxi, takeoff, and landing weights.

The load planner designated where to load baggage so ground crews along the route could easily remove their city's luggage. Connecting bags were stacked separately according to destination so the Houston rampers could quickly transfer them to connecting flights.

Finishing up, Peggy touched on the variables managed by the pilots and Dispatch: the fuel load, takeoff power settings, usable runways, inoperative aircraft systems, and even air temperature—all of which influenced critical parameters like the runway distance required for takeoff. As a cross-check, the captain and dispatcher had to concur on the most important elements for the flight to operate legally.

When all was said and done, she double- and triple-checked her figures, arithmetic, and the center of gravity graph.

"Don't ever, *ever* forget," Peggy said, holding up the load sheet, "this isn't just a bunch of numbers or a math problem." The implication was clear: lives were at stake.

She signed the form at the bottom, added her employee number, and indicated a blank box. "See, the captain signs there and keeps a copy, and we get one for the file. Did it all make sense?"

His head was spinning. "The big picture does, but it seems pretty complicated."

Bert's voice interjected, "New Orleans Ops, Tumbleweed Eight fifty-five in range with six point four."

Drew thanked Peggy, donned his parka, zipped it all the way up, pulled a wool beanie down over his ears, added his hearing protector, and tied the hood tight. Tugging on his gloves, he headed out.

Despite these precautions, the wind howling in over Lake Pontchartrain slapped away any residual drowsiness with a backhand that felt straight from Siberia. The chill factor had to be in the teens. Drizzle blew sideways so hard it stung his eyes. Under the overcast, only a few golden halos broke the dreary gray where misty little raindrops swirled past the powerful apron lights.

Twenty-five minutes later, he lay sprawled against a mound of luggage in the belly of Flight 855. As taught, he had stacked the bags quickly but carefully, always seeking to minimize the space used. Somehow the items, many dissimilar in shape and size, often fit together as if by design. The neat pile he had created, mostly blacks and grays with a colorful piece here and there, looked like something from an airport edition of Jenga. The hum and rumblings of aircraft systems and ramp activity were a subtle soundtrack.

No one yet knew that an Orlando Skycap had short-checked three Austin bags. The trio was circling the Moisant carousel while its owners chatted on the Super 80 about to depart.

Tish, the baggage service CSR, knew the most basic premise of customer service: most people understood, and would even forgive, a mistake. What counted was how it was handled. So before Flight 855 even reached cruise altitude, Tish would notice the unclaimed bags and, from experience, suspect they might be short-checked. After confirming her suspicions by checking Flight 855's passenger list, she would send a message to Austin with a copy to Orlando.

An Austin CSR would fill out a lost bag report, page the customers on arrival, apologize, and explain what had happened. Instead of growing increasingly frustrated waiting for bags that weren't coming, then stalking angrily into baggage service, the customers would sign the report and leave knowing exactly when they and their belongings would be reunited.

The dog-tired CSR awaiting last minute bags in the Super 80's aft bin knew none of this. Irritating rivulets of sweat streamed down under his uniform despite the freezing weather. His hearing protector was a slippery mess, sliding around every time he turned his head. Occasional shivers struck as he reflected on how much work those benign-looking numbers on Peggy's load sheet represented.

His thoughts drifted idly. He was glad to have helped Gail see her son's play, long day and all. Yawning, he took a deep breath of bitingly frosty air and stretched as best he could. The cold metal floor stung his legs and butt right through his pants. He wished he could lay back against the overstuffed garment bag behind him and take a nap.

A scent of sensual perfume, or perhaps a sachet, arose from it, conspiring with the pungent odors of jet fuel and exhaust to twist his stomach around his lunch of cold leftover pizza. After this trip, he would guzzle some Pepto and unwind for the 20-ish minutes of downtime.

He didn't fall asleep, but may have drifted into that nether zone barely south of awake. In any case, when the lights went out and the bin door slammed shut, he sat up, instantly alert but not quite sure what was what. There was a muted *ka-thunk* usually heard from the other side of the door—the locking handle swinging home into its recess. The darkness was utterly complete. He crawled quickly in what he thought was the direction of the door, instead locating the bin wall with the top of his hearing protector. The impact punched the hard plastic band down right across the top of his skull, a painful blow that did nothing to clarify his thinking.

Feeling his way aft, he found the seam where the door met the fuselage, shouted, and banged on the door. Nothing.

Where's this thing going? Right, Houston.

He didn't panic but fear was prowling nearby.

I'll be okay. It'll be cold but animals ride in here all the time. They won't be at altitude very long anyway.

The initial adrenalin rush was subsiding. The darkness bothered him most. He yelled and banged on the door some more; nothing. Should he try the ceiling, which was the cabin floor? Maybe a passenger would alert an ISR, who would probably offer the customary reassurance that odd noises were nothing to worry about.

How long till they push? Till somebody figures out I'm in here?

Just as the battle between calm and trepidation got interesting, the bin door swung open and there stood Rob, laughing his ass off.

Drew was livid.

"You *dick!*"

Rob laughed even harder, doubled over, snorting and braying. Grayson was snickering too but must have noticed the time because he yelled, "All right, knock it off, we got to push!"

After Drew clambered out, Rob tossed a late bag into the hold.

"That was priceless," he said, gasping for breath. "And why were you sitting there in the dark? The light switch is right there."

And so it was, right inside the door.

He was too tired to really be mad and when he thought about it, the prank was actually pretty funny. Still, he hoped as he pulled the chocks that they hired somebody soon. The newbie treatment was getting old.

After Tumbleweed 855 taxied away, Drew deposited coins into the vending machine, chose hot chocolate and waited with high hopes the cup would drop before the beverage flow began. It was always a crapshoot, once taking three increasingly aggravating tries, but this time his luck held. Skipping the sofa, he settled onto a chrome-legged chair whose faded orange plastic was roadmapped with hairline cracks. It felt great to sit down and relax, though wrapping his stiff fingers around the cup took some effort. His hands gradually warmed and the feeling returned to his face.

He asked Peggy if she had time to answer a few more load planning questions. She did, but soon the next arrival was on the ground.

Grayson stationed him in the tunnel at baggage claim to help unload inbound carts. The job quickly revealed itself to be tough money. Not the hard work; what sucked was standing around in the cold waiting for the inbounds. Bone-chilling gusts constantly blew through the little tunnel, yet it was too far to go back inside. Being bundled up to keep warm made it hard to move freely and left him sweat-soaked and overheated after unloading one or two carts.

Once the arrivals were in and unloaded, the focus shifted to departures. He happily shifted with it, over to T-Point to help load the outbound carts.

The L.A. and Miami trips were about to push when late bags came down, one for each destination. Both had Voluntary Separation tags, so they would have to go out later.

Rob motored into T-Point, saw the bags, and hopped off the tug. Chucking one onto the hood and the other onto the back, he yelled, "Come on!"

As Drew climbed aboard, Rob said, "Grab the one on the back!" He turned and clutched the handle as Rob uncharacteristically crawled out of T-Point, steering with one hand. Grabbing his radio, he said, "Ops, T-Point! Hold 'em both right there, we've got a late bag for each one!"

He checked both ways for traffic, then stomped the gas so hard Drew's head snapped sideways.

The two jets sat nose to tail. Donna was in front of the first one with wands crossed over her head. Rob did a terrible imitation of a safety stop before screeching to a halt next to the L.A. trip. Drew jumped off and Rob punched it again, such that it wasn't so much a case of taking the suitcase as catching it when it flew off.

The late customers had no doubt taken their seats brooding over leaving their belongings behind. After pushback, they may have wondered why the plane sat motionless, probably never suspecting that the noises from below were the bins being opened and their luggage loaded.

As the flights taxied away, Drew again felt the pride and satisfaction that came with doing more than customers expected. He mentioned this to Rob, who replied, "That, and two less a-holes bitching in baggage claim. Win win." But cynical humor aside, he could tell Rob shared his feeling of accomplishment.

The rest of the shift flew by, relatively speaking. One more arrival and this long, miserable day would be over. They rode to Ops and as everyone filed in, Grayson said, "The last inbound is running late. Who wants overtime?"

Drew grimaced, knowing what was coming.

Damn it, of all the nights!

Two people were needed; only one raised her hand. He didn't have to; his bottom-feeder seniority automatically "volunteered" him.

Grayson said, "Okay, Brenda, it's you and Drew."

You and Drew. How many times had he heard that little rhyme? At least he'd caught his second wind and simply staying awake was no longer a struggle.

A thought occurred and he looked at Peggy. Before he spoke, she demonstrated either her lengthy experience or her mindreading skills.

"They won't cancel it," she said. "We need an airplane for the Houston originator tomorrow. If anything, they'll swap equipment and keep that one to work on. ETA is 2340…for now."

About a half-hour past sked. No big deal but such estimates were often hopelessly optimistic.

Later, after everyone but Brenda was gone, he checked again. The screen flickered and the flight information, FLIFO in industry vernacular, appeared.

```
RX848/17DEC
HOU          2205 26
MSY 7B       2312 TERM
HOU/ETD      2330 MAINT
MSY/PRE 0026/18DEC
```

Flight 848, originally scheduled to leave Houston's Gate 26 at 10:05 P.M. and arrive at Gate 7B in New Orleans at 11:12 P.M., was now expected to depart at 11:30 P.M. due to a maintenance issue. It wouldn't arrive until 12:26 A.M. at the earliest.

Drew swore to himself, walked down to the locker room, and knocked loudly. He opened the door an inch and called, "Hey Brenda? No rush, it's twelve twenty-six now."

"Damn it!"

They sat at the beat-up table and talked, vapor rising from her coffee and his third hot chocolate of the night. After briefly speculating on how late the flight might actually arrive, Brenda unwittingly confirmed a rumor.

"By the way, I think that pool they have on you is stupid. You'll make it. For crying out loud, Eli got to customer service training in no time but his first time meeting a terminator on his own, he went to the wrong gate. He was at Five Bravo wondering where the plane was and a hundred people were waiting to deplane at Nine Bravo wondering why the door wasn't open yet. *He* made it. And I heard this thing is up to over fifty bucks!"

He acted as if he already knew, chuckling in agreement and changing the subject. This only hardened his resolve to prove the naysayers wrong.

After a while, both too tired to talk further, she found a tattered magazine and he started on Mary's latest newsletter.

The supervisor distributed periodic updates on Ruff Air's fortunes, and the coverage had since expanded to the rest of the industry. She wrote that Ruff Air's system load factor was a robust 58%; the FAA was out in force ensuring employees were challenging anyone in restricted areas without visible ID; and the holidays had moved Barb to extend the deadline for the mandatory monthly ALM lesson.

Mary had also recapped Mr. Ruff's recent session with industry journalists. The CEO stated that he would consider raising pay rates once Ruff Air was consistently profitable; suggested the company might redraw its route map with a greater focus on long-hauls; expressed excitement over the Miami market's performance and potential since its addition the year before; and confirmed the airline was evaluating a potential new destination. The latest Moisant scuttlebutt had San Diego as the leader in the clubhouse.

There were two ominous notes: Ruff expected the David-vs.-Goliath dogfight with Continental at Houston Hobby to intensify, and his namesake airline had reported a small profit the previous quarter. The latter would usually be celebrated but the boost into the black came from selling aircraft delivery positions. Another carrier had paid to take several new jets originally being built for Ruff Air.

FLIFO confirmed that Peggy's prediction was accurate. The code MAINT had been replaced by EQ CHNG and the departure time pushed back yet again.

"This blows," he told Brenda. "Now it's one-fifteen."

Though airlines based estimated times on the best information available, it grated on everybody when revisions were posted only to be changed yet again. Employees hated a creeping delay as much as customers did. This one probably wasn't done creeping yet.

I would have been sound asleep by now. Oh, well. Might as well be productive.

He began another ALM lesson.

Ninety minutes later, shivering, he climbed atop the pushback tractor. The engine whine grew and three white glows appeared through the mist. The dropdown landing lights went out, retracting into the wingtips as the jet came into view. The two on the nose gear faded as the plane turned into the gate.

Drew guided the pilots up the line, brought the lighted wands together above his head, crossed them, and signaled Brenda to place the chocks. He hopped down, plugged in the ground power, indicated to the pilots it was connected, and trotted over to the forward bag bin. His watch read 1:41 a.m., nearly 22 hours since the alarm had awakened him. It was well past two by the time he clocked out and headed home.

* * *

Drew rarely slept past seven or so, eight at the latest. On Tuesday, he didn't even stir until twelve-thirty and then only for a one-eyed peek at the clock. He rolled over and instantly fell back asleep. When he awoke, he was out of sorts, very hungry, and urgently needed a bathroom visit. He was also quite surprised to find himself fully clothed in his uniform complete with shoes and ID. What was he laying on? A reach under his ribs yielded his crushed ball cap, an item always stowed in his locker.

He glanced at the clock, which said 4:07 p.m.

Oh shit, I'm late!

He quickly rolled over and sat up, instantly regretting this upon discovering that someone had emptied his skull and filled the cavity with quickset cement. What day was it? Tuesday, right? Okay, it was his day off, but had he traded for hours?

Generating any useful cerebral activity proved a challenge. Thinking felt like walking would if the floor suddenly became a rope bridge spanning a windswept gorge. No, he concluded a long moment later, he hadn't done a trade today.

Rubbing his face, he stood up gingerly, wishing his head would just explode and get it over with. There was something underfoot—his hearing protector.

What the hell and where are the aspirin?

Foraging through the medicine cabinet produced a couple or three Tylenol. The capsules went down with a swig from a Dr. Pepper two-liter that turned out to be flatter than Florida. Returning to the bedroom, trying to dig the grit out of his eyes, he thought back to the night before. The memories were spotty at best. Rob's idiotic prank, the late flight…but who had worked it with him? It took real concentration before Brenda's name drifted in through the fog. There were vague recollections of the extended delay, a few tidbits from Mary's newsletter, doing some ALM lessons, and the walk up to the office to clock out. But try as he might, he couldn't remember anything after that.

THIRTEEN

December 22nd, a Saturday, marked Drew's last day of probation. He was tired and glad for once that no one had offered any extra hours.

In his mail folder was a card from none other than Mr. Hoppy himself. Taped on it was a snapshot, slightly blurry but obviously Gail's son, David, on stage. Inside was written, "Thank you Mr. Drew for helping my Mom see the play." Under David's name, Gail had added, "Being there meant the world to me. Thank you!!!" The dots under the exclamation points were little smiley faces. He was touched.

Twenty minutes later, he zipped his parka and jogged out to meet the first arrival. Time sped by with things so busy and suddenly it was time to clock out. No one had said anything about his probation. He walked into Ops, shedding his outdoor gear and wondering what to expect. Everyone but Donna was outside. She was on the phone, though she smiled and gave a little wave. He waved back, shrugged, and started for the locker room.

Grayson stepped out of the supervisors' office and beckoned him over.

Drew felt reasonably confident, but this didn't prevent an icy splash of unease.

Grayson closed the door, indicated Drew should sit, took his own seat, and said, "I guess you know what we need to talk about."

Drew nodded, trying to project calm while in fact perching on his chair like an apprehensive gargoyle.

"There ain't actually a lot *to* say, I guess," Grayson said, looking down at the desk, "so we might as well get it over with."

Drew's anxiety redlined.

No. No way. They wouldn't wait until the end of my last shift to tell me.

A silent second.

Would they?

Grayson said nothing further, just toyed with a pencil, glancing up after a moment to return Drew's furrowed gaze with a somber one of his own. The only sound was the muted roar of a takeoff.

A few more seconds passed. Grayson was never chatty but when there was something to say, he said it.

Fine, two can play this game.

Forcing himself to relax, Drew sat back, folded his arms, cocked his head, and raised his eyebrows.

Grayson gave in, rising and extending his hand.

"All right, couldn't let you think this was that easy. Congratulations and merry Christmas. You are oh-ficially off probation. Oh, and let me have the fish. There's a new gal starting on Monday."

Drew was still smiling when he fell asleep several hours later.

* * *

As usual, the news traveled fast. Gail fell in beside him on the way to Ops the next day and said, "Hey, congrats! I'm glad you made it."

"Thanks."

Holding up his RAATS notebook, now fat with formats, shortcuts, and advice, he said, "You helped. A lot. I appreciate it. And thanks for the card."

She smiled. "I was going to buy you one. Making it was David's idea. I'm proud of him for that."

"You should be."

They showed their IDs to the contract workers at security, bypassing the waiting passengers by going through the exit side.

Gail said, "I'm glad you liked the card but...I mean, it meant *so* much to David and to me for me to be there. Let me thank you properly. Dinner, my treat."

Drew stopped and said, "You don't have to."

"I know. I want to."

"It was no big—"

"Look, quit being courteous, or humble, or stubborn, or whatever you're being! We're going. I insist. Besides, there's something to celebrate and it's only right that you're there."

With a fleeting rumination on that, he said, "Fine. Okay. Where?"

"Anywhere you want. Well, within reason."

"Don't worry, I'm not a Commander's Palace kind of guy. More like Bud's Broiler."

"Perfect, I love their burgers. You're off Tuesday and Wednesday, right? Tuesday is Christmas, how about Wednesday?"

"Wednesday's fine."

"Wednesday it is then. About six? Good."

He gestured toward her left hand. "Bringing your husband? I'd like to meet him."

"Nope," she said. "We're separated." She started off toward 7B.

"Gail, hold on, what are we celebrating? Is it somebody's birthday or something?"

She stopped and did a cute about-face, blushing and unconsciously assuming a little girl pose.

She spoke with a sheepish grin.

"I won the pool."

* * *

Christmas was slow since most customers were already at their destinations. As a bonus, the light loads kept most flights on time. Drew made the rounds with his camera before and after his shift, lining up colleagues, airplanes, and the airport itself in his viewfinder. On breaks, he went to the other side of

Concourse B, shooting the jets and thinking about Gail's invitation.

At the distinctive A-frame restaurant on Veterans Boulevard, she ordered a number 6, no pickles or tomatoes, with mayo and mustard. This was coincidentally the same way he liked his burger, so he said "Make it two like that, please," and instinctively took out his wallet.

Gail's expression suggested he put it away.

Dinner was fun. They first discussed work, then shifted to other topics and talked through dessert and a drive along the lakefront.

At her door, she hugged him and asked if he'd like to hang out after work on New Year's Eve.

"We can watch Dick Clark and see the ball drop in Times Square!"

Her almost childlike enthusiasm brought a smile to his face.

I really enjoy her company!

So a few days later, Drew, Gail, and David had pizza before the youngster left for a friend's sleepover. Drew listened while the little boy described the Christmas play and read aloud the book on which it was based. After they dropped him off, Gail looked over with her expressive eyes and said, "Thank you. You were a good sport about that."

"No problem. It was fun, and nice to know more about what I was suffering for." She smiled and lit some candles, then they sat on the sofa to watch a movie and the local news.

Candles? Was the atmosphere meant to be romantic? He cautioned himself not to assume. He liked Gail and found her attractive. The last thing he wanted was to seem forward or boorish.

She fought off yawns all evening but assured him that her early starts were to blame. At midnight, she turned with a shy, curious expression, slowly leaned in, and laid on a long, deep, and very memorable kiss. Afterward, she grinned mischievously, snuggled up close, and said "Happy New Year!"

The kiss, her perfume, and the softness of her body were all stark reminders of his barren personal life. The job quest and hectic work schedule had consumed his time and energy. Gail's affection was a welcome wake-up call and he hoped the kiss wasn't the end of it.

She switched off the TV and blew out the candles when the program ended. Smoke drifted up through the dark, hanging like silver strings in the dim light. Drew started over for his coat but she intercepted him and took his hands in hers. The silence was such that he thought he heard his own heartbeat. Heat seemed to radiate from her skin and the intent in her eyes was clear.

"I've been separated for ten months," she said in a low voice. "I don't want a relationship, maybe not even to date. I'm not ready for all the…complications. There's David and work and technically, I'm still married. If you're okay with that and this being…this, then stay with me."

An ex's voice echoed through his memory: "Guys say they want more when they really just want to screw," she had complained. "A woman needs more. We need to feel a connection."

Do we really have a connection? Or was Gail an exception to that?

Their lips touched again, short-circuiting any further debate. He closed his eyes and let go of everything else in the world.

* * *

Drew lay awake as dawn approached, reflecting on the turns his life had taken. Could only six months have passed since Kelly's phone call? It seemed much longer, as if his life before had been spent floating down a serene river that abruptly turned to rapids, sweeping him along, the ride bumpy and often electrifyingly wild and unpredictable, mostly fun with occasional dashes of uncertainty, and a touch of fear or doubt here and there. If pressed for a one-word summary, "exhilarating" would fit nicely.

Passing probation, the promise of the new year, the time spent with Gail, a sweet and kind soul whose pent-up passion might even have exceeded his own…all felt like harbingers of even better things to come. Another corner had been turned, anxiety and strife left behind. He had seldom felt such utter peace and contentment.

The moment felt like a keepsake to be soaked up and savored, each detail noted and etched in memory. The fall of Gail's long brown hair, her milky warm fragrant skin, the peaceful innocence of sleep on her face, and how her arms and hands lay together before her as if in prayer; the silence, broken only by the slow rhythm of breathing and a little rattle from the heater when it cycled on; the soft lavender sheets, cool on his skin; and the emerging glow of sunrise filtering through the blinds. As the minutes ticked by, the golden light painted bold stripes on the walls and floor, burnishing the metal buttons of her hastily discarded jeans until they glinted like a handful of scattered coins.

* * *

He breezed into January with fresh confidence. A week after New Year's, Grayson called him in on another chilly, misty afternoon. True to form, he wasted no time getting to the point.

"You're off Barb's shit list. Meet Mary at the ticket counter at zero six hundred sharp on…"—he consulted the calendar printed on the desk blotter—"…Thursday the seventeenth for customer service training. Wear your Class A uniform. You're with her till fourteen-thirty, then work your normal shift, but at T-Point. No counter training on Mary's days off. The extra hours are straight time. Any questions?"

There were none but his face must have shown his surprise.

Grayson said, "I didn't get it either till I saw these." He slid two pages across the desk.

The first was RAATS' now-familiar grayish paper, each edge pierced by printer feed holes. Drew's name and employee number headed a list of his completed ALM lessons. After Gail suggested them, his interest and love of learning had taken over, so the list was lengthy and covered many subjects.

"Barb appreciates initiative," Grayson explained. "Even if a little birdy got you started, you've gotten a lot of work done there."

Elvis on a pony! Does the grapevine ever miss anything?

The other page was a secret shopper report. Ruff Air occasionally called random customers and offered a voucher toward future travel as an incentive to evaluate the employees they encountered. By chance, this shopper's itinerary started in New Orleans the day Drew worked for Gail. She noted he had used her name and had handled her transaction—admittedly an unchallenging one—in a timely and courteous manner. In the "Remarks" section, she wrote, "Seemed genuinely interested, chatting with me about my trip while checking me in and writing my boarding pass. Double-checked that my luggage was correctly tagged, which I appreciated, directed me to the gate, and wished me a good flight. Very friendly, professional employee who represents your airline well."

"Must've come through later in the morning," Grayson quipped.

Barely an hour later, as Drew unhooked a cart of bags planeside, Rob looked back, grinned behind his aviators, and said, "Damn, man, bedding Gail, coming to T-Point, *and* training upstairs? Happy fuckin' New Year...so to speak."

"I'm not—"

"Hey, don't be modest. I'd bang that like a bongo drum." Then he was gone, whipping around the tail of the Southwest jet at 5B on his way back to T-Point.

What...the...hell is going on here?

The employee network was impressive but this was ridiculous. Gail was perplexed at first, then made a face as the realization hit.

"It's my fault," she said. "Rob's brother lives in my complex and he hangs out there a lot. I completely forgot! He must have seen your car at my place all night. We're so screwed." Her face brightened. "But congrats on the other stuff!" She looked around, saw they were unobserved—*Why bother at this point?*— then hugged him.

They waited for the inevitable firestorm and were both mystified when no one even mentioned it. Nothing was said the next day either. Meanwhile, the latest new hire was already taking fire like a SWAT practice target. Could he have turned that corner and graduated from newbie status too?

When he mentioned it to Gail, she said, "That's what I'm thinking too. Don't say anything, just see what happens."

What happened was nothing. No more of Rob's demeaning nicknames—which had grown to include "Doofus Drewfus," "Mister Mischeck," and "Doctor Chockenstein"—no pranks or pools, only the same give-and-take ribbing and ragging as everyone else.

It was a welcome relief. There would be bigger fish to fry when the new training started in a couple of weeks.

FOURTEEN

As expected, nothing could stay under wraps for long. Drew and Gail were soon the worst kept secret at Moisant. They took some trips during David's visits with his father, doing the Clearwater Beach day thing and spending a few days in Vegas. They hiked Red Rock Canyon by day and played a little blackjack, fed the one-armed bandits, and people-watched on the Strip by night. She enjoyed the outdoors as much as he did and they had plenty of fun back in the room too. They might have slept six hours the whole trip.

They grew very close, but whenever love seemed inevitable, one or the other would disengage. He wanted a deeper relationship—or thought he did—but she wasn't ready. Gradually, he came to understand he wasn't either. Gail was concerned about David's feelings, too. Their opposing schedules and his extra hours made things easier. They could remain, for the most part, ships passing in the night.

In the meantime, check-in training was a breeze. He excelled throughout thanks to his past customer service experience, greater self-assurance, plain old zeal, the probation monkey off his back, his RAATS primer and all the ALM lessons, or some stew of those ingredients and perhaps others unconsidered. Operating the system became much easier with practice, though many called the complex menus the "RAATS nest." The formats themselves were something like algebra but with names, seat assignments, bag tag numbers, ticket data, airport codes, and flight numbers playing the variables.

Some valuable advice also helped. The third time in a shift that Drew asked Henry a question, his usually genial colleague quietly snapped, "Did you even *check* RAATS?" The abrupt tone took Drew aback, but he dug around and found what he was looking for. Then the counter got busy and he forgot about it.

Later, Henry said, "Look, I didn't mean to sound harsh earlier but don't get in that habit. Nobody likes an 'asker' and you won't either once you have more experience. A lot of newbs do it because they're in a hurry or lazy. You're not lazy, but the formats and technical stuff are all in RAATS and you'll be a lot better off learning to find them on your own. The passenger can wait. Say you need to double-check something to be sure it's correct. I don't mind helping you understand *why* we do things a certain way and that kind of thing but otherwise…figure it out."

He enjoyed the counter but was glad to head down to T-Point in the afternoon. Split days didn't seem nearly as long. Like Express Check-In, T-Point might strike the uninitiated as a fairly straightforward endeavor, but little at the airport was as simple as it seemed.

The T-Point ramper, AKA the bag runner, presided over a decidedly modest domain anchored by a metal desk so dilapidated that calling it surplus was charitable. Initials were inked and carved here and there, the gum stuck underneath resembled an inverted lunar landscape, and opening the "library"—a deformed drawer holding a few well-worn paperbacks—required deft use of a screwdriver. The chair was worse. Some internal malfunction left occupants leaning to one side or the other and the stained cushions emitted an odor the origins of which were best left a mystery. One armrest was AWOL and in general the thing looked like someone had used it as a pinata. This setup was crammed into a narrow space between the metal conveyor chute slanting down on one side and the building wall on the other.

Ruff Air was only the latest lessee. Generations of people had left their marks in various ways as the years and airlines came and went. The side of the chute sported enough stickers to make a stock car jealous. Actually, one *was* a stock car, Petty's famous blue number 43 Superbird. Others were as varied in origin as the individuals who had left them. Next to "Make it in Massachusetts" was a miniature Texas license plate plugging a radio station, with an "O" and "L" represented by a steer skull and a cowboy boot. Others declared Cape May, New Jersey to be "our nation's newest seaside resort" and saluted Hughes Airwest and its yellow aircraft as "Top banana in the West!" Right where the bags emerged was the most apropos one of all: "Next stop…The Twilight Zone."

The belt was so close that anyone seated at the desk had to scoot sideways whenever a large bag came along. Somehow, many people seemed to know precisely when to lean over, and just how far, without even having to look.

Two roll-up doors provided the entry and exit. Rampers operated them by hauling on chains hanging from a pulley fifteen or so feet above. One door was so close to the desk that the bag runner had to contend with freezing gales, scorching heat, and even blowing rain if the wind gusted from a certain direction. Many disliked the stretches of solitude and boredom, the belt's constant rumbling and clanking, and the semi-exposure to the elements, but Rob loved it.

"As long as everything shows up where and when it belongs," he explained, "I can basically do whatever I want." He grinned. "And the bags never bitch."

The bag runner loaded luggage onto a line of empty carts, one or more for each departure depending on the load. Each held fifty or more bags if stacked well. These were periodically hitched up and towed planeside. For inbounds, the process was reversed, the carts brought into the tunnel where Drew had spent a couple of teeth-chattering hours. The conveyor there carried them inside and onto a carousel for their owners to reclaim.

The goals were to load every bag, even if checked late, on the right flight, never causing a delay; to promptly get the inbounds onto the carousel, verifying each was tagged for MSY and hadn't been unloaded in error; and to provide timely, accurate outbound counts, which the Ops agent needed to calculate the weight and balance.

Easy enough for a single flight, or when loads were light. But when they weren't, or multiple flights were on the ground—

or, worst of all, both—the job assumed a Whack-A-Mole quality that had the bag runner and assistant darting about like squirrels on speed. When three full flights were checking in, keeping the belt from backing up and dumping bags on the floor was an achievement. Racing from the conveyor to carts to planes to baggage claim, back and forth, again and again as departure time approached was mentally and physically exhausting. Almost every second off the tug was spent transferring bags, some of which felt like they were loaded with rocks and lined with lead.

Drew quickly knocked out T-Point and finished check-in training within a few weeks. Still, he wasn't done, not by a long shot. Next was issuing and reissuing tickets. Ruff Air maintained an elementary set of fares between city pairs: one peak, one off-peak, and one non-refundable super-discounted rate. The contrast in complexity between this and a major carrier's fare structure was roughly the same as that between staging a kindergarten recital versus a Broadway musical.

Ruff Air's ticketing process lagged the industry standard as well. In fact, calling it "archaic" was kind. Most airlines, and even many travel agents, used their systems to automatically price fares, after which a printer clattered out tickets on cardstock. The toughest part was arranging the cards in order and stapling them together. RAATS calculated the fares but CSRs had to write the tickets by hand. This dumbfounded the American agents on one side and the Piedmont staff on the other, and garnered a few side-eyes from customers too. Of course, the giggling at the adjacent counters abruptly ceased when their systems went down. Dead screens transformed the Ruff Air agents from punch lines into savants.

Everyone hoped a rumored upgrade was really in the works. Only later would most trainees come to appreciate how writing tickets forced them to read and really understand fare ladders—the breakdown of base fare plus taxes and fees listed on each ticket—along with what all the fare combinations were and how to apply the rules.

Learning to book, sell, and write a ticket was challenging, but reissues were where the rubber really met the road. Reissues were essentially trading one ticket for another. Sorting out two or more sets of rules and prices and ending up with an accurate result required knowledge, patience, and an occasional huddle with the lead or an experienced colleague. Working through the details, even with the system doing the calculations, took serious concentration and a knack for digging deep into RAATS.

A few weeks into ticketing, Mary assigned Drew to train one day a week in baggage claim and one at the gates. The baggage office was a lightning rod and proved to be as thankless and challenging a job as there was. The only décor was a large chart with pictures of different types of luggage, each with a standard identification code number. Instead of trying to describe the lost item, customers could point to the corresponding picture and say the item's color.

People constantly streamed in and out. Some actually needed assistance with lost or damaged bags. But most just had questions, questions, and more questions. The topics were limitless. Policies, directions, where to meet unaccompanied minors, refund procedures, how to apply to be a flight attendant, departure times, arrival times, how long it took to get here or there, the best place to eat upstairs, what year the airport opened, the distance to Bourbon Street, what the Wright Amendment was and why it was enacted…with his trainer Carla's help, he answered or redirected these queries and more in just his first few days.

"See, BS doesn't only stand for 'baggage service,'" she whispered after one particularly odd inquiry.

Half the people asked about other carriers, seemingly unaware of the script logo behind the counter. This demonstrated the value of his trainer's first lesson: "As soon as they come in, ask what airline they arrived on. We don't have time to hear their life story then find out they need to go to Delta or wherever." The reason why initially seemed counterintuitive: regardless of which airline they checked it with, the passenger's arriving carrier was responsible for their luggage.

"Wait a minute," Drew objected. "One time I was coming back from San Francisco—"

"The hard way, right?" said Carla with a smile.

"Damn skippy. Anyway, American rebooked a bunch of people on us. You're telling me *we* were responsible for delivering whatever bags didn't get here?"

"Yep," she said. "That's the rule, but think about it: the arriving carrier is, or should be at least, the last ones to physically have the bag. Sometimes the original airline might not even have an office wherever the passenger ends up. We don't interline internationally but suppose somebody checked their bag with BA in London and connected here on AA? Who would *they* file with?"

Okay, that makes sense.

Mastering the RAATS baggage formats took real focus. Like ticketing, it was a matter of inserting information in the proper order, but there was a lot of data and the codes from the big laminated baggage identification chart had to be entered carefully. One typo could turn the search for a wayward train case into a mistaken quest for nonexistent golf clubs. Carla had him complete pages of exercises where trainees wrote the appropriate entries for various lost items.

Taking a couple of damage claims drove home another lesson. Using kid gloves obviously wasn't practical on the ramp but he had seen luggage thrown ten feet down into a cart. That was uncalled for, and why anyone who had worked in baggage service would ever do it was beyond understanding.

At the gates, the CSRs had far more to do than check in passengers. On an empty jetbridge, Mary handed over the key and asked, "What do you think should be the first thing you do?"

The obvious thing would be to put in the key, but that seemed a little *too* obvious.

"Well, on the ramp Grayson always goes on about everything being clear of the jetbridge."

"Yes! The first thing you do, *every* time, without fail, is be sure everything is clear. Do *not* put your key in until you look. It doesn't matter how late the flight is, or that our bridges don't have tires and can't move very far. That might change someday or you'll transfer or something but no matter what, it's the right way on any jetbridge. You'll be surprised how often something has to be moved, and people have a habit of standing around down there too, so *always* look all around first."

They leaned out, searched all around and underneath then walked over to the door leading out and peered around from the stair landing.

"Okay, now put the key in."

It didn't take long to get the hang of the controls.

"Good," Mary said. "Once you're about a foot away, go slow and gentle. You can rock the plane pretty hard if you're not careful. We'll practice on a terminator soon. The next thing is knock twice and stand way back."

"To give the door room to open?"

"Yes, but also to be as clear as you can be if the ISR forgets to disarm the slide. Always let the ISR open the door. It's heavy so it's human nature to want to help them but you don't want to be standing that close if the slide blows. A CSR in Austin got knocked out and his arm broken a few years ago."

"I thought the seatback card said you have to pull a handle or something to inflate the door slides."

"That's to be sure. Opening the door should blow the slide. And anyway, remember to expect the unexpected around here."

They went up to the podium and reviewed more gate duties: juggling seat assignments to get friends and families together; resolving the occasional dupes that left two passengers assigned to the same seat; printing paperwork the pilots and ISRs needed; coordinating timely boarding, including preboards; making the necessary announcements; clearing the standby list; and handling any snags that arose. If the flight was overbooked, add soliciting volunteers, determining whether their seats were needed, and getting the right people aboard. All this with the non-negotiable deadline of departure time looming. Afterwards came post-departure, a set of administrative chores.

"The trick at the gate," Mary said after a particularly hectic scene at 7B, "is to push everything out from departure time as much as possible. Say you have standbys. If there are seats, clear them right when they reach the gate. A lot of people wait until they release seats ten minutes before departure, even when there's space, but why? If you need volunteers, same thing. This flight wasn't oversold by much, so they took a chance and it bit 'em in the ass. Go ahead and get volunteers early. What's the harm? Better to have them in your back pocket than to have to scramble later when everything's hopping."

They were in Ops, and Peggy added, "Yes sir, start early, especially on the volunteers. Your worst nightmare is standing on the airplane at departure time begging for somebody to get off. That gets ugly fast."

Mary went on, "Stuff will always pile up around departure. A runner shows up who doesn't have a boarding pass, there's a late wheelchair passenger they forgot to put in the flight notes…something. You rush around and get everything done and feel good 'cause you shut the door on time, then you get back to the podium and there are those standbys you meant to clear standing there looking at you. I've seen it happen. You can always take the seats back if you need them."

The next assignment was working a flight with Rob, a mid-morning through trip from Houston heading to Tampa and Miami.

"This will be a good one to observe," Mary explained. "It's only about half-full so it's as close to easy as we get."

Drew had seen Rob upstairs before, but couldn't quite get used to this version of his usually scruffy colleague: hair neatly combed, no raggedy ballcap or mirrored shades, in a crisp, pressed uniform, and holding entire conversations without a single f-bomb. Perhaps Rob felt the same way. He looked uncomfortable and occasionally tugged his collar away from his neck without seeming to realize he was doing it.

Unchanged was Rob's ever-roving eye. While going over gate entries, he glanced up and whispered, "Flight Ninety-nine, ten o'clock."

"What?"

"Flight Ninety-nine, ten o'clock, on final."

"We don't have…"

Rob nodded to the left, where a young woman in a snug sweater and jeans was approaching. After she passed, he snickered and said, "Nobody covered Flight Ninety-nine? We really have to update our training."

Soon there was no time for gate processes or anything else. A line began building, 25 people or more so far, some surly and most clutching Eastern tickets stamped "Rule 240." Drew, fresh from counter training, knew Rule 240 was an endorsement authorizing travel on another airline after cancellations or long delays.

The next person in line said loudly, "You people have some deal with Eastern? They canceled our flight. Are they bringing our bags? Do we get our miles? Are you people safe?"

Rob answered: yes, yes, check with Eastern, and yes. Then he excused himself and radioed the gate lead, Sylvia, who arrived a minute later. After a quick update and a glance at the line, now well into the concourse and growing, she drafted Gail from the counter and outlined a plan. Drew went out front to answer questions and direct Eastern re-routes to Gail, since she was faster at rebooking. Everyone else went to Rob. Sylvia helped where needed.

Twenty minutes later, the line had dwindled. The phone rang and Rob answered, listened for a moment, and said with exaggerated politeness, "No, no, thank *you*."

He motioned Sylvia over.

"Perfect. Maintenance is onboard." He lowered his voice to a near whisper. "Glad we busted ass. This blows. Give me T-Point any day."

Sylvia said, "You want to tell them, or shall I?"

Rob picked up the mic, cleared his throat, paused for about five seconds, then said, "For those passengers traveling on Ruff Air Flight Five Forty-four to Tampa with continuing service to Miami, maintenance is aboard looking at what we're told is a minor problem. We'll let you know as soon as we have more information."

Those gathered let out a collective groan. One loudmouth went off about how they should all go back and insist that Eastern rebook them on Delta.

Rob ignored her and went on, "For those from the Eastern flight, Operations has advised that we have your luggage.

As for frequent flier miles, please refer any questions to Eastern at your convenience. Thank you."

Gail asked Sylvia, "Why'd you guys wait so long to call somebody? Eastern called about forty-five minutes ago and said they might send people. We were checking in three flights so Mary said to send 'em straight here. Didn't anybody call?"

Rob shot her a look.

"I guess not," she said.

Drew asked, "Rob, what was that pause after you picked up the mic?"

Sylvia answered, "First rule of announcements: think it through. Otherwise, you'll get a sentence or two out then start babbling."

The flight left thirty-five minutes late. Despite a general air of annoyance among the reroutes, the crowd settled down and waited quietly until the first boarding call. Their placid mood was much different than other delays CSRs talked about, where people hounded the agents mercilessly.

As the flight taxied away, Drew asked about this. Gail replied, "Well, did you notice anything different from those times?"

"I don't know, I guess maybe you guys made more announcements."

"Ding ding, we have a winnah!" Rob said, imitating a carnival barker.

Gail went on, "What were these people stressed about?"

"Bags, miles, and when they'd be leaving."

"Exactly. So we answered that. Every ten to fifteen minutes, say something. When there's nothing new, tell them that. Say you're sorry about what's happening, 'cause aren't you? You've been on delayed flights, and it sucks, right? Oh, and you have to explain stuff. Like weather, you can't say 'the flight from wherever is late because of weather' when it's sunny outside here, they'll go bananas. Find out what's going on and say something like, 'there's a line of storms between here and Florida and the pilots need extra time to find a safe way through.' People understand that and they like feeling someone is looking out for them. You can't fake it or try to BS them, and you might still have a couple of yahoos to deal with, but once they know they can trust you to shoot straight and keep them updated, most of 'em will sit there and read their newspapers."

The phone rang. Mary told Rob to tell Drew to take his break, then meet her at the counter.

"Good," said Gail. "You can walk me back if you want to."

"Aw, how sweet," said Rob. "Yeah, walk her back."

After Gail turned away, he glanced longingly at her behind and made a face that left no doubt where his mind was. But just in case, he mouthed "Yeah!" while pumping his fist sideways.

Drew knew it was a lost cause. He looked up and shook his head with consternation, much like Rob had done on that first day outside the cafeteria.

Rob just laughed.

FIFTEEN

Carnival came and went. Buried under an avalanche of hours, there wasn't time to see a single parade, a first since moving to the Crescent City.

For a while, the work crush obscured a growing disconnect with Gail, but their relationship was clearly tailing off. Granted, their schedules didn't mesh, but gradually, Drew realized there was more. She was troubled, but wouldn't talk about it. He asked her to a parade, thinking she would be as excited as she usually was about such things. Instead, she demurred, citing some half-baked reason he could tell rang hollow, even to her.

Someone said Gail and her estranged husband were going to counseling. That couldn't be true; she would have told him. Maybe they were like puzzle pieces that seemed to match at first but didn't quite fit together. Trying to figure it out was frustrating, especially since none of the likely possibilities involved a happy outcome.

The longer this dragged on, the more discouraged he became. One morning, exasperated after yet another stilted conversation, he spent his break on the observation deck. The platform, outfitted with benches and pay binoculars on gimbals, had become a haven. He could think and get some fresh air, figuratively at least given the proximity to the apron.

He leaned on the rail, absentmindedly taking in the comings and goings around Moisant.

Why won't she talk to me?

He finally decided that as hard as it was, he had to let things play out. A drawn-out mess had to be avoided at all costs.

That's what he told himself at least. Maybe he wasn't willing to risk the hurt of having to read the writing on the wall.

Brock cut to the chase when the old Streak gang got together for pizza at a place in Kenner.

"That ship has sailed, my friend. You're the only one who doesn't get it. It's over. O-V-E-R. The sooner you get that through your head and move on, the better."

Stan agreed. "Let it go. You had a good time, right? Come on, why would you want a girlfriend anyway, especially one with a kid? Besides, it's like the streetcars on St. Charles. You miss one, wait a little while. Another one will come along."

"Yeah, but not the same one."

"No, but maybe a better one," Stan countered.

But letting go proved tougher than it sounded.

* * *

In mid-March, Mary administered a comprehensive final quiz and signed Drew's ticket counter qualification. She complimented his well-organized notebook and the RAATS format flashcards he had created, even requesting copies to use with the next trainee.

A week later, Gail stopped by the counter on her way out. She asked if he was free for lunch the following day. Had this not been such a pleasant surprise, he might have noticed the shadow of sorrow in her eyes. Even without that clue, his realization of her likely purpose grew through the evening.

They met at the Bud's Broiler where they had celebrated her win in the newbie pool. Gail's eyes welled up as soon as they sat down, confirming his fears.

"Damn it, I promised myself I wouldn't cry," she said, dabbing at her eyes with a napkin. "I wanted you to hear this from me and not through the grapevine. Bobby and I are getting back together."

He had thought himself prepared, but hearing Gail nail the coffin closed on the special time they had shared was a blow that left him searching for words.

"I'm glad for you and for David," he finally managed, and he meant it, though a part of him was also very sad.

"I'm not a hundred percent it's for the best but Bobby really seems to have changed and David misses him so much."

"But is it what *you* want? Don't do it for David."

"No, it is, if Bobby can go back to being the guy I fell in love with, and I think he can. I'm sorry I didn't say anything about us going to counseling. It just felt too weird to talk about with you. But I want you to know how much 'us' meant to me, to have someone who accepted me for who I am and the situation for what it was and who didn't try to force something that wasn't there."

Sometimes I really wish it had been there.

She added, "Drew, I will always treasure that."

Recalling some of the scuttlebutt around the station—and, he would admit to himself later, wallowing in some self-pity—he said, "Some people seem to think I took advantage of you."

Anger flashed in her eyes.

"'Some people' should mind their own damn business. You know the truth, and so do I, and that's all that matters."

"I couldn't agree more."

"Good."

Gail managed a wan smile and stuck out her hand.

"Friends?"

Setting the pain aside for the moment, he shook her hand.

"Always. You know that."

"Good," she said again. "Besides, now more than ever I'll need a source for the inside scoop on how guys look at things."

This was the definition of mixed emotions. He was genuinely happy for Gail and especially for David, but he deeply missed the intimacy, honesty, and fun he and Gail had shared. He hoped to find that with someone again someday.

Working more than ever became emotional first aid. By late May, Mary and Grayson had signed him off on everything but Ops, and a new bid was out. There were recent hires with less seniority, but neither could yet hold a line. His shift remained unchanged, but now he had a day on the counter, one in Baggage Service, one at T-Point, and two on the ramp. When staffing allowed, he assisted the Ops agent, the last step before that certification.

If experience is the best teacher, he thought one day, *this has to be the best Airline 101 anywhere. It's a hell of a lot of fun, too.*

His new qualifications leveled the shift-trade playing field. There were now as many hours as he cared to pick up. The savings nearly consumed by the job search had been replenished and watching the balances grow a little with each check was a relief.

There was some traveling too, with one trip even more memorable than his first. Someone said after the San Francisco debacle that nonrevving sometimes went as off kilter but in good ways. But what more could be hoped for than the trip going as planned? The answer came one fine morning when serendipity evidently clocked in for some OT and decided to ride his shoulder like a friendly parrot.

He had splurged on a second-hand zoom for his Canon and Miami International would make the perfect proving ground. British Airways' Concorde came in several times weekly, a Speedbird if ever there was one. A Concorde had visited Moisant once years before. Everyone heard it—the takeoff rattled Streak's windows and shook the walls—but they only managed a distant glimpse. Word was that MIA was a photographer's paradise.

First Class was open on the morning one-stop through Tampa. After dozing most of the way, lifting the shade admitted an eye-watering dazzle of sunshine. Below, boats left random foamy streaks on the Gulf and breakers followed each other toward sand so white it appeared to glow. A few clouds drifted lazily, casting irregular shadows on several pristine barrier islands whose wild beauty had so far escaped the explosion of coastal development coming into view. In some places, the condos and hotel towers were packed in so tightly it looked like a golf cart would scrape the walls if driven between them. Swimmers, sunbathers, and beach walkers were everywhere.

The bay side had manmade peninsulas, some in irregular shapes resembling the Japanese alphabet he had seen on Okinawa, others so linear they looked like combs. All were covered with residences, each with a dock and many with pools. Pleasure craft of every description crowded the waterways and marinas. Across the bay, Tampa International looked something like an asterisk from the air, its core a large central terminal connected by raised tracks to several outlying concourses.

The taxi in revealed that whoever tended the extensive landscaping took pride in their work. Palms swayed among vivid tropical blooms, above which people movers zipped back and forth. Atop the terminal sat a multi-level parking garage and the three-winged structure alongside had to be a hotel. A tall, streamlined control tower completed the ensemble. The airport had a pleasant, modern, efficient look to it. Moisant seemed dated and more than a little frumpy in comparison.

Oddly, the rampers meeting the flight wore Eastern uniforms.

What's with this?

He'd have to ask about that when he got home.

An Eastern captain was among those who boarded for the hop to Miami. His crisp mannerisms, sharp uniform, and crewcut exemplified what Dad had called "good military bearing." After an ISR took his coat, the pilot stowed his gear in the overhead and sat next to Drew, who debated whether to start a conversation. If the newspapers were right, Eastern was in crisis, its future uncertain. Their ground employees at MSY often seemed sullen. Besides, he didn't want to intrude.

Finally, after takeoff, he asked, "What do you fly?"

"These days I'm an instructor on the DC-9," the man replied, stirring sugar into his coffee. "But I've been pretty lucky. Started on propjobs, then the DC-8 and 727. Pretty exciting stuff compared to the Aeronca Champ I got my license with back in Pennsylvania."

"You weren't military?"

"No, I went to Embry-Riddle then got on with Eastern."

"Are you based in Miami?"

A sip of coffee and another nod.

"Just got in from LaGuardia. I'm deadheading home. You a pilot?"

"No, I'm an airport agent with Ruff Air in New Orleans. I'm headed to shoot some pictures of the Concorde." He extended his hand. "I'm Drew."

The captain shook hands and said, "Don Evans. No kidding, all the way to MIA to shoot pictures? Good for you. Ever been there?"

"No, first time."

"You'll enjoy it. There are plenty of good vantage points and every kind of big iron you'd ever want to see. A bunch of old piston stuff too."

"I'm looking forward to it. I'll have most of the day and the weather's supposed to be good."

"Yeah, the forecast is severe clear."

Drew had plenty of questions and like Bert, the captain was more than happy to oblige. Much too soon, the Super 50 was descending over the vast, mottled green Everglades to the theme from *Miami Vice*.

"Hey, thanks for talking with me, I really appreciate it."

The captain smiled.

"When it comes to flying, the only thing pilots like better than doing it is talking about it. Come to think of it, how about this? My wife's a flight attendant and her trip won't be in until later this afternoon. I was going to go catch up on some paperwork rather than drive home and back. But you have a few hours before the Concorde gets in and tell you the truth, I hate paperwork. So why don't we go over there to our training center and I'll show you around? If you've never seen a full-motion sim…well, they're pretty impressive."

Surprised at the captain's kind offer, Drew replied, "Man, that would be great! Really, it's no problem?"

The pilot smiled again at the obvious enthusiasm and said, "Hell no, we have visitors all the time!"

The heat was already getting oppressive by the time the shuttle arrived at the training facility. The visitor paused at the dedication plaque honoring the building's namesake, a first officer named James Hartley.

He looked at the captain, surprised.

"'Died defending his passengers'?"

Captain Evans described the 1970 hijacking during which a deranged passenger shot Hartley and Captain Robert Wilbur, Jr., in the cockpit of their DC-9. Before dying of his injuries, Hartley heroically wrested the gun from the hijacker's grasp and shot him. Still, the wounded captain had to fight off the crazed assailant several more times while flying an emergency approach into Boston.

"Damn, I don't remember hearing about that."

"You must have been a kid back then," the captain accurately observed. His voice grew somber. "I don't know how the hell Wilbur got that thing on the ground. I knew Jim Hartley too. We were on DC-8s and transitioned to the DC-9 together. He was a good guy. After he died, the pilot union lobbied for more cockpit security, bulletproof doors and so on, but nothing ever came of it. Said it was too expensive. They'll be sorry when the next nut comes along."

Those words drifted down into the deepest reaches of Drew's memory, remaining there until a horrific September morning in 2001.

The air inside was cool, almost chilly. They toured the ground school classrooms, where life-sized photographs familiarized students with cockpit panel layouts and schematics illustrating various aircraft systems covered the walls. His host was gracious, but many others appeared tense and there was a pervasive melancholy that hung in the building like fog.

Then an elevator opened and a peppy group emerged and went off down the hall, talking and laughing.

"I'm guessing new-hire flight attendants?"

"Yep, the first class in quite a while," the captain replied.

"Seems like a good sign," Drew said as they stepped into the elevator.

"We'll see. I have friends at OALs who say they've had classes get laid off, sometimes a week before graduation."

"That's pretty rugged."

"So it goes these days. Deregulation turned everything upside down. Nobody was ready for it. Look at Pan Am. When

I got out of school twenty years ago, every pilot I knew wanted the same thing: a seat in the pointy end of a shiny new 707 with a blue meatball on the tail. They sold the Pan Am building and are still swimming in red ink. Buying National was a disaster and sooner or later they'll run out of things to peddle and that will be that. *Pan American,* for Christ's sake. And a lot of people here think we're in the same boat, or will be soon. You're with Ruff Air, right?"

"Yes."

"I don't know how they're making it. Hell, I don't know how anybody's making it right now."

I just hope we keep making it.

They went through a door onto an elevated catwalk, greeted by faint electrical odors and muted mechanical whirring. These emanated from two rows of about a half-dozen flight simulators, all in use. The devices rode at least ten or twelve feet high on hydraulic pistons resembling gigantic auto shock absorbers. Each had six such legs, three sets configured in an "A" shape and anchored at their apex to a platform holding a white pod. Some were cube-shaped and others domed like the Quonset huts Drew remembered from army posts. Each was windowless and marked with Eastern's logo and the name of whatever aircraft type it impersonated—L-1011, A300, 727, 757, and DC-9. Metal gangplanks were folded back against the catwalk, so the simulators' doors and the little gates in the handrails opened to nothing at the moment.

The simulators bobbed, tilted, and rotated as the unseen occupants flew their training scenarios. The scene made for an odd panorama, like watching two orderly columns of gigantic marshmallows being randomly tossed about on a stormy sea.

Could a machine really credibly replicate flight?

"Does it feel real?"

"It's pretty darn close," Captain Evans replied. "You can't tell from here but every movement creates a physical sensation to match whatever phase of flight you're in. Acceleration, centrifugal forces, braking, turns, even stuff like that…what would you call it? You know, that stomach-in-your-throat feeling you get on a roller coaster or when a plane drops suddenly in turbulence."

The nearest sim, marked DC-9, leveled itself and hissed softly as it lowered slowly to rest. A flashing light and buzzer accompanied the gangplank's lowering, folded handrails rising on either side.

Three pilots emerged, one of whom addressed Captain Evans.

"Hey Don, how's it going?"

"Keepin' the blue side up, or trying anyhow."

"We're heading down to grab some chow, want to join us?"

"No, thanks, I'm showing Drew here around. If you guys are out for an hour, okay if I take him for a spin?"

"It's all yours. Keep it in one piece."

"No promises," replied Captain Evans with a chuckle.

Drew tried to keep his amazement in check.

Is this really happening?

The pilot stopped at a control board inside. He directed Drew to the right side of the replica flight deck, where he clambered awkwardly into the seat and looked around with a mixture of interest and awe.

The captain punched buttons and entered settings. The instrument panel lit up and a depiction of Miami International appeared beyond the windows.

"Okay," said Captain Evans, sliding effortlessly into his seat, "let's get strapped in." He fastened the lap belt into a circular buckle, then reached back over his shoulders, grabbed a shoulder belt in each hand, and brought them down to the buckle as well. Drew fumbled for a minute but got all the harness straps set in short order.

"These are the controls," the captain continued, pointing out the yoke, rudder pedals, and thrust levers and describing their functions. Taking out a laminated card, he went on, "Now, there are way too many procedures and contingencies to trust even the best memory, so we use checklists. Let's crank her up." It was hard to believe how quickly the pilot ran through the callouts and how fast his hands flew over the switches, knobs, and levers. Soon came the sound of engines spooling up.

The captain pointed down to his left at what looked like a miniature steering wheel with the lower third cut out.

"This is the tiller," he explained as his guest leaned over to look. "It's for steering the nose wheel when we taxi and on the runway until there's enough airflow to make the rudder effective. Here we go." He pushed the thrust levers forward. The rising whine and forward motion sounded and felt exactly like leaving the gate in a real DC-9. So did the little jolts as the simulator's non-existent landing gear bumped over imaginary imperfections in the fictitious concrete. Drew moved the flap handle at the captain's direction; the sim faithfully mimicked the whirring sound of flaps extending. Any skepticism was fading fast. The visuals weren't entirely lifelike but everything else was, and the effect was uncanny.

After lining up on the runway, the captain said, "See the gear handle there? When I say 'gear up,' grab that handle, move it to the right and then up." The pilot added power, keeping the brakes on.

"Watch these," he said, pointing at two dials marked PRESS RATIO. "Those show us the difference between the pressure of air going into the engine with the air going out. That's one way to measure how much thrust the engines are producing." The needles stabilized and he said, "Okay, let's go up to takeoff power, about one point nine." He advanced the thrust levers again. When he let off the brakes, acceleration pushed them back into their seats.

Seconds later, the captain said, "Eighty knots." His left hand released the tiller and moved to the yoke. A few moments later, he said, "Vee one…and…rotate." He pulled smoothly back and brought the nose off the runway. The low rumble of tires rolling stopped and there was the lifting sensation of takeoff.

"Positive climb, gear up."

Drew seized the handle, easily identified since the knob looked like a miniature tire or wheel, pulled it to the right, then moved it smartly upwards. Gear retraction noises commenced, concluding with thuds as the wheel well doors closed.

Captain Evans suddenly pushed the U-shaped yoke forward, bringing the runway into view.

"Hang on," he said. "We're gonna have some fun."

The "plane" banked into a sharp left turn, a startling move so close to the ground. They streaked over the terminal toward a hangar across the airport. A sign atop it said FLY EASTERN AIR LINES in huge red neon letters. Drew ducked instinctively as they "crashed" through the sign.

"I shouldn't do that," the captain said, looking over with a cat-that-ate-the-canary grin as they climbed away.

They flew past Miami Beach and out over the Atlantic. At Captain Evans' insistence, Drew took the controls for a few thrilling minutes. With coaching, he completed some simple maneuvers with reasonable success. He resolved to learn more about the technology, unable to fathom how the experience could possibly be so authentic. Little jostles of turbulence, dynamic readings on the instruments and gauges, and other aircraft were all present.

"Okay, hold it straight and level," directed the captain, his cool manner clearly inspired by something other than his visitor's white-knuckled grip on the yoke. He got up and went to the control board. The outside screens went dark.

"What happened?"

"Nothing," the captain replied, returning to his seat. "We're going to do some night flying."

"It's hard to tell what's up when everything's black," Drew observed.

"Yes it is. That's one of the things that can play tricks on your equilibrium."

The captain pointed to the panel.

"See? Watch it there, cowboy."

Based on the physical cues, Drew would have sworn the sim was still in level flight. The artificial horizon disagreed, showing a descending right turn. Absent Captain Evans, he would have thought everything was peachy right up until the imitation DC-9 struck the projected water.

"Pull back and ease the yoke left," Captain Evans said, before noticing that his pupil was already correcting. "That's it, a little more…there you go."

Drew was incredulous at how completely his senses had fooled him, and not even in a real airplane!

The captain continued, "Spatial disorientation has killed a lot of pilots. Without visual references, it's tough to figure out which way is up. We train hard on that because even on instruments, your brain wants to reject information that disagrees with your senses. It can get you in a hurry in solid clouds or over water at night."

They turned west. A glittery line appeared in the distance.

"That's not all Miami, is it?"

"No," the captain replied. "That's everything from Homestead to Jupiter." This was where the visuals came into their own. The technology could reproduce nighttime scenes with enough fidelity to complete the illusion of being airborne.

Drew was intrigued by the view and intently focused on maintaining level flight. That's why he nearly jumped through the overhead when a loud bell jangled and a large red light flared on the panel. There was a muffled *whump* and they slewed sideways.

Captain Evans was all business.

"Okay, we got an engine fire in number one. My airplane."

The next fifteen minutes were a blur. The pilot completed the engine fire and emergency landing checklists with remarkable speed, all while flying a smooth single-engine approach. He delegated lowering the gear but otherwise completed the first officer's duties as well as his own. If he was trying to impress his spectator, the effort was supremely successful.

A thud and they were down, white runway lights streaking by. Playing his part in the practice emergency to the final curtain, Captain Evans called, "Stand by for ground evacuation."

An escape rope was stowed near the windows. It almost seemed possible that he could shimmy down it and find concerned rescuers waiting at the other end.

The whine of the operating engine spooled down as they slowed to a stop. The lights came up and the sim settled.

"Wow! That was unbelievable!"

"So," the pilot asked, "does it feel real? And how did you like my little surprise? It's nice to have sims for stuff like that so pilots can practice until their reactions are second nature. Airlines lost quite a few crews and airplanes in training accidents, and of course using a real plane is more expensive too. Come on, let's get a cup of coffee."

In the breakroom, Captain Evans said, "Funny story about that fire bell. Years ago, when I was still pretty new, I was at Hartsfield, flying with this captain who was a crusty old bastard from the Rickenbacker days. You'd almost need a crowbar to pry one of those guys out of the left seat to do a pre-flight but it was a real nice spring morning so he decided to get some fresh air.

"A little boy about three or four was boarding with his parents. He kind of stopped and peeked into the cockpit so I said, 'Hi there, want to come see where we fly the plane?' So his mom brings him in and I tell her to sit him in the captain's seat. I'm showing him this and that and I hit the test button for that fire warning. The bell went off and he jumped the same way you did. It just scared the hell out of him. He started crying, and I mean wailing, and when his mom picked him up…well, the poor little guy had peed his pants.

"That sheepskin seat cover soaked it right up too. We waited twenty minutes for a mechanic to change it. We left late and the captain was pissed, no pun intended. So were the parents and the maintenance foreman 'cause they've got plenty to do already in Atlanta. Everyone called me 'Diaper Don' for about five years after that." He grinned ruefully and shook his head. "Still hear it now and again for that matter."

Back at the shuttle stop, Drew shook the captain's hand warmly and thanked him with heartfelt sincerity. Captain Evans said, "Hey, it was my pleasure. Any time you're down here, give me a call. Take care and good luck to you."

Riding to the terminal, he reflected on the man's exceptional kindness and remembered Peggy's words about how friendship and camaraderie often crossed company lines. Little did he know that another demonstration awaited.

He got some great shots of the Concorde's droop-nosed landing, then hustled out to the concourse to get the gate arrival too. A few minutes later, a BA agent approached.

"Excuse me, sir," she said with British formality, "have you checked in here at the gate? We're very full today and prefer to have everyone check with us before boarding."

On learning his affiliation, origin, and purpose, she said, "Good heavens, you've come all this way to see our Concorde?"

"Yes, I'm here on a day trip."

"May I see your airline identification?"

This seemed odd, but he handed it over. She inspected it, handed it back, and said, "Please excuse me for a moment."

She walked to the podium and made a phone call.

Who in the world can she possibly be talking to?

The answer astonished him. The agent waved him over and said, "We've only a few minutes but the captain would be pleased if you would come on board for a look around. You'll have to be quick though, we'll be boarding straightaway."

Stunned again at his good fortune, Drew got a hurried tour and a brief stop in the cockpit. His main impressions were the surprisingly tight quarters in the cabin, the small windows, the crew's civility in each introducing themselves and shaking his hand, and the unusual control yokes, shaped like an inverted "W" instead of the wide horseshoe in Ruff Air's Douglas jets.

He headed home two hours later, again in First Class. What a shockingly good day it had been! His airline counterparts' kindness touched his heart, and he promised himself he would pass it on every chance he got.

* * *

Kelly called out as he clocked in on his one-year anniversary.

"Drew? Barb wants to see you." Her tone wasn't ominous but the summons still clenched him up.

Barb stood up and said, "I have something for you." She handed him a small box. Inside was his one-year service pin.

She smiled wryly and said, "All things considered, I thought it was only fair to give it to you personally." She offered her hand and said, "Congratulations!"

Downstairs, he placed the box in his locker. He almost couldn't believe it was real, that a whole year had passed, or that he had managed to regain Barb's trust. He wasn't alone; there were several double-takes at the counter the first time he wore the pin.

When he stopped by his parents' house on the way home, Mom noticed the new uniform addition. After he explained, she said, "I'm so proud of you for following your heart and sticking with it. Even if you never make a lot of money, when you love what you do, you're rich in ways that are much more meaningful."

Dad clapped him on the shoulder and added, "Good job, son."

But even with things going so well personally, ignoring the bigger picture was impossible. A strike had crippled Pan Am for almost a month and every day seemingly brought reports of mergers and bankruptcies. Corporate raiders were after TWA, including some who supposedly planned to draw and quarter that venerable airline then auction off the pieces. As if that wasn't enough, terrorists had taken hostages aboard a hijacked TWA 727, crisscrossed the Middle East for several days, and killed a U.S. Navy diver who was among the passengers. The siege lasted for seventeen days. Several tragic crashes rounded out the airline news.

Closer to home, rumors ran the gamut. Depending on who was talking, Ruff Air was ordering Boeing 757s, trying to unload some current planes to meet expenses, or seeking a merger. Load factors had declined and while the financial losses weren't crippling, they were maddeningly consistent. The battle at Hobby burned hotter than ever. Continental ran an ad about their fares being "insanely low;" Ruff Air fired back with an ad featuring a man in a straitjacket, conspicuous enough without the Continental logo emblazoned on it. The copy declared, "Our fares are so low you'd have to be crazy to fly Continental out of Hobby!" Even more distressing were news reports that occasionally referred to his airline as "financially troubled Ruff Air."

The contrast between his personal fulfillment and the industry's struggles felt a little like trying to enjoy a picnic in the middle of a forest fire. While time was helping his heart heal from the breakup with Gail, he missed her and hoped to find someone special to share the ups and downs. Alone at home one evening, down in the dumps more than usual, he switched off the TV and sat in the dark. Somehow that rough morning at the counter flashed into his mind and he could almost hear the kindly passenger saying the words: "It can change."

SIXTEEN

The Gulf of Mexico spans 600,000 square miles of water, cobalt blue in the deeper reaches and bright aqua where waves caress a beach. Nearly every conceivable type of vessel operates on and under its surface and an amazing variety of sea life inhabits its depths. The Flower Garden Banks alone boast over 20 types of coral and 200 species of fish; whales, dolphins, sharks, rays, sea turtles, and various crustaceans and mollusks round out the aquatic cast. Drilling company helicopters shuttle between hundreds of oil and gas platforms, whose towering steel legs create the perfect buffet for the undersea food chain.

But in nature, there must be balance, and each year, the darker side of this awe-inspiring beauty reveals itself. Some storms spin harmlessly away from land. Others bring a few days of wind and rain to the places they touch. And occasionally, unimaginable violence collides head-on with civilization. The forces unleashed are sometimes difficult to comprehend even after the evidence comes to light. Entire villages and their inhabitants simply gone, swallowed by storm surges; winds that scrape homes and businesses down to naked gray foundations; vehicles piled up and crushed into junk; bodies wedged in trees; and ocean-going ships deposited inland as easily as driftwood.

Those who have witnessed this fury or its aftermath are often left either deeply questioning their faith or devoutly reaffirming it. Many years had passed since such a calamity had raked southern Louisiana, but there were still places where the mere mention of names like Audrey, Betsy, or Camille clouded faces with sorrow and caused eyes to well.

Grand Isle has seen its share of mayhem blow in off the Gulf, perched as it is on a narrow barrier island between wetland bays and the open sea. But this summer day was picture-perfect, the kind where mothers turn off televisions and shoo their children outside to play. One such evictee was a ten-year-old who was ready for a snack by mid-afternoon. A Popsicle sounded good, so after asking permission, he shook some quarters from his piggy bank and rode his bike to the town's small supermarket. He sat on the curb in front of the store a few minutes later. The treat was already starting to melt and he was careful not to let any drip onto his clothes.

The boy looked up after a bite or two and noticed a fast-moving speck, flickering with the sun's reflection and trailing a bright white line in its wake. He knew nothing of airline schedules or routes, just that high-flying jets frequently crisscrossed over the little town and that he liked to watch them. He would gaze up and wonder who the people were and where they were going. Would he someday go somewhere so far away it would take an airplane trip to get there? By the time the Popsicle was gone, so was the speck, its contrail scattering in the wind.

Far above the summer haze that sometimes hugs the water's surface, the object of the youngster's curiosity— Tumbleweed 819 from Houston to Miami—cruised in smooth air beneath a blue sky worthy of the Empyrean. Soon after captivating the little boy, the jet passed a navigation waypoint and banked into a gentle turn as the autopilot steered it toward the next fix on the flight plan.

The ISRs in First Class were serving lunch and the customer's beverage of choice. It was much the same in Coach, though the meal was less elaborate and the liquor for sale.

The Bascombs, a couple from rural south Texas, were in 20E and F. They planned to have a late dinner in Miami and get a good night's rest before boarding a cruise ship the next day. The husband dozed fitfully, trying to find a comfortable position, alternately leaning on the window and then his wife, who was absorbed in a novel.

Mrs. Bascomb wasn't feeling well. There was some queasiness, fatigue, and a persistent ache in her upper back on the flight from Brownsville. She began feeling a little short of breath after take-off from Houston but assumed it was the altitude, her age, or the excitement of the trip, one she and her husband had long dreamed about. She didn't say anything, not wanting to cause a fuss and figuring she would feel better after relaxing with her book.

No one else noticed when it happened, but they had been married for so long that her husband instinctively woke up. Something was terribly wrong, the terror in her eyes conveying a message she could no longer speak. Usually a reserved, quiet man, Mr. Bascomb shouted "Help!" so loudly that nearly every passenger's head whipped around and the entire cabin crew hurriedly converged from forward and aft.

In the few seconds it took the first ISR to arrive, Mrs. Bascomb had slumped over against her husband, unconscious. Responding to their training, two flight attendants quickly unbuckled the woman's seat belt, pulled her out into the aisle, and laid her down. Another retrieved a portable oxygen bottle.

The lead ISR, Rachel, knelt, loosened the passenger's clothing, and checked her ABCs—airway, breathing and circulation. Mrs. Bascomb's face was ashen and slick with sweat and she gasped for air with a sound like snoring.

Rachel checked at the wrist and neck and said, "No pulse." She crawled backwards into the space between the row of seats next to the passenger's head, the only place from where she could perform rescue breathing. Her colleague Allen shifted around to the other side, got his hands in the right spot, said "Go!" and started counting with the chest compressions.

This eliminated any question about needing to land. An ISR scurried toward the cockpit and the seat belt sign clicked on a moment later. A P.A. asked any medical professionals to identify themselves, instructed everyone to fasten their seatbelts, and cautioned that the urgent diversion would involve maneuvers that were "more abrupt than usual."

Despite this warning, an involuntary, collective "Ohhh…" resonated through the cabin when the Super 80 rolled into a sharp left turn and dropped into a steep descent.

Rachel braced against a seat to keep her balance. She knew the odds were long. They had to be a good half-hour from the nearest airport.

* * *

That Friday started innocuously enough for Drew. He had qualified in Ops soon after his one-year anniversary and had traded his evening shift there for the morning one. He then worked for a gate CSR until five. These machinations freed up the evening for dinner and the latest Bond movie with Brock, a devoted 007 fan. He was taking his girlfriend, Stacy, who was trying her hand at matchmaking by inviting her friend Desiree.

He clocked out when the gate CSR arrived. There was a change of clothes in his locker and he wasn't meeting his friends until six-thirty, so he returned to Ops. There, the conversation centered on a pushback tractor that was—supposedly—riding a flatbed their way. If true, would the apparatus, a hand-me-down made redundant by new equipment elsewhere, replace one of Moisant's pair or augment them? The second possibility implied additional flights, a welcome and encouraging development.

Someone wondered what Continental's emergence from bankruptcy might mean for the fight for Hobby. The talk turned to that until the radio interrupted with a short scratch of static followed by a loud voice that startled everyone in the room.

"New Orleans Ops, Tumbleweed Eight-nineteen overhead."

SEVENTEEN

Peggy acknowledged as Drew, Chuck, and Donna walked to the counter, curious. Hearing from a passing trip was rare. What was up?

Chuck checked the schedule and said, "Houston Miami."

The pilot continued, "New Orleans, we've got an unconscious female passenger who appears to be in cardiac arrest. We're coming your way, should be there in eighteen to twenty minutes. We've got ISRs attempting resuscitation and we'll need all the medical help you can find."

Donna ran behind the counter and dialed the airport emergency number.

Peggy responded, "Roger, Eight-nineteen, we're calling 'em now. Give me your fuel on board and we'll mark you in range." She was thinking ahead as usual, giving the crew one less thing to worry about.

"Okay, good plan, we'll call it in range with…stand by…make it nineteen point six."

Peggy looked at Donna, who nodded.

"Tumbleweed Eight-nineteen, copy in range with nineteen point six and CPR in progress. Take gate Seven Bravo on arrival and the paramedics are on the way."

"Roger, Seven Bravo for Tumbleweed Eight-nineteen."

Peggy radioed Grayson, then said, "Drew, can you call Southwest and see if they can move their next arrival so we can use Five Bravo?" Bringing an ambulance planeside took a long time because the access gate was across the airport. If they had to wheel the patient to curbside, 5B was the closest gate Ruff Air could use. Any competitor would gladly cooperate in such an emergency, but Southwest had an inbound due around the same time.

He called, then informed Peggy, "Their other jetbridge is down but the inbound is early. Five Bravo is fine if it's gone by the time ours gets here."

"Okay," Peggy said loudly so everyone could hear, "we'll set up for Seven but we'll go to Five if it's open." Donna called the CSR meeting the flight and explained the plan.

Grayson hurried in and Peggy quickly described the situation.

"Okay, got it," Grayson said. Spotting Drew, he motioned toward the office, closed the door behind them, and asked, "Aren't you off now? Can you stay and help with this?"

"Yes, sir, no problem."

"Good man. Them ISRs doing resuscitation won't be in any shape to go anywhere. Crew Sked might not want to pull 'em but they're comin' off anyway. Well, if it's a full crew. We need three to go on to Miami."

"Peggy checked. It's a full crew."

"Okay, good. I need to call Kelly and I have to talk to Dispatch and Crew Sked too." He picked up the phone and went on, "Gail's headed up there and I'll be there as soon as I can. Tell Gail, if the lady has kin or someone else with her, help 'em out however she can. What I want you to do is look after them ISRs. Get them something to eat, drive 'em to the hotel, whatever they need."

The CSR nodded and opened the door. Grayson hung up without dialing and said, "One more thing."

Drew paused in the doorway.

"Close the door." The supervisor lowered his voice. "If the worst has happened and I'm not there yet, get the paramedics to bring this lady out on the jetbridge before a doctor examines her. She can't die on that airplane."

"What? Why?"

"Nobody dies on an airplane, ever. If she's declared dead onboard, that plane's not going anywhere until the coroner releases it and that's not good for anybody, especially all those people got on in Houston expectin' to go to Miami."

Processing this potentially awkward tidbit, he looked back at Grayson.

"Well…okay."

After calling Brock to cancel his evening plans, he watched Gate 5B and wondered how anyone was supposed to carry out those instructions with even the slightest tact.

The radio crackled again. "New Orleans, Eight-nineteen on the ground for Seven Bravo. The passenger is still unresponsive."

Drew called out from the door, "Peggy, Southwest is pushing but we'll have to wait a minute if we go to Five."

"Okay," Peggy answered, "we'll stick with Seven." She keyed her mic and said, "Eight-nineteen roger, take Seven Bravo and the paramedics are waiting."

Drew radioed, "Eight-nineteen is on the ground. We're sticking with Seven Bravo, repeat Seven Bravo."

"Gate copies Seven Bravo."

"Ramp copies Seven Bravo."

Drew walked briskly toward Gate 7B. Taxiing from even the nearest runway took at least a couple of minutes. Nonetheless, the Super 80 suddenly appeared in his peripheral vision, passing at a startling clip, slowing only to turn into the gate. He bounded up the jetbridge stairs two at a time, feeling it move even as the jet shuddered to a stop.

The CSR knocked, the door opened, and the paramedics rushed aboard. Drew followed, stopping a few rows from where the woman lay.

A man, presumably her husband, stood nearby. His face was drawn with the strain and anxiety of watching strangers try to save his wife's life. The ISR counting compressions could be heard above the passengers' murmuring. Almost all were on their feet, craning their necks to see. The drama playing out was written in their expressions.

The paramedics took over resuscitation. One continued compressions while the other forced air into the patient's lungs by squeezing a rubbery bulb attached to a mask.

Two more paramedics appeared, waiting forward in case they were needed and studying their colleagues' efforts with professional interest. Drew happened to glance at the new arrivals just as one looked up and caught the other's eye. The corners of her mouth dropped and she gave a sad little shake of her head.

He couldn't help but gawk at the ISRs who had been aiding the stricken passenger. Each slouched in an empty seat, one behind the other, breathing hard, almost panting, their uniforms askew and dark with sweat as if they had run five miles at a record pace. Was CPR *that* hard to do?

Having never taken a class, he didn't know that even the fittest would-be rescuers found it tough to sustain for long. These two had been at it for over twenty arduous minutes. Perhaps they should have traded places with the other ISRs, but with adrenaline pumping, the hectic landing preparations underway, and already being in a rhythm, they had elected to keep going themselves. They had swapped several times between compressions and mouth-to-mouth, awkwardly due to the space constrictions, but it had to be done; a triathlete would have trouble performing twenty straight minutes of compressions. All things considered, each had given a heroic effort.

Something began stirring in his mind, a perception that would begin materializing only to dissolve away an instant later. It was about the woman, who seemed familiar somehow, though it was hard to tell much with her makeup ruined and soaked hair laid flat against her skull. But those striking blue eyes…

The memory clicked.

She's the one who dropped the trash bag that first day!

He forced himself to look elsewhere, then stole another glance. Yes, it was her.

Remembering his instructions, Drew turned to go forward only to see Grayson and a Jefferson Parish deputy come aboard. The supervisor spoke quietly to one of the paramedics, who nodded, left, and reappeared a moment later with a backboard. An airport regular, she knew the score. Grayson and the captain cleared a path to the ill passenger. With practiced precision, the paramedics secured the patient then recruited the deputy and a couple of burly passengers to help carry her. This proved a daunting task in the narrow aisle; making the turn out the cabin door required standing the backboard almost on end.

The first officer, her expression grim after a glimpse of the patient, went down the jetbridge stairs to do the walk-around. Tragedy or not, the flight had to depart as soon as possible.

An ISR named Grace was in the galley with one of the rescuers, Allen. He had unbuttoned his red serving vest, readjusted his tie, and finger-combed his hair but still looked shaken, his face flushed and beaded with sweat.

It was hard not to feel bad for him.

What's it like to be serving lunch one minute and fighting for someone's life the next?

Introducing himself, Drew caught Allen's gaze, the flight attendant's eyes as moist and red as his face.

"We did everything we could," Allen said, his tone defensive, as if an unspoken accusation was hanging in the air. "We did. We did everything we could."

"Of course you did," Drew replied, squeezing Allen's shoulder.

They heard a rumble as the paramedics and gurney hurried up the jetbridge. The husband and Gail followed, striding to keep up.

Maybe she still has a chance. Founded or not, hope was a comfort.

Grace had thoughtfully retrieved the couple's carry-on, the husband's Stetson, and some other belongings. The bag was just a bag but Mrs. Bascomb's glasses and book saddened him. Someone's life might have ended in their midst. Grace had recovered a bookmark from the floor and placed it inside the novel's back cover, an unintentional, poignant little allegory that fit right into this somber narrative.

She saw the flash of sorrow on Drew's face and said softly, "I hope she gets to finish that."

Grayson leaned in the door and waved him over. All business, he said, "Here, I'll take those up to Barb's office. Kelly's on her way and the captain says they'll be ready as soon as the fuelers are done. Peggy has the release and weight and balance.

Wendy will be down to close the door once she has the paperwork together. Make a P.A. then take care of the ISRs like I said. Whatever they need. Get petty cash from Mary if you need money and get receipts for anything you spend."

Drew made the announcement. As he replaced the handset, the trash tosser emerged from the lav. Her wings said Rachel and she held her serving apron bunched in one hand. She had washed her face, straightened her uniform, and brushed her hair, which was now tied back in a ponytail.

She hugged Allen and whispered, "It's okay. It'll be okay."

The stress of having someone's survival placed in their hands was obvious in her face too. She glanced at his name tag and said, "Drew, I'm Rachel. Do you know how she's doing?"

There was no need to speculate or to mention the one paramedic's silent assessment.

"They were still working on her when the paramedics took off up the jetbridge. Are you guys all right?" He caught himself. "I'm sorry, I know you're far from all right, but is there anything you need?"

"Do they have replacements for us by any chance?" Rachel asked. Her tone was about ten percent hope and ninety expectation that she and Allen would soon be serving sodas again on the way to Miami.

"That would be me," said Kelly, coming in with her purse and a small carry-on in hand. "You guys are out of here. Crew Sked has you set at the hotel and Drew here is going to get you over there."

Relieved in more ways than one, Rachel asked, "You have your manual, flashlight, and key? I'm sorry, what's your name?"

Kelly held up her carry-on. "Kelly and yes, complete with the latest updates."

Rachel said, "Aces. Okay, Grace takes over as the First. We didn't use the oxygen bottle so it's okay. Kelly, it's Captain Nolan and Rae Kilgore up front. Any questions?"

She fixed those incredible blue eyes back on Drew and said, "Give us a sec to grab our stuff."

God, it would be her. I hope she doesn't remember!

He thought it unlikely and so far, so good, not even a twinge of recognition.

At the hotel, he waited while the ISRs checked in.

"You don't have to stay," said Rachel when they were done. "We both need a shower so we'll grab something to eat later. Allen's planning to deadhead back to Hobby on the last trip tonight and I might do the same."

"It's no problem. There's not much within walking distance and I don't mind waiting while you get ready. No reason for you guys to screw around with cabs or shuttles after the day you've had."

"Don't you have to get back?"

"No, I'm off. Stopped in Ops on the way out to talk about a rumor that's going around and then you guys showed up."

"You're off the clock? Go home. You don't need to babysit us or drive us around."

"It's really no problem." Surely overtime would be approved, but it didn't matter; he was more concerned about his two colleagues.

Rachel asked Allen, "You game for dinner? It beats room service, and it'll be good to talk."

"No, I don't feel up to it," said Allen, looking at the floor, still obviously upset. "I'm going to try and get a couple hours of sleep." That's all there would be time for. The last Houston flight left at 10:30 p.m.

She turned back and asked Drew, "You're sure?"

"I'm sure." He told himself, not at all convincingly, that he would have answered the same had Rachel been the one heading off to bed.

"Well, thanks, that's sweet of you. I'll be down in ten." She and Allen headed for the elevators, their rolling bags clack-clacking across the tile floor.

Drew sat and leafed through a magazine, but the scene onboard wouldn't leave his mind. The wife lying in the aisle, slack and pale; her distressed husband's look of foreboding, as if he knew the thing he feared most in the world was happening right before his eyes; how they were both dressed in Sunday clothes like air travelers of bygone eras; the other passengers, spellbound by the unfolding tragedy, some near tears and a few already crying at what they were witnessing; a couple of toddlers clinging to their parents, not comprehending the situation but unsettled nonetheless by the unmistakable ambiance of urgency, dismay, and sadness.

He tossed the magazine onto the side table and deposited a dime into a pay phone.

Rachel returned fifteen minutes later in jeans, a short-sleeved blouse, and sandals. Drew stood as she approached and when she saw his expression, she stopped and looked down at herself.

"What, is something wrong?"

"No, no," he stammered, "not at all. It's just odd to see someone in regular clothes when you always see them in a uniform." That was true, at least partially, the real story being that the sight of her had gridlocked his neurons again.

You better watch that, Chief.

"Yeah, I guess it is now that you mention it." She nodded back toward the elevators. "Allen's pretty shook up."

"No prob, do you need more time?"

"No, he's asleep. Look, I can't even think about eating. Can you call and find out what hospital she went to?"

"I already did and would be happy to take you over there."

"Really? I mean how did you know I'd want to go?"

"I wasn't even there five minutes and I want to, so I figured you would too."

The blue eyes reappraised him and he was pleased by what he saw in them.

Rachel left a wakeup call for Allen, then asked, "You're really okay on time?"

"Yes, I work tomorrow at three."

The fifteen-minute ride passed in near silence. Rachel stared out the window and he couldn't think of anything to say given the situation.

Gail stood as they entered the emergency room, her eyes red.

"She didn't make it."

Rachel, crestfallen, sat down and said, "Damn it!"

Gail went on in a small voice. "They took her husband to tell her good-bye. The doctor said she would've been gone long before you even landed if not for you guys. You were too far out, but you gave her a chance."

Rachel nodded glumly, looking at the floor.

A woman came out from somewhere and asked, "You're from the airline? Mr. Bascomb wants to go home but he's in no condition to travel alone. He says he can call his daughter in Dallas. Can you arrange a ticket for her to come travel with him?"

"Yes, ma'am," said Gail. "From Dallas she could be here by about nine tomorrow morning."

"Oh dear," said the woman, "tomorrow?"

"Yes," replied Gail. "We don't fly from Dallas nonstop to here and I'm afraid it's too late to connect through Houston tonight."

Rachel said, "I have a better idea. I'll go with him if he's okay with it."

Everyone looked at her in surprise.

"He needs to be home asap, right? I'm off the next two days. We'll book him at our hotel in case he needs anything tonight and if we go out on the first trip, we'll be in Brownsville by the time his daughter could get here. She can meet us there. Better yet, if she gets the first flight, she can probably meet us at Hobby."

"I'll drive you guys to the hotel and pick you up in the morning," volunteered Drew, impressed by Rachel's selflessness.

Rachel turned to the hospital rep and asked, "What about Mrs. Bascomb?"

"There's nothing suspicious about the cause of death so the remains can be released immediately. Does your company have someone local for…these circumstances?"

Gail said, "Let me see what I can find out. Is there a phone I can use?"

Mr. Bascomb was agreeable and, amazingly, everything was in place an hour later. Barb called the Ops VP, receiving carte blanche to do whatever she deemed necessary. Mary booked Mr. Bascomb at the hotel and arranged special positive space passes for Mr. Bascomb, his daughter Kimberly, and Rachel, ensuring they would be accommodated even if their flights were full. A funeral director was on the way and had recruited a friend at the coroner's office to fast-track the transit permit. He also promised to personally work as late as necessary to ensure Mrs. Bascomb could travel with her husband.

Meanwhile, Carla had contacted her baggage service counterparts in Miami, who assured her they would expedite the luggage back to Brownsville. Finally, the Ops VP had called the chief pilot and the director of in-flight service, and Barb the station managers in Dallas, Houston, and Brownsville, to make sure crews and ground staff alike were aware of their special passengers.

Rachel was helping Mr. Bascomb finish up the hospital paperwork, so Drew walked Gail to her car.

"What is this?" she marveled. "Sometimes it takes an act of Congress to get an extra carton of boarding passes for Thanksgiving week but we pulled *that* together in an hour?" She had a point.

"Tell me something," she went on while unlocking her car door. "Do you like this Rachel?"

The question caught him off guard.

"I don't know. She's okay, I guess. Why?"

Gail wasn't buying it. "Okay, you like her, that's what I thought. Well, good, because there's something about you two I can't quite put my finger on. You just look like a couple."

"What are you talking about?" he protested. "I've known her about fifteen minutes!"

"You'll see," Gail said with an enigmatic little smile.

"Uh huh. So what else is in your crystal ball?'"

"Scoff if you want but she seems sweet. You could do a lot worse."

With nothing to rebut that argument, he said, "See you tomorrow, Carnac," and closed her door.

Gail made a face and stuck out her tongue as she started the engine.

Rachel came out, beckoned to him, then mimicked driving with her hands on an imaginary wheel.

He brought up the car and she emerged with Mr. Bascomb a few minutes later. He was tall and thin but had the muscle, rough hands, and lined, leathery face of someone used to doing hard work under a hot sun. His clothes were Western; he wore a Bolo tie and held his Stetson in both hands. Drew's first impression back on the plane had been of a tough, self-reliant type, maybe a rancher. But his wife's death had staggered the man and he looked to have aged a decade since.

Wait, how does he have his hat?

Rachel insisted Mr. Bascomb take the passenger seat and squeezed into the back. They rode in silence. Drew got occasional glimpses of his passengers, each of whom was staring out a window. Rachel looked dispirited, as if replaying the scene looking for flaws in her actions or something more she could have done. Aside from his obvious sorrow, Mr. Bascomb was as clearly unaccustomed to having to count on others or to deal with raw, life-changing events in the company of strangers.

Still, he hadn't forgotten his manners. Nearing the hotel, he said in his deep Texas drawl, "Rachel, I thank you for everything you did on the plane and for coming to the hospital."

Rachel looked at Mr. Bascomb, eyes wet, and put her hand on his shoulder.

"I'm so sorry we couldn't save her."

"The steward who helped you, will he be at the hotel?"

"Allen? Yes, but I don't know if we'll see him."

"Well, I would like to thank him too."

Mary was waiting in the coolness of the hotel lobby.

"Our condolences for your loss, Mr. Bascomb."

"Thank you, Miss."

"I have your room key and here's your carry-on and some toiletries. Rachel's room is right next door in case you need anything."

Allen appeared from the hall leading to the elevators. He had the same downtrodden expression as Rachel.

Mr. Bascomb spotted him and said, "There he is. Come here." He took Allen's hand in both of his own, shook it warmly, and said, "Thank you for all you did."

Allen was trying hard to keep himself together.

"I'm so sorry— "

"Just stop right there, son," Mr. Bascomb interrupted. Face wrenched with emotion, he turned to include Rachel and continued, "I had forty-seven wonderful years with the love of my life and for that I'm grateful. If you two are saying you're sorry for my loss, that's fine, and I'm obliged. But it sounds more like you're apologizing, and I won't have that. You both did your very best. It was Millie's time and nobody but God could have changed that."

Rachel and Allen both looked as if a great weight had lifted.

"Now," Mr. Bascomb went on, "I've got to go and do something awful tough. Tell my little girl that her Mama has passed." He brought out a handkerchief and snuffled into it. "So Rachel, if you'll tell me what time to meet you tomorrow?"

She wasn't about to send him up alone. Once he was situated, Rachel made sure he had whatever clothes he needed, ordered him dinner through room service, then returned to the lobby.

"Did Allen go back to the airport with Mary?"

"Yes, they just left. Quite a day."

"Definitely wasn't your garden variety Miami turnaround, that's for sure. Did you notice he had his hat?"

"I was wondering about that. The last I saw of it was when Grayson took it on the jetbridge."

"Gail said Grayson knew he would feel uncomfortable without it, so he gave it to one of the agents who lives over toward the hospital and asked her to drop it off on her way home."

"Have to say that wouldn't have occurred to me. Hey, aren't you hungry? You probably want to stay here in case Mr. B needs anything but I could bring you something."

"I'm not, really, but thanks."

She hugged him.

Surprised, he asked, "What was that for?"

"Just thanks. You've been great."

"I'm glad I could help."

A spark of mischief crept into the blue eyes. "Yeah, you did pretty good for a guy who can't catch a bag of trash."

Drew looked at the ceiling, the floor, then back at her. "I was *really* hoping you had forgotten that."

"Oh no, my friend, oh no. Upstairs uniform or not, I knew the minute I came out of the lav. And I've waited a long time to hear exactly what *that* was all about."

This unanticipated turn called for an intense collaborative effort by every power of reason he possessed. It produced exactly one syllable.

"Uh…"

"Oh, not now. I'm much too tired to enjoy it. Mr. B and I are on the seven-ten to Hobby in the morning. Are you still game to pick us up? It'll be early, say around six?"

"I'll be here."

"Good, I'd like that. We won't have time to talk tomorrow but I'll be back Monday on a layover. It'll be late for dinner but if you're not working or…busy, let's have a drink."

"Busy?"

"Hey, I don't see a ring but you might have a girlfriend for all I know. Wouldn't want any misunderstandings."

"I'm off at eight-thirty and have no plans whatsoever." Any he might have had would have been jettisoned immediately regardless.

"Good. Monday it is."

Drew headed home, tired and saddened by the day's events. The lights were coming on downtown and those nearest the river left rippling reflections on its surface. Driving down the Westbank side of the GNO, he said a quiet prayer for Mrs. Bascomb and all who loved her.

EIGHTEEN

The alarm never sounded the next morning. Drew was already relaxing over breakfast on his tiny balcony. He took a deep breath, savoring the still, relatively cool air, flavored with the scents of earth and tropical plants. Dawn was his favorite time to be outside, even on a typically humid day like this when the air was so heavy with moisture that white mist layered the canals and crawled around the cypress roots under limbs strung with wispy gray-green moss.

He couldn't keep his mind off of Rachel. A lot of guys would probably hesitate to approach her at all. Those who did would have a tough time seeing past her looks, or wouldn't care much what they found if they bothered to try. The emergency had allowed him to sidestep that trap, providing a fortunate glimpse right into her kind and selfless heart.

When his raisin bran was gone, he stretched his arms over his head, took another look at the morning sky, and went in. He dressed in his Class A uniform. Although he wouldn't be on duty until hitting the ramp at three and would come home in between, the uniform felt more appropriate for this occasion.

Rachel and Mr. Bascomb were waiting when he arrived at 5:55 and they arrived at the airport ten minutes later. Rachel took Mr. Bascomb in while Drew parked in short-term.

"Barb took them into her office," said Mary when he walked in. She was filling in for Kelly, who was on her way back from Miami. They looked at each other uncomfortably when they heard faint crying, both feeling helpless.

Rachel came out a few minutes later.

"He was doing pretty well until we gave him his wife's book and glasses," she explained. "I can't begin to imagine what he's going through."

She asked Mary for the Ops number. Mary dialed and handed Rachel the receiver.

"Hi, it's Rachel. I'm the ISR escorting Mr. Bascomb to Brownsville. Who's this? Okay, Marissa, can you do me a favor and call Barb's office when the hearse is headed planeside? Okay…okay. Great, thanks."

"He wants to be at the gate when the hearse gets there?" asked Mary.

"He does."

"I'd think that would upset him more," said Drew.

"That's what I thought too," replied Rachel. "But Barb asked and he said yes."

"Live and learn," said Mary.

Drew looked at his watch. "The outbound crew should be here. Do you need to talk with them?"

"No, I caught 'em last night at the hotel. They'll take good care of us. I also got ahold of a girlfriend from college who lives in Brownsville. We're having dinner then I'll fly home tomorrow."

"What about breakfast, should I bring something up from the cafeteria?"

"No, thanks, we ate at the hotel."

Marissa called ten minutes later. Barb, Mr. Bascomb, Rachel, and Drew made their way down to 7B, arriving as the hearse, led by Grayson in the company pickup, rounded the end of Concourse C across the way.

Rondell, the gate CSR, told Barb, "We can board them whenever, ma'am, just let us know."

Grayson parked and joined the flight's captain and three rampers, who waited near a belt loader borrowed from Ozark. Curiously, the pilot was wearing his coat. They always wore their hats outside, but never their coats in summer.

There weren't many passengers so early on a Saturday. Most came over to see what was going on.

The Ruff Air group and the two funeral home representatives reverently transferred the human remains container, known as an airtray, to the belt loader. Then one ramper climbed up into the belly while the other two, Grayson, and the captain formed a line next to the belt loader. The funeral home duo started toward the hearse but realized what was happening and hurried back.

A hush had fallen over the spectators, which now included virtually everyone near the gate and even two Trans Global agents who would soon work a flight at 9B.

Grayson started the belt. The cadre next to the loader came to attention and the captain executed the slow hand salute usually seen at military funerals. Now the coat made sense. The airtray disappeared and the two rampers followed to help position it in the hold.

Mr. Bascomb's face showed what the expression of respect meant to him. Drew was proud to have colleagues who would think to do such a thing. They didn't know her husband would be watching; it was just who they were.

Mr. Bascomb had long handshakes and heartfelt words of gratitude for all. Drew walked back to the terminal with the station manager once the flight departed, knowing her well enough not to make small talk.

In the hall behind the counter, she said, "Come into my office for a minute."

She stood behind her desk and said, "Rachel and Grayson said some very nice things about the way you handled yourself yesterday and this morning, staying over and coming out early today. I appreciate it." Drew thanked her and headed out.

Wow…feels damn good to have come so far since the chocks mess!
Henry waved him down on the way out.

"Hey, you interested in some hours?"

"Always. When?"

"Now." Trades were supposed to be prearranged, but Mary approved it. Drew had learned to keep his steel-toed shoes and a spare ramp suit downstairs. He moved the car to employee parking, rode the shuttle back, and went to clock in.

Grayson looked up from a report he was filling out.

"You got receipts from yesterday?"

"No, I didn't spend any money. They weren't hungry or anything."

"Good. Use an expense form for your mileage and I'll have Barb approve that and the overtime."

"How about we call it even? I wouldn't feel right taking money for helping out on something like that. I was glad to do it. Rachel isn't getting paid for going to Brownsville, is she?"

"I reckon not," he said, his approval evident.

Henry was working Express Check-In so Drew grabbed his validation stamp and headed out front. An idea was bubbling around and once he had relieved Henry, he worked on it whenever there were no customers. By noon, everything was ready.

* * *

Yesterday, it had seemed like a great plan. Gail loved it; first she smiled and said, "I think it's sweet!" She went on with a mock pout. "In fact, I'm kinda jealous."

Somehow Drew kept *Oh, don't even…* off his face.

But now second thoughts crept in as he waited at a concourse window in Houston.

Is this maybe going a bit overboard?

Too late; the marshaler climbed onto the pushback tractor and the gaggle of hobnobbing rampers broke up, its members tugging at gloves and hearing protectors. The familiar jet whine grew and a Super 50 taxied into view.

To his relief, Rachel's face lit up when she emerged from the jetbridge. She looked a little pale and a lot of tired.

He hoped all that had happened might have exiled the garbage thing from her mind. But while the emergency and her unexpected escort duty had clearly taken a toll, her memory and sense of humor were both quite intact.

"Where's a big ripe sack of trash when you need one?" she asked with one of her dazzling smiles.

Drew looked around, grinning self-consciously. "I could probably find one if you'd like, but I really hope that's not all you think of when you see me."

"Nah, just razzin' ya. Where ya headed?"

"Here."

"Cool, so what's up, they sent you over for training or something?"

"Not exactly."

Surprised, she said, "Don't tell me you're here to see *me*."

"Guilty as charged. I wanted to make sure you were okay. Maybe buy you lunch if you're up for it? I listed on the two o'clock back to New Orleans."

"That's really sweet of you. I'm okay, or at least I think I am."

"Well, whatever works for you works for me. Please feel free to take a raincheck. I can leave on the next trip if you'd rather go home and sleep."

She thought it over, then said, "Lunch sounds pretty good. Come to think of it, I'm starved."

"Okay, as long as you're not 'busy.'"

She smiled.

"Touché!"

She took his arm, a pleasant surprise, and they started down the concourse.

"Let's go somewhere outside the airport," she suggested. "It's early enough."

"Sounds good. Dodging the rumor mill?"

"No, anybody with nothing better to do than talk about my love life is welcome to it. I'm just sick of airport food. And airports for that matter."

"That doesn't seem like a good thing for a flight attendant. Wait, your love life?"

"Reel it in, Romeo. I was going on what they'd assume."

"Okay, good. Don't want you getting your hopes up or anything."

"Ooooh," she said, squeezing his arm. "He gives it as good as he gets it, huh? I like that, I like it. But let's see how it works out for ya."

Her tone turned thoughtful.

"You're leaving when? Two?"

"Actually, I work tomorrow at twelve, so I can go whenever." He stopped walking and went on, "But I'm guessing you're beat and I did show up unannounced so seriously, like I said, a raincheck is fine."

She looked at him thoughtfully.

"I have to say I'm impressed. You really wanted to check on me."

"As opposed to…"

"Being some presumptuous jackass making nice while really hoping to get laid."

Damn, she says what's on her mind!

He thought a moment, then said, "Well, I can't say the fact you're attractive had *nothing* to do with it, or that I would've met Allen's flight, but getting laid? Nope."

"Fair enough," she said. "Granted, I haven't exactly been pageant material the last couple of days."

His tone grew serious. "You've been through a lot. Most people go a whole career without a situation like that."

She said nothing but he could see sorrow on her face. She gave his arm a little squeeze.

Rachel's car was an older Honda, its interior spotless and the body polished under the inevitable metropolitan dust. They headed south to a Mexican place Rachel frequented.

"I'm such a regular there," she noted, "they probably wave when my trips fly over."

The hostess greeted her by name and showed them to a booth, where they each quickly decided on chicken fajitas and dug into the chips and salsa.

"So that's about it," she said after recounting Saturday's events. "Like I said, Mr. B.'s daughter Kimberly met us at Hobby and what looked like the whole rest of the family was there in Brownsville. What a nice man. He introduced me to everyone and treated me like I was one of them. He'll be okay. It's just going to take some time."

"A long time, I'd think."

"Yes." The sorrow returned to her face. "They'll be in my heart for a long time too."

"Same here," he replied. "So I'm curious. I was really surprised when you volunteered to fly home with Mr. B. What made you do that?"

Rachel tilted her head, thinking. Her eyes welled, she looked down at the table, and her lip quivered slightly before she said, "My dad died about eight months ago. Cancer. He was in hospice near the end and the people there and at the hospital before were amazing. I'd never lost anyone close to me and I learned first-hand what it does to you. I'd have had trouble tying my sneakers right after he died. It…I don't know, your heart just swells up with pain and hurt and sadness to where you can't even think straight. The nurses and hospice workers knew how it would be and they helped so much.

"Daddy's doctor said he could go in an hour or three weeks, there was no way to know. I couldn't afford not to work so I was flying a week or so later when he took a turn for the worse. My mom didn't call and one of the nurses asked why. Daddy looked pretty awful by then and Mom said she didn't want that to be my last memory of him. The nurse asked, very gently but very firmly, 'Shouldn't that be Rachel's decision?' Mom knew she was right so she called Crew Sked and I barely got back in time to see him. I will be grateful to that nurse *forever* for giving me the chance to hug my father one last time and tell him good-bye."

Drew was moved. He reached out and took her hand as she rubbed away a tear with the other one.

"I'm so sorry about your dad. I can't imagine." And he couldn't, not Mom or Dad being gone. It seemed like it should be a long way off, but you never knew.

"I'm sorry for asking, too," he added. "I didn't mean to upset you."

"It's okay, I don't mind talking about it. Anyway, I knew Dad was terminal and it still wiped me out. But when it's unexpected, like this? One minute they're leaving for a vacation they've put off for years and the next she's gone? Forty-seven years, over like that? I thought maybe I could kind of look out for him like the hospice people did for us until his world got right side up again, or at least until he was with his family. It felt like repaying the kindness we were shown."

"Well, it was amazing. What you did? I'm a little ashamed to say it never would have occurred to me."

She smiled a little, squeezed his hand, and said, almost shyly, "You're sweet."

"Did you guys save room for dessert?" asked the server, who had seemingly appeared out of nowhere.

For reasons neither knew, they clumsily withdrew their hands as if a teacher had caught them under the bleachers.

"The sopapillas with ice cream look pretty good, want to share?"

"Nothing for me," Rachel replied, "but you go ahead."

"Just the check, then, please."

The server left.

"Not in the mood for dessert? Don't tell me you don't like sopapillas."

"I'd kill for dessert and I love sopapillas but I have to weigh in Friday."

"Weigh in? *You're* on a diet?"

She laughed. "No, silly, for work."

Stewardesses had to meet all kinds of standards in the old days, but that was ancient history, wasn't it?

"Seriously, they still do that?"

"Oh yeah. Big trouble if you're over, especially if it's a supe you don't get along with."

"How much can you weigh? Is there a chart or something?"

"Yep, and if that chart ever goes away, laxative sales will take quite a hit."

"*What?*"

"People will do almost anything to make weight. Starve themselves, hit the Ex-Lax, make themselves barf, all three if their backs are against the wall...you name it, somebody's tried it."

Surprised, he made a face, then asked, "Is it a Ruff Air thing?"

"No, it's everybody. My girlfriend applied at American and they flew her to DFW for an interview. But they weighed everybody first. She was a pound and a half over. They told her she could reapply in a year and sent her straight back to the airport."

"Damn, that's rough. What about age limits and being single and all that?"

"No, that stuff at least is gone now, thank God. Did you know Pan Am stews even had *girdle checks?* That must have been something to see. But we still have plenty of rules."

"Such as?"

"Let's see…well, your hair can't be too long, and neither can your nails."

"But how would they know?"

"They measure."

"Actually measure, like with a ruler?"

"Yep. Our makeup has to be done a certain way and our nails have to be painted too."

"Damn, they keep you guys on a short leash."

"Yes, they do."

Should he get the trash thing over with?

Might as well.

"Okay, you ready for the trash story?"

"I already know it."

"How do you mean?"

The blue eyes steadied on his, a sparkle of amusement evident.

"I was screwin' with you in New Orleans. Hey, it's not rocket science. The wind's blowing, we're hanging out a door ten feet up wearing a skirt with a slit up one side almost to…well, you know, and some newbie is looking up expecting…well, not that. You weren't the first guy to go goo-goo and you won't be the last. The funniest is when some clown is trying to look all cool and casual while he's about dislocating his neck trying to get a peek. That's when my drop might be a little high and inside."

"Are you kidding?"

"Nope. I've nailed a couple too."

Drew chuckled. "Good to know. And thanks for not making me stammer through the story."

She frowned but the twinkle in her eyes remained. "Damn…that would've been fun."

"I think you've had quite enough fun with that." Switching gears, he added, "You know, once I started working gates, I figured I might see you again sometime. On a trip I mean."

"I don't get to New Orleans much. I like the long hauls so I always bid the Houston non-stops to Miami, L.A., San Francisco, maybe Vegas now and again for a change. Makes for a long day on turnarounds but I don't mind. I had traded trips the day we dropped in."

"Lucky me."

She smiled self-consciously.

Is she blushing?

In the car, Drew said, "Okay, back to the weighing in thing. If you can't have dessert, how is it you drink? Isn't that a lot of empty calories?"

"Yes, but it's only one, and only on special occasions. So, you want to catch a movie or something? You can go back later, right?" A yawn almost swallowed the last word.

"I'd like that, but why don't you grab a nap? You can drop me at a coffee shop or wherever."

She looked over. "I look that bad?"

"Just a slight case of raccoon eyes, nothing horrible. Like I said, you have to be beat."

"A nap sounds heavenly, but I don't want to be rude."

"What would be rude would be to show up from out of town and drag you to a movie or expect you to keep me entertained when you're this tired."

"I'd only need an hour."

"Take your time."

"I don't feel right dumping you somewhere. Would you be okay watching TV at my place? I mean, you won't raid my medicine cabinet or rummage through my closets while I sleep, will you?"

"I never rummage without express permission."

"Well, *that's* a relief."

The eclectic furnishings of Rachel's tidy apartment reflected the fiscal constraints of small carrier pay scales. She had united the various elements into a pleasing whole and added a spectacular gallery of photographs that told her story through the years. Large and small, the images were a lovely blend of family, pets, travel, nature, and their airline.

Here she was next to a tuk-tuk in Bangkok, her arm around the driver, who looked uncomfortable with the attention; on the steps of the Sydney opera house, arms outstretched and mouth open like a diva immersed in a soaring aria; leaning on a Paris streetlamp with mock seductiveness, the Eiffel Tower as gray as a pencil drawing against a misty evening sky; glowing with pride and camaraderie in her ISR class graduation photo.

"The ones you're not in, did you take them?"

"Every last one," she called back from the bedroom.

When she returned in a faded Broncos t-shirt and sleep shorts, he said, "You have a good eye!"

"Thanks!" she replied, beaming. "I love it. I wish I had room for all my favorites."

"I'm in the same boat."

"You shoot too?"

"Every chance I get. Took a day trip to Miami a while back to get the Concorde. What an incredible airplane."

"It is. I saw it at DFW. So, Canon or Nikon?"

"Canon, of course."

"Oh well," she said, with snobby pretense. "Nobody's perfect."

"Nikon fan, huh? Ever tried a Canon?"

"Nope."

"You can borrow mine sometime. In the meantime, you can at least dream about using a Canon."

"Oh yeah," she said sheepishly, "a nap is what we came for, isn't it? The remote's there on the coffee table. I only have basic cable so I hope you're not bored. Help yourself to anything in the kitchen. Oh, and there's beer in the fridge."

"Thanks, but I don't drink beer. Or much of anything for that matter."

"You're from New Orleans and you don't drink?"

"I don't like a lot of seafood either."

"*What?* Oh, you are warped. Okay, see you in an hour."

Just making the rounds admiring the gallery of photos took nearly that long. She had captured several subjects from unique perspectives and had a talent for using light to add texture and impact to her work.

He grabbed a soft drink and settled in on her sofa to watch TV. The Astros and Reds were in extra innings. Somewhere between a sac fly and a double play, the surreality caught up to him.

Two days ago I didn't even know her name. Now I'm sitting in her apartment watching baseball?

The emergency, the shared sense of mission, had broken down the barriers, fast-forwarding them past many of the awkward rituals. Not that he was complaining.

A couple of outs later, there were footsteps in the hall, then Rachel plopped down on the other end of the sofa.

"I hope you feel special," she said. "I used to think I'd never even let a husband see me like this."

"You look pretty good compared to yesterday."

"Wow, thanks," she replied. "That helps. Yeah, that *really* helps."

They both laughed. He couldn't get enough of her smile.

"Hey," Rachel said, turning serious, "thank you for listening at the restaurant. I don't know if *I* even understood why I wanted to help Mr. Bascomb until you asked me. I hadn't really thought about it."

"You're very welcome."

"Honestly, I don't feel much like going out. Would you mind if we hung out here? Maybe we'll get a pizza if you're okay taking a later trip home."

"Sure, how much later?"

"Maybe the eight o'clock?"

Res said the flights were wide open, no surprise on Sunday evening. Suddenly Rachel waved to get his attention then held up both hands splayed and mouthed, "Do the ten-thirty!"

Well, that's a very pleasant surprise.

After he hung up, she said, "Sorry, this is more fun than I've had in a while."

"I don't know whether to pity you or be flattered."

"Maybe both?"

More laughter, then they spent the evening talking, sharing war stories, and looking at box after box of pictures.

"Where is this?" he asked, holding up a snapshot of Rachel and two other ISRs, smiling from a wing with a backdrop of towering bluish mountains capped with snow.

"That was a charter to Salt Lake."

"How'd you get out there? Pull an emergency exit?"

"Yep. You can't on a widebody 'cause some have slides in the wing exits but it's no problem on a Mad Dog."

Rachel grinned. "You know what I remember most about that trip? The group was staying a week so we ferried the airplane back empty. See the blonde there, Angie? She'd done charters before and knew the pilots like to hot dog a little with no passengers, and the airplane's light so it really goes. You don't have to buckle up like on a regular trip—well, you should but who's the wiser? So on takeoff, you start by the galley, sitting on a serving tray—"

"Sitting on a serving tray?"

"Bear with me. You let go when the nose comes off and as the climb gets steeper, off you go, sailing down the aisle like you're sledding down a hill! It was a blast! Well, except one time where we didn't know there was a noise abatement turn. Angie crashed into an armrest and busted her lip pretty good."

"The secret lives of ISRs!"

She grinned. "We have some stories, my friend."

He recognized a couple of Rachel's classmates in her ISR graduation photo.

"Isn't that Valerie?" he asked. "I didn't know you're a Pioneer. I didn't see a pin the other day."

"Wow, you don't miss much, do you? No, I'm thinking it fell off during the CPR. It was gone when I changed at the hotel, so that's all I can think of. Nobody's turned it in. Breaks my heart to lose it after all these years. They're sending another one, but it's not the same, right? But anyway, yes, that's Valerie.

We were the three and four on the very first flight, Hobby to Love and back. Look, here's a picture."

There were balloons, cakes decorated like the cities' destination posters, news crews, and even a trio of classical musicians.

"What the heck is that?"

"A champagne fountain. Can you believe that? And the airplane was straight from overhaul, clean, everything worked, and those leather seats were brand new and smelled soooo good. We were all jazzed and so were the customers." She smiled wistfully. "That was a great, great day."

Everyone knew Valerie, who was legendary for her poise with even the rudest or most demanding customers.

Rachel asked, "Have you ever heard why Valerie became a flight attendant? She tells it better but what a story!"

The airline bug bit Valerie on her very first flight. Fortunately, the bat didn't.

Her university's European tour charter to Paris devolved into an almost inconceivable series of delays and diversions. Shortly after takeoff from Chicago, a warning light forced the pilots to dump fuel and return to O'Hare. Hours later, the flight departed again, but soon the dispatcher and operations center manager were trying to decipher a curious message: RTRNING ORD ACCT LIVE BAT IN LAV.

"That has to be a typo," the dispatcher said.

It wasn't. The stowaway, *Lasionycteris noctivagans* to be exact, had sent a shrieking passenger bolting from a bathroom just after the flight reached cruise altitude. The dispatcher informed the O'Hare station to prepare for another return only to receive a follow-up communication a few minutes later:

BAT DCSD, PROCDNG PARIS.

Rachel explained, to which he replied incredulously, "The flight engineer *killed* it? How?"

"He caught the damn thing in a freakin' blanket and crushed it! I mean, you don't want to go back to Chicago again but holy shit, right?"

So the charter U-turned again, resuming course for Paris only to divert to Gander after a passenger fell ill. On the ground there, the pilots reached their legal duty time limits, so a fresh crew had to be sent. Finally, thirty-four hours after boarding, the exhausted students finally dragged themselves off the plane in Paris. Despite all the issues, Valerie had returned home knowing she would earn her wings one day.

"Your turn," Rachel said.

"Well, I can't top that, but on a through trip from Houston going on to Tampa, this woman got off to stretch her legs—"

Rachel knew what was coming, at least in part.

"And missed the flight?"

"Exactly." It happened often; despite announcements, passengers unused to such short stops deplaned, used the restroom, picked up a newspaper or candy bar, browsed the magazines, and returned to an empty gate.

Drew continued, "Her husband told the ISRs right after they pushed. The captain was going to hold and drop the airstairs so we could run her out on a tug. But the husband said no, it wasn't right to hold up the whole plane."

"No way! I mean, good for him for being considerate, but wow!"

He nodded and said, "It gets even better. When the crew called the times, they said the guy wanted his wife to get a cab to their hotel because he wasn't going to waste one minute of his vacation waiting for her at the airport!"

"Nooooo way!" she exclaimed again. "I would have *loved* to be a fly on the wall when she finally got there."

"Can you imagine?"

They laughed, looked at each other and laughed some more. One or the other would recall a funny moment from that story or Valerie's or another they had shared and crack up again. The laughter fed on itself until neither could stop.

But suddenly something was different. Rachel's expression changed and she slumped over, her face in her hands. She wasn't laughing anymore, she was crying.

"Whoa." He scooted over to get his arms around her. Her body shook as she sobbed and wailed. He had never witnessed such pain and sensed it was best to just hold her.

Finally, she quieted, sat up, and took a handful of tissues he offered from a box on the end table. Clearly self-conscious, she patted her eyes, wiped her nose, and said, "I'm sorry. I don't know where that came from. Well, I guess I do…I miss my Daddy so much and I never really had a good cry when he died. There was so much to do and my mom was so broken up and then I had to go right back to work. This whole thing with Mr. and Mrs. Bascomb was so sad and it…I don't know, cranked the handle on the jack-in-the-box or something. Sorry you had to be here when the clown popped out."

"I'm not. We all need someone when our clowns pop out."

Her eyes widened in surprise and his in embarrassment at this reply, kindly intended but monumentally goofy. She giggled and said, "God, don't get me started again, I don't know if I have it in me."

"Sorry, that didn't come out quite right."

"You think?"

It was almost time to leave. Rachel washed her face and changed into jeans.

Nearing Hobby, she said she would walk him to the gate. Drew insisted she drop him at curbside so she could get home and sleep as soon as possible.

Slowing in the Departures zone, she said, "Are we still on for Monday night? Holy cow, that's tomorrow! God, this weekend flew by."

"What time do you get in?"

"It's pretty early for a layover trip…I think it's a little before seven?"

"Yeah, from Orlando, right?"

"That's the one."

"I'll come by the hotel when I get off."

This was rough. Drew wanted to kiss her so bad he could taste it, but it didn't feel right.

He decided not to push it, and would have been astounded to know she was thinking the exact same thing.

He reached over and squeezed her hand.

"Are you going to be okay?"

"Yeah," she said, "I got it out of my system. I needed that and I feel a lot better actually. Hey, wait a sec when you get out, okay?"

He did, and Rachel came around the car and hugged him tightly. When she stepped back, she was blinking back tears.

"Thank you, Drew. For helping with Mr. B and coming over here, because I was afraid I'd lose it when I got home and I did but you were there to hold me. And for being a gentleman, too. Like I said before, with me being so upset and tired and all…well, some guys might've tried to—"

"I wouldn't ever want it to be like that."

"I know," she replied. "And that's just one of the things I like about you." She kissed the tip of his nose and said, "Safe travels. See you tomorrow."

They thought about each other all the way home.

NINETEEN

Rachel's flight from Orlando was fifteen minutes late. This worked well since Drew could delay his counter break until the flight was in range. Also fortunate were Gail being the CSR meeting the trip and it being a terminator with no outbound passengers. He could thus talk with Gail without garnering undue attention or dropping quarters in the gossip-go-round.

She knew why he was there and was delighted to play armchair Cupid.

"Flowers," she declared, head tilted slightly with a look of mild disapproval. "Why don't you have flowers?"

"Yeah, that would be subtle," he replied, leaning on the wall behind the podium. "Forget the station, Whiskey Whiskey would hear about that before these guys are on the hotel van. I'm only here to tell her hello."

She rolled her eyes. "Right, old man Ruff's got a special red phone for updates on you and your chicks."

"Chick, singular, and she's not mine."

"Yes, she is," Gail said, looking into his eyes. "Just like *I* told you. *You* just don't get it…yet."

"This is way too early for flowers," Drew asserted. "I'm trying to hit all the right notes. I don't want to screw this up."

"Don't *try* to do anything," she said. "Be yourself. If there was one thing I wish everybody understood about relationships, it's the value of wissywig."

He shook his head, brow furrowed. "What? What the heck is 'wissywig'"?

"W-Y-S-I-W-Y-G—'what you see is what you get.' Like when we were together, there was no pretending, no trying to be something or someone we weren't. A lot of people start off trying to be what they think the other person wants, or what they think they should be. But that can't last. Sooner or later, they either fit or they don't. Better to know from the beginning."

"Makes sense."

A voice blasted out of the radio. "Ops to Nine Bravo, Five Seventy-one's on the ground." Someone must have cranked it up in a noisy moment and forgotten to reset it.

"Damn," said Gail, lowering the volume. She said, "Roger," unclipped her keys, opened the door, and went into the jetbridge.

She was calling from halfway down, her voice echoing off the walls as if she was shouting through a cheerleader's megaphone. Thinking she needed something, Drew started for the door until he recognized the drawn-out word.

"Flooowwwerrrs!"

Good grief, he thought, shaking his head.

A few minutes later, he smiled at the sea of bobbing mouse ears as happy children, and more than a few exhausted adults, trooped out of the jetbridge. Sometimes it seemed everybody was wearing the ears or some kind of theme park paraphernalia. Once, he and the rest of the ground crew had done a double take as a Super 80 inbound from Orlando taxied into view, the unmistakable mouse ear profile visible on both pilots' heads.

The plan was to play it cool, but that wasn't easy when the crew emerged. She wasn't on the same page anyway.

"Hi! I wasn't expecting you up here. Hey guys, go on, I'll catch up. Don't let 'em leave me." Her crewmates waved and headed up the concourse.

Rachel still looked tired. She saw Gail, hugged her, and said, "Gail! So good to see you!" She then hugged Drew and said, "They weren't being rude, we're all beat and can't wait to get to the hotel. I am *so* ready for that drink! See you at what, eight forty-five or so?"

"I'll be there," he said. "You're up for it?"

"Absolutely!"

Rachel took the handle of her rolling bag and hurried off, leaving him wondering how she moved that fast, much less gracefully, in her heels.

Gail caught his eye and mouthed, "Flowers!"

* * *

He found Rachel in a quiet booth way back in the hotel bar, a cozy place with muted lighting, a slight buzz of conversation, and a mellow jazz playlist.

"Long Island tea," she said to the server. To Drew's bemused look, she went on, "Hey, if I'm only having one, I'm making it count."

"Rum and Coke, please."

"This for the man who doesn't drink?" she asked.

"It's a special occasion."

"So it is," she replied, "so it is. Hey, you mentioned a rumor the other day. Which one? Let's see, Northwest is taking our Super Fifties, we're buying somebody, somebody is buying us, we bought some Eastern seven-five delivery positions, we're opening LaGuardia, no, we're closing LAX. One, some, or all of the above?"

Recalling that conversation took a moment. Friday already felt like long ago.

"Actually none," he replied. "This one's local. Supposedly we're getting a new pushback tractor. We're wondering whether it's a replacement or we'll be needing another one."

"Big news, big news," Rachel said. "That would mean more flights, right?"

"That's what we're hoping. Hey, what was that about the flashlight when Kelly relieved you?"

She paused.

"Oh, the reserve? You can't fly unless you have your service manual, a working flashlight, and a key to the cockpit door."

"Didn't know that."

"Yep, that's why."

They sipped their drinks. Somehow there was no need to fill silences with idle chatter.

Setting down her glass, Rachel turned the topic to her trip to Brownsville. "Mr. Bascomb's daughter got in touch yesterday."

"Kimberly, right?"

"Right. Anyway, she said it would mean a lot to her and her dad if Allen and I could come to the funeral on Saturday. I think we're going. Would you want to come with? We could fly back to Houston and you can crash at my place if it's too late to connect back here. You work at three Sunday, right? I'm flying Sunday afternoon but I'll run you up to Hobby that morning. You'll be back in plenty of time."

He could trade his Saturday shift and hadn't picked up morning hours Sunday, so it would work.

"I'd be honored," he said. "Thanks for asking me. But are you sure they wouldn't mind?"

"Yes. Barb and Gail are invited too. Which by the way, can you pass that on to them?"

"Of course. Hang on, how did Kimberly get in touch with you?"

She answered as a timetable appeared out of her purse. "I gave her the Brownsville station manager's name and told her to call him with any messages. He put it in my PNR."

"Nice! Great idea."

They came up with a plan then talked until the bartender ushered them out.

* * *

On Saturday, Rachel wore the more formal peplum-style ISR uniform jacket. Allen was equally sharp in his camel-colored suit coat, white shirt, tie, and navy trousers. The CSR's garb differed only in that his coat color matched the pants.

Mr. Bascomb had recovered from the initial shock. Spotting the airline trio near the back, he approached and said, "There you are. What are you doing back here?" He insisted they sit near the family. Drew expressed Barb and Gail's regrets and passed along their condolences as Mr. Bascomb led them up the aisle.

Several sizable flower sprays surrounded the casket along with a portrait of the beloved Millie. She was a pleasant-looking woman with kind eyes and a genuine smile who hardly resembled the gravely ill passenger Drew remembered.

Many people shared remembrances of Millie as a strong woman with deep faith, a sharp sense of humor, and compassion for everyone. When the service ended, Mr. B wiped his eyes and spent a few minutes composing himself and comforting his daughter. Then he took Rachel, Allen, and Drew in tow and introduced them to everyone. The mourners were obviously aware of the events aboard Tumbleweed 819. Rachel and Allen received many long, tearful embraces and sincere expressions of gratitude.

Rachel was in her element, poised, sincere, her empathy and thoughtfulness shining through again and again. She had become close to this warm, close-knit family and their sorrow touched her deeply.

When everyone said their goodbyes, it was all Rachel could do to convince Mr. Bascomb that they couldn't stay for dinner. A minor uproar erupted when Rachel asked about using a phone to call a cab back to the airport. Soon the only question to be resolved was who would drive them.

As Tumbleweed 526 climbed into a lemon sky afire with reefs of orange and red cloud, Rachel raised the armrest and snuggled against Drew's shoulder. She was asleep before the post-takeoff announcement.

He gazed out at the deepening lavender twilight that came into view as they turned east. He could have sat there forever feeling the slow rhythm of her breathing, looking at the sky, and taking in the scents of her hair and perfume.

Focus, bro, you've got thinking to do.

Rachel was special. He had seen it over and over, on the plane at Seven Bravo and at the hospital, in the car and the hotel lobby and at the funeral. Truth be told, he had harbored a bit of a crush ever since the trash drop, based on nothing more than her wonderful smile, beautiful face, and the flash of spirit she had shown in response to his reaction that day. His feelings had grown exponentially since they met. He enjoyed being with her, liked her sense of humor, and was touched by her genuine heart. He had even come to treasure some little quirks, like her habit of unconsciously repeating a phrase when she talked.

But every time this little love song began to play, a slap of reality sent the needle screeching across the vinyl before the intro even finished. Part of him just wasn't on board. He barely knew her. Was he about to sprint through a dark room yet again, using his shins as furniture detectors?

And what about Rachel's feelings? Were they romantic? It seemed so sometimes, but now doubt raised its ugly head and lobbed a few grenades. Had he only been a convenient friend, an emotional crutch to help her navigate the stress of the emergency and the grief she had repressed since her father died? Who was he anyway, thinking he could operate so far out of his league?

There was much to learn from his experience leaping before looking, but objectivity proved elusive with the lovely subject of his introspection leaning against him.

Disastrously pursuing the sales job had eventually— thankfully—been canceled out by quitting and finally getting on at Ruff Air, but he was determined to avoid a repeat.

On the other hand, too many people live as if they have an unlimited supply of tomorrows. Take the Bascombs, whose dreams went unfulfilled despite the best of intentions. Several eulogizers had mentioned the oft-delayed vacation that had ended so tragically before it even began. The message was clear: life is short. You only get one ride around the carousel, and nobody knows when some ghoul with a scythe will take you by the arm and insist it's time to step off. If the brass ring suddenly appeared right in front of one's face, didn't it make sense to reach for it?

Yeah, buddy, tell her how you feel! It'll be great, right up until your heart ends up like one of Gallagher's watermelons.

Yes, there was emotional peril, but wasn't this the definition of a risk worth taking?

An overarching truth shouldered its way past denial to enter the discussion: he was in love, plain and simple.

Crap. What now?

Reason made a stand and hammered out a compromise. Patience often wasn't his strong suit, but if there was ever a time to let things play out, this was it. If he played it cool and it went nowhere, at least his soul would be crushed in private.

He sighed, accepting the decision but far from satisfied with it.

As with the time he had wanted to kiss her, he wouldn't have dreamed that Rachel was struggling with the same dilemma. She had stared at the Texas landscape on the way to the airport and said little as they boarded. He had attributed this to being physically and emotionally spent, which was true enough, but she too was telling herself how insane it would be to date someone she had only just met, especially considering the circumstances. Her head and heart argued the same case, presented identical evidence, and reached essentially the same result before she drifted off to sleep.

As foolish as it seems, I like this guy. He probably won't even ask me out, but if he does, I'll say yes, but one way or another, we're going to take it very slow.

An attention chime sounded and the "fasten seat belt" signs in the ceiling illuminated. A voice followed a few seconds later.

"Ladies and gentlemen, our Super Fifty flight to Houston is almost complete. To prepare for our landing, we will be collecting any remaining cups and glasses. Thank you."

Rachel stirred. "Hey," she said, her eyes not quite open. "Hey."

"Every time you're around, I'm sleepy."

"I sometimes have that effect on women."

"Not this woman," she said.

Seems like a good sign.

Rachel fluffed her hair into reasonable shape then took out a compact. By the time the Super 50 rolled up the line, she had gone from tousled sleepyhead to pert and alert. They walked Allen to his connection and saw him off to Miami for some time with his family.

"I think he'll be okay," she said. "So how about dinner and then that movie we were going to catch the other night?"

"There's no way it'll be over in time to catch the ten-thirty."

"Yeah, I know. It was fun hanging out and talking and looking at pictures like we did. I was thinking see that movie then some more of that and you can crash on my sofa and fly home in the morning. But if you don't want to risk going back tomorrow or it's too much of a hassle, I understand."

Drew crossed his arms, reached up with one hand to stroke an imaginary goatee, and said, "Hmmm…"

"Uh huh," Rachel said, seeing right through his performance, "you have to think this over?"

"Not really. And since the loads looked a little iffy tomorrow and I felt bad that you might have to get up and drive me up here, I traded my shift just in case. I'll ride with you and try for the two o'clock trip."

"You didn't have to do that," Rachel said, "but I'm glad you did. I'll never turn down a chance to sleep in. Okay, that's settled. I'm starved. You up for Mexican again?"

"Always."

The restaurant near her apartment was cozy, dimly lit, and had outstanding fajitas. They talked about the funeral, then Rachel said, "You know, we've been wrapped up in all that ever since we met. I know a little about you but I need the whole story. Let's hear about your life, love, likes, dislikes, where you're from…everything."

"Sure. Quid pro quo?"

"Deal."

The first topic—his nomadic wanderings as an Army brat—invited a question.

"No way. You've moved *eleven* times?" she asked.

"Yes, including the one to my apartment."

He was as amazed that she had only moved twice, from her parents' home near Denver to a Houston stew nest then to her apartment.

"It was me, Valerie, and two other girls forever," Rachel explained, "and it was still a stretch to make it to payday. It was only last year I could afford my own place, and I may still have to find a roomie."

"You lived at home even when you went to college?"

"I wanted to go to Colorado," she replied, "and Gunbarrel wasn't even a half-hour away. I thought about a dorm, but home was cheaper, plus my parents were already making sacrifices even with my scholarships so that felt kinda selfish."

"Do you miss Colorado?"

"I do. I love the Rockies. Hiking in the summer, skiing in the winter...I go back whenever I can."

More music to his ears. He loved the outdoors and though he had never skied, he now had a good idea of who to ask for lessons.

She was a fan of Colorado's Buffaloes and the NFL Broncos, and followed pro football closely enough to know of the annual endurance test that was being a Saints fan. Still, she was surprised by one tidbit he shared.

"Seriously? You went to your first game in 1969 and they *still* haven't had a winning season?"

"Sad but true, and they actually came into the league in '67, we didn't move there until '69. I heard they may replace the fleur-de-lis on their helmets with Eeyore."

By and by they got to how her former boyfriend's infidelity had broken her heart six months before.

"How did you find out?" Morbidly curious, he went on, "You didn't walk in on it or anything, did you?"

"Worse."

"What's worse than *that?* I mean, if you're okay talking about it."

"Oh yeah," she said. "It stung for a while, but honestly, looking back now, I almost can't believe it. It's so pathetic it's almost funny. But it's a long story."

He smiled. "I have till tomorrow at two."

"All right, but remember, you asked for it. He worked for us but he also had a 737 rating. He was from Chicago, so when Midway offered him a job, he went. Maybe that should've been a clue that he wasn't as serious as I was about 'us,' but it was right after Christmas and I thought he just missed his family. It was hard after he left because we didn't see much of each other.

"Pretty soon things started cooling off but I told myself it was the distance. I should have seen it was hopeless but I really thought I loved him and that we could make it work if we wanted it bad enough. And that's probably right, but *we* didn't want it bad enough, *I* did. So come Valentine's Day, I decided to surprise him—"

"Oh, no."

"Right, and that's bad enough, but I also had to trade two trips and start from San Francisco to get to Chicago on time. I couldn't afford an ID ticket to go nonstop so I had to go to Hobby and use a buddy pass from a friend who flies for Southwest. We got into SFO at eight at night so the only trip I could take to Hobby left at like two in the morning. I couldn't believe anyone still has a flight with so many stops."

"Oh, I'd believe it."

The blue eyes turned curious.

"Sorry, my own long story," he explained. "Go ahead."

"So I got to Hobby and caught Southwest, and it stopped in St. Louis, and then we had a weather hold over Chicago. I'd been traveling something like twelve or thirteen hours on top of my trips and was beat, but I was really excited about finally having some time together. It was snowing and with the traffic, it took another hour to get to his place. I'm standing there with a big smile and my little bag of presents and I ring the bell and who answers? Some bimbo wearing nothing but panties and one of *my* t-shirts!"

He shook his head in disbelief.

"Yeah. So we're staring at each other and she finally says, I swear to God, 'Oh, Rick's in the shower. I thought you were the pizza guy.' You go to the door like *that* for the pizza guy? And that's your date on Valentine's Day, order a pizza? I said, 'Honey, right now I don't care if Rick's at the bottom of the Chicago River. You tell that worthless, two-timing, lying asshole that Rachel said hi.' I turned around and walked through the snow to a drugstore and called a cab back to Midway. At least she looked pissed. He probably ate his pizza alone."

"Damn."

What kind of moron cheats on a woman like this? And only a few months after her father died?

Tears filled her eyes but before he could speak, she said, "It's okay, I'm just still pretty mad. At myself, mainly, for being so stupid."

"He was the stupid one. That had to cut pretty deep, but next Valentine's Day will be much better."

"Oh, big words, big words," she said. "Promise?"

"I promise. Of course, the bar's pretty low. I could swipe some chocolates off a meal cart and cut a ticket jacket into a heart and still be way ahead."

Rachel tried to look indignant but couldn't quite hide her grin.

"Oh, we need to book you for open mic night at the comedy club. Okay, wise guy, tell me about your flight of many stops."

She anxiously bit her lip at several junctures, chuckled at others, and laughed out loud when he took on Grayson's accent and told how the supervisor yelled about lollipops and lemonade.

"Holy hell, the same endless flight! But yours sure came out better than mine."

Storms were rolling through so he brought her car to the door. A downpour greeted them at the theater, with lightning veining the sky and streams rushing between the drain grates. The only parking spot was far from the entrance so Rachel suggested skipping the movie again.

"Works for me."

They were on Rachel's living room floor long after midnight, photos strewn all around. The storms had faded away, leaving a soft, soothing rain. He mentioned the late hour and they reluctantly began boxing up the photos.

Rachel got some bedding. While her guest made up the sofa, she went around turning off lights until only a dim table lamp was left.

"Come here," she said. She hugged him and snuggled against his neck. It was quiet except for the rain.

"What a week," she said with a sigh.

"It was pretty crazy. I'm still amazed at what you did for Mr. B."

She said nothing, but held him closer. Her perfume reminded him of jasmine.

"This feels pretty good," she whispered a minute later. "Really…I don't know…comfortable."

He wasn't about to disagree.

"Let me ask you something," he said.

"Mm-hmm, what?"

"We barely know each other, but…"

Silence.

"Yes?"

Nervous, but emboldened by their growing connection, he said, "Tonight kind of felt like a date."

She tilted her head and replied, "It did, didn't it? It was fun."

Okay, that's progress. Now quit while you're ahead.

With difficulty, he did. For exactly three seconds, after which he heard himself say, "Would you be open to us dating?"

Well, smart guy, so much for your big plan! Hopes, stand by to be shattered!

The blue eyes met his. "No, Drew," she whispered. "I can't."

"I understand," he replied quickly, already kicking himself for pressing her.

"No, hear me out. I'm not ready to date but I really like you and being with you. I would love to have a guy like you in my life. So instead of dating, I'd rather be together. Like exclusive. Would you be up for that?"

That's taking it slow? she thought, as surprised at utterly failing to keep her promise to herself as he was.

Her words were such a shock that he was interrogating himself as to whether she could possibly have said what he thought he had heard.

She looked at the floor. This was obviously difficult; she wasn't impulsive like this. Or was she? He couldn't really know, but told himself that anybody who had recently been burned as she had was apt to be gun-shy.

"I've thought about it a lot," she went on. "And I know, it's kind of ridiculous. I was going to say let's wait a while, then I thought okay but we have to go slow, but with all that's happened, I feel like I know you way better than if we'd been out on dates or whatever. But you're right, we hardly know each other. I don't know, it's probably way too fast."

He understood perfectly well that it *was* too fast, way too fast. But his psyche's voice of reason was faint, as if calling from far away, and it began to fade even as it peppered him with objections. Then the voice was gone and he fully committed to exploring this great unknown.

"It's not too fast."

It was so easy to say what he wanted to believe!

"But Drew, just know that I won't do games or drama or lies, not ever. I can't, so all our cards are always on the table. Always tell me what you mean and what you feel, not what you think I want to hear. If I seem skittish, remember Rick and be patient with me. I want all of you, and you'll have all of me. But there's one thing we have to agree on."

"And that is?" Not that it mattered; short of giving up both kidneys, he was in. This felt right, like a chance worth taking.

"We promise each other that if it ever stops working for one of us, we'll say so, and try to work it out, and if we can't, we go our separate ways as friends."

"Absolutely."

Rachel looked up and their eyes met.

"We shouldn't…" she said, and he knew it was true, too early for the relationship and too late on a night when they had to be up in a few hours.

Their lips touched, lingering, as if relishing the anticipation. Her voice dropped to a whisper.

"We really, really…"

They both caved, kissing deeply.

By the time they broke away a minute later, both were breathing raggedly, hearts pounding.

Rachel stepped back and said, "Look, it sucks big time, but we have to stop this right now. Right now, 'cause if we don't, I will invite you into my bed and there will be *no* sleep. I shouldn't tell you how bad I want to right now, but it's *definitely* too soon for that. And anyway, you're right, we've got to get some rest. But don't worry, pretty soon you're not getting off the hook this easily."

After their goodnights, Drew switched off the lamp and stared at the ceiling, grateful and almost in disbelief at having the chance to experience life with someone like Rachel.

Yet, something nagged at his heart—the long, sad shadow cast by the dreadful event that had unexpectedly brought them together. He felt guilty, almost ashamed, that such a radiant silver lining of excitement and anticipation could form around such a terribly dark cloud.

TWENTY

Calling it a long-distance relationship was something of a misnomer. They saw each other almost daily once Rachel began bidding routes through New Orleans, though most of the encounters were about as long and romantic as a green-flag pit stop. When time off could be coordinated, they bounced back and forth like ping pong balls between Houston and New Orleans.

There wasn't much travel elsewhere since free time together and extra money seldom coincided, but that was okay; being together was enough. They were kindred spirits, both sort of homebodies with no need for expensive restaurants or five-star resorts. Hanging out to watch TV or having a picnic, out on Lakeshore Drive or at the beach down in Galveston, was all the fun either needed. They also loved movies and the only thing better than a discount matinee on a rainy afternoon was a double feature.

When enough was enough with the brief hellos, Drew traded shifts and worked consecutive doubles so they could plan a couple of days off together. He was surprised when Rachel wasn't waiting at the gate as usual, finally spotting her in an empty corner, tears streaming down her face.

Alarmed, he hurried toward her. She saw him and spoke before he could.

"I'm okay. This was in my mail folder today." She handed him a photocopy of a handwritten letter. He sat next to her and read:

Dear Mr. Ruff,

I am writing on behalf of my father, Lamar Bascomb, my mother, Millie, and our family and friends. As you may know, my mom passed away on August 9th after suffering a heart attack on Ruff Air Flight 819 from Houston to Miami. The pilots made an emergency landing in New Orleans but it was too late.

We cannot begin to tell you how much your airline's compassion meant to our family at such a terribly difficult time. Your stewardess Rachel and steward Allen did everything possible to save my mom's life. We so appreciate that, but the care we received in getting my mom and dad home to Brownsville was far over and above anything we could have imagined.

Rachel, who volunteered to travel with my dad, the station managers and staff in New Orleans, Houston, Brownsville, and Dallas, and the stewardesses and pilots on my dad's flights and mine (I'm sorry, I don't have all their names)—every one of them opened their hearts and treated us like we were part of their own family. When my parents' luggage came back from Miami, we even found a touching condolence card inside!

My dad has told everyone he knows about these kindnesses and about how your pilots and baggage handlers paid their respects as my mom was put on the plane in New Orleans and again in Houston, and when she was taken off in Brownsville. That meant the world to him and made losing her a little easier to bear.

Thank you for having such special people at your airline. We will never forget them and I know my mom is hugging each of them from Heaven.

Sincerely,

Kimberly Bascomb Ross

"Wow," Drew said, his own eyes threatening to overflow. "What a beautiful letter."

"I sure wish she'd never had to write it."

"I know," he whispered as he leaned over and hugged her.

She hugged back, then stood up and dried her eyes, resilient as always.

"Come on," she said, starting down the concourse. "I know a great pancake place that will tide me over until you can buy me a margarita or three."

* * *

Somehow, the new couple kept a low profile. Ruff Air's deepening troubles provided unfortunate camouflage. The usual operational struggles were a given, but a few recent financial hits were downright bizarre, like the Super 80 that arrived with an apple-green tailcone.

Drew and Gail had finished unloading the inbound bags when Bert descended the jetbridge stairs.

"Bert! What's with the tailcone?"

"The Rams finally signed Eric Dickerson."

The rampers exchanged baffled looks. What did football have to do with it? The apron was loud but that response didn't fit anything that might have been asked.

Did it?

Drew spoke up, walking over and pointing toward the tail, Gail tagging along.

"No, what happened to the tailcone?"

"Just what I said," Bert replied. He went on, paraphrasing the prison captain from *Cool Hand Luke,* complete with a fair imitation of the delivery: "What we had here was a failure to communicate."

As Bert explained, the supervisor for Ruff Air's Los Angeles cabin cleaning vendor loved the Rams, spoke no Spanish, and kept a small black and white TV in his office. On the Monday night in question, he was glued to the game in which L.A.'s star running back had returned from a contract holdout. He was thus ignoring his subordinates, none of whom spoke more than rudimentary English or wanted to sit around waiting on the supe when they could be cleaning Ruff Air's terminators. Nobody could go home until each was ready for the morning departures.

The CSRs locked the jetbridge door and left once the flight deplaned, so the cleaners had to depend on their boss to lower the airstairs from outside. He was the only one authorized to operate them, but Dickerson was running wild through the Seahawks and the task was simple enough. What would it hurt to delegate it this once?

The supervisor pulled aside a trusted crew member during a commercial and delivered a quick tutorial in broken Spanish and pantomime. Missing from it was one essential detail: that there are two sets of accessible controls near a Super 80's tail. One lowers the airstairs; the other, for emergency use only, jettisons the tailcone and deploys an escape slide.

"Oh no," Donna said. "How much will *that* cost us?"

"I don't know," Bert replied. "They had to cancel a bunch of flights, then there's the new tailcone, a new slide, painting over that green primer when they get a chance, probably the next B check…the short answer is a lot. One thing's for sure, that clown will have plenty of time now to watch football."

The grapevine thus had plenty to chew on without delving into Drew's countless flights to Houston or why a certain ISR had a new affinity for New Orleans.

Things stayed that way until the last day of October.

Halloween in a major airport is seldom dull. Tonight, Cinderella, Blackbeard, and the Wicked Witch of the West worked Ruff Air's counter; angels, demons, and mummies manned the gates. Even the staid old Americans and Easterns of the world had let their hair down, with many of their people costumed too.

Rob admitted the outbound crew into the jetbridge and hurried back to the podium. He made a passable Zorro, though security had refused his sword.

"It's plastic for Christ's sake," he complained, still ticked about having to take the fake blade back to his locker.

"Tumbleweed Five Oh Five on the ground for Seven Bravo," squawked the radio.

Rob acknowledged before turning back to Drew, who couldn't resist this special opportunity to spill the beans.

"Whoa, hold on bubba, let me get this straight," Rob asked. "You're here with flowers to meet *who?*"

He repeated himself and Rob's eyes narrowed with suspicion. "Bulllllsshiiiit!" he whispered, mindful of the customers already milling around in anticipation of boarding. Tactful as ever, he added, "I mean, I heard you were sniffing around some ISR but you're saying that stone-cold fox who tried to save the old lady? No way."

"She's on this trip. You think I'm here on my day off to bring *you* flowers? We're going to see Heart at UNO."

He would have played it cool with anyone else, but this was too good to pass up.

"You're going to a concert with Rachel? *That* Rachel, the tall one with the eyes and the—"

"Hey! Watch it. But yeah, that Rachel."

"Dream on," Rob said dismissively. "I think you have your holidays mixed up. It's not April Fool's Day."

"Check the crew list."

Rob typed, glancing over his shoulder to watch for the plane, which promptly taxied into view.

"Lucky you," Rob said, hurrying away to meet the flight.

Passengers began streaming out. Rob returned and checked in a couple of people while watching the jetbridge door. He looked victorious when the pilots and three ISRs emerged, none of whom was Rachel.

"See? You're jerking my chain. Show's over, Bozo. Go take your flowers back to Schwegmann's."

Drew gestured toward a couple of thirty-somethings near the jetbridge. "Is there a UM? Rachel likes to handle them personally." Rachel loved kids and always made sure unaccompanied minors had a memorable time.

Rob's face fell into uncertainty. "What? Yeah, there is one as a matter of fact." Okay, an ISR was unaccounted for, but it couldn't be—

Rachel and a girl of about six walked out of the jetbridge. Rob looked like a man whose world was on the verge of turning upside down.

Rachel checked the parents' ID and chatted with them for a minute, her smile lighting up the vicinity as it always did. The child proudly showed off her plastic wings and the coloring book of airport scenes the cabin crews gave out.

The family left and Rachel walked over with her rolling bag in tow. "Hey there! Awww, flowers? Thank you! You didn't have to do that but I'm glad you did."

She took the bouquet, hugged Drew, and said, "I can change downstairs if there's not enough time for the hotel."

He checked his watch. "No, we'll be okay if we hustle."

Blowing the lid off their secret was well worth relishing Rob's poorly concealed shock. The person for whom he was writing a boarding pass was the only thing keeping his jaw off the floor.

* * *

The next morning, Drew reluctantly surfaced from a deep, refreshing sleep. Snug in the comfort of fragrant sheets, it took a beat for the surroundings—Rachel's layover hotel room—to register. He sighed contentedly.

Comfortable as it was, the bed was not the source of his fulfillment. That honor belonged to Rachel, whose head was wedged beneath his chin and whose body half covered his own. She twitched and murmured through a dream as a deep gold band of morning sun invaded the room, dividing the bed into two dark triangles. Specks of dust floated lazily through the intense shaft of light.

This is it, he thought. *This is everything I ever wanted. This amazing woman, the job...it was all worth waiting for.*

His thoughts wandered to last night and it took an effort not to laugh out loud.

The look on Rob's face!

Carefully extracting himself from Rachel's sleepy embrace, he slid to the edge of the bed, moving slowly so as not to wake her. She turned over, her body rearranging the bulky bed linens into another delightful collection of girl-curves.

He pulled on his underwear with that odd modesty people often feel despite the depth of intimacy recently shared. Stretching, arms over his head, he looked at Rachel and counted his blessings again.

She peeked out from under the covers when he returned and said, "Hey, you."

"Hey."

"You still up for breakfast later?"

"Later?"

"It's only ten after seven."

"And?"

She moved the covers aside. "Get back in here and find out."

The time was soon the last thing on their minds, but Rachel had set an alarm so they could get breakfast before he drove her to Moisant. A few minutes later, a loud *click* was followed by a voice from the clock radio: "…when the Saints take on Atlanta on Sunday. In business news, a Houston-based equity group—"

"Sorry," Rachel said, reaching for the off button.

"—has reportedly purchased financially troubled Ruff Air."

They sprang up, gaping at each other in shock.

"A spokesman said founder W.W. Ruff will step down but stressed that the company is not bankrupt and will keep flying to the Crescent City and the airline's other destinations. Stay tuned for local reactions to this developing story along with all your favorite soft rock hits…"

"Hooolllllyyyy *shit!*" Rachel rooted around for her t-shirt and underwear. "I've got to call crew sked!"

Fifteen minutes of busy signals later, she got through. She listened, hung up, and said, "It's for real! Old man Ruff is cleaning out his office right now! Nobody really knows anything, but all the flights are going."

* * *

There were a million questions and no answers. Rachel said it was the same with the crews.

This changed soon enough. The equity group's point man, one Harrison Kirby, proved to be a prolific communicator, firing off such frequent memos that they soon spilled over the bulletin board's edges and began eating up wall space.

One described how Ruff Air's purchasers planned to "remake" the airline. Apparently, nothing associated with W.W. Ruff could stay, so a contest to choose a new name was already underway. With it would come a new logo and paint scheme along with a "refresh" of the airline's service level "to be more in keeping with an upscale clientele."

The last bit set eyes to rolling all over the system. More sobering was the realization that Ruff Air would be but a memory after all the "remaking."

The overall effect was deeply discouraging. Before, there were peaks and valleys and it often felt like swimming upstream, but everyone knew where upstream was. This was like being along for the ride, the transaction suddenly and unwillingly strapping them into a roller coaster car that was now careening through the dark.

His colleagues' reactions were strikingly like those among the nonrevs waiting for boarding passes: withdrawal, indifference, acceptance, anger, and even some optimism. Maybe it was all for the best and the new owners would finally end the constant oscillations between red ink and black.

Kirby soon thanked everyone for submitting 437 potential names and announced the winner: AirStar, which had been entered by…no one.

"Regrettably," the message explained, "potential trademark conflicts ruled out the ten most popular submissions and none of the remaining entries reflected our fresh, bold vision for the airline—to deliver *air* transportation of *star* quality."

Gail, Henry, Donna, and Drew discussed this development during lulls at the counter.

"Do you think they already had the name?" Donna asked. "I mean, was the contest them trying to be warm and fuzzy when they already knew what it would be? And I love the italics, like we weren't going to get it. Good grief."

The same foursome was on the counter again a week later. A little after eleven in the morning, Barb and Kelly emerged from the back office. The station manager was somber, almost mournful, while the supervisor looked as if she had either witnessed someone throwing up or needed to herself.

"Hey guys, what's up?" Henry asked, concerned.

"We're going to grab something at the cafeteria," Kelly replied.

Henry knew them too well to be dissuaded. "But is everything okay?"

Barb, uncharacteristically, shook her head and looked at the floor, leaving an awkward silence because nobody wanted to risk talking over the boss.

Finally, Kelly said, "You're not going to believe what's at Seven Bravo."

Barb added, "I don't know what to say, other than this is going to take some getting used to."

The two walked away toward Concourse C.

Donna looked around at her colleagues. "What is 'this,' and have any of you *ever* seen Barb like *that?*"

Everyone's impulse was to go see, but obviously they couldn't all leave at once. The solution was easy; seniority was so ingrained that Henry going first was simply the natural order. He, Donna, and Gail all went back in turn and returned moments later, their expressions a mix of astonishment, disbelief, and heartbreak. Donna in particular, her heart nearly always on her sleeve, looked crushed, with tears in her eyes and her lips making those little quivers that are a telltale sign someone is struggling not to cry.

What in the world?

There were enough customers around that nobody could explain, so Drew would have to see for himself.

He stapled an SFO tag on a boarding folder and said, "Okay, we have one bag checked to San Francisco. You'll use this boarding pass here and this one is for your connecting flight in Houston. Your gate is seven B, like 'boy,' down that way and to the left. Have a great trip!"

Gail was also finishing a transaction. No one was in her queue but a couple was waiting in his. She called out, "I'll help you over here, sir," while motioning them over, then looked at Drew and nodded toward the back office.

The mystery was solved at the window by Kelly's desk, the same place his wonder had caused her to declare him an "airline guy." But there was no wonder this time. The Super 80 at Seven Bravo was the same familiar cream as always, but the tail was blank, the logo painted over. Also gone was the distinctive mark a prominent national newspaper had called a "signature of dashing elegance." In its place, large, plain letters spelled out AirStar.

Knowing it was coming did nothing to dull the shock and disappointment of actually seeing the new name. The Frankenstein application didn't help, but repainting was expensive, so ownership changes often left planes in such "hybrid" schemes, the new name plastered on with few other changes. This usually lasted until the next major maintenance check, which could be many months away, unwittingly creating an interesting—and sometimes rather less than aesthetic—visual depiction of the turbulence within the industry.

More planes soon showed up this way, including a couple obviously rushed back into service because neither had a name at all. Drew was alerted to this when a customer saw the arriving jet and remarked to her friends, "Good God, what's this we're riding? Generic Airways?" They all chortled, but one was concerned enough to approach the podium a few minutes later and quietly ask, "Excuse me, seriously, why is the plane like…blank? Is it safe?"

The CSRs, one of whom dubbed the unmarked jets "Caspers," felt bad for such customers. Media coverage framed the public's view. There was little depth about such transitions, but plenty of juicy coverage whenever things went awry. There were even inferences that the churn had the potential to compromise safety, which wasn't entirely untrue. Airlines had latitude when customizing new aircraft, including flight deck configuration. When one carrier acquired planes from another, some controls or switches could be in different places than those in its existing fleet. Pilots flying the dissimilar aircraft received training on the changes, but it wasn't hard to imagine muscle memory causing them to end up like drivers in a rental, trying to signal a turn as they would in their own car and switching on the wipers instead.

Kirby scrambled to clarify things, but press releases couldn't make the stew of planes—some marked AirStar, others still in Ruff Air paint, and a few unmarked "Caspers"—any tastier. The Ruff Air brand remained everywhere else, at least for now, forcing the CSRs to explain over and over.

Things got even more interesting when the chain-smoking Kirby abolished Ruff Air's nonsmoking policy. Smokers obviously loved the change, but it brought an avalanche of new headaches for employees along with complaints from long-time customers. Gate agents faced the tricky task of appeasing both smokers and nonsmokers, many of whom held strong views on the topic; the smoky odor permeated cabins despite the cleaners' best efforts; ISRs bore the brunt of enforcing the NO SMOKING sign, sometimes clashing with people who became more agitated with each cigarette-free moment; and nonrevs often ended up stuck in smoking—tolerable on short hops but miserable on long hauls.

Another consequence festered for a while before revealing itself. Mechanics were dealing with more and more cabin ventilation malfunctions, and rampers began noticing brownish stains streaming back from a fuselage vent.

"That's the cabin outflow," Bert explained. "It opens and closes to regulate cabin pressure."

Investigation traced the issue to valves gummed up with tar residue—which was brown. A consultation with OAL counterparts led to an unlikely fix: automotive carburetor cleaner, which dissolved the goo and unstuck the valves but did little to ease the stress.

There was also the safety angle. New rules governing the flammability of cabin materials were already in the works, the result of a tragic in-flight fire that had killed 23 passengers on an Air Canada DC-9 just a couple of years before.

Morale was descending fast and in danger of nosediving. Nobody liked the gloom permeating the station, especially Barb, who called on her most experienced people for input and ideas. Henry told her about a Braniff colleague, and Kelly was busy typing a memo for Barb's signature with that and a couple of other perspectives.

In the meantime, Henry shared it firsthand at the counter.

"I met Doris when I moved here," he said. "She passed away a few years ago but talk about a story! She started with Pacific Seaboard Air Lines right out of high school in 1933."

Quizzical looks all around.

"I had never heard of them either. They flew on the west coast for a while, then for whatever reason, the owner bid for an airmail route between Chicago and New Orleans. They changed the name to Chicago and Southern and kept expanding, and eventually flew from here to a bunch of Caribbean islands. I guess that explains Kelly's guest chair. Anyway, that's how Doris got here. She left the industry when she got married but she missed it, so she came back and got on with Braniff.

"She told me how Delta bought C&S in the early '50s and actually went by 'Delta-C&S' for a while. She said everybody felt the same as we do when Delta bought them, but then somebody said, 'Look, I don't like it any more than anybody else, but I can't change it. Whatever name is on the planes, all I can do is give my best for you guys and the people who buy the tickets, same as always.'"

Everyone looked at each other.

"Makes sense to me," Gail said to nods of agreement. "Okay, I guess we rock on as best we can."

Kirby next declared that AirStar was shifting focus to long-haul markets, carrying out a strategy that Ruff himself had considered. The longer a segment, the lower the cost per seat mile, an industry standard for measuring such things.

"Wow," said Regina during a discussion in Ops between arrivals. "What will they do with places like Brownsville, Midland-Odessa, and San Antonio?"

Peggy piped up from behind the counter. "Probably depends on how much feed traffic they're sending to Hobby. If you're talking whoever doesn't have long-hauls now, that would be Austin too, and Dallas for that matter. Can those stations stick around just with connecting traffic?"

"Time will tell, I suppose," offered Drew.

"I heard we may get non-stops to L.A. and Miami," Peggy went on. "And that's for starters, they might even add Vegas and San Fran. But don't quote me on that."

Regina read the message's ominous final line aloud.

"What's this mean? 'Rebalancing the company's workforce may eventually become necessary.'"

"Oh, I've heard that before," Grayson said dejectedly. "That's how the big shots say they're cuttin' people loose."

"What's an equity group anyway?" asked Rob. "I need a dictionary to understand half this crap."

"Only half?" needled Donna.

"Nice to know you still have your sense of humor," Drew told the redhead.

"By the time this Kirby character is through with us," she said with a sigh, "that may be all any of us have left."

TWENTY-ONE

Uncertainty aside, the world kept turning. Resilience is a survival skill for airline people, so everyone kept their happy faces on for the customers even as a bitter, frothy milkshake of apprehension churned their insides.

Drew and Rachel escaped the turmoil at every opportunity. On a lovely fall morning, they parked near Jackson Square and lucked out at Café Du Monde, waiting only a few minutes for a table. They ordered hot chocolate and beignets, then began talking at the same time.

"How—"

"Can you—"

They laughed. He motioned for her to go ahead.

"I was just going to say, can you believe everything that's happened?"

"That's what I was going to ask you. It's insane how much has changed."

"C'est la vie, right?" she replied, her usual upbeat tone noticeably absent. "I hope this Kirby knows what he's doing. But enough of this BS. Is there anything to see around here?" She asked it flippantly, as if they weren't surrounded by world-famous tourist attractions.

They walked the Quarter after helping each other brush off the inevitable blotches of powdered sugar. They bought po-boys and colas from a deli then rode the streetcar uptown to Audubon Park for a picnic. There were no tables but a live oak's massive root was a workable substitute.

Rachel looked up, taking in the magnificent canopy of limbs and branches, many draped with moss.

"I *love* these trees," she said. "The way the years have shaped them, and the way the bark looks, it's almost like they're wizened old people with wrinkled faces. This one, think how long it's lived and how much it's seen! Centuries, right? I would love to hear the stories it could tell."

The oak would certainly have tales to share. The magnificent specimen on which they perched had poked up through the fertile soil not long after Jean-Baptiste Le Moyne de Bienville found some (relatively) high ground in a bend of the mighty river, established a community there in 1718, and called it La Nouvelle-Orleans.

They unwrapped their sandwiches, enjoying the gentle breeze that rustled the irises and elephant ears surrounding a nearby pond. The voices of children playing competed with the falling water from a fountain in the pond. A few resident ducks paddled aimlessly while across the way, musicians were gathering on a small bandstand, chatting and taking instruments from black cases.

Between bites, Rachel asked, "Where's the New Orleans zoo? I'd like to go someday." Like many, she pronounced the second word "Or-LEENS."

Drew smiled.

"What?" she asked.

"Look, I'm telling you this because…you know what, never mind."

"No, come on, what?"

"Okay, but only 'cause I know you won't let it go. Natives usually say 'New OR-lens,' not 'New Or-LEENS.' 'New OR-lee-uns' is okay too, just please don't ever say 'N'Awlins.'"

He pointed and continued, "As for the zoo, it's about a five-minute walk down that way. We can go when we're done eating if you'd like."

"I'd love to." Eyes agleam with the mischievous twinkle he had come to love, she continued, "But first, tell me: how should I pronounce 'kiss my big round ass'?"

Like with Marty, he knew to give the bluster right back, covering the most critical item first.

"Look, your ass isn't anywhere near big. Round, yes. Quite pleasingly plush, absolutely. But big? No. As far as pronouncing that last bit, you have it down pretty well, but it's nippy out here and besides, NOPD really frowns upon nudity in public parks. Come on, don't get fussy. I'm trying to help you blend in."

"Uh huh."

"If you really want to hit the zoo, we should go before it gets too late."

They spent the rest of the afternoon among the animals. All were interesting and engaging in their own ways, but the two beautiful white tigers stole the show by lolling around back-to-back, creating what looked like a mirror image when they settled down for a nap.

When Drew opened the car door for her that evening, she kissed him before getting in.

"That was just about a perfect day," she said once he took his seat. She reached over, took his hand, and looked him in the eye.

"A perfect day...here in New *Orleans,*" sprinkling a little sass with a spot-on pronunciation.

The next was memorable too. They wandered several of the famous cemeteries, both captivated by the inscriptions. Feeling so many souls' presence, their mortal remains housed above ground in deference both to tradition and the city's unusually high water table, humbled their hearts and hushed their voices.

After lunch in the Quarter, they drove to Slidell for a swamp tour, an experience that offered quite a stark contrast to reflecting on the lives of the departed.

"What's with that?" Rachel asked when the guide held a wiener on a stick out over the side. She squealed with surprise as an eight-foot alligator erupted from the black water to its hind legs, tearing off the wiener and a third of the stick.

"I can't believe it did that!" Rachel said when they got back to the car, which was covered in white dust from the parking lot's crushed shell surface.

On the way to Moisant, Drew impulsively asked, "Hey, how would you feel about meeting my parents?"

She reached over and laid her hand on his. "I would like that."

She flew over early the next Sunday. He traded off so they could have lunch at the house in Terrytown where he had grown up. After, they watched the perennially wanting Saints drop their sixth straight. At halftime, Mom went to work on a painting, her way of relaxing after the long days she put in as a successful real estate broker. Rachel joined her in the guest bedroom that doubled as a studio. They returned to the living room as Dad switched off the TV in disgust.

"I'll be dead before they win anything," he groused. Remembering their guest, he went on, "I'm sorry, Rachel. We don't usually have witnesses to our misery."

Rachel said, "I'm spoiled being a Broncos fan. Well, except for the Super Bowl, but we'll win one sooner or later."

"A worry we have never had," Drew said.

"For now," Rachel replied. She excused herself to use the bathroom.

Mom waited until she was gone then said, "I like her. A lot."

"She's a keeper," Dad agreed. "Smart and beautiful, just like your mother. And a sports fan too? Don't let that one get away."

"I won't," Drew promised, to them and to himself.

* * *

Kirby's next missive, in glossy color, featured a contrail curving sharply across the sky. "We're changing course!" shouted the headline. Underneath was an invitation to a series of unveilings, complete with light catering, soft drinks and a cash bar. The first was the following week at a hotel near Hobby; more would follow so as many people as possible could attend.

Aside from revealing the new livery, the meetings would introduce the new leadership team, a necessity given the brisk, thorough HQ housecleaning. The rumor mill said new uniforms would be shown too, but this seemed a reach since keeping costs down was surely fundamental to the new strategy.

Drew, planning to go, left a message in Rachel's PNR. She replied a few hours later.

FLYING BUT WOULDN'T MISS IT. ARV HOU RX864 @ 1655. XOXO

The day couldn't come fast enough. Drew hopped Tumbleweed 547, scheduled to arrive 20 minutes before her trip from LAX. They had an early dinner, headed to the hotel, and found seats a few rows back from the stage.

Someone pointed out a circular platform back in the shadows. A drape covered a tripod-mounted aircraft model that looked to be a Mad Dog about six feet long. It was the kind that grace headquarters lobbies and window displays at big travel agencies.

The lights dimmed at precisely 7:30. People were still filing in as a voice boomed through the speakers. The announcer drew out each syllable as if two silk-robed heavyweights were bouncing with anticipation in opposite corners of a boxing ring.

"La-dies and gen-tle-men...*Harrrrrison Kirrrrbyyyy!*"

Kirby was polished. Dark, tailored suit, white shirt, and red tie; full head of graying hair, perfectly styled; and gold-rimmed aviator style glasses. If nothing else, he looked the part. He stepped into the spotlight amid a noticeably light smattering of applause.

"Good evening," Kirby said, pointedly glancing at his watch. "You'll notice we're going right on time tonight. That's no coincidence. From now on, we will go on time, every time. Every day, every flight. Our people are going to set new standards for punctuality, efficiency, accountability, and cost-effectiveness."

Eyes rolled all over the room. Someone whispered, "What's this clown think we're doing every day?"

"But first," Kirby went on, "Our new identity."

Workers rolled the platform to center stage.

"Ladies and gentlemen, as you know, our priority is to consistently deliver air transportation of star quality. Our name personifies our commitment to that goal. Now we proudly present our new visual identity, one that will become synonymous with style, elegance, and exceptional service in the air and on the ground."

The drape fell away, revealing an MD-80 painted midnight blue from radome to tailcone. "AirStar" was rendered in a plain, light blue font below the windows. Three horizontal stripes, pink, green, and the same light blue as the wordmark, ran across the tail. Murmurs, more than a few of them dismay, echoed through the room.

"I would be pleased to take any questions or hear any comments," Kirby said from beside the model.

"He's a brave soul, I'll give him that," Rachel quipped.

There ensued the kind of awkward silence that grows more uncomfortable by the second.

Finally, a hand went up.

"Yes, over here, what's your name, sir?"

A man slowly stood, his expression suggesting he already wished he had kept his mouth shut. Rachel whispered, "He works in Brownsville. He helped with the Bascombs."

"Mr. Kirby, my name is Merrill Hoskins. I work in Brownsville. Sir, that plane is real pretty to look at but I can't help but wonder about that dark color. It's upwards of a hunnerd in the shade just about all summer long down there in south Texas and God knows how much hotter on the ramp." His desire to be done quickened his tempo until the words almost ran together. "Dark colors soak up the heat so seems an airplane of that color might get awful warm inside, that's all, sir. Thank you, sir."

Kirby's reaction, a perturbed glare toward someone offstage, said everything about whether the brand designers had considered such concerns.

"Oh," he replied stiffly, "I'm sure it will be fine. Any other comments? Questions?"

Mercifully, no one else cared to comment, so Kirby moved on to the Go Long strategy. Highlights included cutting seat-mile costs by focusing on lengthier segments; adding underserved markets; a frequent flier program; upgraded meals; and "Indigo Club" VIP lounges, the first planned for LAX and MIA.

Kirby was persuasive, and the slick presentation didn't hurt. Those who could see past their bitterness to objectively evaluate the plan admitted, if only to themselves, that it might make sense. Some even left feeling a surge of hope.

Drew had to fly home and they discussed the meeting all the way to Hobby. He was cautiously optimistic; she, not so much, though she conceded that Kirby's bunch had a plan.

A couple of jets were soon repainted in the dark blue and the others would follow soon. Drew, at Hobby to meet Rachel one day and always alert for photo opportunities, managed to catch a shot of two company jets tail-to-tail, one the lone Super 80 still carrying the Circle R logo and the other with what one customer had coined the "party stripes."

Less than a week after the first blue plane appeared, HQ issued a directive instructing ISRs to ask passengers to lower their window shades after landing to help keep the cabin cooler.

"Apparently dark blue airplanes get hot inside," Rachel observed, sarcasm dripping from each word. Merrill Hoskins, the Brownsville CSR who had raised the issue, had become a bit of a folk hero as the tale spread.

Other developments explained Kirby's mention of accountability. Crews would no longer radio their times; an onboard system enabled by new RAATS programming—purchased at considerable cost—took over that function. CSRs didn't escape the new scrutiny either. The computer could also determine the interval between the pilots setting the brakes and the opening of the main cabin door. Taking longer than 45 seconds to accomplish the latter would now deliver an alert to the station manager with a copy to HQ to ensure the offending agent received "appropriate discipline," as Kirby's memo phrased it.

The monitoring didn't bother most. They prided themselves on keeping to the schedule as best they could anyway. But what about the enormous expense even as HQ was yammering about survival depending on pinching every penny?

They also clearly underestimated employee ingenuity. Nothing could be done about alerts for tardy door opening, but a wad of tissue or paper towel held over the door frame sensor while the captain released the brakes tricked the system into issuing a bogus out time.

So HQ's heavy-handed approach was a minor annoyance—until Rob stalked angrily into Ops a couple of weeks later, so enraged that he threw his hearing protector across the room.

"What the hell, man?" asked Chuck.

"They shitcanned Hoskins!"

"What are you talking about?" asked Donna.

"Hoskins, the guy from Brownsville who said blue planes would be hot. Those assholes in Houston fired him! A Pioneer! *For asking a goddam question!*"

This news hit everyone hard. Apparently, loyalty and common sense were now speed bumps for Kirby's steamroller. As if to underscore the point, "AirStar" began replacing "Ruff Air" on signage and equipment. Ticket jackets, bag tags, and stationery followed as stations replenished those items.

As nonsensical as firing Hoskins was leadership's insistence on replacing the callsign "Tumbleweed." Their first suggestion was "Bluebird," a nonstarter with the flight crews according to Bert. The pilots won, but only to the extent of using "AirStar" instead.

"What we can't figure," Captain Michaels said in Ops one day, "is why even waste time and money on that? Nobody hears it. It would be like changing all the N-numbers. Who cares? There's a fee to do it and most passengers never even notice it's on the plane."

"Well, Cap," Grayson replied, "that might go along with them runnin' Whiskey Whiskey out of here like a rabid raccoon. A friend back home does stocks and oil investments and such. Seems Whiskey Whiskey used to work with this Kirby years back and those two went beak to beak a few times. Explains a lot."

This was as good a theory as any. Regardless of the rationale, pissing off most of the pilots while ostensibly working to rally the troops seemed questionable. The crews had no choice; carriers submitted a list of every plane that would use the new callsign to the FAA. Once approved, the feds notified controllers of the effective date and bitter feelings or not, the pilots would have to comply.

* * *

While the Saturday before Thanksgiving began the holiday crush, Turkey Day itself was a breather, with far fewer passengers and far more timely arrivals than usual.

Drew and Rachel feared there might be nothing more than a passing hello, but he swapped for a gate shift and she for a rare flight with a thirty-minute stop at Moisant. Another ISR kindly covered for Rachel until departure time, and as kindly, Grayson—in the concourse for a change and well-informed as always—pulled Drew aside and said, "I'll set up for your next trip. No need to rush back." This yielded twenty precious minutes.

Rachel picked her way down 7B's external stairs, mindful that the metal grating was notorious for snagging high heels.

"Doesn't feel like November," she said. "What is it, seventy?" Close; the latest observation reported 69° F in light rain.

Everyone had pitched in for turkey sandwiches from a 24-hour place on Williams Boulevard. He grabbed a couple from the tray, got her seated at the table in Ops, then bought sodas and chips from the machines down the hall. Modest as it was, this qualified as a veritable holiday feast in the airline world.

Too soon, it was time to go. They said a quick goodbye at the jetbridge door. Ten minutes later, Drew pushed aside the ache of longing and loneliness swelling in his chest as her trip taxied out of sight.

* * *

"Twelve days of Christmas? That felt like about two!" Rachel exclaimed during a harried hello they squeezed in the first time she passed through Christmas morning.

Their "celebration" later felt like déjà vu. They jumped through the same hoops as on Thanksgiving, and her flight arrived early so they had a few extra minutes. The brisk weather felt more like the holidays and someone had softened the drab walls, cold fluorescent glow, and worn furniture in Ops with makeshift decorations—some tinsel taped to the counter, a small, scraggly tree perched on a filing cabinet, and paper snowflakes hung throughout.

Drew again bought sodas and chips from the vending machine. They ate, then exchanged gifts.

"Ladies first."

Rachel tore off the wrapping, her eyes widening with excitement.

"How did you *do* this?"

"It took a little horse trading," he admitted. Rachel had commented on the crisp, tight closeups captured by his Canon 300mm zoom lens. A similar Nikon to fit her camera was beyond what either of them could afford. But he doggedly combed local shops until he found a used one in near mint condition. Cash, a couple of seldom-used lenses, and a behind-the-scenes airport tour for the store owner and his twelve-year-old son sealed the deal.

"All that? Oh my God, thank you! I love it! I can't wait to try it out. But can you keep it for me until we get together next week? I don't want to leave it in my bag on my layovers."

"Of course. The tour was fun. The kid loves airplanes. Reminded me of myself at that age."

"Oh really, you love airplanes? Then hurry and open yours."

She couldn't have done better: a pocket-sized aviation band radio complete with earpiece. Now he could listen to Air Traffic Control any time.

"This is great." He was touched by her thoughtfulness.

Her face lit up. "You really like it?"

"You know I do. I've wanted one of these for a long time. Thank you."

"Moisant Ops, AirStar Five Forty-five in range with six point six," squawked a voice from the Ops radio, bringing the curtain down on the moment.

They stood up, hugged, and then she looked into his eyes and said softly, "Merry Christmas. I love you."

"Back at you."

Drew caught another amusing glimpse of Rob on the way out. Even months later, he still looked as if he suspected the whole thing would eventually be revealed as an elaborate ongoing gag.

They walked back to her gate and said goodbye like on Thanksgiving. A colleague had draped the podium with garland and strung Christmas lights around the jetbridge door, but it was tough to embrace the festive spirit.

He was on the headset as her flight pushed. He saluted and waved to the pilots and they began to taxi away. That empty, hollow feeling again gnawed at his heart as he watched the blue jet disappear around the far end of the concourse.

TWENTY-TWO

Mary posted a notice in early January seeking lead agent volunteers. Drew was a couple of weeks into the training when deregulation's ever-churning jetstream again rocked the industry. Ostensibly a means of increasing competition and lowering fares, the law had backfired. Mergers and acquisitions whittled ten or so major carriers down to four, devouring smaller airlines or forcing them out of business. Especially hard hit were less profitable regional markets, where consumers found a lose-lose combination of higher fares and fewer flights—or none at all.

The latest step backwards had Northwest acquiring Republic, consigning no fewer than eight rich and distinct airline heritages to the dustbin of history in the process.

Somewhat ironically, Republic itself resulted from the first post-deregulation merger, North Central's 1979 acquisition of Southern Airways.

North Central's origins were unusual to say the least. A Clintonville, Wisconsin, firm first known as the Badger Four Wheel Drive Auto Company formed a flight department in 1939, seeking faster transportation than roads or rails could provide. The company traded a truck for a used Waco biplane and before long, the flights were useful enough to add a second aircraft. They even allowed local residents to tag along when space was available.

This proved so popular that charging fares became feasible, eventually resulting in Civil Aeronautics Board approval to form a "local service air carrier" in 1944. This was the remarkable genesis of Wisconsin Central Airlines, the "Route of the Northliners."

Post-World War II growth led to a 1947 relocation to Madison and the birth of a beloved and widely recognized logo—Herman the duck. The airline moved to Minneapolis in 1952 and adopted the name North Central Airlines to acknowledge their expanded reach.

Merger partner Southern Airways, another local service carrier, began spreading its wings over the southeast on June 10, 1949. The DC-3 operating Southern Flight 1 departed Atlanta that day for Gadsden, Alabama; Birmingham; Tuscaloosa; Columbus, Mississippi; and, finally, Memphis. Southern illustrated the Civil Aeronautics Board's leisurely pace prior to deregulation, having applied for its operating certificate some five years prior to the inaugural flight.

By the time North Central purchased it, Southern had grown from 39 employees to over 4,500; from DC-3s to a fleet of modern DC-9 jets; and the "Route of the Aristocrats" served 50 cities in 17 states along with Grand Cayman. But the 1970s brought two fatal accidents, a high-profile hijacking, and soaring costs that shredded the viability of its short-haul routes. Meanwhile, new highways fueled customers' growing willingness to drive rather than fly. But Southern's routes complimented North Central's nicely, so Herman got a companion, if ever so briefly—Dixie the duck. The airline soon rebranded as Republic so the fowl-in-formation version of the venerable mark only found its way onto some internal materials and never onto an aircraft tail.

Republic picked some bananas a year later—flying bananas. Acquiring Hughes Airwest and its canary yellow fleet gave the network a western component. Barely a decade old, Hughes Airwest was the product of a 1968 union between Pacific Air Lines, Bonanza Air Lines, and West Coast Airlines that created Air West.

That carrier had barely left the gate, figuratively speaking, when the very rich and even more eccentric Howard Hughes began pursuing it, achieving his goal of buying Air West in 1970. By late 1980, North Central, Southern, Hughes Airwest, and their ancestors were joined in the form of Republic.

A smorgasbord of hybrid paint schemes ensued. Republic at first kept North Central's colors, with Herman on the tail. This transitioned into a rather bland look someone nicknamed the "MTM scheme" because the font was the one used in the titles of *The Mary Tyler Moore Show*. Admirably, it honored Herman, though most passengers likely couldn't imagine why a tiny mallard was painted by the boarding door.

Northwest had swallowed them all with a few pen strokes in some sterile law office and yet again Republic's jets were a mishmash of liveries old and new.

In early February, Drew shook his head and sighed as he watched an example taxi by while Mary graded his lead agent coursework. The red "Northwest" titles looked strangely out of place against Republic's original teal and navy, and he could almost imagine a tear running down the tail under Herman's eye.

"Congrats," Mary said. "You aced it!"

He could now fill in as an acting lead when needed or trade for lead agent shifts and the forty-cent-an-hour bump that went with them. The wait wasn't long; it was Carnival season and plenty of people wanted time off.

Mardi Gras had seemed tired a couple of years ago. Having Rachel to share it with made it all new again. They didn't make Fat Tuesday but attended several parades. They both loved people-watching and there was no better place for that. As always, Rachel's tall, graceful beauty always turned heads. She didn't have to shout "Throw me something, mister!" to prompt a bead and doubloon barrage whenever a float rolled by.

"This is crazy!" she yelled amid the usual jostling of people scrapping for trinkets. "I love it!"

It got even crazier at Bacchus when Brock and his girlfriend Stacy, also a striking young lady, came along. Even King Bacchus, star of a popular TV comedy, targeted the two with a shower of throws.

The theme that year was "New Orleans, We Love You." Floats honored the local cuisine, the oil industry, famous people like Louie Armstrong and de Bienville, the Sugar Bowl, and the Saints among others. Seeing the famous Clydesdales up close really brought home their size, though they looked miniscule compared to the enormous "Bacchugator." Stretching over a hundred feet, the reptile honoring local swamps and bayous claimed the title of largest Carnival float ever.

The foursome gave away most of their haul because they couldn't carry it to the car.

Brock, hair tousled and eyes red from draining Jax longnecks all evening, was always good for a quip. "Thank God you girls didn't flash your boobs," he said with a tired grin, "they would have needed a steam shovel to dig us out."

Five days later was Valentine's Day, a hectic Friday on which Drew was working a counter/ramp double and Rachel a full slate of turnarounds. They had agreed to postpone celebrating until the following Tuesday, planning to have dinner at her favorite Mexican place. Still, both were disappointed when her last trip passed through without even a chance to say hello.

He had, however, arranged for the gate CSR to hand Rachel a small box neatly wrapped in red right before closing the cabin door. As planned, Rachel only had time to quickly stash it away. The short segment was too busy for her to open it, and she was too tired when they landed. Finally, after showering and climbing into bed, she read the note taped to the top.

"See," he had written, *"I told you."*

What was inside brought a smile onto her face and into her heart. There were some chocolates from a meal cart and a ticket jacket cut into a heart.

* * *

March brought open slots on the ISR reserve class waiting list. Drew eagerly applied, reflecting afterwards on how the chocks fiasco had become an unexpected blessing. His curiosity, inclination to pitch in, and hunger for extra duty had, by necessity, morphed into a survival tactic. Now all were second nature and there was always a process to master, more training to take, or another nuance to learn about the company or industry. The ISR course would fit right in.

Rachel's eyes grew wide and her mouth dropped open when he told her over pancakes one morning. "Oh, I can't *wait* for *that,"* she said with a smirk.

"Wanna bet I'll make it? How 'bout this: if I pass, you pin me."

By tradition, only another flight attendant could pin on a graduate's wings.

"It's a bet. But don't forget, I'm buds with most of the instructors."

"I know, and that will make it *so* much sweeter when we toast my victory."

"Something will be toast all right," Rachel shot back. "You!"

"We'll see," Drew said, confidence written all over his face. "Just start thinking about where you're going to take me. Maybe that barbeque place in Denver you rave about."

"You're on. Oh, and that reminds me," she said. "Remember I mentioned a while back my mom put her house on the market? Well, it sold and she's moving to a senior community, though I don't dare call it that. Anyway, she needs help moving. Would you want to come with?"

"I'd like that. When?"

Her calendar book was already out. "Let's see…I'm going up Friday the twenty-first and I figure I'll stay till Sunday night."

"Sounds good. Looking forward to it."

He swapped his shifts and she her trips. Both would make up the lost time since neither could afford not to. With ID90 tickets on Frontier, they left Hobby on a chilly April morning. The open flight spared them the usual NRSA handwringing, and they were grateful because the only place worse than the bottom of your own airline's standby list was the bottom of somebody else's.

"Shoot, the agent goofed," Rachel said when she saw their seat assignments. They both tried to be "good little nonrevs" and knew Frontier only allowed ID90 travelers in Coach.

She returned to the podium. "Excuse me," she said softly. "I think this is a mistake. We're on ID—"

"Shhh," replied the Frontier agent, smiling. "Have a nice trip."

Their good fortune continued at the rental car agency.

"I'm sorry, we're all out of compacts. Will this be okay?" the Avis agent had asked, quite ridiculously since the proffered replacement was a silver Eldorado that smelled of new leather and had 15 miles on the odometer.

"I thought she was kidding about honoring the rate," Drew said as they drove away. "I thought for sure we'd have to try somewhere else."

Strangely, there were people who frowned upon such blessings, always sure the other shoe would inevitably drop. Well, maybe, but why not enjoy their luck in the meantime?

They reached Gunbarrel around eleven. After Rachel and her mom hugged and said hello, Drew introduced himself.

"Call me Marilyn," said Rachel's mother. "It's so nice to finally meet you." Gesturing at the car, she went on, "What in the world? I thought you guys were poor airline employees."

Rachel explained and added, "We got First Class on the way up too, and seats together!"

"Well," Marilyn said, "isn't it nice sometimes to be lucky!"

They grabbed their bags and used the guest room, which was cluttered with boxes of all sizes, to change into working clothes. Both were glad to have packed t-shirts since the weather was unseasonably warm.

Rachel tied her hair up into a high pony tail.

"Hey Pebbles, you forgot the bone."

"Listen, smart guy, it's not *that* high. And you try working hard in this weather with hair this thick laying on your neck."

Marilyn had everything packed and each box marked with the contents and whether it went to storage or her new place. Drew remarked about how organization makes moving easier.

"Trust him," Rachel said. "He knows. He's moved eleven times!"

"Military brat?" asked Marilyn.

"Yes, ma'am, my dad was career Army."

There was still plenty to do despite the preparation. After dropping items at a charity thrift store and a self-storage, they began bringing out belongings. He was working hard but the women were nearly a blur. It was more than tackling the task at hand; both had obviously resolved not to pause long enough to let memories or nostalgia get a foot in the door.

As the pile outside grew, Marilyn fretted that she had hoped to avoid making two trips.

"Let me see what I can do." he said, sizing up the space in the truck.

Marilyn and Rachel made a final sweep. Nothing was left, so they started cleaning. When they came out forty-five minutes later, Marilyn was shocked.

"Where is everything?"

Drew wiped sweat from his face as he walked around behind the truck. The boxes and furniture were neatly stacked to the ceiling. Granted, squeezing in a tennis ball would have been trouble had she come out with one, but they could close the door.

"The stuff marked as needed right away is in your car," he said, gesturing to Marilyn's station wagon.

"That's amazing!"

"It's actually just like stacking baggage in a plane. You find what fits in whatever space you have."

"Yet *another* hidden talent," Rachel said kiddingly, but he could see in her eyes that she was pleased.

Drew drove the rented truck with Rachel beside him. She had insisted on driving Marilyn, whose refusal to be chauffeured was every bit as stout. That had been an interesting standoff, solving any mystery as to the origin of his girlfriend's stubborn streak.

It was tough keeping a straight face when Rachel climbed into the truck cab, slammed the door shut, and exclaimed, "God! I cannot *stand* it when she gets like that!"

"Like what?"

"So damn headstrong!"

"No comment."

After a lengthy side-eye, she said in a carefully measured voice, "I am *not* as stubborn as she is. Not even close."

"Not…even…close," he replied with a sidelong glance of his own.

He could see Marilyn's reflection in the side mirror as they drove away. She sat with her hands at ten and two on the wheel of the square-nosed Subaru, face set with determination not to let emotion overwhelm her.

The sun had dipped behind the mountains in a warm glow of pink and amber by the time the truck was empty. Marilyn's apartment smelled of fresh paint and recently installed carpet. Marilyn directed the arrangement of furniture, then Rachel opened a box and handed out wine glasses. She poured, and Drew reflected for a moment before raising his glass.

"To all that was," he said, "and all that will be." Mother and daughter both looked touched.

When the goblets were empty, Rachel started to put dishes away.

"No, no, no," Marilyn protested. "Out, both of you."

Rachel looked at her. "But—"

"But nothing," Marilyn interrupted, taking a stack of plates from her daughter and setting them on the counter. "Take the rest of the weekend and have some fun. I'm going to relax for a few minutes and then I've got a lot of work to do here."

Her voice didn't match the conviction of her words and Rachel's expression made it clear she wasn't buying it. Still, the daughter gave in gracefully this time.

Rachel hugged her mom at the door, and she in turn hugged Drew and said, "Thank you for your help today." Her eyes, as blue as Rachel's, filled with tears. "Take good care of my little girl. She's all I have left now."

"I will. You can count on it."

In the truck, Rachel said, "'Work to do' my ass. She misses my dad so much and there were so many good times in that house. She needs time to cry and no way will she do it with me around." Her hand found his. "I probably need a good cry too but not now."

"Now is okay with me," he said, squeezing her hand in return.

"No," she said. "We have the rest of the weekend so let's come up with a plan."

"Shouldn't we come back tomorrow and help your mom?"

"No, she and I talked when you were outside. She wants to settle in on her own so she meant what she said."

"Okay then, a plan." Drew thought for a minute and said, "You know, I lived in New Orleans for fifteen years before I finally took a tour of the Cabildo. I felt like a knucklehead for never doing it. Is there anything you always wanted to do here but never did?"

"That's a good question," Rachel replied. "Let me think."

She stared out the window on the way back to the old house, trying to focus on fun ideas rather than the sadness in her heart. When they arrived, she took the Cadillac keys and said, "Actually, there *is* something I've always wanted to do." He agreed it sounded like a blast.

They filled the truck with gas and returned it, dropping the keys in a lockbox and the paperwork through a slot. Drew checked in at the hotel as Rachel perused a rack of brochures. He grabbed a quick shower while she made some calls.

She hung up as he returned and said, "We lucked out again. Nobody rented the Simons' cabin this weekend and they're not going up either. Mrs. S. said we're welcome to it and told me where to find the spare key. The Jeep place closed at seven but the message said we can get in tomorrow as long as we're there in Breckinridge by eight forty-five. It's a couple of hours' drive and a lot colder up there so we'll have to dress warm and beat the roosters out of bed. You up for getting out of here first thing?"

"Absolutely, as long as we're not up too late tonight."

She leaned across the bed, brought her nose to his, and rubbed the two together.

"Sorry, buddy," she whispered. "No promises."

* * *

Rachel was brushing her teeth when her boyfriend awoke.

"Leth go, theepyhead," she said.

"What?"

She removed the toothbrush.

"I said, 'let's go, sleepyhead.' That Jeep won't drive itself."

Peeking out into the morning twilight, he asked, "What time is it anyway?"

"Quarter to six," Rachel replied, walking to the edge of the bed. "Fifteen minutes," she went on, "before this fine establishment starts serving a delicious, and better yet free, Continental breakfast. Then we're off to spend money we don't have on an adventure we will never forget."

"Is that line from their brochure?" he asked, still looking at the slopes emerging from the darkness.

He turned from the window and laughed. Rachel was as beautiful as ever except for the frothy ring around her mouth.

"Whuh?" she said, brushing again.

"Nothing. Never mind."

Back at the sink, she looked in the mirror and sheepishly said, "Oh."

The breakfast wasn't bad and soon they were headed south to pick up I-70 into the mountains.

"I'm glad I brought a few tapes," said Rachel as she pulled out a small plastic case of cassettes.

"What do you have there?"

"How 'bout some Fogelberg?"

"Who?"

A *you've got to be kidding* glance.

"Dan Fogelberg. Don't tell me you don't know Dan Fogelberg."

"Oh yeah, him. I've heard some of his songs. *Same Old Lang Syne, Leader of the Band,* right? Yeah, that's fine."

"The thing about Fogelberg," Rachel went on enthusiastically, "is a lot of his best stuff has never been on the radio. And the lyrics…I love the way he can tell stories in his songs, how he captures how it feels to be in love or lose someone you'll miss forever." Slipping the cassette from its case, she said, "Let's listen to this album. It's my favorite ever, by anybody."

"What's it called?"

"Nether Lands."

"Like Holland?"

"No, it's two words, not one. *Nether…Lands.*"

"Is that him on the front? Looks like Jesus. Should I base my expectations on that?"

"Good grief, will you hush and listen? Just give it a chance."

"Okay," he promised, settling back into the seat.

Rachel popped in the tape and fiddled with the audio controls.

"Not a bad setup," she said, quite facetiously since it was far nicer than their cars had. "I'm glad there's a tape deck. We could've been stuck with the radio and the reception's not so great once you're out of Denver."

She adjusted the volume and asked, "How's that?"

"Perfect." His answer encompassed much more than the sound level. The sky was clear and the rising sun lit the tops of the peaks ahead, rendering them a hazy mauve. The light gradually brightened and traveled downwards, turning the highest mountains into angular gray cutouts and coloring the pine trees and pastures on the lower elevations various shades of green. The weather alone was the kind that makes people glad to be alive; adding the scenery, the plans for the day, and the lovely lady sharing it all left him happier than he could ever remember.

The music made for a nice accompaniment. In fact, it was really pretty good and Rachel's singing wasn't bad either.

"Well?" she asked when the album ended.

"Not bad. You got any more?"

Rachel grinned behind her sunglasses.

"Oh, yeah, I have more. See, I knew you'd come around."

"He's pretty good," Drew admitted, "but I'm bringing Boston next time. just so you know."

"Bring whatever you want," she replied. "And really sorry Marianne walked away on ya. Guess it wasn't more than a feeling after all, so now you're stuck with me."

He played along, managing to meld several of his favorite band's hits into his response. "Yeah, it's been a long time since I had any peace of mind. But you know what they say: don't look back."

"Oh God," she said, making a face, "that's *so* bad."

An hour later, they were halfway through *The Innocent Age* and rolling into Breckinridge. Twenty minutes after that, they were bouncing along a rutted trail in a rented canvas-topped 4x4. The plan was to cross the Continental Divide then circle back to Breckenridge. They would return the Jeep and take the gaudy rental out to the remote cabin belonging to long-time friends of Rachel's family.

"Stop here a sec," she said, taking off her sunglasses and parking them atop her Colorado Buffaloes ballcap. She was obviously frustrated with navigating the unmarked trails using the crude map provided by the rental agency.

Some llamas peered through a barbed wire fence to see who had pulled over to get their bearings this time.

"I think," she said, then paused. "Hold on…crap. I think we missed a turn back there. This will get us where we're going, but it'll take longer."

"Good."

"Good?"

"What all have we seen already? Those llamas, who look amused by the way, the buck, that eagle over the ridge, mountains, streams, all while smelling pine trees and wildflowers…did I miss anything? I finally get *Rocky Mountain High*. As long as we get the Jeep back by seven, who cares if we're lost? We'll get up there by lunch time."

"There" was Georgia Pass. They parked near the marker sign, spread a blanket, and had a picnic surrounded by the snow-capped peaks of the jagged, majestic Rockies.

"Look, mountain goats," Rachel said, pointing. "That's so cool."

"This whole place is incredible." His thoughts drifted back to the shuttle bus trip to SFO. He had wished for someone with whom to share special moments and places like this. So many wishes had been granted and he was profoundly grateful.

Around three they pulled off into a secluded clearing for a break. Rachel leaned over for a kiss. Drew kissed her back. One thing led to another until the Jeep's cramped confines brought things to a disappointing halt. Both were too shy to take it outside so the romance stalled somewhere between second base and third and soon they were back on the trail.

"I'm telling you, we're going to be sorry we didn't throw the blanket down and go for it. You know what they say, it's the things you don't do that you end up regretting."

"Hey, I would've if you would've."

The Jeep skidded to a stop. He popped the gearshift into reverse and started to back up.

"Hey, wait! What are you doing?"

"Turning around! Or was that all big talk?"

"No, no, no you don't," Rachel stammered. "No changing your mind now. Besides, we have to get back. The sun will be going down soon."

She was right; the shadows were growing long and this was no place for novices after dark. Reluctantly, he continued down the trail.

Yep, that saying is right on target.

* * *

They returned the Jeep just in time. After picking up some food at a market, they set out to find the cabin. Though Rachel had been there many times, finding it at night was a whole different animal. Forty-five minutes, several dead-ends, and some wolf howls later, they pulled into the gravel driveway, exhausted.

The luxurious Caddy made for an interesting juxtaposition parked next to the rustic cabin. Rachel, laughing, said it looked like an underworld kingpin had come to call on some bumpkin cousins.

After dinner, they layered up against the chill and snuggled up in the hammock behind the cabin.

"It's colder than I thought," Rachel said. "Back inside, maybe start a fire?"

"One more thing before we give up," he said as they clambered out of the hammock. "I saw something inside that might help." He returned a couple of minutes later with a down-filled sleeping bag with room for two. Getting into the sleeping bag and the hammock was quite a feat of teamwork and balance.

Now comfortably warm, Drew stared at the sky, more mesmerized by the second as his eyes adapted to the dark.

As if on cue, Rachel said in wonder, "I've never seen so many stars!"

The moon rose and crowned the mountains in silver. There was no need to intrude on the peaceful quiet of the forest. He treasured that about their relationship; silence was as comfortable as conversation.

They had never discussed the future, not the long term anyway. Someday they would make plans, he figured, but for now the present seemed to be everything they wanted. He trusted that the rest would take care of itself.

His cares fell away, leaving nothing in the world but the girl, the sky, the mountains, and the crisp air laced with pine and a hint of wood smoke. Like on the plane climbing out of Brownsville, he would have been happy for the moment to last forever.

Far above, a blinking white speck appeared, leaving a contrail that the moonlight turned into a gleaming strand. It arrowed along at an angle that made its trajectory appear to rise higher and higher.

Again, Rachel seemed to read his mind.

"See that?" she whispered. "Looks like angels could follow it home."

* * *

Drew woke the next morning feeling rested.

I wish we had more time.

He got up, stretched, pulled on some clothes, and found Rachel in one of the porch rockers. She was cozied up in jeans and a Broncos sweatshirt, her long legs pulled up under her and hands cradling a hot cup of tea. The sun had barely begun to light the high overcast.

He kissed her on the forehead and said, "Morning."

"Good morning. I hope I didn't wake you."

"You didn't."

"Good." She nodded at the scene before them. "I love watching the dawn. It's almost spiritual the way the light transforms everything."

"Save that thought. I'll be right back."

He made a cup of cocoa and joined her. They enjoyed the silence as the new day made a breathtaking entrance. Gray, unremarkable clouds became works of art and the color soon spread to the peaks and trees and finally to leaves and blades of grass. For a few spellbinding moments, the whole world was made of polished brass.

"'Nature's first green is gold,'" Rachel said softly. "May not be the poem's exact context, but that's what comes to mind."

"'Her hardest hue to hold.' That kinda fits here too."

She turned to him. "Not bad, not bad," she said. "He can quote Frost."

"Don't give me too much credit. I didn't know it was Frost and I can't remember the rest."

"Well, I can, and now that the dawn's gone down to day, we better hit the road if we're going to make our flight."

They washed their cups, put fresh sheets on the bed, again cranked up Fogelberg in the Caddy, and headed for Denver.

* * *

Late that evening, Drew unlocked his door, tired and ready to get to bed. He was working at ten the next day but had a clean uniform so the only thing he needed right away was his toothbrush. Wrapped around it was a lavender-colored page from the little notebook Rachel always carried.

I hope that for me, she had written, *"all that will be" will be with you.*

TWENTY-THREE

Through attrition and transfers, Drew slowly climbed the part-time seniority list, reaching fourth just before his second anniversary. The next bid, issued a few days later, listed only two schedules with weekend days off: a Friday/Saturday and a Sunday/Monday, both afternoon starts. On a lark, he chose them as his first two lines.

He smiled incredulously when Kelly posted the results.

Holy crap – Sunday and Monday off!

"Good for you!" exclaimed Donna, delivering one of her patented hugs. "You know what they say, 'Bid what you want—'"

"'Not what you think you'll get.'" It was good advice but seldom paid off in reality.

"You got it, buddy."

He shook his head and said, "Not to look a gift horse in the mouth...but I don't get it."

"One used to be a morning," Donna explained. "Marissa didn't want to take afternoons to have a weekend day off, and I heard Demarcus is taking night classes so he needs to work mornings. That left you and Connie."

"Lucky me!"

"Enjoy it," counseled Gail, who was high in the full-time pack but tolerated Wednesdays and Thursdays off to work mornings. "You're very, very lucky. You wouldn't believe how long that takes at majors. Decades, and I'm not kidding."

He counted his blessings for six weeks. That's when Kelly called out from her desk as he clocked in on a muggy June afternoon.

"Hey there, congrats!"

"On what?" Drew asked over the *ch-chunk* of the time clock.

"Oh crap. Barb didn't tell you?"

"Tell me what?"

"That you're our newest full-timer," said Barb from her office door.

"Sorry," said Kelly, sheepishly. She had been off the day before.

"No big deal," said Barb. "I got tied up yesterday and never got a chance to call him in."

"Whose spot? And what about Connie and Demarcus?" Henry preferred part-time but the others wanted full-time.

"Brent's transferring to Houston," explained Barb. "Connie's been accepted for ISR training and Demarcus has decided to go to school full time. You can pass and hold the second part-time line but full-time is all yours if you're interested."

Here was every part-timer's Holy Grail, placed before him on a silver platter. Yet suddenly the choice wasn't so obvious. The pros and cons bounced around in his head.

Moving up to number two part-timer would change everything. Partial weekends off were pretty sweet but at number four, that schedule was only certain until the next bid. Now it was his indefinitely. Going full-time would mean a cliff dive right back to the bottom of the bid.

This meant declining, once unthinkable, was now an option. Any subsequent full-time slots would again be his to consider. Still, such things were unpredictable. The next opportunity could be weeks away or years.

But so what? His greater concern was time with Rachel. What would be the fallout there?

The ISRs bid every month. Rachel was senior but cabin crew schedules were much different than CSRs'. Some people valued layovers while others wanted out-and-backs so they could be home most nights. Some, like Rachel before, preferred long-hauls but others enjoyed the short hops that skipped around the map like stones on a pond.

The ISR and CSR lines had one thing in common: neither made it easy to coordinate days off with someone else. ISRs could trade their trips, but the bottom line was that Rachel's schedule was as fluid and unpredictable as his. They had to patch together a day here and a few days there whenever they could.

Full-time shifts would be easier to trade; there was, as always, an eager flock of part-timers chirping for stray hours like hungry nestlings. He was still among them despite his ascent up the part-time list.

That tipped the scales. The endless scrapping for hours was a miserable existence. This was a priceless opportunity to escape.

"Yes," he told Barb. "I'll take it."

Would they just slide him into Brent's spot, mornings with Thursday/Friday off, until the next bid? Fat chance! Kelly issued a special bid the next day, sending him full circle—right back to a 3:00 p.m. start with Tuesday/Wednesday off. A shame, but he was grateful to have 40 guaranteed hours every week along with the flexibility to trade.

This quickly proved to be the right choice. The relative stability combined with more practice syncing their schedules meant more time with Rachel. Soon they were even able to start a fun tradition—a mini-vacation whenever they had some extra money. The trips were brief, a few days at most, and they took turns choosing destinations. This quickly turned into a "Gift of the Magi" competition where each tried to choose the perfect place for the other.

Drew scored first, capitalizing on Rachel's love for movies. They flew to LAX and toured Universal Studios and Hollywood, followed by a romantic evening walk along the Santa Monica pier. They went to Long Beach the next day, checking out the Douglas factory, Howard Hughes' massive Spruce Goose flying boat, and the *Queen Mary*. Then they headed down the Pacific Coast Highway to Laguna Beach. They toasted the sunset from the sand and it didn't matter a bit that the wine was cheap or that they drank it from plastic cups.

Rachel proved up to the challenge. She procured ID tickets on Piedmont from Houston to D.C. but refused to disclose their ultimate destination. They boarded a 737 with *Lone Star Pacemaker* coincidentally painted on its nose and departed into a light predawn fog. The captain's post-takeoff announcement closed with a request to keep seatbelts fastened "in case we encounter any unexpected rough air."

Rachel turned at his chuckle. "What's funny?"

He described asking Grayson how "Ruff Air" sounding like "rough air" had failed to raise a red flag.

The supervisor had smiled and said, "Oh, them smart college types at the ad agency tried to tell Mr. Ruff, but he's a stubborn man proud of his name. The way I hear it, he said, 'Boys, when you got your own airline, you can call it whatever you damn well like. But for now, kindly shut up and start paintin' airplanes.'" Grayson had laughed. "Then later this reporter asked the old man if he didn't think the name would be confusing like that. He said, 'The smart ones will figure it out.'"

They connected in Charlotte and *Bluegrass Pacemaker* touched down at Washington National just after eleven, the requisite robust use of brakes and thrust reversers on the short runway leaning everyone forward. They took the Metro to L'Enfant Plaza and exited by way of an escalator so long and steep that it seemed possible St. Peter was greeting riders at the top.

Rachel suggested grabbing a quick bite, warning, "You're not going to want to stop and eat once we get there."

They ate sandwiches at an outside table, then she took his hand and led him over to 6th Street SW. As they approached Independence Avenue, Drew nodded toward the massive white building across the way. There was a sign, but it was too far away to read. Still, the place seemed familiar.

"Are we where I think we are?"

"You tell me," Rachel replied, pointing toward one of the tall windows.

The sun was bright and seeing what she was talking about took a few seconds. The dark silhouette was barely visible through the deeply tinted facade of the National Air and Space Museum.

"Holy crap! That's the Wright Flyer!"

"Yes, it is," she said, beaming behind her sunglasses at his excitement.

The pedestrian signal blinked to WALK. Rachel stepped off the curb; Drew, transfixed, didn't move.

"They close at five-thirty," she prompted as people streamed around them. "Ya gonna just stand there and gawk?"

* * *

Eventually they hiked in Yosemite, reprised his bicycle crossing of the Golden Gate—this time, hilariously, on a tandem—snorkeled in the Florida Keys, and rafted the Arkansas River through the Royal Gorge. So much love, happiness, and adventure filled this magical time that it became the benchmark against which Drew would measure experiences for the rest of his life.

Their airline even cooperated, chiseling out a reasonable market share, continuing to bow up to Continental in Houston and keeping a tenuous hold on solvency.

Everything he had ever wanted was within reach. How could life get any better?

* * *

"Didja see Tampa posted a TDY position?" Donna asked as Drew clocked in one day. "It's only a couple weeks but it's full-time. Those are usually part-time. And I know you love that airport." They had talked about TPA's charms after his monumental nonrev trip to Miami.

That would be pretty amazing. But—

"Well? What do you think?"

He wanted to jump at the chance, but the drag chute of possible rejection he had struggled with at Streak surfaced again.

"I think I have about half a snowball's chance. Everybody wants to work somewhere like that."

"You never know," she replied, always seeing the glass half-full. "Remember the bid? Plus, lots of senior people have kids and stuff so they're not interested in TDY. You could go to the beach every day!"

"Come on, the bid was a fluke." He couldn't argue the other point; Clearwater and its neighbors were nothing short of spectacular.

"Well," Donna continued, "someday you'll do something different or want to transfer, so why not meet the manager and get some interview practice?"

He shrugged. "I don't know. Seems like a waste of time."

She put her hands on his shoulders and looked into his eyes. "Hey, believe in yourself. I do."

Wait, does she believe in me, or herself? Both?

He wanted Rachel's perspective, so he dropped a note in her PNR. She often couldn't check it until after her last segment, but today she found a moment. Her response lacked nothing in brevity or enthusiasm.

TDY 4 2 WKS IN TPA? GO 4 IT!

Okay, why not.

A Manila envelope showed up in his mail folder a few days later. The grapevine and his colleagues' kindness had struck again, for inside was a copy of the Hillsborough County Aviation Authority's master plan for Tampa International. A sticky note on the cover said, "Always helps to have a little background. Good luck! Capt. M." Leave it to Captain Michaels to have such a thing, to know it would be of interest, and to want to help.

The document described how TPA began operations in 1928 as a general aviation airport, coincidentally called Drew Field. In World War II, the military leased, expanded, and modernized what became Drew Army Airfield. Some 120,000 pilots and airmen, mostly bomber crews, trained there before the facility was returned to the city at war's end. Several airlines began service in April 1946, moving their operations from Peter O. Knight Airport, which was on one of the Davis Islands near downtown and couldn't be enlarged to handle the larger airliners entering service. The name became Tampa International Airport in 1952 and steady growth continued from there.

Amazingly, the layout and people mover system that seemed so futuristic had been completed way back in 1971. More growth was already scheduled, and the city showed admirable vision by setting boarding number targets that would trigger expansion through the year 2000. The airport's innovations ranged from the design itself, which allowed passengers to move from parking to check-in to gates quickly, to the color-coded signage that made navigating the airport much easier.

The candidate arrived on a gray, rainy Saturday, relieved of the usual interview jitters thanks to his assumption of the outcome. Even the dreary weather couldn't make TPA's sleek design and tropical setting less alluring. It was just...inviting.

A supervisor, Annette, met his flight. They chatted on the walk to the back office, which looked much like MSY's and probably every other one too.

Paul, the station manager, introduced himself, and the trio took seats around a small table. They began with the usual questions about his background and why he was interested in this opportunity. Then they shifted to a different track, taking turns presenting operational situations and customer service dilemmas, asking how he would handle each and why.

Next was the schedule, a split shift from 6 a.m. to 10 a.m. and 6 p.m. to 10:00 p.m., with Monday/Tuesday off. The evenings involved two hours at the counter, then closing it and meeting a couple of arrivals, one scheduled for around nine and the other at 9:45 p.m. "Scheduled" was the operative word since the last daily arrival was seldom on time. Paul explained that having to stay late for the terminator would not excuse tardiness the following morning.

"How would you feel about those hours?" asked Annette.

"No problem. If that's what you need, that's what I'll do." It was true; he'd had many tougher days and had to stifle a chuckle when the Mr. Hoppy morning popped into his head.

Finally, they explained that Eastern handled ramp services under contract. Ruff Air's only role below the wing was working operations in a small corner of Eastern's office.

Annette led a brief facilities tour, and when they returned to the counter, she shook hands and wished him luck.

There was an hour until his flight boarded, so what else would he do but explore the airport? He walked it for 45 minutes, then headed out to the gate on Airside B. Among the murmur of conversation there, he realized it was an anniversary of sorts: a year since Ruff Air 819 had diverted to New Orleans. He used a computer behind an empty podium to write Rachel, noting the anniversary and telling her the interview had gone well.

But from there, his spirits fell. He stared glumly out the window as the Super 50 pushed off the gate.

I never should have listened to Donna. Competing with senior CSRs who are way more experienced? Yeah, good luck with that.

Smitten with TPA before, now he wanted this assignment more than anything. So what if it was temporary and involved wacky hours?

But he knew he wasn't going to get it.

* * *

Mary came out to the counter the next morning.

"Drew? Phone call."

He looked at her, surprised.

Who's calling me at work at seven on a Sunday morning?

The lead agent answered the unspoken question as they approached Kelly's desk.

"It's Paul from Tampa," she said.

His surprise showed. Mary shrugged before punching the blinking button and handing him the receiver.

Wow, that's really nice of him to call everyone and not just whoever they picked.

"Drew? Good morning, it's Paul in Tampa. Hey, thanks for taking the time to come down yesterday."

"You're very welcome. I appreciated the chance to meet you and Annette."

Convinced of the outcome, he was already mentally drafting his next response, and thus utterly unprepared for what Paul said next.

"We really liked what we heard from you. Can you be here by Wednesday?:"

TWENTY-FOUR

Sunrise the following Tuesday was a multicolored spectacle. The beautiful dawn felt like a portent of something new, beckoning all who saw it toward a future brimming with fresh, exciting possibilities.

Drew, cruising east on I-10, laughed at himself.

Dude, it's TDY. You'll be back dragging the lav cart around Seven Bravo in nothing flat.

True, but the lovely, peaceful moments still felt like a gift after the whirlwind following Paul's call. Working, packing, and tying up loose ends had barely left time to breathe, let alone deal with the apartment office's reminder that his lease expired in six weeks. Moving closer to Moisant would significantly cut his commute, but sorting that out would have to wait.

Soon an unmistakable silhouette loomed against the bright orange horizon—the superstructure of the magnificent USS *Alabama*. He had toured the old battlewagon and the adjacent submarine, USS *Drum*, years ago. The visit was memorable for quite a rare occurrence: Dad getting choked up.

The family had stopped at the Memorial Park on the way to a Florida vacation. Drew captured each of the aircraft on display with his Instamatic, the last being a Marine Corps Corsair.

Dad stood quietly in front of it for a long moment.

"We called them the 'Angels of Okinawa,'" he finally said, his voice almost a whisper and tears in his eyes. "There were so many times we thought we'd had it, about to be overrun, banzai charges, a lot of my buddies shot to hell or blown to pieces…and then those Corsairs would come screaming in so low we thought they might leave some of that blue paint on our helmets. They gave the Japanese hell. Those six fifty-calibers, rockets, bombs, anything they could strap to the wings. I think they even dropped napalm. Afterward, it was a wasteland—nothing left alive. Nothing. Only smoke and the stink from everything burning."

Dad was standing in Mobile but the sight of the gull-winged fighter had taken his mind back to a muddy island in the East China Sea. Shaking his head, he said. "That noise they made, almost like an artillery shell coming in. A buddy told me later the enemy called Corsairs 'the Whistling Death.' Once you heard it, you understood why."

Drew was astonished. He had never seen this raw side of his father, and was heartbroken by the realization of how deeply the war had torn his soul.

Dad shook off the haunting reverie, wrestling the horrifying memories back to wherever he kept them. Putting his arm around his son, he said, "Your old man wouldn't be standing here if not for those brave Marine pilots, that's for sure. I wish I could have found every one of them to shake their hands like we did that time on Leyte."

That remarkable tale was the only one Dad ever told spontaneously. The story compelled his son to spend hours building a model with the markings of America's top World War II ace, Major Richard Bong of Poplar, Wisconsin. The famed pilot, flying one of his last combat missions, had helped provide air cover for a beach assault. The landing craft plowing through the turquoise surf toward Leyte on that third anniversary of Pearl Harbor carried elements of the Army's 77th "Liberty" Division, including Drew's father, then barely twenty-one years old.

Still far from shore, the soldiers spotted an enemy bomber approaching. As Dad told it, time seemed to stop. Every man's focus was absolute. Most were veterans of Guam, so it wasn't their first time in mortal danger. But in battle, most guys never saw it coming. The sudden stitch of machine gun fire from ambush, the grenade sailing into a trench, the sniper's round from a jungle nest, a random step onto a buried mine...all brought a quick and violent end, often with little chance for perception, much less contemplation.

Not this time. There was nowhere to hide; everyone had a ringside seat.

Step right up! See death delivered right into your lap!

The bomb and the plane from which it fell were painted on a sky dappled with black puffs of anti-aircraft fire and white cottony clouds. The color and sound, depending on who you asked later, was suddenly either vivid or gone. As the bomb fell, seconds seemed to stretch to minutes. There was plenty of time to reflect on all the wishes and regrets, to wonder how parents or sweethearts would react when Western Union delivered the telegram: *The Secretary of War expresses his deepest regret…*

In that moment, a visceral understanding took hold—everything mattered, yet nothing did, because this was going to be close. If it hit, the brief remainder of their lives would flash by like the last few feet of broken film rattling through a projector. Consciousness, vitality, potential—all they ever would have been wiped to empty white light in a flickering instant.

The bomb detonated alongside with a thunderous concussion, raising a massive geyser that drenched the ducking troops and rolled the boat to starboard. Shrapnel peppered its side and whistled overhead. Miraculously, the vessel wasn't seriously damaged and no one was killed or even hit, though the blast temporarily reduced many to lip-reading.

Relief swept through the boat, but then somebody yelled, "Don't cheer yet, boys, this bastard's got another egg!" And sure as hell, the plane was circling for a second try. Dad said some of his buddies cursed, others prayed, and one even emptied his rifle at the plane in defiant, impotent rage. The rest simply stared upwards in silence, reliving their vile vulnerability and hoping the practice run hadn't improved the bombardier's aim.

As the bomber came out of its turn and lined up to drop, a brief burst of bullets and cannon shells struck its left engine, setting it afire. Shedding pieces and trailing black smoke, the bomber traced a long arc out of sight, eventually crashing with an orange flash on the mountainous shore of a nearby island. The sudden deliverance came courtesy of an American P-38 Lightning. The troops roared their approval as their savior zoomed by, rocking his wings twice before wheeling into a sharp turn and heading off in search of more targets.

"It was a great shot," Dad always said. "He was far away and it was just a short little 'rat-tat-tat' from his guns."

Days later, Dad's platoon, already minus several casualties, used a precious break from the fight to do something seldom possible in the anonymity of war: personally express their gratitude. At Tacloban Airfield, a sea of mud surrounded by palms sheared off by bombs and artillery, someone directed them to the Operations tent. Their sergeant described the action to the officer there and pointed to the bomber's silhouette on the recognition chart.

"A 'Sally' over Ormoc Bay on the 7th?" the officer said. "Well, you fellas are pretty gosh-darn lucky. You had Major Bong himself looking after you!" He gave them an idea of where to find the major, but there were many long rows of parked aircraft so Sarge flagged down a muddy jeep driven by a shirtless mechanic covered with grease, oil, and dirt. It was hard to tell where he ended and his equally filthy fatigue pants began.

Sarge asked where they might find Major Bong.

The man's face lit up. His accent was heavy and Southern.

"Major Bong? He's got thirty-eight kills now, the most in the whole dang Air Corps!" An old-timer, he still used the obsolete name for the Army Air Forces. He pointed and said, "Over that way."

They finally found Bong talking with his crew chief. Few war memories brought a smile to Dad's face, but that one always did, he and his buddies gathering around Dick Bong himself to shake his hand, pound him on the back, and offer their heartfelt thanks for his handiwork.

Dad, seeming to leave the painful remembrances behind, gestured toward the *Alabama*. "You know, the old gray lady there was at Okinawa too. Let's go take a look."

They had a great time touring the grand ship, with Dad adding interesting context from his wartime service. At a weapons mount, he explained, "These are twenty-millimeter anti-aircraft guns called Oerlikons. Why do you think those words are there?"

The guns had armor plate welded on each side. Stenciled on them in a vertical stack was LEAD DAMMIT LEAD.

"Is it like when you throw a football to someone who's running? You have to throw it where they'll be, not where they are. So the same with shooting at a plane? I guess unless it's coming right at you."

"That's right, son. The same with a plane." A shadow of regret crossed his face again, and his voice was quiet when he added, "Or a man."

"But it seems so obvious."

"Well, standing here talking on a beautiful day like this, I suppose it is. But you have to remember, the boys manning these guns were kids, maybe a year out of high school and a lot of times even less than that. Most had never been even a hundred miles from home and had sure never seen anything like war. Here they were, separated from their families, friends, heck, everything they had ever known, dead on their feet from a lack of sleep a lot of times, seeing things no one should ever have to see, and sometimes there might not have been even a chance to eat for a few days. So maybe having a reminder like that helped when they were at battle stations and hitting the target was the only way to keep themselves and their buddies alive."

Dad's tone had flattened out as he spoke. His voice tailed off at the end and that haunted, faraway look returned to his eyes. Drew realized his father wasn't talking only about anxious young sailors on a battleship.

Remembering Dad's melancholy that day again brought guilt over pestering his father to talk about his experiences. Drew was too young then to see war as anything other than glorious and heroic, and only realized later the emotional toll. Except for the Leyte story, Dad never raised the topic himself and would only reluctantly tell a brief story or two after being egged on by his son.

He felt terrible about it, yet the time to say he was sorry had never felt quite right. He resolved to apologize as soon as he got back to New Orleans.

* * *

Working exclusively above the wing was a big change, and Tampa's CSRs didn't even do all of that. Eastern employees even drove the jetbridges, presumably as a condition of their contract and the Airside B gate lease.

Finding the best plane-watching spots in and around the airport was a fun challenge. The garage's top level offered excellent sightlines as did Airside E, where the gates were three stories above ground rather than the typical two. The unique configuration routed passengers down an escalator to the jetbridge door. Not ideal for efficient boarding, but the layout made for terrific high-angle views. A sharp shot of a red New York Air DC-9 pushing back was among his first efforts from that vantage point.

While the split shift took some getting used to, sunshine and sea spray on various beaches washed away any displeasure. Time at the hotel was rarely spent on anything but showering, changing clothes, and sleeping. A modest per diem helped cover meals.

The heady rush of earning the assignment and the excitement of working at TPA sustained him through the first hectic week—then vanished. He would have spent his first day off watching TV from bed but for having to pick up Rachel. She had worked the inaugural between Houston and San Diego the day before, arriving home at nearly midnight. If she could be at Hobby before dawn so they could have a couple of days together, he wasn't about to be late because his ass was dragging.

She smiled when she saw him, but the blue eyes were subdued and her face didn't light up like usual.

She's got to be exhausted; that's all it is.

They hugged and started toward the people mover.

"What did you think of San Diego?"

"It's beautiful," Rachel replied, "and the weather is incredible. We'll have to go one day." But her usual spark was missing along with any excitement about working the first flight to a new city.

"What's going on? You just tired?"

"That's part of it," she said with a glance around the crowded concourse. "Let's talk somewhere quiet."

A few minutes later, she tilted her face up to the sunshine pouring through the people mover's tinted windows as it glided toward the Landside terminal. "I am *so* ready for some beach time."

"We'll be there in half an hour," Drew assured her.

Soon they were alone on the walkway to employee parking. He sensed she would talk when she was ready. Halfway to the lot, she was.

"Okay, the inaugural. Having the cake and balloons and champagne and all at Hobby was just weird. We weren't even going nonstop to San Diego! The trip wasn't close to full and only about eight people were even going all the way there. Coming back was worse." She stopped and turned to him, holding up three fingers. "Three passengers, Drew. *Three!* Why even bother if it's tags off the L.A. trips? Pay the same fare as Continental but make a stop? Who's going to do that?"

"Tags" were short segments appended onto existing service that enabled carriers to add cities without having to fly more aircraft. Three of Ruff Air's daily flights from Houston to Los Angeles now continued to San Diego, then went back through L.A. on their way back to Houston. Continental operated three daily nonstops.

She shook her head, as frustrated as he'd ever seen her. Seeing her optimism so utterly crushed was alarming, especially since her instincts were usually spot on.

"C'mon, you know how it is. We don't have enough planes yet, and markets take time to develop. They'll put on nonstops when it does."

"Not when, if. It's stupid to fly there if we can't go nonstop from the get-go. Even if we start nonstops, people will have told their friends about making a stop. Whiskey Whiskey is on that giant ranch of his either laughing his ass off or shaking his head, or maybe both. He was a lot smarter than this."

This wasn't her characteristic fire; this sounded more like pessimism, something he had seldom heard from her.

In the car, she continued, "It should have been Seattle."

"And take on Alaska?"

"Why not? They're strong on the West Coast but I don't think they even fly down this way."

"That's a long trip on a Mad Dog," Drew pointed out.

"American flies Seattle-DFW with narrowbodies," she countered.

"That doesn't mean the passengers like it. Besides, DFW has more feed traffic in a day than Hobby does in a month. And that's another reason too. American and TGA already fly it. Those are two bears we don't want to poke."

"Whose side are you on?" she demanded.

This is not the Rachel I know. What's going on?

"Nobody's," he said as they exited the employee lot, trying not to sound defensive. "I'm only trying to see it from all angles."

"Seattle would be bonkers from day one," she insisted. "Bonkers!"

She was right, but he wasn't about to hose *this* fire with jet fuel.

"You may be right. I hope we get to find out."

"Me too," Rachel said, sighing and sinking into her seat. "Enough of that. What's this surprise you mentioned in my PNR?" In a blink, the petulant tone was gone.

"Have you ever been to that hotel Sandy mentioned last time we saw her?"

"No, but I've heard it's amazing. You can walk right out of your room onto the beach. What about it?"

He didn't have to answer. His grin gave it away.

"No way!"

"Way. We're there for the next two nights."

"Seriously? Two nights? Don't you have to work the day after tomorrow?"

"Yeah, but I'll be back in time to hit the beach for most of the day. But I could only afford two nights, even at the airline rate. We'll have to stay at my hotel the night before you leave."

"How in the world…no, not now, tell me later over the biggest drink they've got," she declared, sounding a little more like her usual self.

Getting more into the spirit, she did her best Meg Ryan as they merged onto the Courtney Campbell Causeway. "Buy me margaritas or lose me forever!"

He glanced over with a mock frown and asked, "Wait, what about the 'take me to bed' part?"

"Yeah," she replied, rolling her eyes. "Like you've ever had to worry about *that.*"

* * *

The Belleair Beach hotel lived up to its billing. Worries like new routes and their airline's future were soon and completely forgotten. They swam and sunned until dinner, for which she ordered fresh local seafood and he a steak. Then they laid in chaise lounges at the water's edge, holding hands as a panoramic, soul-soothing sunset unfolded.

The next day was much the same. They were basking in the chaises again, this time under a warm morning sun with a soundtrack of waves crashing and seagull cries. Drew checked his watch a couple of times, then pulled binoculars from their backpack around ten-thirty.

Rachel glanced over. "Do you have somewhere to be, or something to see?"

"As a matter of fact, there is something I want to see."

"Okay, I'll bite. What are you looking for? But word to the wise, it better not be bikinis."

"No, a Tumbleweed," he said, handing her the binoculars and pointing at the sky offshore. "I'm still calling us that regardless of what those dickheads in Houston say. And here it comes I think."

She examined the dark speck approaching from the northwest, already well into its descent. Through the binoculars, she could make out the wordmark along the fuselage and in any case, the midnight blue was unmistakable. Still focused on the jet, she said, "That's so cool! What would that be, five sixty?"

Meanwhile, out came the ATC radio she had gifted him. He hoped they might catch at least a snippet of radio traffic. He smiled as the radio crackled to life as if on cue.

"Good morning Tampa Approach, AirStar Five Sixty with you, six thousand descending four thousand."

"AirStar Five Sixty, Tampa Approach, radar contact, descend and maintain two thousand."

"Down to two thousand for AirStar Five Sixty."

Rachel was floored. "That is *so* freaking cool! I *love* it!"

As she handed back the binoculars, he said, "The New Orleans flight will be along in a bit if it's on time too."

She side-eyed him, perplexed. "How can you possibly know…ohhh, all that time you have now to sit out by the ocean!"

He chuckled, glancing at the DC-9 again, and replied, "Well, it helps that my amazing girlfriend gave me this ATC radio so I can hear them coming." Gazing around at the sand and sea, he asked, "Can you imagine living here? Not 'here' like this hotel obviously, but in a place like Tampa?"

"I might not ever come in from the beach," Rachel replied. She reached out and took his hand, squeezed it, and said, "I love you." Finishing her drink, she went on, "Even more than this very delicious Screwdriver."

"Good," he quipped, "maybe I'll be around longer than it was."

* * *

They headed to Caladesi Island State Park the next morning. Neither had been shy at the breakfast buffet and the boat ride was a little choppy, an unfortunate combination. They exchanged a look, both having to laugh at the other also being green around the gills, though the hilarity ceased when giggle nearly came to yak.

"Thank God!" Rachel said when they reached the calmer water near the dock. A nearby bench suddenly seemed like a great place to spend the next few minutes.

"Here," Rachel said, handing him a couple of Tums and tossing two into her own mouth.

"Thanks."

Ten quiet minutes calmed their churning stomachs, after which they rented a two-place kayak despite the outfitter's good-natured warning.

"You know, we call the tandems 'divorce boats,'" she said. The reason soon became apparent as the couple tried to mount a coordinated effort capable of at least moving them clear of the put-in.

That finally accomplished, Rachel stopped paddling and said, "Well, we're idiots. We forgot to put on sunscreen." There wasn't a choice, so they glided to a stop in some mangroves and took amusing turns trying to get everything covered. Eventually they did and went on to explore as much of the wild island as they could.

Not wanting to risk being late, they paddled back to the kayak shack with a half-hour to spare. They sat in the sand enjoying the steady, pleasant breeze that offset the heat, to a point at least.

Rachel was staring out at the Gulf. He thought nothing of the silence, assuming she was soaking up the moment.

"Hey," she said a minute later, "can we talk about something? Nothing about us...well, I guess it is about us, but not in a bad way. Remember me telling you about my girlfriend Lexi?"

"Sure, she works for Trans Global, right?"

"Right. She told me they're getting ready for a huge expansion later this year, huge. They need a lot more flight attendants. She said I should apply."

"Really?"

"Really. She said they're hiring two thousand people, and that's just cabin crew!"

Absentmindedly watching some pelicans glide by, he asked, "Damn, that's a bunch. Was she bummed when you said no?"

Seconds passed with nothing but the sounds of waves breaking and seabird calls. He turned to see a mix of sadness and sorrow on her face, strikingly similar to the paramedic's expression when she saw Mrs. Bascomb was likely gone.

"Rachel…are you actually considering it?"

"No. I mean, no, I didn't when she brought it up. But with what's going on? 'Going long,' 'upscaling our service,' come on. We've done that and we're still treading water. I thought why not fill out the application, you know, just in case."

"Why didn't you tell me?"

"I should have, but the time never seemed right and who knew if or when they'd even call." Her use of past tense verbs went right over his head.

"That's pretty lame, Rachel. But okay, now we can at least talk about it."

"No," she said softly, "we kinda can't."

He stared at her, then shook his head. "They offered you a job already? When did you apply? Never mind, it doesn't even matter. You took the job without even telling me you applied?"

"You're right, I'm sorry. I only sent the application like ten days ago. I didn't want to tell you through our PNRs and you know we can't afford a big discussion on a long-distance call. Then they called right before the inaugural so it was in my head the whole trip. Cake and champagne but nobody on the plane and all that while we're ignoring places like Seattle. And not just that, it's all the stuff that's happened since we got sold." Her tone turned bitter. "Sold out is more like it."

"And?"

"I should have told you the second I saw you the other day, the first second. But I couldn't, and then you sprung this wonderful surprise and there was no way I was going to spoil it. No way."

She turned to him and went on, "I get now what people have been saying: we can either compete or we can grow, not both. I never worried about this stuff before but I'm seriously wondering if we're going to make it in the long run. If we don't, I'd rather make a move now, on my terms, instead of being in a big scramble. You see what I'm saying?"

He did, even if he didn't want to. He couldn't hide his surprise, sorrow, and—fair or not—some anger.

"You're pissed," she said.

"You wouldn't be? Not that you're going, I get that. Don't like it one bit, but I get it. Things aren't looking great and I can't love you for how you think for yourself then get mad when you follow your heart. So I guess I'm more sad than pissed, though at least a conversation would have been nice for a decision this big. And I'm calling bullshit if you say you're not at least a little worried about what this could mean for us."

She went on, "Look, being apart is going to make for a tough couple of months—"

"Come on, Rachel! It's more than a couple of months. In fact, it'll be worse when you're done training. Where's their academy? L.A., right?"

"Yes."

"At least you'll be in one spot for that. Then you'll be sitting reserve for God knows how long and who knows where that will be? Right?"

Sitting reserve meant just that—being present at the airport for immediate assignment. Reserves at many carriers spent months, even a year or more, waiting in airport crew lounges. "Home reserve" wasn't much better; though allowed off the airport, they had to report to work within a couple of hours after notification. Either way, for eight to twelve hours each duty day, reserves had to be ready to fly away on a moment's notice. This erratic, unpredictable, stressful existence rendered normal sleep, much less making personal plans, nearly impossible. Even packing was a challenge since the fledglings could end up laying over anywhere from Barbados to Boston. To top it off, reserve pay barely covered the bills, and earning more by being called up to fly was never a certainty.

She lowered her eyes. "Okay, yes. It's going to absolutely *suck*. But we're going to be fine." She took his hand. "You can count on that. Trust me…nothing is stronger than this." She squeezed to emphasize the "this."

Letting go to mockingly use air quotes, she went on, "Whether Kirby and his 'air transportation' of 'star quality' works or not, whether you're still there or somewhere else, and wherever I am, we're still going to be us. *TGA* could go bankrupt and we'll still be us."

The ludicrous thought that a massive, worldwide carrier like Trans Global could ever go bankrupt forced a rueful laugh.

"Riiiiight," he replied. "Trans Global, that's been flying since before Lindbergh landed in Paris, they of the six hundred plane fleet, with what, two hundred destinations, ten thousand pilots, seventeen thousand flight attendants, oh wait, excuse me, seventeen thousand and one—"

"Hey, I was trying to make a point. Oh, and nice shot there at the end."

"Okay, you made your point and I guess I did too."

"Look," she went on, taking his hand again, "Why don't you do the same? Like I said, Lexi says they're hiring tons of people and they train everybody at one campus. With a little luck, we might even end up there at the same time."

"Where would I work? You know Tampa is way too senior for me to have a prayer of getting hired here. We might end up worse off than if I ride this out. You're a Pioneer and you'd really bail on everybody who's trying to make this AirStar thing work?"

"Do you think it's *going* to work?"

He had his doubts and it showed. Still, quitting had never occurred to him. Finally, he said, "I don't know."

Rachel squeezed his hand. "My class date isn't until January. If we turn things around by then, then we'll see. Will you at least think about it?"

"Okay, I will." And he would, but already knew he wasn't going anywhere.

"We will always be us," she reiterated, offering to etch this declaration into stone with the epitome of commitment. "Come on, we'll pinky shake."

So they did.

* * *

The ride to TPA the next morning was unusually quiet. The gunmetal sky matched the mood.

"Trust me, I get it," Rachel said, rather randomly. "I most definitely get it."

He parked in short-term, wondering which "it" she was referring to—her leaving AirStar, the implications for their relationship, or both.

They were early and sat in silence while other travelers took suitcases from their cars and headed toward the elevators. Neither knew how to handle the awkward moment.

Finally, Rachel said, "You know what I said about the inaugural and the company, that's just the truth as I see it. That doesn't mean I like it or it's what I want."

"I know," was all he could muster, so they fidgeted and feigned interest in anything other than the unfamiliar, uncomfortable vibe. When the time came to go, there were still no words, but their eyes met, and after a kiss both long and longing, they headed for the terminal.

Out on the airside, a downpour began as the gate agent announced boarding. At the cabin door, Drew hugged her and spent a brief second lost in her eyes. Back at the gate, he gazed at the MD-80 in its gaudy blue paint and festive stripes. The announcements and bustle of people gathering their things and lining up to board had become so familiar that he unconsciously tuned them out.

For all the times he had watched her leave, this was different. As the jet taxied off into the rain, he felt a vague disquiet, the kind that only makes sense in hindsight—when you realize your heart knew something you didn't.

TWENTY-FIVE

The drive back to New Orleans felt twice as long. No lovely sunrise this time, only a low, dark overcast. He drove on autopilot, the white lane markers flashing by mile after mile, none of the little things he typically noticed and enjoyed able to compete with his melancholy.

Rachel's decision to leave for TGA had been a profound shock. He had to make peace with it as best he could, but that was easier said than done. He brooded over it the entire way home and while he unpacked, checked his uniforms for tomorrow, and fell asleep around midnight.

The next morning was no better, but that wouldn't work on a busy Friday. Drew was acting counter lead, having picked up a shift from Mary. He enjoyed the role, ranging back and forth helping where needed instead of being tied down. As usual, the tide of passengers ebbed now and again, giving the CSRs time to catch their breath. Unfortunately, this provided unwanted time to further dwell on his troubles.

He had to focus. The lines were growing; keyboards clicked and the hum of conversation increased. Several customers were casting uneasy glances at watches and wall clocks.

Rachel's trip, 867 from Miami, should be calling in range soon and would depart for Houston and San Francisco in about 35 minutes. It was overbooked, as was the LAX nonstop; Tampa and Orlando were full. Would they get a chance to say hello?

He chided himself for letting his mind wander—again.

Get your head in the game, bro!

The queues were flowing well, the CSRs instinctively shaving a few seconds off each transaction as the pace subtly quickened.

Henry keyed the P.A. and called for any remaining Hobby passengers to come forward. Some people booked on other flights grumbled but managing the process worked far better than a free-for-all. This was the last opportunity to check baggage and head for Concourse B with a reasonable chance of making Flight 867.

As Henry hung up the mic, an overweight man in a rumpled, sweat-spotted business suit surged forward, bumping a couple of people sideways. A plump hand tossed a ticket folder onto the counter.

"Jesus, thanks!" the customer said. "I'll bet my fat ass will be on standby all afternoon if I miss this flight!"

Managing not to laugh out loud was an effort for Henry, Drew, and even Regina, who was one position over and covered as best she could with a sudden fit of fake coughing. To be fair, the man's assessment was accurate on both counts; his ass was quite large and subsequent Houston flights were full or oversold. Yield management was an inexact science at best and CSRs' opinions of it—and fairly or not, of the fresh-from-business-school MBA hotshots brought in by Kirby's bunch to practice it—couldn't be repeated in polite company.

Henry, his fingers a blur and keyboard chattering, said, "All I have are middle seats, sir, but you can check with the gate to see if anything else opens up. It's Seven B, down that way and left. You'll have to hurry."

Henry alerted the gate, but Drew's thoughts had already wandered back to Rachel.

Does she realize what this could mean for us? Or does she have that much faith in our relationship? Am I overreacting?

Regina's elbow interrupted. She nodded across the lobby.

"He's really hustling."

The man had joined the line at a snack bar down the way.

Drew elbowed Henry in turn and said, "Look at this."

Henry took in the scene then startled everyone by abandoning his usual gentle nature. He cupped his hands around his mouth and bellowed, "Hey! Sir! What are you doing? You have to move, that flight leaves in less than fifteen minutes!" People looked at Henry and then the man, who turned away, pretending not to hear.

Regina blinked, astonished. "Henry, what the hell was *that?*"

Henry smiled innocently and replied, "He doesn't have his priorities in order. I was trying to help."

Regina shook her head and said, "Hey, I'll be back in a sec." She flipped the sign overhead to "Position Closed," hopped through the bag well, and headed toward the restrooms across the way. Thirty feet on, a young woman intercepted her. The passenger was canted over toward the huge, battered hardsider she carried. A little girl clutched her other hand. The woman asked something and Regina replied, pointing at Henry. The woman hurried on.

Regina caught Drew's eye, pointed at the pair and then, animatedly, at her watch.

Drew called, "Ma'am," waving for her to come right to Henry's position. Out of breath, the harried woman struggled to the counter and dropped the suitcase.

The little girl looked around, wide-eyed, clutching a stuffed Bugs Bunny tattered from years of attention.

Henry said, "Yes, ma'am, where are you going?"

The woman plopped a ticket folder down, examined the departure board, then looked plaintively at the terminal clock. Her face slowly scrunched up and she began to cry, softly, as if her spirit had finally been broken after a long fight. The little girl looked up with childish worry.

"Mommy?"

Drew handed the mom a tissue. She squeezed her eyes shut and finally managed, "Well, we *were* going to Houston and then to Midland, but it doesn't look like we're going anywhere. My damn car wouldn't start!"

Confusion and disappointment joined the concern twisting the little girl's face. She looked up again and said, "Mommy, we're not going to Aunt Maggie's?"

Henry glanced at the acting lead. The answer to the child's question was maybe or maybe not, a quandary that came with the extra forty cents an hour lead pay. They could reach the gate before departure and would be no worse off if they didn't. Runners were common and while holding a plane for one or two passengers was a myth, latecomers were accommodated whenever possible. The problem was the overbooking. Getting any trip out on time was a challenge; sending these two could light the fuse on a delay.

The airline would pay no compensation due to "10-minute rule," under which reservations could be canceled ten minutes before departure if a passenger wasn't at the gate.

Henry, despite his experience and seniority, respected Drew's temporary authority and left the choice to him. He did, however, offer some subtle advice. Motioning with his eyes toward the flight coupons, he gently tapped a finger on the fare basis code. Drew caught the hint. These were non-refundable discount tickets, worthless the moment the flight pushed, invalid even for standby.

Such draconian measures were controversial, unpopular, and ruthlessly enforced—ironically this time—as part of the constant battle against no-shows. Still, oversold flights often went out with standbys, empty seats, or both.

The mother obviously assumed they were out of luck and he could simply play along, but in reality, he would be the one sentencing her and her little girl to a miserable trudge back to their unreliable car, their vacation ruined and fares forfeited. That wasn't his idea of customer service. Gail was working the trip and would get it, not griping about the extra workload or having to break the news about 10-minute rule if that became necessary.

Henry eyed him expectantly.

If we don't send these guys and find out they would have made it…well, screw that.

Drew said, "Let's see if we can get you down there."

"Really?" the woman asked, "There's a chance?"

"If we hurry," Henry replied. "Listen, your bag won't make it and the flight is full. They may or may not have seats for you, but we'll give it a try." He checked RAATS for available seats, knowing it was fruitless. The expected response appeared: FINAL. Check-in was now restricted to the gate. He added the names to the standby list. It didn't look good, with three volunteer oversales topping the list.

Drew dialed the gate. The phone rang eight times before Gail snapped, "Seven Bravo."

"Two more runners, a mother and child. Mom's in a blue dress. That's it for Hobby."

Gail barked "Got it!" and hung up so quickly that her second word was clipped by the receiver hitting the cradle. Minutes before an oversold departure was no time to expect manners or chitchat.

Drew stepped through the bag well to get the luggage, though boarding it was beyond a long shot. He grabbed the scraped and dinged piece, then set it back down.

"Careful, it's heavy," understated the mom, trying to be helpful.

The slang term for such bags was crude hyperbole: a nutbuster. This thing weighed at least 75 pounds.

How did she even carry this thing?

He got a two-handed grip on the handle, bent his knees as trained, swung the suitcase into the bag well, and squeezed back through. He slapped on a Hobby hub tag and a red "HEAVY" warning. There wasn't time to collect the usual fee, so he scrawled the flights and city pairs on a Voluntary Separation tag. In legalese, the VS tag was a customer's acknowledgement that the luggage was unlikely to make the flight and if this held true, the airline wouldn't deliver it upon arrival.

Henry explained as he presented the tag and a pen to the mother, who hesitated.

He and Drew exchanged a glance, both thinking the same thing.

Don't do it. Do not *stand here crying ten minutes before departure then balk at signing a VS or whine because your bag won't make it!*

She scribbled a signature. Drew tore off the claim check and handed it to Henry, double-checked that the tags were secure, and carefully moved the massive suitcase onto the conveyor while hoping the goddam handle didn't rip right off in his hand.

Henry handed the folder to the mother and pointed. "It's gate Seven B like 'bravo,' down that way and left. Hurry, ma'am. They won't wait for you."

Drew started to call the gate again but hesitated.

Gail will find a way to seat them together if they make it.

The bag didn't have a prayer but Henry motioned for the receiver and dialed T-Point anyway. "Never hurts to at least let them know," he said, and it was true.

The mother was trying to stuff the ticket folder into her purse. She was moving slow, barely making headway. The little girl looked back and waved, all big brown eyes. Drew, focused on getting the mother's attention, distractedly waved back. They would never make it at this pace. He gave up on subtlety, leaned from behind the counter, and was about to shout like Henry had. No, a more definitive course of action was in order. He hopped through the bag well and quickly caught up with the passengers.

"Ma'am, we have to hurry. Here, let me take your carryon. Come on!" She finally picked up the pace. At security, he waved at a screener and pointed to the pair. A minute later, they were through. The mom picked up some steam, at last seeming to recognize what was on the line.

When Seven Bravo came into sight, a few people were still in line at the jetbridge where an ISR—not Rachel, this one was a petite blonde—was collecting tickets. Good; the runners would make it to the gate. Would there be enough no shows?

"That's it on the left, ma'am, Seven B," he said, handing back her carry-on. "Don't slow down!"

"Thank you so, so much!" the mom said.

"You're welcome. I hope you make it."

"Bye-bye, thank you," the child said in her little girl voice, making him smile.

Back at the counter, he hoped things would calm down. The busy morning and worrying about Rachel's move had tied a tight knot right behind his eyes. He raided the breakroom first aid locker but found nothing for a headache. Maybe he would pick up something at the newsstand. Paying ridiculous airport prices might be worth it this time. In the meantime, he could at least sit down for a minute.

Literally a minute as it was. After one sip of soda, Regina stuck her head in the door.

"Hey, Eight Sixty-seven has a mechanical. Gail says they could use you down there for a few minutes."

There had been no reason for the latecomers to hurry after all. He parked his soda in the fridge, happy to see Rachel before she left yet hoping the problem was minor and that the Trans Global mechanics weren't tied up elsewhere.

Gloomy gray light washed away the color outside. Rain had begun ahead of a squall line that had lackadaisically drifted down from Texas and Arkansas until it reached Baton Rouge. Then, a powerful jetlet—an unusually strong jet stream current—intensified and accelerated the front, bowing its middle out into an arc.

Bert was copiloting Rachel's trip and was concerned about the weather. "Man, it's black out there to the northwest, looks grim. Hope we beat it out of here," he said as he slid back into his seat after the walk-around.

"Hey, you know the drill," Captain Doherty replied, "the weather's cold or the weather's hot, we go whether there's weather or not." He wasn't serious; this was standard cockpit humor. "Kidding aside, if it's too dicey we'll wait it out, but let's ask ATC for a deviation. Turn right to get out of here on the climb."

Bert caught his drift. "Circle south till we're on course?"

"Exactly, that should get us clear of that line."

Pilots usually took turns flying throughout the day. This was Captain Doherty's segment, so Bert would be handling the radios. "When I talk to tower," he said, "I'll tell 'em we'll need a minute on the pad to take a look."

No one was at 7B except Chuck, who looked up from the post-departure work and said everyone was on board.

Thank goodness we sent the runners to the gate. The bag should make it too.

Rain drummed on the jetbridge's canvas canopy and streamed down the fuselage through the inevitable gaps between the two. Gail and Rachel chatted at the cabin door.

Uh oh, he thought, but quickly reconsidered. How could Rachel know?

"Hey guys. Gail, it was way late but I had to send those runners."

"I'd have been mad if you didn't. That child is precious."

"Did you make an announcement?" One of his pet peeves was when departure time passed without an explanation and customers were left wondering what was going on.

Rachel's eyes widened. "Did we make an announcement? Do you believe this guy?"

Gail, eyebrows raised, obviously agreed.

"I'll take that as a yes," he said. "So we're hanging out until we know whether we need to rebook the connections?"

Gail said, "That's the plan. I'm going back up. Call if you need anything."

"Thanks, Gail," Rachel replied. "Great to see you."

"You too. Take care."

CSRs and crews were always friendly, but the emergency diversion had forged something deeper between these two.

A glance into the cockpit revealed Bert conversing with the mechanic. The illuminated dials, numbers, and buttons drew a sharp and colorful contrast against the rain-streaked windows and the monochromatic blur of the concourse beyond. Passengers often glimpsed gauges and knobs and levers but few knew what the cockpit of these heavily utilized workhorses looked like up close—a cramped, worn space, painted an unusual, pale turquoise, with a faint odor suggestive of electronics at work.

"Hey," Rachel said, motioning him into the galley. "So, about Gail…I heard you guys had a thing."

The correct question to ask himself a moment ago would have been, "How could Rachel *not* know?"

"Yeah, we dated for a while," he said, shrugging casually then toying with a cabinet latch.

"And?"

"She was separated when we met. She and her husband went to counseling and they decided to try again. They have a little boy and I think that was a big part of it." Enough time had passed for him to admit, "But we never clicked like you and I did."

"Well, selfishly, I'm glad, but she seems sweet. You could have done a lot worse."

He grinned and chuckled.

"What?"

"She said the same thing about you that day at the hospital."

Taken aback, Rachel said, "Seriously? We had barely even met."

"That's what I told her. Her exact words were, 'You just look like a couple.'"

"Wow, she called it. Funny how things work out sometimes."

Drew nodded forward and asked, "So what's the deal?"

"Supposedly the mechanic says it shouldn't be long, but you know how that goes. And I guess the weather looks pretty rough."

"Thanks. I'll go try and smooth any ruffled feathers."

Making his way aft, he answered questions and assured people, understandably anxious about their connections, that they should be on their way shortly. He remembered many of the customers from the counter. Even snack bar guy had made the flight. He was stuffed into a middle seat way aft.

As he knew she would, Gail had seated the little girl with her mother. He told mom that the delay shouldn't be long, then called T-Point to confirm that Rob had run the bag out to the flight.

"That's a roger," said Rob's voice, scratchy with static. "The bricks are aboard." Several passengers chortled but the mother must only have heard "roger" because she just smiled and nodded.

Her child solemnly announced that her name was Jessica and she was five years old, accompanying this fact with an upraised, spread-fingered hand.

"I'm going to see my Aunt Maggie. She's my mommy's sister. Her name is Margaret but I call her Aunt Maggie."

She had big plans for the trip and related them with certainty that everything would come out right.

"That sounds like a lot of fun," he told her, smiling at her innocent sincerity.

Rachel touched him on the shoulder and said, "They need you up front."

The pilots were talking earnestly with the mechanic, who was on the jumpseat with the plane's maintenance logbook open on his lap.

Drew waited, smiling to himself at the way many pilots stuck pictures under the clear lining of their hats, which hung on little clips. Captain Doherty's snapshot showed his family on the Great Wall of China. Beside him was a pretty woman and a boy who had inherited his mother's blond hair and his father's broad shoulders and square jaw. The imposing serpentine structure extended so far out behind them that the nearest mountains shone a lush, vibrant green while the most distant were hazy blue silhouettes.

Bert's looked like a scene lifted from a Caribbean vacation brochure. He and a lovely bikini-clad woman, both smiling behind their shades, leaned against the railing of a sailboat moored in a beautiful lagoon.

Catching Bert's eye and nodding at the headwear, Drew grinned and said, "Wow, must be serious, her picture made the hat."

The captain and mechanic chuckled.

Bert shrugged and self-consciously flashed his news anchor teeth. "What can I say man? She keeps me in line."

Captain Doherty motioned toward the mechanic, who was scribbling in the logbook, and said, "Looks like we're about ready to roll."

Bert snapped his fingers. "Meant to call about the connections," he said, picking up the radio mic. "Ops,

Tumbleweed Eight Six Seven, confirming Hobby is aware of the connections?"

Peggy answered, "Affirmative, we let them know."

The mechanic tucked the logbook into its place and got to his feet.

"All set, Captain, shouldn't give you any more trouble." He stowed the jumpseat and addressed Drew. "You're good to go my friend."

"Drew!" called Bert. "Take it easy man. See you next time through."

"You too," he replied.

The ISRs had everyone seated, so after mentally rehearsing as taught, he keyed the P.A. mic.

"Ladies and gentlemen, we apologize for the brief delay. Maintenance has corrected the problem and we're ready to go. For those with connections, our Houston staff knows you're coming and will do their best to help you make your flight. We appreciate your patience and your understanding that safety is our first concern. Thank you for flying AirStar."

Rachel, oxygen mask and seatbelt demo piece in hand, nodded with mock admiration.

"*Very* nice," she said quietly, trying her best to peg the sass-o-meter. "*Very* reassuring, *very* comforting."

Drew rolled his eyes and said, "Good grief. Maybe this move is a good thing. A little TGA structure might calm you down."

"Ha! Good try, but nothing's changing here but the uniform. I'll still be in all my glory."

"I have *no* doubt about that," he said, stepping out onto the jetbridge. Starting to swing the cabin door closed, he managed for once to get the last word.

"Have a good trip, smartass."

Her radiant smile filled the little round window in the door as he cranked and seated the locking handle. He waved a sign language "I love you," then maneuvered the jetbridge away.

An ordinary departure on an ordinary day—with no way of knowing that the next ten minutes would determine whether he ever saw Rachel's smile again.

TWENTY-SIX

Marissa and Donna were getting drenched despite their yellow raingear. The headset earphones bulged Donna's hood out amusingly and her face had a reddish fringe of soaked hair. She spoke into the cupped mic. Drew obviously couldn't hear but he knew what she was saying.

"Jetbridge is clear, ready to push."

Bert spoke in turn, also out of earshot, but experience enabled lip reading.

"Moisant ground, AirStar Eight Six Seven with Juliet, ready to push from Seven Bravo." The ground controller must have approved because Bert nodded and the captain spoke next.

"Brakes released, clear to push. Clear to start?"

"Roger," Donna replied, "clear to turn two and one."

The tractor growled and belched black exhaust in response to Marissa's gentle push on the gas pedal. Bert and Captain Doherty gave friendly waves as the plane rolled backwards. Drew waved back, secured the jetbridge, and headed back up to the concourse. He could still squeeze in his lunch break before the counter got busy again.

In the cockpit, there was radio traffic and background noise, then Donna again.

"Set your brakes for me, please."

The captain acknowledged and she answered, "Roger, stand by for the pin and have a great trip!"

"She is such a sweetheart," said Captain Doherty. Donna stood ahead of the aircraft with the steering pin over her head, the blowing rain running down her face. The REMOVE BEFORE FLIGHT streamer flapped like a flag in the stiffening wind. Captain Doherty flashed the landing light. She saluted and waved as the jet began to taxi.

Meanwhile, the storm front had crossed Lake Maurepas and the western shore of Lake Pontchartrain, now minutes away and barreling toward Moisant at almost fifty miles an hour.

The gear thunking over concrete seams punctuated the pre-takeoff routine. In the few minutes it took to reach Runway 01, the squall line had strengthened further and traveled over four miles closer.

Bert keyed his mic. "Moisant Tower, AirStar Eight Sixty-seven request, we'd like to hold short to look at this weather. What are your winds?"

To uninitiated listeners, many controllers spoke at a pace rivaling a Gatling gun.

"AirStar Eight Six Seven, winds three four zero at one-six, gusts two-four. Hold approved. Let me know when you're ready."

In one of the towering gray cauldrons, a waterfall of air, rain and hail began plunging toward the ground, growing and accelerating at an astonishing rate. The resulting surface swirls were beginning to tickle the anemometers along the airport's perimeter. Those first disorganized gusts only hinted at the violence about to erupt from the roiling thunderhead.

Bert inspected the weather radar. "Man oh man…looks like *mierda.*"

They lowered the radar's sensitivity to spotlight only the most severe activity and raised the antenna's tilt for a more comprehensive picture.

"Christ," Bert observed, "now it *really* looks like *mierda.*"

"The worst looks like it's still out past the marker," the captain replied, his voice low. "But we're not seeing the gust front."

The hail within the plummeting cascade of cold, dense air and extremely heavy rainfall had mostly melted to insignificance when the torrent reached full force off the distant end of Runway 01. The ground, an unyielding obstacle, sent the air blasting outwards in all directions with enough velocity to flatten trees and bend traffic signs over at odd angles. Along its edges, vortices formed, powerful horizontal whirlwinds waiting in ambush. If visible in its entirety, the microburst would resemble an enormous, inverted mushroom over two miles wide.

But it wasn't visible from the cockpit of AirStar 867.

* * *

At the 7B podium, Chuck set up the signage for the next departure as Gail finished the flight paperwork and needled Drew.

"Remember the guy who told me I was full of it in the hospital parking lot?" she asked, an impish gleam in her brown eyes. "Yet there he was—again—at the window. You watch her flights leave every time, don't you?"

"Sure, when I can. And?"

"And nothing, but my dad was a merchant marine, and he always said it's bad luck to watch a ship until it goes out of sight. Do you think it's true for planes?"

"Well, obviously I hope not."

"Me too. You going to lunch?"

"Yeah, I have to get some aspirin or something on the way back but I'll eat in the breakroom."

"I've got a bottle of something in my purse. Give me about five and I'll meet you there."

"Cool, thanks." He paused. "And okay, you were right about Rachel and I. How, I'll never know, but I have to give credit where it's due."

She smiled. "That was easy. I know you, so half the job was done. You couldn't have hidden it if you tried. She was more of a challenge, but there was a vibe there too."

Drew grabbed his lunch and soda then sat at the beat-up table. Someone had left the morning paper. As usual, the headlines were mostly depressing: a bizarre natural disaster had killed many hundreds in Cameroon; a community was reeling after a massacre in an office; and authorities had recovered a stolen Picasso. Tossing the paper aside, he rubbed his temples and hoped Gail would hurry.

She walked in a second later with her own lunch. Setting down a pill bottle, Gail said, "There ya go," then noticed his sandwich. "PB and J *again?* Don't you live about a block from a supermarket?"

"Hey, PB and J is cheap, fast, and easy." Opening the aspirin bottle, he continued, "Win win win."

"Yeah, yeah, whatever." She dug around in her vest pocket, withdrew some coins, frowned at them, and asked, "Can I borrow a quarter?"

He fished one out, handed it over, and teased, "See, I have an extra because I brought a PB and J *again.*"

She rolled her eyes and groaned on the way to the soda machine.

* * *

Bert turned to the captain. "We gotta go if we're gonna beat it."

The briefest pause. "Yep, let's get out of here."

Bert thought the captain looked tense and the weather spoke for itself, but he kept any reservations to himself.

"All right, boss," he said, "I'll sit the girls down."

The cabin speakers came alive. "Good afternoon, ladies and gentlemen, this is First Officer Dios from the flight deck. On behalf of myself, Captain Doherty, and our truly fine cabin crew, welcome aboard. We're planning a smooth trip for you today but it may be a little bumpy as we clear these showers here in the vicinity of the airport. We apologize for the delay and we'll do our best to get you to Houston as quickly as we can. We're number one for departure so flight attendants, please be seated for takeoff."

Bert switched to the radio. "Moisant Tower, AirStar Eight Sixty-seven is ready. Request ninety right for weather."

"AirStar Eight Six Seven, winds now three two four at one seven, peak two six. Climb and maintain two thousand, deviation approved then as filed, cleared for takeoff Runway One."

The Super 80 taxied through the silver rain onto seven thousand feet of dirty gray concrete smeared with the residue of countless landings.

"Two thousand and cleared for takeoff, AirStar's rolling."

* * *

Coming back into the breakroom, Gail asked, "Have you heard the latest?"

"No, what?"

"My girlfriend Tracy in Res is dating a guy who works at HQ. He swears he saw a memo talking about a purchase agreement for eight A320s. Saw it with his own eyes."

"Airbuses? Supposedly we can barely make the interest on the Super Eighty trust certificates as it is. And why A320s? I could see seven-threes maybe."

"No, he said it was definitely A320s."

"I'll believe we're getting anything when I see one taxi in."

"Well, me too, but who knows?"

"How are things at home?"

"They're good," she said with a smile that felt a bit artificial and a hint of uncertainty in her eyes.

Don't go there, he cautioned himself.

She went on, "David asks about you now and then."

"He's a good kid. I kept the card he made for me."

"Thanks, I couldn't agree more." The smile was authentic this time. Her maternal pride was never far below the surface.

* * *

The raindrops became glittering diagonal slashes in the Super 80's powerful lights. The engines, roaring with nearly 40,000 pounds of thrust, left a wispy trail of black exhaust. Speed built quickly.

"Eighty knots," Bert reported.

The rain increased. Captain Doherty said, "Wipers on high, repellant my side only."

The captain used the rudder to keep the accelerating jet on the centerline, utterly focused on the task at hand. Yet subconsciously, the wisdom built while practicing and studying his craft was hard at work. Decades of experience and learning, from his first flying lesson to his latest check ride; countless hours of "hangar flying"; aerodynamics and aeronautical engineering courses; brutally honest military pilot debriefs; poring over everything from accident and incident reports to *Flying* magazine's "I Learned About Flying from That" and "Aftermath" features; each scrap of knowledge feeding a deep personal and professional curiosity about the miracle of flight. All of it helped forge something called "airmanship."

Few can fully define this critical attribute past a dictionary description, which is accurate but not quite complete: "a measure of a pilot's awareness of the aircraft being flown, the environment in which it operates, his or her capabilities, and the relationship between each." Airmanship shares much with its forebear, seamanship, which esteemed British mariner Erroll Bruce described in part as "...knowledge, preparedness, vigilance, and coolheadedness...honed to a fine edge by constant practice." Many agree there's something more, an intuition, an innate sense of oneness with the machine and the air.

Whatever the ingredients, the result had a little voice in Captain Doherty's head murmuring restlessly.

Bad weather and hub systems never played well together. The captain had heard other pilots say things like, "We fly through this stuff all the time, hasn't killed us yet. Besides, these people have connections to make." And it was true. But he also knew that decision-making bias had proven deadly in the past. People, including pilots, sometimes justified risky choices based on past results as opposed to an objective assessment of the present circumstances.

One of the captain's buddies from Navy flight training served as a sad example. Delayed by a rented airplane's balky electrical system, he couldn't depart until it was too late to complete the flight before nightfall. The destination airport was in mountainous terrain and oriented such that an approach from either end of the single runway was often challenging even in daylight.

A pilot friend, the mechanic who had repaired the airplane, the manager of the flying club from which it had been rented, and the pilot's wife all suggested waiting until morning.

"Aw, we'll be fine," he had declared confidently, "I've flown in there a hundred times and plenty of those at night." But those times weren't *this* time. Factors change; weather, fatigue, routings, traffic, aircraft system performance, unpredictable mountain winds, rusty skills—each potentially dangerous and likely disastrous in combination.

Locating the crash site took two days and another passed before the Alpine Rescue Team could climb to it. They found the captain's buddy and his wife dead in the wreckage.

None of these were thoughts; more just a quiet unease that suddenly coalesced.

Captain Doherty barked an order.

"Reject! Reject!"

Stopping on a wet runway in these conditions was risky, but countless simulator practice sessions paid off. The captain pulled the thrust levers back to idle and disengaged the autothrottles, calling "Throttles!" Then, in nearly the same motion, he raised the spoilers and applied maximum allowable reverse thrust as both men mashed on the brakes.

Bert executed his "memory items," actions so urgent they can't wait for a checklist: applying gentle forward pressure on the yoke to help keep the nosewheel on the runway, verifying things were working as expected, and calling out confirmations: "Spoilers, buckets are out, on the brakes!"

Then he notified the tower, with stress sparking a reversion to old radio habit.

"Tower, Tumbleweed Eight Six Seven rejected takeoff, repeat, Tumbleweed is stopping." Quickly switching over to P.A. mode, he announced, "Remain seated! Please remain seated!"

* * *

Gail looked out the window. The rain beating against the glass was heavy even for New Orleans. The wind howled and sheets of water washed down the building and rushed into the storm drains. Lightning flashbulbed the room and the rumbles of thunder were strong enough to feel.

"Glad we're upstairs today. Wonder if they've closed the ramp with the lightning and all? Good thing that trip got out of here when it did."

Drew, chewing, nodded in agreement and went "Mmm-hmm."

* * *

"Roger," acknowledged the tower controller. "AirStar Eight Six Seven rejected takeoff."

Bert again called, "Eighty knots," this time as the jet decelerated. Accordingly, Captain Doherty closed the thrust reversers.

The wind picked up as the captain turned off the runway, stopped, and set the brakes.

"Tower," Bert radioed, "AirStar is clear of the runway at the last turnoff, no assistance needed."

As the captain called for the Rejected Takeoff Checklist, a lightning show of epic proportions erupted with startlingly loud accompaniments of thunder. An absolute downpour began tattooing the MD-80 from nose to tail, with gusts so strong that the jet bobbed and rocked on its landing gear.

"Looks like a good call, boss," Bert said, comically stating the obvious as he dug for the checklist.

"Seems so," Captain Doherty said quietly, brows furrowed, his face the portrait of someone contemplating the road not taken—and where it might have gone.

"You want me to talk to 'em?" Bert asked.

"No, I've got it." Further reflection would have to wait.

"Ladies and gentlemen, Captain Doherty from the flight deck. I regret the need to stop so abruptly but I think you see now why we did. The storms around the airport are very strong and they got here a little bit faster than we anticipated. We're going to delay our departure until things calm down. It should only be ten to fifteen minutes, but unfortunately those of you making connections will likely miss them. I appreciate your understanding that our commitment to safety sometimes comes with some inconvenience. We thank you for your patience and we'll get our Houston ground staff started on making alternative arrangements for you."

"Nice job explaining," Bert said, sincerely.

They ran through the checklist, after which the captain said, "Let's get clearance back to the other end and we'll wait down there for this to pass."

Bert nodded and radioed, "Tower, AirStar Eight Six Seven would like to taxi back to Runway One."

"Roger, taxi to Runway One via Sierra."

Back at the hold line for Runway 01, there was time to talk.

"What's the real lesson here, Bert?"

"Should have called it here on the pad?"

"Damn right. Ninety knots isn't the time to make that decision."

Bert replied, "I thought the weather looked pretty sketchy."

"Well, don't ever hesitate to speak up, with me or anybody else you're flying with. I learned a long time ago that checking your ego at the door usually achieves the best outcomes. When you get to where you can't learn a lesson or consider the opinion of the guy or gal next to you, it's time to hang it up."

"You got it, cap."

Captain Doherty went on, "My first instructor was a character. Old school guy, started on DC-3s and eventually retired as a 747 captain. He said, 'Whether you're by yourself or have two hundred passengers in the back, any time you have a doubt—something doesn't sound quite right, feel quite right, smell quite right, weather's real iffy, whatever it is—remember four simple words: better late than never. People miss a connection, they'll forget about that in a week. But some things can never be undone.' That might be the best advice I ever got."

"You think the chief will see this one the same way?"

"Demerest? Won't be the first time if he doesn't." Ruefully, he went on, "Or the last, I'm sure. But he's fair, and remember, he's been there. Helped get a 707 back on the ground after some nut set off a bomb in a lav. Blew a hole in the side of the airplane. God knows how that thing held together. But they also had a couple that didn't end so well."

Airline disasters' profound repercussions ripple out, shattering lives and families. They touch everyone affected: survivors, the families of those lost, responders, witnesses, investigators, and the community. To some degree, all suffer the trauma of coping with a life altered beyond recognition. The pain, grief, and loss manifest in emotional, psychological, and physical ways, leaving scars that often last a lifetime.

Yet eliminating all risk would mean never leaving the ground, so how much caution is enough? Evidence exists on only one side of the debate. We can only know what was, not what would have been. The former exists to be comprehended, scrutinized, quantified—and, far too often, criticized—while the latter does not. Whatever horrors are actually prevented by prudent decisions remain unknown.

Had AirStar 867's takeoff continued, subsequent events would have included preparation of something colloquially called a "blue cover." In Box 16, "Abstract," of the "Technical Report Documentation Page," a National Transportation Safety Board staffer would have typed:

On August 29, 1986, AirStar Airlines, Inc., Flight 867, a McDonnell Douglas MD-82, N947RX, was a regularly scheduled passenger flight from Miami, Florida, to San Francisco, California, with enroute stops at New Orleans, Louisiana, and Houston, Texas. About 12:58:26 Central Daylight Time, Flight 867, with 6 crewmembers and 143 passengers on board, began its takeoff from runway 01 at New Orleans International Airport…

More immediate consequences would have played out in the AirStar breakroom, where Drew and Gail were halfway through lunch.

Some kind of commotion from the office next door, like people rushing around. Indistinct voices, then many footsteps echoing down the hall.

Looking at each other, wondering what was happening.

Kelly at the door, her face weirdly pale and torqued into an expression so out of character that the two CSRs just stare, then simultaneously put down their half-eaten sandwiches.

"The tower called and Barb needs everybody right away." Her voice, off somehow, like an instrument slightly out of tune.

"What?" They push back their chairs to get up, more curious than concerned. "What's going on?"

Kelly, trying to speak but nothing comes out. She points down the hall. "Just come on!" Gone as quickly as she arrived.

Another glance exchanged, a sharp edge of unease added to their confusion.

"What the *hell?"* Gail, rhetorically.

The answer to that question would have carved everything that followed indelibly into their memories.

* * *

In the timeline where Captain Doherty ignored his intuition, seasoned experts led by a relative NTSB newcomer would have dissected everything related to the brief flight and tragic end of AirStar 867. The lead investigator would eventually develop a worldwide reputation for compassion, integrity, determination, attention to detail, and sharp appearance. The last came courtesy of a penchant for crisp suits, impeccably styled hair, and distinctively loud neckties. Under his direction, the team would have crafted a comprehensive report detailing the facts, conditions, and circumstances surrounding the disaster.

As always, the most anticipated passage would begin with a sentence in which no one ever wishes to be referenced: *The National Transportation Safety Board determines the probable cause of this accident to be…*

In this instance, the continuance would have said, …*the captain's decision to depart into an area of known convective activity resulting in an encounter with downburst-induced wind shear. The abnormally strong wet microburst was associated with a newly matured severe-to-extreme thunderstorm embedded in a fast-moving multi-cell line. The crew's properly executed windshear escape maneuver was unsuccessful due to the prevailing conditions.*

Specialists would have meticulously analyzed the Cockpit Voice Recorder tape. They would play the sounds captured by Cockpit Area Microphones (CAM) again and again until reaching consensus on the source and meaning of noises and conversation. Yet for all their efforts, it is of course impossible for a transcript to convey a person's tone, pace, or inflection, or to describe their physical appearance, personality, gestures, accents, nuances of expression, backstory, or any of the myriad habits and idiosyncrasies that make people unique and engaging individuals.

Captain Doherty would have simply been CAM-1, not the hardscrabble kid from rural Oklahoma who flew crop dusters as a teenager, earned an improbable Naval Academy appointment, and flew right wing for the '63 Blue Angels before bagging a MiG over Vietnam.

Bert, aka CAM-2, wouldn't be known as a proud naturalized citizen who had worked his way through Embry-Riddle and paid his dues building hours as a flight instructor. The public would never know how he welcomed newbies rather than tormenting them and sometimes amused CSRs with his favorite prank: leaving one of those cardboard Whiskey Whiskey cutouts propped up in a parked plane as if the owner was in the copilot's seat.

News outlets would have feasted on cherry-pickings, taken out of context as such things often are, with headlines like "CRASH CAPTAIN: 'WE GO WHETHER THERE'S WEATHER OR NOT!'" His addendum of "Kidding aside" would have been conveniently ignored.

Two lifetimes reduced to lines of text, judged for one error while the pressures on them to make schedule were ignored, adding another layer of grief for those who knew them as the committed professionals they were.

CAM-3, CAM-4, and CAM-5—Rachel, Drew, and the Trans Global employee—were "voice identified as no. 1 flight attendant," "male gate agent," and "contract mechanic," respectively.

The lines would have felt surreal, like reading the script for a production in which he had appeared. At 1249:31, "((sound similar to closing of cabin door))" would have marked his exit but could never dim the memory of Rachel's smile framed in the tiny round window, those blue eyes sparkling with mischief and love…

He had hoped events he hadn't witnessed would be easier to bear. But his imagination did not labor under the limitations of impassive microphones or tapes encased in fireproof steel or clinical explanations of their contents. The mental movie played on as if he had never deplaned.

The callouts, checks, and radio traffic were as with any other takeoff. But just seconds after lifting off, the MD-80 was bouncing and rattling in heavy turbulence, much rougher than usual so close to the ground. Still, it was climbing.

"Positive rate," called Bert.

"Gear up," replied the captain. The *clunk* of the gear handle being raised, followed by nearly simultaneous thumps announcing the arrival of the wheels in their wells.

There were several exclamations the experts would have labeled as "non-pertinent words."

Bert, yelling to be heard. "Airspeed's all over the place!"

Shoving the throttles forward to their limits, the captain eased back on the yoke and called, "Flaps fifteen, ignition override!"

The engines' spooling added to the cacophony of rain, wipers, and controls wrested to and fro as the plane shook wildly in the insanely churning channel of air.

The words summoned a multilayered, true-to-life snapshot into Drew's mind: the complex and beautiful machine, suspended in a black convulsion of wind and water; along for the ride, a random and unique subset of human beings like those on thousands of daily flights worldwide, usually existent only between when the last passenger boarded and the first deplaned—but forever connected if tragedy intervened.

The windshear escape maneuver had stopped the descent. The Super 80, its nose as high as the captain dared hold it, even climbed a few feet.

The decisive seconds would have again demonstrated the contrast between the subjectivity of perception and the objective depiction thereof. The airflow into one or both engines became too unstable to sustain the normal compression sequence. In the aft cabin, what registered on the cockpit mics as "((sound of irregular popping similar to engine compressor stall))" would have been heard as a staccato series of terrifying concussive blasts that sounded like shotguns at point-blank range.

When every pound of thrust might be the difference between life and death, the only thing the crew could do to keep the compressor blades from disintegrating—reduce power—was also the very thing they couldn't do and keep flying. The captain had tried to walk the razor's edge of the cruel contradiction by coaxing everything he could from the fanjets without causing them to tear themselves apart. It would have been a heroic effort that never had a chance.

The Ground Proximity Warning System whooped a call for attention and delivered its message with mechanical indifference.

"Terrain! Terrain! Pull up! Pull up!"

Rachel's final act would have been no surprise to anyone who knew her. She would have died the same way she had lived, one hundred percent committed to whatever was in front of her. Somehow pushing the terror of the moment aside, she would have fulfilled what she must have known could be her last duty to her passengers. Overlapping the chilling, robotic chant of the GPWS would have been one final line from CAM-3.

"Heads down! Heads down! Heads—"

"((Sound of impact))"—words that couldn't begin to describe a 70-ton jet crashing into a construction site.

The thousands of people who had loved the 149 irreplaceable souls aboard Flight 867, and the eight workers killed on the ground, would have also lost their lives in a sense. The soul-shattering news would have created a moment after which nothing would ever be the same. Many would struggle with guilt and regret over things said or unsaid, and the tragedy's massive shadow would touch countless others in one way or another as all of them do.

The families of those lost would have begun feeling their way along the darkest path of their lives. No airline would have had the knowledge, skills, and training that would eventually bring about a way to help support such people, and no government agency was charged with ensuring they were supported. AirStar's overwhelmed staff, the equally unprepared authorities, and many well-meaning others would have done their best, but the resulting mishmash of inconsistent and often ineffective assistance would have often made things worse.

Then there were the first responders, who included some motorists passing by, all of whom fearlessly ran out into the fiery, ghastly devastation only to find there was no one they could help; others who witnessed the airliner's fatal descent; residents of Kenner, faced again with an unthinkable blow to their community like the Pan Am 727 crash four years prior; AirStar's employees; and even the tower controller who had cleared the flight for takeoff.

Drew's grief over Rachel's loss would have been matched only by his regret over sending Jessica and her mother to the gate. The silent anguish was common among the reservations, counter, and gate agents who had, through the years, unknowingly sent passengers to their fates.

If I had only told them it was too late…

That battle would have lasted the rest of his life. On one side, his rational understanding that he couldn't have known what was to come and thus bore no responsibility for their deaths; on the other, the crushing guilt that spat on such consolatory logic, dipping his heart in an acid bath every time the memory surfaced.

Load factors would have nosedived under the glare of media coverage and negative customer reactions. Some employees would have begun changing out of their uniforms when leaving work, ashamed about how the press was, fairly or unfairly, portraying their airline. And eventually, inevitably, AirStar's already fragile financials would have crumbled into dust.

Kirby and company would have pulled the plug soon after, this final cruel consequence stranding hundreds of passengers.

Captain Doherty's moment of clarity, and his courage in acting upon it, relegated the disaster and its dreadful aftermath to the realm of what never was. AirStar 867 departed 22 minutes after the rejected takeoff and flew to Houston through smooth, clear skies. The passengers read, slept, or talked, blissfully unaware of their recent proximity to the hereafter. Several even busied themselves with writing letters thanking the crew for choosing safety over schedule.

* * *

In the breakroom, Drew and Gail had just finished their sandwiches when, coincidentally, Kelly also appeared at the door during the actual course of events.

"Drew, phone call. It's Paul in Tampa."

"Oh boy," said Gail. "More Florida sunshine in the forecast?"

He shrugged. "Beats me, but I can't imagine why he'd call unless it was more TDY."

He hung up three minutes later, incredulous at what he had heard.

TWENTY-SEVEN

Rachel had a New Orleans layover a few days later. Courtesy of PNR messages—carefully circumspect, since AURA was essentially an electronic party line—they each knew the other had something important to discuss.

They ordered appetizers, then he said, "Okay, the big news. Ladies first."

"Thanks, but I'd rather you go first." She smiled, but something was off. There was a shadow in her eyes, like the day Gail had come by the counter to ask him to lunch. Alarm bells might not have been ringing, but their hammers were twitching. He swallowed his apprehension but couldn't help pausing with a slight head tilt and furrowed brows.

"Well, okay. Paul from Tampa called me again."

"Wow, more beach time TDY? Lucky you!"

"No, not TDY. I still can't believe it. Rachel, he offered me a full-time job! Well, if things work out the way he thinks. I promised an answer by tomorrow and—"

"Don't," she interrupted, her face set and tone resolute. "Don't go."

He shook his head, perplexed. "Don't take the job? Are you serious?"

The blue eyes assured him she was.

He went on, still in disbelief. "Don't take a *full-time* spot in *Tampa?!* The same place that causes a stampede of any airline's most senior people anytime even a part-time spot opens up?"

"I know how it sounds, but I've been hearing stuff. The—"

"Come on, there's stuff going around all the time. How much of it ever pans out?"

She took his hands in hers. "Let me finish. I've been hearing stuff, and you're right, what's new? But I ran into Valerie at Hobby and she told me about her Miami layover last week. It was a Super Fifty and some Eastern mechanics came on the second the last passengers were off."

Seeing his mouth start to open, she continued, "Yes, I know, they do our maintenance. This wasn't that. They showed the captain a work order and started taking measurements in the cockpit. The captain asked what it was about and the lead said, 'All I know is they told us to get the cockpit layout on account we might be getting some of your Fifties.' This isn't crew lounge gloom and doom, Drew. She was there."

She waited but he said nothing. "You know as well as I do, we wouldn't be selling off airplanes if things weren't bad. They're closing Midland and Brownsville, and supposedly they're even looking at leaving Dallas Love. Love! One of our first-ever stations! So I don't want you to get down there and…you know."

Sure, some of the talk going around was dire, and the station closings were troubling to say the least. No one he knew had heard anything about dumping airplanes, yet here was concrete testimony from someone Rachel trusted implicitly.

He sighed and whispered, "Damn."

After a few silent seconds, he mounted a halfhearted defense. "So the mechanic said they *might* be getting some of our planes. It must not be a done deal."

An exasperated look from across the table. "Come on, Drew…"

He knew he was grasping at straws even as he reached for another. "The other day, Gail said she heard somebody at HQ saw a draft purchase order for A320s. Plus there's the station closings and the 'Go Long' thing. I'll bet that's why they're starting to unload the Fifties." But he wasn't sure he believed that one himself.

"Before we buy anything else? And don't you wonder how is it they're not posting the job?"

"Paul said usually they would have to, but he got permission because I had been down there already on the TDY. Transferring me saves the time and effort of doing interviews again."

Rachel, unconvinced, said, "Maybe so, but it also conveniently avoids uprooting a senior CSR with a family who would be a lot farther up the creek than you if it doesn't work out."

"Seriously? Come on."

"Am I wrong?"

She wasn't, and he had no rebuttal.

"Rachel, I thought you'd be on board with this."

"Hey, a week ago, I would have helped you pack."

He shook his head dejectedly. "Wow, okay, on to your big news."

Uncharacteristically lowering her eyes, she paused, then said softly, "TGA moved up my class date."

Drew sat back and stared at her, taken aback for the second time in as many minutes.

"To when?"

"Three weeks from today. Someone in the next class was in a car wreck so they're swapping our dates. I would have said no before the Miami thing but I'm serious here. I don't know if we'll still be around come January. I know it's a lot to ask and it's going to be tough on us for a while, maybe a good while. But please understand and support me on this."

She smiled, albeit halfheartedly, and went on, "One good thing is I heard this next class is all but set to get Miami. I guess if that works out, and you decide to take your chances in Tampa, and you guys stick around, maybe it won't be so bad."

His eyes widened. "Jesus, we're already 'you guys'?"

"No. I mean, I gave my notice today so maybe yeah, but trust me, it's as weird and uncomfortable to me as it is to you."

He said nothing, just shook his head again.

She looked into his eyes, squeezed his hands, and said, "Like I said on the beach that day, what I know for sure is that nothing is stronger than us. We'll get through it, one way or another."

Drew thought it over as he tried to fall asleep. The Eastern story was unsettling, but he'd been around long enough to know that rumors turned out to be drama more often than not.

Some people are freaking out about everything they hear. Eastern's probably doing some kind of instrument replacement or cockpit refit work. I'll bet she leaves me a note tomorrow saying it was all a misunderstanding.

* * *

There was no note from Rachel the next day, only a statement from Kirby that launched out of HQ with more spin than a Nolan Ryan curveball.

"We are thrilled to share some exciting news regarding our efforts to enhance and streamline our operations. In a carefully considered move to optimize our aircraft portfolio and position AirStar for sustained growth, we have entered into an agreement to sell two of our DC-9 Series 50 aircraft to Eastern Air Lines. This transaction signifies a pivotal moment in our journey toward operational excellence and financial resilience. By divesting these specific assets, we are aligning our fleet to better meet the evolving demands of our markets and to support our ongoing transition to longer routes.

"AirStar's leadership has taken this decision in the context of ensuring our airline's long-term success. The proceeds from this sale will be reinvested strategically, fortifying our balance sheet and laying the groundwork for targeted enhancements across various facets of our business, including the possibility of acquiring additional aircraft better suited to our overarching plan."

"Do they get paid by the buzzword?" wondered Regina as she finished reading the RAATS printout.

"And we're going to 'sustain growth' by *selling airplanes?* To a *competitor?*" added Henry. "How dumb do they think we are?"

"Wish I had a buck for every time I've wondered that since Kirby's bunch took over," Gail said. "I could tell them where to stick their 'Go Long' plan."

Meanwhile, Rachel's days at AirStar counted down. They "talked" through their PNRs every day, and a couple of times on the phone. Her flights passed through, sometimes with a chance for the usual rushed hug and hello, and they even had another layover dinner date, albeit a short one because both had to be back at the airport before sunrise.

In short, life went on as it was before. But there was a noticeable undertow in this sea of apparent normality. The banter wasn't quite as effortless, the kisses a little shorter, and there was obviously no scheming to manufacture a few days off exploring some new place. Crossing the bridge early one morning, the flare stacks of the Chalmette refineries etched in sharp relief by the rising sun, an apt comparison came to mind.

It's like shooting pictures with a colored filter. The scene is the same but there's something there that wasn't before.

Both felt the unfamiliar chasm yet neither spoke of it, perhaps hoping the pall was residue from her decision and not a crack waiting to spread. Part of it, he realized, was that this was the first real, life-altering choice either of them had made since somewhat impulsively becoming a couple. Feeling excluded from it was rough enough, but he also had to shake his head at the irony: Rachel insisted they would be fine—despite having shared her own misgivings when her ex did essentially the same thing by taking the Midway job.

People always think it's going to be different, and I guess sometimes it is. Maybe it's up to us to make it different.

That they might decide the outcome was a reassuring thought, but his apprehension continued to deepen.

* * *

Things worked out the way Paul anticipated, forcing a decision. The allure of TPA and living on Florida's coast proved too much. He rolled the dice and accepted the transfer, glad he had waited to decide whether to end his apartment lease.

The move was hectic; he packed his car, drove down, found a small apartment in Tarpon Springs, and flew back to New Orleans the next day without missing a shift. A rented truck took care of the rest of his belongings, but eight boxes just wouldn't fit. He offhandedly mentioned this to Donna, activating the lightspeed grapevine. A few minutes later, Grayson summoned him into the supervisors' office.

"I hear you need some boxes sent to Tampa."

"Yeah, they won't fit in the truck. I'll leave them at my parents' house."

"How about you drop them off at the counter? We'll keep 'em at T-Point and load a couple a day as COMAT. Barb's good with it."

This thoughtful gesture worked well. The Eastern rampers unloaded the boxes with the inbound luggage and Drew picked them up from the baggage service office after work. Everything arrived in less than a week.

He loved Tampa—the airport and the area. His new colleagues were nearly all highly experienced, fun to work with, and made him feel welcome. Nothing changed with Bert, Captain Michaels, and other pilot and cabin crew colleagues, who passed through TPA as they had New Orleans. The beaches remained a terrific perk. He went regularly, enjoying the typical beautiful weather even if it was sometimes too cold to go in the water. Perhaps the only disappointment was missing the Saints' first winning season, though they cratered in their first playoff game anyway.

Despite choosing Tarpon Springs almost by happenstance, Drew soon discovered it was more than a cool coastal town with an apartment he could afford. Known as the "Sponge Capital of the World," Greek immigrants and their Mediterranean traditions had shaped the area's identity. Sponge diving had flourished since the 1890s, and the industry was such a part of the community that the local high school proudly displayed a diving helmet on a pedestal out front and called their athletic teams the "Spongers."

His parents flew down for a visit and fell in love with the area as he had. The food was terrific and eating it soon spotlighted another drawback of no more ramp duties—tighter clothes. He had grown accustomed to eating plenty of whatever he pleased with several fat-blasting shifts a week on his schedule, but now some moderation was in order.

A pleasant surprise was the fantastic Fred Howard Park. The total trip time from his front door to its beautiful beach was about ten minutes. Lunch on days off often consisted of a picnic under a palm followed by a swim or a walk along the surf line. Just as often, he was back that evening to lie on the sand and watch the high clouds burn over the Gulf like molten metal flung against a cyan canvas. Gradually, they would fade to plum over neon pink and finally to silvery brush strokes on an indigo backdrop sprinkled with stars.

His visits soon included a fun little mental game too, counting the park's out-of-state license plates. The tally quickly exceeded 30, with several from Canadian provinces and a couple from Mexico thrown in too.

Yet, even though his new chapter was starting off well, he soon realized an oversight in his decision to leave New Orleans: his time there had been uniquely special. Barb had opened the door to finally achieving his dream and granted a chance to keep it alive, if on life support for a while. In overcoming those early struggles, he had come to treasure and rely upon Gail's lovely soul, Grayson's quiet leadership, Peggy's wisdom, Henry's kindness and perspective, the live wire that was Donna, and even the rankling provocateur Rob. They, and many others, had shown him the ropes and encouraged him, each in their own way, and those bonds had grown into something far beyond the workplace.

He even missed working the ramp. Well, maybe not dragging that damn lav cart around, but the hands-on work, the aircraft, the persistent odors of fuel and exhaust that often defied even the heavy-duty wash cycle, and even the weather. That was the raw, elemental side of aviation that had excited him when he had clamped his hands over his hearing protector and watched that first arrival rolling up the line at Moisant. There was something about the grind outside that felt inherited from those intrepid souls who, decades before, had committed themselves to a fledgling industry with an uncertain future.

In their era, customers going coast-to-coast rode "luxurious trains" by night and "safe, swift planes" by day, cutting the travel time between New York and Los Angeles from a week to "just" two days. The setting, some of the processes, and certainly the planes had evolved, but it all still echoed those early days. Standing at a podium in an air-conditioned concourse, with freshly shampooed carpet underfoot, shielded from the brutal Florida sun by deeply tinted glass, with aids like AURA that were inconceivable not so many years before, felt like something entirely different.

Time flew by as if someone was fanning through the pages of a calendar. Resourceful as always, Rachel managed to keep in touch while in training. She would call a friend at LAX, who entered the notes into Drew's PNR. The friend would pass along his responses when Rachel called again. This is how she scheduled a phone call a few days before she would earn her TGA wings.

Her boyfriend correctly surmised that base assignments had been announced. He less accurately anticipated that she would excitedly report being assigned to Miami.

Near midnight, his living room dark except for light dancing on the walls from the muted TV, his phone finally rang. He impatiently assured the operator that he would accept the charges, then said, "Hello?"

Static and clicks from the line.

"Rachel?"

"I'm here," came the response in a small voice.

"What's wrong? Are you okay?"

"Nobody got Miami."

He had resolved to stay positive whatever the outcome.

"Damn. That would have been too easy, right? Okay, fine, I'll have a little farther to go. Where then? New York? Chicago? D.C.?"

More static. Then, finally, another soft response, almost a whisper, barely audible.

"Anchorage."

He couldn't have heard correctly. *"Anchorage?"*

*"*Yes, Anchorage."

"TGA has a crew base in *Anchorage?*"

"It just opened. My whole class got it. Nobody with enough seniority to hold another domestic base wants to go there. It's all because we got Far East routes and we'll lose them unless we start service before the deadline. The MD-11 deliveries are delayed again and the DC-10s can't make it without a fuel stop."

He would never get used to hearing her refer to another airline as "we."

"They call the line we'll be getting the 'Arctic Circle,'" she went on. "The international crews based in Seattle fly between Anchorage and the overseas destinations. We take over in Anchorage and fly the domestic segments, either Chicago New York Miami L.A. Seattle and back to Anchorage or the other way around. But supposedly we'll only have to sit reserve until the next class graduates, and I'll have two layovers a month in Miami once I can hold a line. We also get some time off before starting our OE."

Operating Experience was on-the-job orientation where new flight attendants work regular flights under supervision and are graded on their proficiency.

"How much time?"

"A week, and I only need three days to move up there. Maybe you could meet me in Denver? I want to see my mom and maybe we can hit some more trails." She was making an effort to stay upbeat.

"In November?"

"Okay, maybe we stay on the pavement but Rocky Mountain National Park is amazing in the winter. Wanna do that?"

He did, so they each started working on making it happen and within a few days, everything was set.

* * *

An envelope awaited Rachel at her mom's place. The contents brought her to tears. A mechanic had found her Pioneer pin, which had fallen off during the desperate resuscitation effort as she suspected. After being found wedged in a seat track during a heavy maintenance check, a quick call to the Director of Inflight sent the memento on its way to Rachel's forwarding address.

Her face reflected the heartache of knowing that what the pin represented—the fun, laughter, and camaraderie she had shared with her Ruff Air family, in good times and bad—were a cherished chapter of her life now gone forever. The mechanic's thoughtful effort to return it underscored the feeling all the more. Drew held her close after she carefully tucked the keepsake into her jewelry box. No words were spoken or needed.

They rented a cottage at the Black Dog Inn in Estes Park, where the winter landscape provided a whole new perspective of the Rockies. A few constants remained; the breathtaking mountain views, the crisp, clean air, and the sun's colorful comings and goings each day. They hiked on rented snowshoes, rewarded by the wildlife out enjoying a break from the tourists; drove up Trail Ridge Road to the winter closure barricade; took a backcountry snowmobile tour; and bundled up for a picnic near a stream that was mostly frozen but still trickled crystal-clear water here and there. Evenings were spent browsing the town's many shops followed by hot cocoa near the fireplace back at the inn.

Time stood still for a few wonderful days. Everything felt as it had before, a warm rush both wished could last forever. But it couldn't, so on a blustery morning at Stapleton, they held each other, neither willing to be the one to stop, wringing out a few more priceless moments before the toughest and most emotional goodbye of their relationship.

He stood quietly at a window, watching her flight depart. A dark shroud of apprehension again squeezed his heart as the TGA 727 taxied off into the snow.

* * *

Thankfully, Rachel's time sitting reserve at ANC was mercifully brief. By late January, she was able to bid a schedule and they met in Miami for her first layover there a week later.

Drew did a double-take when she emerged from the jetbridge in her TGA uniform. Rachel would be stunning dressed in a burlap sack but this ensemble worked especially well for her. The blue beret and scarf were a perfect touch, giving an effortlessly cool and sophisticated vibe.

He stepped back for another look after their hug.

"Wow, you look great! I always liked that gray and yellow color combo. I wouldn't think that pale blue would work with it, but it does. That's the color of the fuselage stripe, right?"

"Yep, but it's not 'pale blue' and this most certainly isn't just gray and yellow. This is 'Nimbus,' 'Sunrise,' and 'Stratos.'"

A raised eyebrow. "Really? Aren't nimbuses…nimbi…whatever the plural is, aren't they storm clouds?"

"Yes, and that's exactly the point," Rachel went on. "As they put it in training—about three times, in fact—Nimbus is for 'weathering the storms—real and metaphorical—we know will come,' Sunrise because 'each new day is a fresh start, for us and the operation,' and Stratos reminds us to 'always strive for the highest aspirations.'"

He chuckled. "Wow, they lay it on pretty thick. But I respect that they put so much thought into it."

"They do, and you know what? It works. The standard is excellence. You see it everywhere and it rubs off on you."

"Well, I'm impressed. I can tell you're proud to work there."

"I am."

He loved her more than ever, and was happy for her, but moments like this hurt his heart. The stark contrast between his world and her new and expanding life only widened the distance between them.

Miami quickly became a ritual and they managed to get together every time she was in Florida. They also spent considerable time on the phone, at least until the first bill arrived. The long-distance total equaled nearly a full day's pay, so they agreed to one call a month, supplemented by postcards and letters. The layovers were obviously the stars of this sad show, with fun in the sun by day and nights whose steaminess had nothing to do with the subtropical Florida weather.

Less exciting was AirStar's sale of four MD-80 delivery slots in May along with two more DC-9-50s the following month—June 22 to be exact, Drew's third anniversary with the airline. The Eastern mechanics conducted their flight deck assessments on a TPA terminator this time, so he got to see it for himself.

These moves stretched the fleet so thin that it had to be a matter of time until Kirby announced the new aircraft acquisitions. That's what the optimists told themselves, followed by plenty of talk about what the CEO would buy to grow the airline. But so far, Kirby had proven to be all hat and no cattle on that front.

Late in July, Rachel revealed a surprise on the monthly call: she had wrangled five days off. Would he like to come to Alaska? She didn't have to ask twice. He had some news too: he had been accepted to reserve ISR training with a class date just a few weeks away.

"Too bad you won't be able to pin me," he lamented.

"I'll find a way to be there," she promised, *"if* you make it."

He decided he might as well get a taste of Trans Global on the way to Anchorage. He would go AirStar from Tampa to New Orleans, taking time to say hello to the old gang before hopping a nonstop to LAX. He would meet Rachel on a L.A. layover and use an ID90 for the West Coast legs of the "Arctic Circle" she would work from there to Anchorage.

Another long-awaited chance to see her, and to visit a place he had long dreamed of going, stoked more excitement about a nonrev trip than he could ever remember. He was listed on the first departure tomorrow and would be headed home to finish packing in a few hours.

Alone in the back office, occupied with copying some pages for insertion into the Read Log, his mind wandered to the impending trip.

Alaska…with Rachel! This is going to be absolutely amazing! That glacier she mentioned, the otters in Prince William Sound…

The printer was clattering and the sound wedged its way into his thoughts when it hadn't stopped fifteen seconds later. Only Kirby prattled on that long.

Uh oh. What now?

He walked over to see if the message was anything important.

It was.

TWENTY- EIGHT

Drew's heart sank and he started feeling a little queasy as he read, slowly shaking his head in disbelief.

```
ALLXXRX ALLZZRX ALLTRRX ALLOORX
.HDQXARX 291545 D91102
ATTN - ALL AIRSTAR EMPLOYEES

AS   MOST   OF   YOU   KNOW..AIRSTAR'S
COMPETITIVE  POSITION  HAS  DETERIORATED
BADLY   IN   RECENT   MONTHS   DUE   TO
COMPETITIVE  PRESSURES  IN  THE  INDUSTRY
AND IN OUR MARKETS IN PARTICULAR. WHILE
OUR OPERATING COSTS HAVE BEEN AMONG THE
LOWEST IN THE INDUSTRY.. OUR YIELDS HAVE
BEEN   UNSATISFACTORY   AND   OUR   LOAD
FACTORS   HAVE   CONTINUED   TO   STEADILY
DROP..PRODUCING   LOSSES   THAT   HAVE
CONTINUED   AT   AN   UNACCEPTABLE   RATE.
MOREOVER..OUR FORECASTS FOR THE COMING
MONTHS   INDICATE   LITTLE   IF   ANY
IMPROVEMENT   IN   OUR   FINANCIAL   AND
OPERATING CONDITION.
```

IN LIGHT OF THE CONTINUING LOSSES..THE BOARD OF DIRECTORS OF AIRSTAR HAS DECIDED THAT IT IS NECESSARY TO ANNOUNCE LATER TODAY THAT THE COMPANY WILL PERMANENTLY CEASE ALL AIRLINE OPERATIONS AS OF THE CLOSE OF BUSINESS ON AUGUST 9..1987 AND THAT AIRSTAR AIRCRAFT AND OTHER ASSETS WILL BE SOLD FOLLOWING CESSATION OF OPERATIONS.

YOU ARE AN OUTSTANDING GROUP OF DEDICATED EMPLOYEES AND YOUR MAGNIFICENT EFFORTS HAVE BEEN TRULY APPRECIATED DURING THIS DIFFICULT PERIOD. NO ONE COULD HAVE ASKED FOR MORE FROM AN EMPLOYEE GROUP. HOWEVER..THE EXISTING COMPETITIVE ENVIRONMENT HAS MADE IT VIRTUALLY IMPOSSIBLE FOR A SMALL CARRIER TO COMPETE EFFECTIVELY..AND INDEED..TO SURVIVE.

TO BEST SERVE OUR CUSTOMERS, WE PLAN TO OPERATE A FULL SCHEDULE IN THE INTERIM AND ALL EMPLOYEES WHO CHOOSE TO REMAIN THROUGH THE CESSATION OF OPERATIONS WILL BE PAID IN FULL FOR ALL TIME WORKED AND WILL RECEIVE A SEVERANCE

PACKAGE. RAATS RECORD /K*CESSATION/ HAS
ADDITIONAL INFORMATION AND FURTHER
DETAILS WILL BE FORTHCOMING FROM THE HR
DEPARTMENT IN THE COMING DAYS.

IF YOU ARE APPROACHED BY THE
MEDIA, PLEASE MAINTAIN YOUR
PROFESSIONALISM AND RETAIN THE PRIDE IN
THE COMPANY THAT ALL OF YOU HAVE
DEMONSTRATED TIME AND TIME AGAIN. WE
SINCERELY APPRECIATE THE MANY
SACRIFICES YOU HAVE MADE.

H.D. KIRBY

He sank into a chair, trying to make sense of the words.
This can't be true. It's like something Rob would pull. Is it someone's idea of a sick joke?

He read the message twice more, struggling to grasp its finality through a bitter haze of denial. This only happened to other airlines!

Rachel was right. I should have listened. Maybe we would have ended up training together at TGA like she said!

Instead, he had dismissed her hopeful suggestion out of hand.

Later, nearly everybody would swear on their souls that Ruff Air might have made it if not for "that asshole Kirby," a reference widespread enough to have spawned the acronym "TAK." They were making the common assumption, the one underlying nearly all regret: that the path not taken would have led to a better outcome. In truth, they would never know, and while assigning blame felt perversely good, it was pointless—the bitter pill still had to be swallowed.

Some karma was in the equation too. The news of other carriers' death spirals was often fodder for the breakroom experts, seemingly without a thought about the emotional wreckage left in their wakes. Some even broke into song: *"Da da duh duh duh, another one bites the dust! And another one gone, and another one gone…"*

Bet they're not singing now!

Annette came in, saw his face, and said, "Uh oh…what now?"

He handed her the message.

Her eyes widened as she read, then narrowed. She slammed the page down on the desk, rattling the pens and pencils residing in a topless soda can.

"Sacrifices? What does Kirby know about our sacrifices? Damn him! Damn headquarters! Damn every one of those 'brilliant' assholes, so smug with their great ideas about how to 'remake' Ruff Air! *Look what it's got us now!*"

She stalked around the office, anger radiating from her entire being.

"How could they—" She froze in midsentence. Her shoulders fell as she slowly unclenched her fists, closed her eyes, and took several deep breaths. After a moment of silence, she whispered, "You know what? Screw them."

She paced around some more, then said, "I have to call Paul," and disappeared into his office.

Drew sat there, gazing at the destination posters in their battered frames, just as he had on his first day back in New Orleans. His jumbled thoughts quickly piled up into a logjam.

How didn't I see this coming? Great call coming down here – what now, genius? Is anybody hiring?

Melissa, the ISR, came to mind. She passed through from time to time and they always took a minute to catch up. How would she react to yet another box of bittersweet memories to hide away next to those from Continental? He remembered her describing the emotional carnage left by shutdowns and mergers. He had heard her words then; now he was living them.

Annette returned and said, "Paul's on his way. No one else sees this. He wants to tell everyone personally. You'll be done at the gate by then so while he does that, you and I will call whoever's off. He doesn't want anyone getting the news from the TV. Anything else you can think of?" There wasn't.

The station manager arrived 45 minutes later. As always, the word didn't take long to spread, a reminder of the joke Peggy had made about airline news traveling faster than light. His colleagues' reactions ran the gamut from quiet, resigned acceptance to rants worse than Annette's.

When the unpleasant chore of calling his off-duty colleagues was done. Drew and Melody set up for the next departure, the last one before his shift's end. Both were thankful that the news wasn't yet public. No one was ready to endure the onslaught of questions they knew would follow. The same questions, over and over and over because such things could not be explained in an announcement.

He shook his head with a wry smile at the ship number on the flight paperwork. The arrival was the very plane he had chocked early that memorable afternoon at Moisant.

Ops called the inbound on the ground. Drew propped the jetbridge door open and made his way down to where an Eastern ramper waited at the jetbridge controls—something that still felt weird. Fortunately, the Easterners were experienced and typically positioned the bridge in seconds flat, enabling AirStar's crew to open the door before a RAATS alert tattled their tardiness to HQ.

Of course, five RAATS alerts, or 500 for that matter, wouldn't matter anymore. Even the auditors must be unhappy. There would be no more employees to hound about inconsequential transgressions while systemic deficiencies went ignored.

He returned the ISR's warm smile and hello but couldn't quite disguise his unease. As he replaced the mic after welcoming the arriving passengers, she silently mouthed, "What's wrong?" He shook his head and held up a finger in response, and she nodded. He hated knowing what they didn't know, hated the thought of the torrent of emotion the message would inevitably unleash.

When the passengers had gone, Drew handed a copy of the message to Captain Michaels, who scanned the page, handed it to the first officer, then slumped in his seat and stared straight ahead. The first officer, a new hire with only a few weeks on the job, read the message then silently handed it back. His expression remained deadpan but he suddenly became intensely interested in straightening the contents of his flight bag.

After a moment, the captain spoke in a tired, quiet voice. "Honestly, I'm almost relieved. Knowing what's happening beats this rumor crap."

Motioning for the copilot to follow, the captain unfastened his safety harness and climbed from his seat, wincing as he straightened up.

"Goddam knee," he muttered as he reached for his uniform jacket and hat. He straightened his tie using the tiny mirror on the cockpit door then went into the cabin. The ISRs waited restlessly, recognizing this must be some kind of unpleasant news.

"It's over, guys." He began reading the message. his voice catching in his throat a couple of times.

Suddenly Drew needed to escape.

"Sorry," he interrupted, "I have to get back." This was half-true at best. He felt guilty at the real reason, his dread of again seeing people he cared about thrashing through the inevitable feelings of disbelief, denial, anger, and sorrow.

He had left the frying pan for the fire. Here came the outbound crew, chatting as they casually walked down the concourse. They obviously didn't know.

Damn, damn, damn! Calling them was the "anything else" I should have thought of!

The fact no one else had thought of it either was no consolation.

The First, Rachel's old roommate Valerie, approached the podium for the flight paperwork. Her smile morphed into concerned curiosity when she saw Melody's face.

Suddenly he was back at Rachel's apartment, laughing with her over the story about Valerie becoming an ISR. She was renowned for her perpetually cheerful, outgoing, optimistic outlook on whatever life sent her way, even the rumors and uncertainty around AirStar's fate.

This raced through his mind in the few seconds it took for Valerie to ponder Melody's expression and accept the sheet of paper held out to her. Her crew mates gathered in a semi-circle around her, craning their necks to see over her shoulders and read along.

In the frequent retrospect of years to come, Drew would always remember this as the moment when AirStar's failure became painful and real. Valerie and her crewmates filled his whole field of vision, as if seen through a powerful zoom lens. Time itself seemed to slow. The noisy babble of the terminal faded. The afternoon sunlight, bright even through the deep gray tint of the windows, glinted off seniority pins and polished wings. As Valerie read, her lips quivered slightly. Her eyes moved further down the page and tears welled, spilled over, and followed each other down her face. They gathered at the base of two vertical streaks of makeup and dripped onto the paper.

Suddenly her composure flew like a startled bird. She turned and groped for someone to hug, mewing and shaking as she sobbed with blind abandon. Startled passengers turned to stare.

Watching her pain tested his self-control. He wanted to hug her, somehow to make it better, but his own feelings were clawing around inside him. Unwilling to let them spill over, he retreated again, back to the aircraft.

He answered the inbound crew's questions as best he could, then felt the jetbridge shudder as their replacements thumped down to the airplane. They looked like everyone did—depressed and defeated. Valerie fussed with her makeup mirror, trying unsuccessfully to pop it open and finally putting it back in her purse. For an awkward moment, everyone just stood there looking at each other as if wondering what to do next. One of the arriving ISRs was a Pioneer, a classmate of Valerie and Rachel. She hugged Valerie tightly.

His eyes stung, and he saw that everyone else was struggling to control their emotions. The anger, fear, and apprehension felt too much to bear. They had given so much of themselves only to have it come down to standing in a muggy jetbridge, crushed by the feeling that it had all been for nothing.

Finally, Captain Michaels said, "Guys, I know this hurts, especially if it's your first time around. It's my fourth, so I know it's tough and it's scary and it takes time but trust me—wherever you land, you'll be okay."

Feeling helpless and adrift, and missing Rachel so much it hurt, Drew wanted desperately to believe him.

TWENTY-NINE

The final ten days were long and difficult ones. Serpentine lines of anxious customers greeted the CSRs each morning. Fortunately, the complex RAATS entries for exchanging AirStar tickets for passage on other airlines quickly became second nature. Everyone worked overtime because rebooking several months' worth of passengers was on top of running the regular schedule.

Most customers were kind and understanding, many wondering out loud how such a nice airline could possibly go under. Yet ironically, deregulation had made the flying public unwitting accomplices. More and more, customers looked only at price when booking travel. Grayson, in his insightful if inelegant way, had pinpointed the resulting squeeze years ago during a bull session in Moisant Ops. Someone had said Ruff Air was too small to compete.

"It ain't how many airplanes or people you got. I think we got it better that way anyhow 'cause a smaller herd is easier to point in the right direction. It ain't the service either, we know how to run an airline. The trouble is it's easy enough to be good and easy enough to be cheap but it ain't easy to be good *and* cheap." The result was that a smaller airline's relatively low costs still weren't low enough to turn a profit.

By day eight, a Friday, just getting out of bed and dressing was an accomplishment, like those dark days right before Kelly had called to offer the interview.

How am I going to make two more days of this?

Late that evening, he got the answer. Standing outside the jetbridge after meeting the day's last arrival, he tried to keep his mind from wandering as the passengers filed by. Some asked for directions to baggage claim; most just nodded or silently shuffled into the concourse. A peripheral flash of gray and yellow brushed against his awareness, informing him that the last person emerging was a Trans Global flight attendant nonrevving in uniform. It was the kind of detail the brain registers without even trying, usually insignificant, not even earning a glance.

He had started toward the podium when a familiar voice said, "And here I was thinking I'd have to track you down."

He spun around, stunned.

"Rachel! Holy sh—"—he caught himself, sheepishly looking around—"cow! What are you doing here?"

"Thought you might need a hug."

"Wow, do I! But I thought you weren't in Miami again until next week."

"I wasn't. I traded trips." She gestured toward the jetbridge. "Had to hustle to catch this one and I have to leave Sunday night."

"I'll take every second." He hugged her as tightly as he ever had, struggling to keep his composure. "Thank you for coming. You don't know what this means to me."

The next thirty-six hours were like those special days in Estes Park—a blur of stolen moments. Despite the frenetic pace, Drew's shifts dragged by, while Rachel forced herself to get out and do something, anything, to pass the time until he was free. When they were together, they laughed and reminisced, desperately grasping at the present and wishing they could stop time or at least slow it down. Holding Rachel close or feeling her hand in his centered him, and the joy they shared became a makeshift barrier against the uncertainty of what lay ahead.

The last day fell on a Sunday. AirStar's final Tampa departure was Flight 888, the 10:30 P.M. through trip from Houston continuing to Miami. Only twenty or so passengers held reservations, and one very special one had a meal listing.

The mood at the gate was subdued; at first, Sarah and Dustin could have been mannequins posed behind the podium. The end could be pushed out of mind when they were busy, but that was over. Now everyone was just trying to drag themselves to the finish line.

The passengers were all present but people kept arriving at the gate. No one had planned for the whole staff to assemble there, or for TPA alumni near and far to show up too, or for someone to bring a bottle of champagne that looked decidedly out of place on the gate podium, but they did. Naturally, the gathering morphed into an impromptu good-bye party, much to the delight of the customers waiting to board.

Not that this was an airline party worthy of the title. Anyone who came expecting a jazz funeral was sorely disappointed. Celebrating the good times would have to wait. Tonight, sorrow and disappointment hung in the air like smoke. There was a touching moment, when Paul was presented with a framed copy of Drew's Ruff Air-AirStar tail-to-tail shot. He couldn't help but get emotional as he read the many heartfelt tributes and well-wishes staff past and present had written on the mat.

Despite the comfort of having Rachel at his side, Drew drifted around feeling like an impostor among his friends. For the first time, he regretted transferring to Tampa. He should be with the Moisant gang at a time like this. Why, he couldn't quite explain; it just felt that way. So, despite his sincere interest, his mind wandered while everyone talked about their plans or hid their pain behind gallows humor. As the evening unfolded, he felt more and more like a scarecrow, slowly shedding straw and propped up on a pole so rotten it would collapse if someone brushed against it.

Eventually the bleak finality closed in and smothered the last of the conversation. Everyone stood around feeling helpless as the clock ticked inexorably toward the end.

Drew and Rachel retreated to a corner. Sensing his mood, she was quiet while he sat contemplating his ID card, which was scuffed, frayed around the edges, and still bore the name Ruff Air. He looked into his own face, which smiled back with the excitement of a dream come true, the eyes behind the clouded plastic bright with naïve optimism.

Sarah's voice interrupted his reverie.

"Ladies and gentlemen, this is the final boarding call for AirStar Flight Eight Eighty-eight, nonstop service to Miami. All confirmed and standby passengers…" Her voice broke and she turned away, embarrassed. Dustin gently put his hand on her shoulder.

"I'm okay," she whispered, as much to herself as to him. She straightened up, gathered herself, and finished strong.

"All passengers should be onboard at this time and ready for an immediate departure."

There were only a few stragglers left. One by one, they gathered up their belongings and went aboard. When they were gone, Dustin wrapped Sarah up in a comforting hug. Her shoulders shook as she cried.

Taking his arms from around Rachel was among the hardest things Drew had ever done. She paused at the door and turned back to him, eyes shining with tears. She touched her vest, then her sleeve, then her beret, and then she was gone.

Nimbus, Sunrise, Stratos.

The message was clear: *Stay strong; persevere; this will pass.* As always, Rachel knew exactly what his spirit needed.

She's right. It hurts, but this is an ending, not the end. I don't know where, how, or when, but I will get back in.

There was no time to dwell on it further; he had one last duty to perform.

Most everyone trooped down to the ramp, where Drew marshaled AirStar 888 out exactly on time. He had requested the honor a week ago; Paul, probably distracted in the moment, had approved, as had the Eastern ramp supervisor. Paul was a Pioneer and should have had the honor. Drew would have gladly deferred, would have insisted in fact, had all that occurred to him at the time. Paul pulled the chocks instead while everyone else looked on from near the jetbridge stairs.

The Eastern ground crew—oblivious that a similar fate awaited them several years hence—seemed surprised that these terminal types actually knew what they were doing. They watched with interest as Drew guided the captain with crisp movements of the lighted wands, concluding with a sharp salute, the usual wave, and a soul-searing rush of loneliness and heartbreak as the jet taxied off into the darkness.

There were a lot of hugs and everyone lingered for a while as if expecting the usual last arrival to land and taxi in.

"It's over," Melody finally said, tears streaming down her face. "It's really over."

Jumping the employee shuttle would have been easier on everybody, but no one did. When his colleagues retreated up the jetbridge steps, Drew stayed behind, compelled somehow to finish his time on the ramp where it had begun. He walked out from Airside B almost to the adjoining taxiway.

Arms crossed tightly, he stared at the familiar T-tailed silhouette awaiting takeoff.

We deserved better. How did it come to this?

Despite the writing on the wall, so obvious in hindsight, shock had been the first reaction around the system. Right on its heels was nearly every coping behavior in the human repertoire. An ISR crew made funeral veils an unofficial uniform accessory; someone in New Orleans cut all the threads on the faded makeshift route map in Ops, the strings hanging from the tacks like so many dead flowers; and a Moisant ramper, too new for anyone to know very well, expressed his feelings clearly if repulsively. Donna said they found his soiled IDs in a locker room urinal, the plastic newbie fish still attached.

That damned fish…

The memories came rushing back: the sack of trash, the chocks, the Bascombs, the cabin in the Rockies…

He and Rachel were cuddled up in the hammock again, gazing up at the moonlit contrail.

Looks like angels could follow it home.

That magical time felt like a lifetime ago. Sitting on the porch in the chilly air as the sun rose the following morning, reciting Frost as they shared the beauty of a new day…the memory began nudging his despair aside until a thunderbolt of irony demolished the nostalgia.

They had never gotten to the last line of the poem.

Nothing gold can stay.

The heartache returned, the kind you're certain will kill you the first time you feel it, which is usually when someone you love very much doesn't feel the same way about you.

He now understood more fully what Rachel had felt when her Pioneer pin showed up, that sense of knowing that something very special is over and will never come again. The hectic days since the announcement had allowed little time to grieve, much less worry about what might lie ahead. That, her unexpected arrival, and some denial if he were to be truthful, had forged a shelter, rickety as it was. Now it had imploded, leaving him freefalling right back into the same bottomless apprehension he had felt before Ruff Air called.

What do I do now? There's no way to stay here. But what then, go back to New Orleans?

Tucked into a back pocket was the radio Rachel had gifted him in Ops that Christmas day. Mercifully, a voice from the earpiece interrupted.

"Tampa Tower, AirStar Eight Eighty-eight request, we'd like to remain in the left traffic pattern for a fly-by."

Pilots called this tower controller "Andy" for the way he unconsciously started many transmissions.

"And AirStar Eight Eighty-eight, a left pattern fly-by is approved then resume standard departure. Wind three four five at seven, Runway Three Six Right, cleared for take-off."

The Super 80 rolled forward, wingtip lights pivoting down into place as it turned onto the centerline, two more strips of translucent white light joining the one from the nose gear.

"A left pattern fly-by then the standard departure, cleared for takeoff Three Six Right, Tumbleweed's rolling."

Was using Ruff Air's old signature a way of paying homage, subtle defiance of the circumstances, or both? The controller, perhaps understanding, ignored it. There was no other traffic anyway.

Drew glanced back at the concourse and saw exactly what he expected: his colleagues, shoulder to shoulder at the windows, the sorrow for all that had been lost etched into every face.

The lightly loaded jet leapt into the air. As the belly doors dropped open to accept the retracting gear, Captain Nolan leveled off, banked, and circled the airport, coming around to fly a few hundred feet above the runway.

As the airplane thundered by, he rolled it gently, dipping each wing twice in an aviator's salute of thanks and farewell.

Andy showed his awareness and some empathy as well. "And AirStar Eight Eighty-eight, contact Departure on one one seven point one. Take care of yourselves and good luck."

"Departure on one seventeen one for AirStar Triple Eight, thank you, sir, good night."

The jet accelerated into a smooth climbing turn. The engine roar gradually faded and soon all that remained was a tiny white flash from each wingtip.

Drew watched the pulsing strobes until they disappeared into the night.

THANK YOU

I sincerely appreciate the time you devoted to reading *Unexpected Ruff Air*. If you enjoyed the book, I'd be deeply grateful if you'd take a moment to leave a review by scanning the QR code below or visiting the book's page on Amazon.

And wherever life may take you…*Nimbus, Sunrise, Stratos!*

Please scan here to leave a review!

ACKNOWLEDGEMENTS

Adequately expressing my heartfelt thanks to everyone who has contributed to the creation of this novel is a tough chore. Their support includes everything from random comments that called up distant memories to giving feedback on drafts to posting remembrances and images that helped me more accurately describe scenes and settings.

To **you, the reader,** thank you for coming along on the journey.

My mom, **Darlina Goodwin Goutierez,** was a gifted writer and artist whose contributions to my life—and this book—are beyond measure. Shortly after TranStar's demise, she gave me powerful advice that launched my airline career to heights I never could have imagined. That moment was so significant that it will figure prominently in a planned sequel.

For this story, her creative spirit found its way to me again long after she passed away. In one of her journals, she vividly described a visit to Audubon Park, and that passage became the inspiration for Rachel's reflections during her picnic there with Drew.

My dad, **James A. Goutierez,** was a good father and a kind, humble man—qualities all the more remarkable given that he lived with what we now call survivor guilt and PTSD. The horrors of his WWII service haunted him for the rest of his life. Serving with the 77th Infantry Division, he fought in Guam, the Philippines, the Kerama Islands, and finally Okinawa. (The 2016 film *Hacksaw Ridge*, which chronicles the 77th and one of its six Medal of Honor recipients, Corporal Desmond Doss, realistically portrays the savage nature of Pacific combat.) I wish I had recognized and understood his pain sooner.

On a related note, **Briana Fiandt** of the Richard I. Bong Veterans Historical Center in Superior, Wisconsin, helped me confirm details of Major Bong's December 7, 1944, aerial victory over Ormoc Bay during the amphibious landing at Leyte in the Philippines. His shootdown of a Mitsubishi Ki-21 "Sally" bomber was the thirty-seventh of the fighter ace's forty victories. As described in this book, it was witnessed by my father and likely saved his life.

All of my family, including **Chica**—who has a few things in common with Rachel, and inspired the Fogelberg/Boston exchange—as well as **Sheila and Michelle,** remained supportive even when it seemed that finishing this book was just a distant mirage. Girls, maybe you'll finally get that ice cream!

To **my former Muse Air/TranStar colleagues:** in real life, I came to the organization relatively late in the game. The pride everyone took in our company was evident from day one. Your commitment to our customers, and to each other, touched and inspired me and earned my deepest respect. I salute and thank you for building such an extraordinary airline and I am proud to say I was part of it.

Special thanks to my station managers at MSY and TPA respectively, **Jeanne** and **Chris,** along with the **MSY and TPA CSRs.** In addition, **Toby Pratt** has provided copious information and encouragement along with superbly showcasing the Muse Air/TranStar experience and the warm, caring spirit of its people through the website museair.com. Much of the material is preserved at departedflights2.com and can be accessed via the QR code at the end of this section.

Captain Mike Martin's astonishingly comprehensive collection of documents, images, and memorabilia is worthy of any museum, and his memories of people and places are just as impressive. Mike's insights into professional piloting, and his images and personal observations, all helped me try to articulate the captivating beauty and wonder of aviation.

I am also grateful to Mike for his permission to use the back cover image of Muse Air rampers walking an MD-80 departure from a Dallas Love Field gate in 1982. Mike and I would later become colleagues again at American.

Another inspirational source was the **Facebook group for former Muse Air/TranStar employees**. Incredibly, over 500 people have connected there as of this writing despite the passage of over three decades since our little airline graced the skies. All have graciously shared their memories and knowledge, with special thanks to:

> **Gene Bathe**
> **Barry Canning**
> **George Cantley**
> **Lane Chenoweth**
> **Nancy Anderson Cooper**
> **Doug Coram**
> **Linda Nevitt Eakin**
> **Cari Everhart**
> **Bill Faulkner**
> **Erin McKinney Fleischer**
> **Ron Freer**
> **Jimmy Gee**
> **Denise Kennedy**
> **Paul Keilen**
> **Tim Kincaid**
> **Michelle LaPine**
> **Judy Coke Marudas**
> **Vince Shobe**
> **Stefanie Solano**
> **Paul Wilson**

The reflections on our shared experiences posted in the group have been invaluable.

John Nolan kindly allowed me to honor the memory of his late father, Muse Air **First Officer John Nolan,** by naming a character after him. **Mary Connor** was a terrific colleague, and later, counterpart. Representing different carriers in the same role, we coincidentally walked into the same meeting ten years after last seeing one another at TranStar.

Other terrific Facebook sources were the **DC-9 Fan Club,** whose members range from fans of the type to mechanics, cabin crew, pilots, and ground staff; **Airline Employees Past and Present;** and **AIRPORT: The Movie (1970).** These gracious people were more than happy to answer questions and provide their personal observations and insight. And finally, special thanks to FedEx **Captain Cliff Leftridge** for his friendship and support, and to everyone in **Blue Skies and a Tailwind** for their patience with the old guy and his stories from way back when.

The front cover photo is © 2000 by **Erik Frikke**. Erik captured his stunning shot of a DC-9 takeoff at Aalborg, Denmark, in 2000. Erik's image captures both the passion for aviation and the spirit of freedom, excitement, and adventure that drew me and uncounted others to the airline industry. I gratefully acknowledge Erik's permission to use this beautiful image.

According to www.planespotters.net, McDonnell Douglas delivered this DC-9-40, Line Number 756, to Scandinavian Airlines System (SAS) in December 1974. SAS registered it as LN-RLZ and christened it *Bodvar Viking*, presumably in tribute to legendary Norse hero **Böðvarr Bjarki**, depicted in literature as a powerful warrior with bear-like strength and loyalty, embodying courage and resilience.

The airline retained that name when it reregistered her as SE-DOM in March 1999. (LN is the aircraft registration country code for Norway and SE that for Sweden.) This aircraft was withdrawn from use in 2001 and, sadly, shares the fate of many DC-9s in that she was eventually scrapped.

Scan the QR code at the end of this section to see more of Erik's exceptional aviation photography.

Captain Dave Savage was the Eastern pilot who took me for a DC-9 simulator ride after our chance 1986 meeting on a flight to Miami. I never forgot that incredible experience or the joy Dave showed in sharing his love of aviation with a wide-eyed industry newb. His kindness left a lasting impression and inspired my determination to pay it forward whenever I could.

After Eastern ceased operations in 1991, I often wondered where Dave had ended up. I tried searching for him from time to time with no luck—until 2019, when we reconnected through

Facebook. Back in 1986, Dave lived in Miami and I was in New Orleans, so you can imagine my surprise when I found out that 33 years later, we were living just 20 minutes apart in the same north Georgia town! We met up for dinner, had a great time catching up, and kept in touch until 2021, when Dave "flew west," as aviators say.

Dave's spirit lives on in extraordinary people like "Mentour Pilot" **Captain Petter Hörnfeldt,** who graciously took the time to review and provide valuable advice on a key passage. Much like Dave, he selflessly shares his wealth of aviation knowledge and experience. His YouTube videos on incidents and accidents explore the nuances that often go unknown, and each of his YouTube channels reflects the depth of his expertise and passion. They are, like his signature signoff, "absolutely fantastic."

As told in this novel, Captain Savage's tour of Eastern's Hartley Training Center was where I learned the shocking story of Eastern Air Lines Shuttle Flight 1320. On March 17, 1970, First Officer James Hartley heroically gave his life to stop an armed hijacker, enabling Captain Robert Wilbur to land their DC-9 despite being wounded himself. First Officer Hartley's granddaughter, **Danila Brown,** kindly corresponded with me via email, providing very helpful information. Captain Wilbur's son, **Robert M. Wilbur III,** has written a book called *Reluctant Hero; The Story of Eastern Airlines Flight 1320.* It was a treasure trove of useful background and is an excellent read for anyone interested in knowing more about that remarkable yet largely unknown chapter of aviation history.

Sue Warner-Bean contributed thoughtful suggestions about my writing and about life. And you were right; I kept coloring and here we are.

Also among those who generously gave their time to read drafts, make suggestions, or offer encouragement are **LeeAnn Hart; Angie Kehnemuyi; Jim Kelly;** my CARE brother, **Ken Jenkins; Jen Stansberry Miller; Brandon B.** from CCSLC; **Vicki Sansom; Kim Fender Collins** (Flying Purple People Eaters!); **Lori Jouty;** and **Erin Hales.**

Mike Machat, noted aviation artist, author, historian, and, most recently, YouTuber (@celebratingaviationwithmik9782) offered encouragement that kept me working on this project long after I might have otherwise given up.

Author **Tom Petzinger** (who wrote the excellent deregulation chronicle *Hard Landing)* corresponded with me, offered advice, and even shared his agent's contact information, which was much appreciated given that self-publishing was not an option then.

Erika Armstrong graciously took time from her "A Chick in the Cockpit" pursuits to read an excerpt and offer suggestions and encouragement.

Artist **Chris Bidlack** of Jet Age Art provided his unique take and had terrific promotional suggestions as well.

Kelly Squires-Henry, sister of my former public safety colleague **Kimberly West,** helped by sharing her experience around funeral homes.

Melissa Turchetta, a veteran of no fewer than *seven* carriers, provided her perspective on the terrible human cost inflicted by deregulation's tumultuous aftermath. She also helped with details about life as a flight attendant and created Ruff Air and AirStar aircraft renderings.

Captain Tony was flying Mad Dogs long before the magenta line. His insights on piloting and flight deck procedures brought home the importance of a pilot's knowledge, experience, and instincts when things can't be fixed by pushing a button. A prime example of such an emergency is US Airways Flight 1549—the "Miracle on the Hudson"—where the airmanship demonstrated by Captain Sullenberger and First Officer Skiles saved everyone aboard. Captain Tony's commitment to his craft and salty dedication to pilot professionalism make the skies safer.

The Cockpit Voice Recorder (CVR) aboard the DC-9-14 N100ME captured **flight attendants aboard Midwest Express Flight 105** shouting "Heads down! Heads down!" during a tragic 1985 accident at Milwaukee Mitchell International Airport (MKE). Though doing so was part of their training, having the courage to carry it out in such a terrifying moment reflected a selfless and heroic dedication to their passengers. It deeply moved me and inspired Rachel's actions during the Flight 867 passage. Out of respect for their families' privacy, I have chosen not to name those courageous young women here.

I'm grateful to **Warren Qualley** for sharing his vast weather expertise and to **Vince Shobe** for his deep knowledge of ATC systems, both of which helped add authenticity.

My former American colleague **Barbara Russell** unselfishly helped me become a much better writer.

Mike Lynn, it's been decades since I worked for you at General Cinema, but your wisdom stayed with me. You were right; deciding what you want is often the hardest part.

departedflights.com provided timetables that helped add realism to my schedules and flight numbers, and the outstanding **Tampa International Airport** site **tampaairport.com** jogged memories about my days working there.

I also owe the deepest gratitude to authors like **Captain Edward L. Beach, Arthur Hailey, James Lee Burke, Herman Wouk, Robert Serling, John D. Macdonald, Tom Clancy,** and countless others whose writing has inspired me. Their words informed my world, expanded my horizons, and often touched my heart.

I did my best to keep notes through the years, yet I have an uncomfortable feeling that this roster is woefully incomplete. To **anyone I have missed**, please accept my heartfelt thanks and a sincere apology for the oversight.

Learn more about Muse Air/TranStar at departedflights2.com:

See more of Erik Frikke's photography at airliners.net:

ABOUT THE AUTHOR

Beyond Muse Air/TranStar, American hired me as an airport agent in Tampa, the next step in a career journey I never could have imagined. The company was expanding, and I wanted to learn and do everything, so it was like the proverbial kid in a candy store. I took on new roles every 12-18 months on average: Lead Agent in San Jose, CA, which at the time was American's West Coast hub; then to staff positions at HDQ in Fort Worth (not Dallas!); and finally at System Operations Control (SOC), still by far the coolest physical location in which I've ever worked.

My career path included Yield Management Operations, Ticketing & Terminal Services, and special projects like coordinating aircraft filming (**Fred Ashman** and Multi Image Productions were terrific) and planning charters. Those memorable 14 years, and three more in International Pricing at Delta managing those fare rules everyone loves to hate, made for a remarkable career (that's practically begging for sequels!).

Rachel's efforts on behalf of the Bascomb family aren't a stretch; I've seen many instances where employees went to heroic lengths to help passengers in need, in both everyday situations and during emergencies.

American pioneered a formal, structured approach to what is now called Humanitarian Support or Special Assistance Teams (SAT) with its creation of the Customer Assistance Relief Effort (CARE) Program in 1993. I was among many who volunteered, spending four years as a team member and several more managing the program. We hoped, of course, that the special skills we were taught for supporting survivors and families following crises and tragedies would never be needed. Sadly, that wasn't the case.

I mention this because my career after the airline industry has been focused on emergency preparedness and response. Making a difference for someone on their darkest day is like the airline industry in that it gets into your soul. I continue to be involved in Humanitarian Support as a consultant, trainer, and responder.

AUTHOR'S NOTE

My first airline job inspired this book. Muse Air operated under its original name from 1981 until being purchased by Southwest in 1985 and rebranded as TranStar. Among its many attributes was being the first nonsmoking U.S. airline. But more than anything, the people were what made it special, something I soon learned reached across the entire industry.

My approach to telling the story was inspired by the gritty realism of authors like the late U.S. Navy Captain Edward L. Beach. The World War II submariner transformed his professional experience into engaging, authentic, and plausible fiction.

I also wanted readers to have a sense of what it was like to work for a small, scrappy airline in the tumultuous 1980s; to better know the special people who operate the airline industry and the many challenges thereof; to gain a broader view of deregulation and its consequences; and to take them along on some of the indescribably fun adventures, planned and spontaneous, made possible by employee travel privileges.

As this is a fictional story set in a historical context, some details—cities served, for example, along with who bought Muse Air and why—won't align perfectly with history itself. Many of the operational happenings come very close to real-life events, but while I had many remarkable friends and colleagues, the romantic relationships depicted are all pure fiction, written to fit into the narrative.

Finally, a word to aspiring authors: writing this book took years—I started on a typewriter and ended doing cover edits on an iPad. A reminder of my unfinished project greeted me every time I saw a contrail in the sky. I often wondered if I'd ever finish, or if anyone would want to read it if I did.

Persevere, and look for ways to make your work better, like connecting with people who know your subject well. Nearly everyone I asked gladly shared their knowledge, even though all I could offer was a mention in the Acknowledgments. Embrace the positives and take heart in knowing that every step, even the setbacks, is contributing in a meaningful way, even if it's not evident at the time.

Nimbus, Sunrise, Stratos. You'll get there, and the arrival is worth the journey!

Made in the USA
Columbia, SC
30 May 2025

58501637R00221